PLAYING WITH FIRE

A Magical Romantic Comedy (with a body count)

RJ BLAIN

Playing with Fire
A Magical Romantic Comedy (with a body count)
by R.J. Blain

Warning: This novel contains excessive humor, a fire-breathing unicorn on a mission of destruction, magic, romance, and bodies. Proceed with caution.

Catering to the magical is a tough gig on a good day, but Bailey has few other options. Spiking drinks with pixie dust keeps the locals happy and beats cleaning up the world's nastiest magical substances. She could live without serving Police Chief Samuel Quinn most days of the week, especially after destroying his marriage.

But when she's targeted with a cell phone bomb containing gorgon dust capable of transforming her home into a stone tomb, she's tossed head first into a mess with her sexiest enemy. Add in his ex-wife angling for revenge, and Bailey must use every trick up her sleeve to survive.

The last thing she needs is to fall in love with Manhattan's Most Wanted Bachelor.

Saving Manhattan will be tough enough.

All rights reserved. This book or any portion thereof may not be reproduced or used in any manner whatsoever without the express written permission of the publisher or author excluding the use of brief quotations in a book review.

© 2017 Pen & Page Publishing

For more information or to contact the author, please visit thesneakykittycritic.com.

Cover design by Rebecca Frank of Bewitching Book Covers.

Dedication

Susan and Caity,

Thanks for sticking with me through the eleventh hour. It was rough, but we got through it. I simply don't have the words to express how much I appreciate your company in the trenches. I really couldn't have done this without you.

Di,

This book is all your fault. I hope you're happy with yourself!

To answer your question, yes, I will be doing another story about Bailey and Quinn in the future. Prepare the bribes. You're going to need them.

Aunt Wendy,

You would have liked this one. I hope your heaven is full of books, music, and friends. You deserve it.

We miss you.

ONE

What a way to start the day.

NO ONE in their right mind would ever license me as a private investigator, but that didn't stop people from coming to me when they needed something found. Fortunately, I liked my job as the only human barista at Faery Fortunes Coffee and Book Shop. Most came for a cup of joe and left too buzzed to read a thing, but who was I to complain? People paid top dollar for their pixie dust infused latte, and they tipped me well not to judge them.

Unfortunately, I wasn't so fond of Chief Quinn. When he walked through the door, bad things usually happened to someone—me. For him to come in five minutes after opening, long before the sun even thought about rising, he needed something, and it wasn't a cup of coffee. Why couldn't he want coffee? I could deal with making him a drink, and I'd double his dose of pixie dust to keep him happy.

I gave the espresso machine a defiant swipe of my cleaning cloth before stepping to the counter to deal with Manhattan's Most Wanted Bachelor. Without my help, he'd still be married, too.

What a way to start the day.

And to think people wondered why I refused to help find anything for anyone anymore. The reason stood across the counter from me. Chief Samuel Quinn, aged thirty, hotter than sin, and my heaven and hell rolled together in one smoking tall, dark, and handsome package, hated me for good reason. It was his fault, too. He had been the one to ask me for help finding his wife. I had found her all right, right in the middle of teaching a college stud the nuances of the reverse cowgirl.

If no one asked me to find something or someone again for the rest of my life, I'd be a very happy woman.

"Chief Quinn, what a pleasant surprise," I lied. "Can I get you something? A dark roast, cream, no sugar, light on the dust?"

Why couldn't I have been blessed with forgetfulness? I knew my worst nightmare's favorite drink, and I had to make it for him first thing in the morning. Of course I knew it. He came in at least three times a week to torment me. Screw it. Who was I kidding? Instead of the coffee, he could take me instead. If I had to put up with the hassle of dealing with him, why couldn't I enjoy it, too?

"Cream, no dust, and make it a large, Bailey."

Alarm bells tinkled in my head. Since when did Chief Quinn address *me* by my first name? On a good day, he snapped my last name like he worried it would contaminate him. "Of course, sir."

The faster I made his coffee, the sooner he'd go away. I'd love every second I spent watching him go. In less than a minute, I had his drink ready, and to lower the risk of him spending any extra time with me, I chirped, "It's on me today, Chief Quinn. Have yourself a nice morning."

If it meant we parted without incident, it'd be well worth the five bucks.

He saluted me with his cup, flashed a hint of a smile, and walked out the door. Facing him was hell, but I glimpsed the heavens when he left, and if my panties hadn't caught on fire under my jeans, I'd be very, very surprised.

"You're drooling, Gardener," my boss squeaked. The moth faery, with just enough pixie heritage to dust glitter when she wanted, fluttered over my shoulder, her tiny arms crossed over her chest. "Reverse cowgirl."

"Stop reminding me!" I wailed, slumping over the counter. "He hates me. Worse, all I think about when he struts in is taking off my clothes and giving him my panties. I think they caught on fire this time, Mary. Why couldn't he have had one of his cops find his wife instead?"

"You just want to indulge in some guilt-free fantasizing like every other hot-blooded American woman in the city."

"Exactly. This is why no one in their right mind asks me for help. I ruin everything."

"Except my coffee, which is a miracle. Now that we've had our daily dose of excitement, can you handle the shop on your own for an hour? We'll call it even on the coffee."

Was she serious? Alone for an hour on a Monday morning forty minutes before rush hour? If she thought I'd be all right alone, she was completely cracked. I could already hear her if I dared to complain about my shift. What could possibly go wrong in an hour? Didn't I like my job? The list went on and on and on. I smiled so I wouldn't cry. "Sure, Mary. I can last an hour."

"You've gotten better at lying. Your smile didn't even slip that time. Try not to die while I'm gone. Good humans are so hard to find." Mary zipped out of the shop through the pixie door and dove through the window of an idling sports car.

Wait.

Sports car? Red, convertible, top up despite the nice summer morning? I leaned over the counter and squinted. Yep. My boss had just ditched me for a ride in Chief Quinn's car. Sometimes life really wasn't fair.

TEN MINUTES AFTER MARY LEFT, every centaur in the city decided to hold a convention in the shop. Not a single one of them seemed to notice—or care—they barely fit through the door. Equine, bovine, and God-only-knew-what bodies crammed together, waiting for their chance to get a taste of pixie dust goodness.

I lost track of the number of species, wondering what sort of idiot decided to call them all centaurs; maybe they got tired of trying to come up with names for them. By the time the first cat hybrid showed up, I decided to just skip past questioning my sanity to weary resignation and kept making coffee.

Since asking a centaur for his species classified as rude, I plastered my best smile on my face, swallowed my curiosity, and asked, "What can I get for you, sir?"

"Small latte, extra dust." He slapped a pair of twenties on the counter. If he'd wanted B-grade dust, he would've dropped a ten and left with change, so I rang him up for an upgrade to something a bit better. While we kept all four types of A-grade in stock, we only offered A and A+ to regular customers.

Without a permit, no one got the best stuff, and I thanked God for that each and every day. It was only polite; I never knew if the poor bastard stuck with the portfolio was listening.

"Keep the change, my guardian angel." While the cat hybrid centaur thing had a human face, orange and black fur covered his skin, and when he smiled, he showed his sharp, pointy teeth.

I checked for wings just in case. Stranger things had happened on shift. "Was my halo showing?" I took his cash, tossed the extra fifteen dollars into my tip jar, and fetched his drink, handling the tiny vial of A-grade dust with care. The last thing I needed was to give everyone in the shop a high they'd remember for years to come.

With a fifteen buck tip and a customer to keep happy, I took advantage of Mary's bribe box on the way back to the counter, snagging a catnip bag. A happy feline mauled no one, including me. "Here you are, sir. Have a great day."

With that much pixie dust in his system, if the centaur cat wasn't grinning from ear to ear by the time he made it half a block, I'd be shocked. Of all the legalized recreational drugs, pixie dust brought the high without the low, impaired so few people no one bothered to test for it, and single-handedly fought off the weekday blues for those who could afford it.

I sure as hell couldn't, even if the dust worked for me, which it didn't. I balked at a five buck coffee. Twenty-five for a morning hit would bankrupt me within a month.

The centaurs kept on coming, which in turn lured in the more curious races, including the faery. I'd never understand why they came to a shop dedicated to selling pixie dust. The bright-colored blighters wanted one thing in life: liquid sugar, and lots of it. We kept it by the gallons in the fridge, and by the time my shift was over, I would need to make more. We even stocked pure sugar cane for the really adventurous, but we made them sign a waiver and an agreement to pay for any damages.

On the heels of the traditional faery, all of whom had butterfly, moth, or dragonfly wings, the bat-winged folk fluttered in. I doubted they called themselves faery, but with hundreds of different 'What the hell is *that* thing?!' critters living in the city, could anyone really blame me for forgetting their proper names?

After the faery stampeded their way in,

taking up every bit of available table space, the cops showed up in search of a little Monday morning cheer. Most of them were frequent flyers from every station in a five mile radius, and it really wouldn't have surprised me if they came because they idolized Chief Quinn.

At least the faery were easy to serve; one had the bright idea of bringing her credit card—which was bigger than she was—and paying for them all, asking for a pitcher and thimbles. I had no idea how the card disappeared into the faery's black tank top, but I wisely didn't ask. I got out the liquid brown sugar and poured it into a cup, dug out enough thimbles to stock a sewing store, and left them to their binge.

When I could serve at least fifty in less than two minutes, I considered it a good day. Unfortunately, at least fifty more people waited for service. On a good day, a line of ten inspired rage and pissed the customers off.

None of the cops, straggler centaurs, or other beasties peeped a single complaint. If I wanted to survive the shift, I'd need to take the methodical, perfectionist approach. As long as I didn't screw up an order, I might survive until Mary showed up. Once she arrived, we could tag team the crowd. She'd take the orders, I'd fill them, and everything would be okay.

I lasted the full hour, but Mary didn't show up. Instead, the first wave of businessmen stormed through the door, and some of them were even human.

Crap.

Humans were the worst. Delays infuriated them, and I still hadn't managed to get rid of all the cops yet. Too busy to cry, I kept on smiling, faking the good-natured spirit Mary insisted made her coffee and pixie dust taste better.

"I thought this place hired faery." The business man glared down his nose at me, his perfect black suit and white shirt tempting me to chuck the fresh pot of coffee all over him. "Isn't your shop called Faery Fortunes? I came here to see the faeries!"

I pointed at the nearest writhing mass of sparkling winged bodies. During the throes of their sugar high, some of them had spread dust and glitter, and I tried not to think of all the health code violations they were committing on the table. When my shift ended, I'd leave that train wreck for my boss to clean up; it'd serve her right for abandoning me. "What can I get for you, sir?"

The businessman stared at the faery, narrowed his eyes, and turned his attention back to me. "You have pixie dust here?"

"We stock C and better, sir. Our regular brews use B, but we have all other grades available." I prayed he wouldn't ask for the two better grades. The last thing I needed was the paperwork and having to confirm his permit.

"Espresso, A+, heavy on the dust."

I bet the human would take flight before he made it out the door. I rang his order up and struggled to hide my shock at the amount. I smiled. I smiled so much it hurt. "That'll be three hundred and ten dollars, sir."

"Credit," he barked, slapping his card on the counter.

I ran his card, handed him the payment terminal, and went to make his coffee. Anyone else who worked in the store had to wear a mask and gloves when handling the vials containing the most potent of the pixie dusts, and I was the only employee certified to handle the best of the best.

Not even my boss could.

Sometimes, immunity was as much of a curse as it was a blessing. Why couldn't I drink my cares away like everyone else? Even the time Mary had shattered an entire vial of A++ dust, I hadn't felt a damned thing while she and the rest of my co-workers spent the following six hours giggling over everything, unable to handle even the simplest of tasks without dissolving into a laughing fit.

I checked to confirm the transaction had been approved before measuring out the dust and adding it to his coffee. I offered it to him, my smile still fixed in place. "Have a great day, sir."

"I better, seeing how much this garbage cost."

I already missed the centaurs and the cops. A glance at the clock informed me I had survived through three hours with no sign of Mary. When she got back, we'd have words, and unless she had a damned good reason for abandoning me so she could take a ride with Chief Quinn on the worst Monday morning shift I'd ever seen, I knew exactly which two words I'd say.

MY SHIFT SHOULD HAVE LASTED six hours. The chaos ebbed to a trickle, but when the pixie sisters should have arrived, the shop remained quiet, the lull before the lunchtime storm. I considered killing the pair, who provided most of the shop's dust and worked the midday hours. No one would miss Evita and Lea Anne in a city full of bubbly pink pixies, right?

The door bells tinkled, and instead of the tardy duo, I got Chief Quinn's former brother-in-law. If I closed the shop really quickly and ran for the hills, would he go away? Before I could escape, Magnus McGee stepped to the counter.

Well, crap. At the rate I was going, my face was going to freeze into a permanent smile. "What can I get for you, sir?"

"Large coffee, black, no dust."

I loved simple orders. It made maintaining a pleasant demeanor in the face of a living nightmare so much easier. I fetched his drink, and he slid a twenty across the counter. I glared at the bill and snatched it up. Why couldn't people carry smaller bills instead of decimating the register's change?

Better yet, I'd really appreciate it if they started using their debit and credit cards. Plastic made things nicer for everyone, especially me. I offered his change by setting it in front of him so I wouldn't have to touch him. "Have a nice day, sir."

McGee took his money, crammed a five into my tip jar, and stared at me. Instead of leaving like a good little customer, his eyes tracked my every move, and I contemplated turning a toothpick into a lethal weapon.

Of all the people on Earth, Magnus McGee came third on my list of those to avoid. His sister came in second.

The polite, professional me took over, and still smiling, I chirped, "Is there something else I can get for you, sir?"

How about a murder: his. I could do that. I had a spoon within easy reach. Surely I could kill someone with a spoon. I blamed my bad Monday morning shift for my inclination towards violence.

"Audrey said you can find anyone or anything. Is that true?"

Oh, God. Why me? Why was the woman I had caught having sex in Central Park telling her brother about me? Who had told her I'd been the one to inform her husband—with photographs—of her deed? I really wanted to kill them, whoever they were. "No, sorry," I lied.

"She seemed pretty convinced."

Of course she probably believed I could find anyone or anything after I caught her cheating on one of the sexiest men alive. The mental image of Samuel Quinn's wife and her college stud would never, ever fade. Every time I thought I could forget, someone had to remind me.

At least I could hide the truth behind the truth. "I'm a vanilla human, Mr. McGee. Sorry."

On paper, I was as vanilla as they got, with my only recorded abnormality—or talent, as they liked to call magical abilities—being my immunity to pixie dust and a few other magical substances. Sometimes the cops called me in and paid me a cute little pittance to deal with some of the nastier substances, including gorgon vomit.

No one wanted that job, especially me, but since a gorgon's bile didn't turn me to stone like it did everyone else...

"That's not what I heard. I really need your help. You're good at finding people who don't want to be found, right?"

That was one way to put it, but instead of voicing my agreement, I pulled out my driver's license and showed it to him. "V for vanilla. I'm qualified to handle dangerous substances, but that's it." Guilt, the type born of having ruined a man's marriage, reared its ugly head. "Tell you what. I know a few people. Give me the info, and I'll see what they can do. No promises. I'm not what you're looking for, but maybe one of my friends knows something."

I was such a miserable, horrible liar. What friends? What help? I needed a life, one outside of making coffee and asking how high when the cops ordered me to jump.

McGee pulled out a slender black cell phone and handed it to me. "Everything you need to know is on here. I'll pay seventy-five thousand if you find him, and an extra twenty-five if you do so within the next forty-eight hours. Please. I'll call you tonight, so keep the phone on you."

I gaped at him. He wanted to pay how

much for me to find someone? Seventy-five thousand was more than twice what I made in a year, and that included all the buckets of gorgon bile I'd shoveled up so some cop didn't get turned to stone trying to do it. Seventy-five thousand meant I could make good on my never-spoken threats of quitting.

"Oh, and Miss Gardener?"

"What?" I asked, tensing as I waited for the catch. There was always a catch. I should have known there'd be a catch.

"This talk never happened."

Of course. I should have known. Someone willing to pay a fortune for someone to be found wouldn't want anyone else to know he was looking. I sighed. "That's going to make it difficult to ask my friends for help."

"Aren't you supposed to be smart or something? Figure it out." He turned and headed for the door.

I fumed. "If I were so smart, do you think I'd be working as a barista in a pixie dust shop?" Why did rich men always insist on ignoring me? Magnus McGee left without acknowledging my question. "Screw you, too, buddy. And your sister sucked at the reverse cowgirl, in case you were wondering!"

Ah, well. It was probably for the better he couldn't hear me. Who could he need to find so badly he'd pay so much for me to do the work for him? Had he missed the memo? I found people all right, in the worst positions possible.

I blinked, and a thought struck me. What if he hadn't missed the memo?

Muttering curses, I shoved the black phone into my pocket to deal with after my hell shift ended.

WHILE I COULD UNDERSTAND the pixie sisters ditching their shift, I expected better from Branden. The satyr loved coffee and pixie dust more than life itself, and he worked at Faery Fortunes part-time for the discount. He had a far better paying job as a desk monkey somewhere, but until now, he'd never missed a shift. With Mary still a no-show, I was stuck with closing.

If anyone expected me to open in the morning after an eighteen-hour shift, they'd get an unpleasant surprise. I locked the front door, flipped the sign, and cleaned up the mess. As soon as I finished, I wrote Mary a scathing note informing her she could find some other certified barista, invoked one of the rare New York employee rights laws favoring the workers, and told her she owed me for all eighteen hours I'd worked solo. In case she had trouble with the math, I gave her the amount along with a reminder she had promised to be back within an hour.

I would regret my decision when it came time to pay my rent. Then again, maybe I wouldn't. My certification opened doors, and everyone wanted someone who could handle dangerous substances without a hazmat suit. If I didn't mind a life as a high-class janitor, I'd be set. There weren't a lot of people who could fall into a vat of gorgon bile and live to tell the tale. I was one of three in New York City, and the other two were gorgons, powerful ones who didn't need to petrify me before crushing me to teeny tiny Bailey bits.

A little after one in the morning, I trudged home. Thanks to the late hour, it took four buses, and I staggered to my door in Queens at a little after three. All in all, I couldn't complain. It could've been worse—a lot worse. I had run into only one drunk, and he'd been more interested in a leggy blond, who had enjoyed shocking the shit out of him with her Taser a little too much.

In the relative safety of my apartment, I flopped on my battered, flea-market couch and dug out Magnus McGee's phone. "Who could you possibly want that you'd pay *me* so much to hunt him down for you?"

To add a bit of extra icing on my day, the asshole had locked the phone. I glared at the prompt. "Seriously?"

Blocking the info behind a passcode meant he either wanted a little revenge or meant for me to earn my keep. Fine. Two could play at his game, and a four-digit passcode wouldn't take too long to hack, especially if I pulled out all the stops. First, I'd try random bullshit luck. I'd save the hocus pocus for later, when I was frustrated enough I wouldn't care if I broke the phone.

I took a few minutes to test the device to make sure it was the real deal. A few swipes of the screen brought up the expected menus, and I even turned on the flash out of curiosity. Maybe after I got paid for the work, I'd buy my very own cell phone. I was probably one of ten people in the entire city without one.

It took me until five after six to brute force my way in. The device clicked, the screen flashed, and it displayed a list of icons showing one missed call. It also clicked and gave an electronic buzz. Before I could do more than suck in a startled breath at the unexpected sound, the device detonated. A cloud of vapor, dust, and glass shards burst in my face. The sharp bite of shrapnel tore into my skin, and my eyes burned with the fires of hell.

With tears streaming down my cheeks and blinding me, I staggered to my bathroom to flush my eyes. I cursed every painful moment I spent splashing my face with water. When I could finally see again, reddish droplets stained my white sink and had splattered on my mirror. I squinted to make out my reflection. The whites of my eyes had turned an angry red, but by some miracle I refused to question, none of the shards had cut me anywhere important. Being blinded would've really put a damper on my day.

I picked out the fragments with tweezers. It was a good thing I hadn't started life all that pretty, as my new collections of scars would ensure no man looked my way twice. At least I didn't think I needed any stitches.

Who the hell turned a phone into a miniature bomb? Magnus McGee, apparently. The dust gave my skin and clothes a greenish cast, and after a few exploratory sniffs of my shirt, I picked up a faint trace of wet earth.

Gorgon dust.

No one in their right mind made the stuff, not even gorgons. Not only could it turn its victims into stone, they ran a chance of becoming a gorgon, too. The authorities refused to give a percentage on how many were turned, but I suspected it was high, as handling the stuff required a top-level permit, one I possessed thanks to my immunity.

The truly insane dosed themselves with it on purpose. McGee hadn't just tried to kill me. He had meant to make me a monster—

one who'd never be able to look anyone in the eyes ever again.

"That son of a bitch!" Had I been anyone else, I would have been transformed into a statue, easy pickings for anyone who came into my apartment. Petrifying someone was a great way to get rid of them—or cart them off before reversing the petrification with neutralizer. Spitting mad, I went to work purifying my apartment, tears pricking my eyes. It hadn't been *my* fault McGee's sister had cheated on her husband. What kind of idiot left someone like Chief Quinn for a college kid?

Audrey McGee, apparently.

At least I had everything I needed to neutralize the gorgon dust thanks to working with the police. They provided me with a new batch of neutralizer every call, and I kept every last pinch of it. After mixing the powder with some water, I'd be able to spritz everything and vacuum the pale residue when it was dry.

Two hours and one thoroughly cleaned apartment later, I collapsed into bed and dreamed of wringing Magnus McGee's scrawny little neck.

TWO

Choices, choices.

I DRAGGED myself out of bed at noon and spent an unreasonable amount of time glaring at the mangled ruins of McGee's phone. Even if there was data on it, there was no way I could access it without exposing someone to the gorgon dust inside. Even after bathing it in the neutralizing solution, I worried someone would be petrified and possibly turned into a gorgon.

I had two choices: I could assume Magnus McGee had lied to me or I could take a walk on the wild side and perform some magic to learn the truth. Choices, choices.

Ah, hell. Hocus pocus it was. Until I got a new job, I needed something to do to fill the time. I'd do another round of spraying to make certain all the gorgon dust was neutralized, too. Thankfully, since I didn't have any real friends, no one came to my apartment without good reason. In a day or two, my place would be safe.

It'd take a lot longer than a day or two to get a reply from my job applications. It took me ten minutes to update my resume to reflect my work at Faery Fortunes and add a few lines to include my certifications. The hard part would be submitting to jobs, but I'd manage.

I always did.

After three frustrating hours, I gave up and decided to get my hands dirty. If McGee had a legitimate job hiding behind his stupid exploding cell phone booby trapped with gorgon dust, I'd find out. Either way, I'd make him pay for every last cut inflicted on me.

To hide my magic so my talents weren't classified, I used rituals and spells to make it appear like I was a harmless practitioner. Without tools, practitioners couldn't work any magic, placing them firmly in the vanilla human category. Given the right tools, enough determination, and time, they could accomplish just about anything. Pretending I needed tools to tap into magic would keep me off the radar—mostly.

Ideally, no one would ever find out there was something more to my ability to find what others didn't want found.

I really needed to sit down and have a chat with Magnus McGee about his exploding cell phone. Thanks to the wretched device, I'd have to do a lot of coverup work to stop anyone from realizing there was something more to me than I wanted them to see.

To make my special brand of hocus pocus work, I needed two components: a piece of paper and some ink. Everything else I gathered, ranging from a big bag of marbles to a light bulb, served as props to trick anyone who might be watching. A little caution never hurt anyone, and I never knew when the walls might grow eyes. Magic worked in mysterious ways, and mine was a little more mysterious than most.

I wasn't even sure how it worked. It just did.

Since the phone was the largest contamination risk, I'd put it in a plastic bag, which I set in front of me along with the paper and ink. I scattered everything else around me in a haphazard circle in a mockery of a practitioner's ritual. Crossing my legs and resting my hands on my knees, I closed my eyes. Maybe one day I'd figure out how my magic ticked and learn to control it so it wouldn't find some way to bite me in the ass.

The first step was to concentrate on what I needed to know, but I often found the simple tasks were the most difficult. I had too many questions. Had McGee wanted someone found, or was he just after some good old-fashioned revenge? Then my thoughts wandered to the day Chief Quinn, easily one of the sexiest human beings alive, had barged into the coffee shop asking if I could help him find his wife.

The camera he'd given me should have tipped me off he knew his wife had been cheating on him.

Was the phone revenge for finding proof of Audrey McGee Quinn's infidelity?

I reined in my thoughts and turned them back to McGee, the phone, and the possibility of revenge. Then I waited until a tingle swept through my body, the sole indicator my magic was working. I cracked open an eye and peeked at the page.

Ink splattered over most of the sheet, leaving behind enough white space to form a single word: yes.

How lovely. Why wasn't I surprised? Yes was an easy enough answer to interpret. Revenge motivated McGee, and he had used the phone to get it—or tried to. Too bad for him I was immune to his stupid batch of dust.

Still, the single confirmation wasn't enough. I needed to take it a step further. Discarding the soaked page, I grabbed another and plunked it down beside McGee's phone. The more specific I got with my desires, the harder it was to get an answer I could use.

On a good day, my magic would seek out the truth and, using a single word, tell me what I needed to know. It tired me, and without fail, there were consequence associated with using my talent. Usually, the magic put me in the worst position possible, like witnessing Magnus McGee's sister doing things I only fantasized about.

With her ex-husband.

I groaned and gave up all hope of concentrating on the problem without my mind diving into the gutter. My magic sucked. Samuel Quinn, quite probably the man of my dreams, was back on the market, and thanks to cheating and using some hocus pocus to do him a favor, he hated me. At least I didn't care if the McGees hated me.

Well, maybe I did. A face full of gorgon dust and glass shards wasn't my idea of a good time. Why the hell would anyone risk contamination to get revenge on *me*? Only an idiotic moron would do such a thing.

There were easier ways to kill or hurt someone.

I opened my eyes. The marbles rolled across the floor and lined up, heading straight towards my door. One by one, they halted in a new position, stretching from my side all the way across my living room.

Someone knocked at my door.

A chill ran through me, and I picked up

the bag containing the contaminated phone. Ink splotches on the page drew my attention, and I sucked in a breath. Written in the clearest words I'd ever seen my magic produce were two words: not you.

Another knock at my door startled me to my feet; my heart drummed a frantic beat in my chest, echoing in my ears and throat. I was immune to gorgon dust. Some people knew. Most didn't. Because most didn't, whenever the police department needed my help, Chief Quinn came personally. He always did.

Oh no.

"Bailey?"

Panic jolted through me. Yep. Chief Quinn was at my door, and unless my guess was way off, Magnus McGee wanted revenge—on him, not on me. I was just a bonus. "Oh, shit. Oh, shit, shit, shit, shit."

I hurried to the door and engaged the deadbolt. Until I could confirm I'd neutralized every last particle of gorgon dust, I couldn't let anyone in. Even with my cleaning and spraying of the neutralizing solution, I had no way of knowing if I'd gotten it all.

If I opened the door, some might get out, and it only took a trace to petrify someone.

"Bailey? It's me. Open up," he ordered.

"I can't. Seal the door, Chief Quinn." If I had to lock myself in until they could napalm the place to prevent a gorgon outbreak, I would. Being napalmed fell really low on my bucket list of things to do before I died, but if I allowed anyone to be infected, I would never forgive myself.

"What? What's going on?"

"Get someone to seal the door. Someone bombed my place with gorgon dust. Just go away, please. I have neutralizing solution here, I just need time to get it all." There. If that didn't send him a clear message, nothing would. "Please."

A string of curses spewed out of the man's mouth, so potent my toes curled. "You're certain?"

"Of course I'm certain. I know gorgon dust when I see it. Don't be insulting."

"Who did it?"

I imagined him standing on the other side of the door, his arms crossed over his broad chest, and the muscles of his biceps flexed beneath his uniform. Damn. I wished my door had a peep hole so I could get a good look at him before I either starved to death, decontaminated my apartment, or was napalmed by law enforcement to prevent an outbreak.

"Bailey? Who did it?"

There was no point in hiding it, but I sighed anyway. "Ma—"

The pressure of invisible hands around my throat cut off my breath. Thunder roared in my ears, and when the sound crested, someone turned out all the lights.

I WOKE to Chief Quinn barking orders. My door shuddered in its frame, lost its will to live, and thumped against my back, shoulders, and head. Ouch.

The universe obviously hated me and wanted me to die.

Before I could gather my wits to do something about getting smacked with my own door—and figure out which end was up—Chief Quinn gave another command. I really wished the man would shut up for once in his life. My door smacked into me so hard it cleaned my clock and shunted me aside. Double ouch.

Why couldn't he follow simple instructions? 'Seal the door' did *not* mean 'batter the damned thing down.'

A white shoe and leg stepped over me, and it took me a moment to comprehend someone wearing a hazmat suit had invaded my apartment. Oh. Hazmat suit. That'd work, too. I blinked and tried to piece together how I had ended up on the floor, but I couldn't remember.

The person in the hazmat suit was either a part of the police containment team or a member of the Center for Disease Control and Prevention. Either way, I was screwed. Plastic crinkled, and I heard the gentle hiss of the oxygen tank ensuring complete protection from any potential gorgon dust lingering in my apartment.

A gloved hand pressed something gold to my throat. I guessed it was a stethoscope of some sort. It could be a gun, too, something they'd whip out if I started petrifying people.

"Sluggish pulse, semi-conscious, sir. Looks like she collapsed in front of the door."

Damn. I recognized the man's voice, although it took me a few moments to force my uncooperative memory into dishing out its secrets. Forensics. He was someone from Forensics. No, that wasn't right. He wasn't in Forensics, he just knew everything. Quinn's… expert guy. The 'weird shit just happened' guy. I was fairly certain he had a name.

Bert? No, that wasn't right. Perky? No. Wait, yes. Perky Perkins. He hated when I called him Perky. Maybe if I stopped giving strangers names they didn't like, I'd have more friends. "Hey, Perky. There's gorgon dust in here, and I don't know if I neutralized it all." My words slurred. Yippee. I sounded like a drunk.

"That's why I'm wearing a hazmat suit, Gardener. On the surface scan, you're showing as clean, but let's not take any chances." Perky removed the metal sensor from my throat, took hold of my chin, and tilted my head so I faced him. Behind his clear face shield, he frowned. "Your face took one hell of a beating. What happened?"

My body really didn't approve of my attempts to move, but I pointed at the trashed cell phone anyway. "Boom."

"Jesus Christ. Cell phone bomb, Chief. She even bagged it for us."

"Bathed it in neutralizer first, too." With Perky's help, I managed to sit up. "Sprayed down the whole apartment, too, but..."

"Better safe than sorry and having an outbreak. Sprayer," he ordered, standing and turning to the door. "Nail the hallway while I take care of the interior."

The other residents of my building were just going to love the mess. It'd get into everything, invade the ventilation system, and coat everything in a pink, glittery residue requiring a great deal of elbow grease to clean up. Someone in a hazmat suit passed Perky a green extinguisher. Pulling out the pin, he took aim and fired, covering everything in my apartment with a pale pink powder. Maybe I was immune to some of the nastiest magical substances known to man, but the purest form of neutralizer could stop the most virulent of plagues dead in its tracks. I tingled everywhere it touched, including my mouth, nose, throat, and lungs when I breathed. It worked its way into my clothes, and within several seconds, I tingled in places I had no business tingling.

It took less than a minute for the itching to kick in. I spat curses at Perky for exposing me to hell. "I thought you said I'm clean!"

"Better safe than sorry, Gardener. Don't be a baby. It only stings and itches for a little while. Look at it this way: if you were sick with anything, you aren't anymore. This is the good stuff. It'll even reverse petrification in a few minutes."

Even my eyes itched, which didn't help me look at anything on the bright side. Scratching wouldn't help; I'd end up spreading the neutralizer into my bloodstream even faster. Within two minutes, I'd be a living itch. "Yippee. I got the good stuff."

Perky abandoned me to scan my apartment for gorgon dust, the meter in his hand beeping away. It squealed like a stuck pig the instant he approached the destroyed phone. "What ratio of solution did you use on this, Bailey?"

"One part neutralizer, three parts water."

"Was the batch stale?"

Was he trying to insult me? While I had expired neutralizer lying around, I kept it separated from the active compounds. I only squirreled it away in case of an utter emergency. The state of my apartment counted, but I hadn't run out of the unexpired formula. "No, it wasn't stale."

Asshole.

Perky sighed. "A man can dream, can't he? Chief, I'm going to need a box. Got a live sample, and it's strong—I'm getting a reading right through the plastic, and it's airtight." Turning to me, the man frowned. "Any symptoms, Gardener?"

A shiver ran through me, and I fought the urge to scratch. The full-body itch could mean nothing. It could mean everything, too. Even with treatment, in a day or two, I might start petrifying people. The human body was filled with inert diseases and bacteria, and the neutralizer killed them all, but it couldn't reverse the gorgon virus. Nothing could.

To add to my misery, if I stayed exposed to the powder for too long, the neutralizer would fry my immune system, ensuring I'd need a new dose of vaccinations on top of everything else. For the next month, I'd catch every little illness known to man.

But I wouldn't spread the gorgon contagion, and that was the important thing.

Why the hell would anyone toy around with gorgon dust? I sure as hell didn't; I knew what would happen if I took a dunk in bile: nothing. But gorgon dust? I'd never breathed in a lungful of it before. Would my immunity hold up? I'd find out soon enough.

I sighed. "No symptoms, but the bomb detonated right in my face. I breathed it in."

With my words, I condemned myself to quarantine, and I knew it. Judging from the way Perky blanched, he knew it, too. "We're going to need the mask and the glass coffin, Chief."

The police chief cursed from his post in the hallway but issued the order. Screaming at the thought of forced hibernation and containment wouldn't change anything. Like it or not, I'd spend a few days in a coma while the CDC evaluated and monitored my health. Begging and pleading wouldn't get me out of it, either.

If I got lucky, they'd reverse sedation, wake me up, and life would go on. If I didn't, one of two things would happen. Depending on my rating as a gorgon, I'd either be tossed to the wolves or packed out for a trip to the mountains where I couldn't harm anyone. If they determined I was a carrier potentially capable of transforming others into gorgons, too, I'd probably be euthanized as too much of a risk to humanity.

Not even other gorgons wanted a carrier among them. Carriers could produce the dust, the dust made more gorgons, and the dust could petrify gorgons, too. I wish I had paid more attention to the gorgon biology courses during my certification rather than yawning my way through most of them.

Immunity gave me an auto-pass for everything relating to gorgons, and their non-typical methods of reproduction hadn't interested me. Their *typical* reproduction didn't, either, but I knew enough about the basics I wanted nothing to do with the whole twisted thing.

I got to my feet to enjoy the last few minutes of freedom, took a single step, and found a marble with my foot. The impact with my floor cut my squeal off and drove the air out of my lungs. "That hurt," I wheezed.

When Perky hurried to my side, he discovered my marbles the hard way. Unlike me, he stayed on his feet. Bending over, he picked up one of the shiny bright blue spheres. "Lose something, Gardener?"

I hated Perky so, so much sometimes.

The man grinned at me, crouched at my side, and touched the marble to my nose. "Don't worry. I'll pick them all up for you. This explains so much. Hey, Chief? I figured out Gardener's problem. She's gone and lost her marbles."

"Screw you, Perky."

He laughed.

THREE

You're really going to make me get into the box, aren't you?

AS PART of the certification process, I'd done several stints in a glass coffin. The devices prevented outbreaks due to mundane and magical sources, and those on the front lines were most likely to be exposed to contagions. My only job was to keep calm. The mask, the part I hated almost as much as the idea of being trapped in a see-through contraption, delivered the initial sedative and doses of the neutralizer. Once I lost consciousness, Perky and anyone else in a hazmat suit would dispose of my clothes, load me in, and flood the box with more neutralizer. If all went well, the mask would keep me breathing.

The neutralizer had no more than seven days to eliminate any hints of contagion. After that, I'd die from dehydration.

Once a glass coffin was activated, nothing entered or left it, and if I didn't survive the process, they'd bury me in it. If I got a viewing, they'd cover my coffin with black velvet to preserve my dignity.

I tried not to think too hard about the whole being stripped part of things. It'd been bad enough with strangers doing it, but I knew at least half the men and women quarantining my apartment. Sighing, I shook my head and waited, my nervousness intensifying with each passing minute.

Had I been inexperienced with hibernation, neutralization treatment, and the glass coffin, someone would've knocked me out with the mask instead of letting me observe their preparations so I could confirm they did the job right. Magic supplied the oxygen, and if something went wrong, I'd suffocate unless they had someone on hand able to penetrate the glass barrier with magic.

Few could.

"You're really going to make me get into the box, aren't you?" A hint of my dismay manifested as a quiver in my voice.

Perky paused in his work and grinned at me. "If you ask me really nice and fetch your nicest lingerie, I'll decontaminate it for you so you can go in partially clothed."

"She will do no such thing," Chief Quinn snarled, stepping into my apartment. Unlike the others, his hazmat suit was yellow with a blue armband marking him as a member of law enforcement with kill authority in the case of a critical contagion.

Yippee. The man who hated me for ruining his marriage could issue the kill order if he determined I was a risk to public health. "Chief Quinn, shouldn't you be somewhere safer, like in the hallway? Back at the station would be even better."

"What she said." Perky snorted and returned to his work setting up the glass coffin for my habitation.

Chief Quinn crossed his arms over his chest. "And miss the chance to strip search you, Gardener?"

My entire body flushed at the thought of his hands on me. Instead of begging for it like every cell of my body demanded, I glared at him. At least his hazmat suit hid his perfection, which helped me control my desire to rub up against him while pleading for him to search me as thoroughly as he wanted. "Yes, please miss my stripping session."

It wasn't until someone laughed in the hallway I realized my words hadn't come out quite right. My face burned. Fortunately, with so much pink powder covering me, no one would spot my blush.

"I'm afraid I'm going to have to disregard your request."

I liked the sound of that a lot, but I made

myself scowl. "That's stupid. Go back to where it's safe, Chief Quinn."

"I'm afraid I can't. I'm the only one here qualified to operate the mask and seal the glass coffin. You'll just have to accept me, like it or not."

Could sedation be faked? I really wanted to fake the sedation. If I ended up dying, I wanted my last memory to be of Samuel Quinn patting me down. That'd be one hell of a way to go. "That's not at all fair."

"You're going in the box, Gardener. Get used to the idea." Chief Quinn already had the mask in hand; I glowered at the plastic device designed to fit snugly over my mouth and nose. I had no doubt he just wanted to do his job and contain a potential outbreak, but I willfully deluded myself into believing he cared what happened to me. A girl could dream, right? My dreams just happened to involve dead ends, impossibilities, and ditching my virginity in a wild night with Manhattan's Most Wanted Bachelor. "Damn it. Fine. I'll get in the stupid box."

"Good. Status, Perkins?"

"It's ready, sir."

Shit. I'd hoped for a little more time. I needed to tell Chief Quinn about Magnus McGee and his involvement with the cell phone bomb before he put me under. "What about—"

Chief Quinn slapped the mask over my mouth, and a puff of hot air filled my lungs. "Nighty night, Gardener. Sleep tight and have sweet dreams. We'll see you in the morning."

It didn't take long for the sedative to pull me under.

LATER, when I wasn't alternating between seizures and full-body spasms, I'd remember surviving revival after hibernation was a good thing. Until the worst passed, I'd remain stuck in the glass coffin with several doctors and nurses hovering in case I required an intervention. I trembled from weakness, which warned me I'd spent several days in an induced coma. It tasted like something had died and rotted in my mouth, and I really didn't look forward to stage two of revival, which involved expelling everything in my body the neutralizer had killed off.

For whatever reason that one of the doctors could probably explain if I bothered to ask, most of it ended up in my stomach.

I bet magic had something to do with it. Magic always found a way to rain on my parade.

I questioned whether survival was really worth the misery of revival. "Please kill me now."

One of the doctors chuckled, and after a few moments of thought, I recognized him as one of the CDC's instructors. "It's your favorite, Bailey. Aren't you excited to go through a live run of top-level containment? You only whined once about it, too. It's a miracle. I'll even give you a gold star this time for your exemplary behavior."

"Oh, look. It's Professor Yale. Did they bring you out of retirement just so you could torture me?" At least Yale understood me. He'd let me crawl out of the coffin on my own and stew in my own vomit if I couldn't swallow my pride and ask for help. While I struggled, he'd laugh. In the end, spurred by his mockery, I'd recover in half the time it took most others.

Everything came at a price, and I'd rather bite off my tongue than ask my cranky ex-professor for help.

I set the bar of victory low: all I wanted was to hit the floor before stage two began. How hard could it be?

"Yes, Bailey. I came out of retirement just so I could torture you. When they called and asked me if I'd deal with our favorite pain in the ass, they actually begged—and offered to pay me for the work. How could I say no? Torture's usually illegal."

God, I had missed the old man's smart mouth. He was a ray of sunshine among a bunch of cantankerous sticks in the mud. With a groan, I rolled onto my back. If stage two hit before I managed to sit up, no one would be happy. Without fail, I'd cry, and then Professor Yale would have to intervene so I wouldn't choke to death. "Yay. I'm so happy. How nice of them. So, how'd I do this time, doc?"

Distractions from the growing discomfort in my stomach would help. No matter what, I couldn't crack, not yet. If I made it to the floor, I'd consider it a win.

"You lived. That's good enough for me. You get a passing grade. I even vacuumed the residue so you wouldn't have to roll in it. Aren't I nice?"

"You're just swell." Clacking my teeth together, I braced for the worst and lurched upright. It went better than I expected, and with a little help from the glass coffin's sides, I got to my knees. With one good shove, I'd topple over the ledge and flop to the floor.

Maybe I'd set the bar a little higher and make it to the trash can before stage two hit. Surely they had one nearby just for my use. Then I could really give the old geezer a hard time when I proved it could be done. Victory was measured in effort, and I'd show him I hadn't been a waste of his time.

I hauled myself over the glass coffin's side and smacked to the tile floor, grunting from the impact. Just because I could, I gave the wretched thing a solid kick. "Stupid box."

It didn't even budge. I'd have to work on my acts of defiance later to make them more effective.

Professor Yale sighed and pointed across the room. "Bathroom's over there."

Game on. I loved the old man so much. Who else would let me make a total fool of myself and only sigh about it? I clenched my teeth and swallowed to hold my nausea at bay. I wasn't able to walk, but I had no issues with crawling my way to victory. Maybe I'd go for gold and take care of all the unpleasantries of stage two revival on my own. That'd teach the professor never to underestimate me again.

Inch by miserable inch, I clawed my way towards the bathroom and made it with seconds to spare. Score. I'd make him eat his words later, after he confirmed I still had guts left after throwing them up.

Victory tasted disgusting.

I GOT to wear one of the hospital's fancy paper gowns while Professor Yale tried to educate a bunch of bright-eyed students about the glamorous reality of surviving a round in a glass coffin. Next time I'd remember to insist on a nurse inserting the catheter. While setting up an IV was an important skill for CDC qualified nurses and first responders, my arms did not appreciate the kid's fumbling efforts. He got it in on the eighth try, and I suspected Professor Yale had picked him on purpose to make me suffer.

The catheter hurt like hell going in, but it didn't compare to the misery caused by a bunch of young men and women eager to show they could handle injections to a professor renowned for demanding perfection. By the time they finished with me, I'd turned into a living pincushion. How the hell could anyone screw up a vaccination injection?

One girl had managed to stab through my arm twice before she got her three syringes emptied into me.

Unfortunately, one of the syringes contained enough active viruses to ensure infection and jumpstart my immune system. Once the viruses took hold, a doctor specialized in magic-aided recovery would work to mitigate the worst of the symptoms and coax antibodies to life so my body could do the rest on its own. Within a week, I'd be a functional human being again, and they'd release me from the quarantine ward.

"Since Miss Gardener required four days within the glass coffin, she will have a lengthy recovery process, requiring a full battery of antibodies plus treatments for dehydration and malnutrition. Any questions?"

Had the requirements for top-level containment at the CDC gone down since my certification, or was Professor Yale taking advantage of a live body for demonstration purposes? Probably both. Gorgon bile incidents happened often enough, but victims of standard petrification didn't require contamination treatment. The dust, on the other hand…

Every last student raised their hand. Spiffy. I had either gotten the ultra curious batch or the green newbies.

"Go, Puck."

Puck? Who the hell named their kid Puck? A girl in the front row bounced on her toes and lowered her hand. "Why is it called a glass coffin? Wouldn't crystal containment sound cooler?"

Good God. Someone had named their daughter Puck, and she cared more about the name of the equipment than the lives of those who needed it for survival—or to prevent an outbreak.

"Miss Gardener, would you please address her question?"

Professor Yale truly loved me. Why else would he be so nice and give me the pleasure of knocking the ignorant girl down a few pegs? I struggled to keep from grinning. "Of course, Professor Yale. While 'crystal containment' sounds nice, it lacks one very important thing. Any guesses on what that might be?"

Every single student shook their head, and Professor Yale leaned against the wall, crossed his arms over his chest, and graced me with a smug smile.

I matched his smile and turned it on the girl. "Puck, what happens when someone has no access to water for seven days?"

"They get dehydrated."

I prayed for patience. "Incorrect."

"What? My answer is most certainly correct."

"Incorrect." How would she handle my direct challenge of her too simple answer? If she was like every other student qualified to join the CDC, she'd probably flip her lid—I'd done it more than my fair share of times before I figured out everything I knew about life was wrong when it came to preventing the spread of infectious diseases and handling dangerous substances.

Puck twisted around and glared at Professor Yale. "She's just a victim. Tell her she's wrong."

Oh boy.

Someone had tried the same stunt when I'd been in his classes, and by the time Professor Yale had finished with him, he left with his tail between his legs and never returned. I wondered how the old man would take Puck's attitude.

If he thought she was worth her spot in the class, he'd handle her gently. Otherwise, I doubted she'd ever show her face at a CDC education center again.

"Miss Gardener has top-level certification in six different branches of the CDC with exemplary performance records handling some of the world's most dangerous substances in live situations. Do you know why she was in a glass coffin?"

The girl had enough sense to slouch and flinch at his words. "No, sir."

"Miss Gardener, please continue your explanation on the purpose of glass coffins. I would appreciate if you forgave my interruption."

Score. I had earned major brownie points from the CDC's meanest professor. It wouldn't buy me a cup of coffee, but I'd savor the moment later, using it as a reminder of my success when I was busy coughing my lungs out thanks to some infection. "In order to prevent any contagions from escaping, glass coffins are completely sealed. The masks used with them provide oxygen to the occupant. If the contagion isn't neutralized, the occupant dies. If the mask fails, the occupant dies. If the neutralizer doesn't scan clean within seven days, the occupant is left to die, however long that may take. Seven days is the typical limit. After death, the victim remains in that clear little box and is buried. That's it, that's all. When you put someone in a glass coffin, you're waiting to see if they can be revived—*if* they can be revived, thus the word coffin."

Every student in Professor Yale's class either blanched or winced.

Puck did both. "Oh."

"You're not going to tell them you inhaled a lungful of gorgon dust, Miss Gardener?" Chief Quinn murmured in my ear.

I screamed, grabbed the nearest object, which proved to be the IV stand, and turned to bludgeon the police chief to death with it. The catheter ripped out of my arm. The man dared to back away, and infuriated over how badly he had startled me, I pursued him while treating the IV stand like it was a giant club. "I'll kill you," I hissed.

Professor Yale sighed. "Miss Gardener, please don't use your medical equipment as a weapon."

Chief Quinn laughed and disarmed me without breaking a sweat. "You're dripping blood all over the floor."

"And whose fault is that?" Taking hold of the IV stand, I strained in my effort to liberate it from him. "What's wrong with you, sneaking up on me like that?"

"I wanted to confirm you'd made it through revival without incident."

I gave up trying to reclaim the IV stand and clapped my hand over my bleeding arm. Snarling a few choice curses, I returned to the examination table and hopped up on it. "Who let him in here, Professor Yale?"

"He activated the seal and mask, Miss Gardener. He's fully within his rights to be here. Perfect timing, Chief Quinn. Perhaps you can impress upon my class the severity of this lesson."

"In ten words or less, please," I muttered.

"A city full of dead people."

Everyone in the room froze, and I had to give the man credit; he'd gotten the point across all right. "That's one way to put it."

"Miss Gardener, on behalf of everyone at my station, thank you for detonating the bomb in your apartment rather than at your workplace. We're very appreciative. Professor, are you almost finished with her? I need to ask her a few questions. I even helpfully removed her IV for you. I also brought her some clothing, which I left at the nurse's station." Chief Quinn set the IV stand down beside the examination table and shook my former professor's hand. "Thank you for coming in to help."

"Of course. Don't tell Miss Gardener this, but she was a very promising student once she figured out how to think on her feet. You can't take her out of this ward, but I'll remove my students so you can have some privacy. Everybody out. Bailey, put a bandage on your arm for now unless you think you're going to bleed to death. I'll ask a nurse to come by later and reinsert the catheter."

I forced a smile when I wanted to scowl at the thought of having the IV replaced. "Thank you, Professor Yale."

"Let's try to avoid a next time, all right?" Without waiting for an answer, he herded his students out of the room, leaving me with Chief Quinn.

Every time I saw him in his blue uniform, I wanted to jump him. Flushing, I turned my head so I wouldn't have to admire the way his clothes clung to his body. "I know for a fact you have at least thirty qualified operators on staff. There was zero reason for you to be the one handling the mask and coffin sealing."

Huh. Maybe I should have said something else instead. A thank you would have done the job without sounding quite so bitchy. Damn it.

"You're welcome." Chief Quinn sat beside me on the examination table. "Made it to the bathroom this time, I hear?"

"Hell yes. Yale can suck it. He told me it couldn't be done."

"Why do I have the feeling everything you

do in your life is prefaced with that statement?"

What an asshole. "Hardly. What do you want to know? I have an appointment with every virus known to man in the next few hours. Wouldn't want to miss it. I'll probably wish I had died." Fine, I was whining, but I had earned a good complaint session or two. A bomb had blown up in my face, and I came too close for comfort to a permanent stay in a glass box.

"You'll be fine. Were you aware someone put a geas on you?"

Someone had put a *what* on me? I scowled. "A geas? Why would someone waste such high level magic on *me*?"

"I don't know. Maybe to hide the identity of the person who gave you a bomb tainted with gorgon dust? Seems like a logical conclusion to me. If they've got the skills to make gorgon dust without becoming infected themselves, a geas is child's play."

Okay, while I deserved the rebuke, did he really have to sound so damned snarly about it? "Someone really put a geas on me?"

"That's what knocked you out in your apartment. We're speculating you were about to say something that would violate the geas, and you were punished as a result. Perkins noticed it, and after I got the mask in place, we called in a few people to remove it. It's gone, but we couldn't figure out the exact conditions to trigger it. We have a few guesses, though."

"Magnus McGee gave me the phone. He said it had important information on it regarding a missing person, and he wanted to hire me to locate them."

"Magnus McGee was found dead yesterday morning in Central Park in a rather compromised position. His partner was a tree." Chief Quinn grimaced, and when I glanced his direction, he was hard at work untangling tubes and righting bags on the IV stand. "I had assumed he was the culprit. A few of my cops had seen him near your workplace."

"I quit." Chief Quinn's small role in my change of employment status shouldn't have pissed me off so much, but it did. It was bad enough Mary had ditched her shift, but to have done it with *him*? I wanted to wring both of their necks over the stunt.

Mary and Chief Quinn. Together. That the thought had crossed my mind at all was proof the universe hated me. Why had I agreed to help him in the first place? If I hadn't taken his stupid camera and gone hunting for his wayward wife, I could go back to my wishful thinking and fantasizing without reality getting in the way.

Chief Quinn sighed. "I heard. Your boss

was rather upset over it, and then she found out someone had tried to kill you on top of it. She didn't take that well at all. I questioned her rather thoroughly along with the rest of the store's staff."

"Did you enjoy taking her for a ride, Chief Quinn?" Shit. Why did my mouth always have to go blurting the bitter things I didn't want anyone to ever hear me say?

"Should I take that as an invitation to explain the situation?"

The anger of having dealt with an eighteen hour hell shift flared back to life. "I really don't give a shit what two consenting adults do in your car. You know what I do care about? Not being left alone to run the shop for eighteen hours. So what if you took her for a ride in your car? I don't care who she dates. At least she could've called someone in to take her place. What happened instead? I soloed my job from opening to closing. To add insult to injury, *your* former brother-in-law bombed me with gorgon dust probably hoping to get rid of *you,* since someone had probably told his wife about the certified barista you called in for consulting work. I was just the bonus. If he took me out, he had a damned good chance of being able to eliminate you from the picture."

Silence.

Crap, crap, crap. I had said too much. My

face flushed, and I scrambled to find some sane justification for unloading all my speculations, one that didn't involve magic.

"I see." His lifeless tone partnered with his completely neutral expression told me everything I needed to know. My barbs had struck true, and he wasn't happy about it at all. "Is there anything else you want to tell me, Miss Gardener?"

How could I possibly be so mad at someone yet still be so attracted to him? At the rate I was going, I wouldn't know which end was up. Since 'I'm not wearing anything under this gown' qualified me for early admission into an asylum and counted as sexual harassment, and 'spank me, I've been bad' wouldn't go over so well, either, I mumbled, "Sorry. I shouldn't have said that."

"I'd be pissed, too, if someone had tried to kill me in his effort to get revenge on someone else. I'm a big boy. I can handle anything you throw at me. That's all I needed to know. Thank you for your time, Miss Gardener. Enjoy rehab."

How did he make sliding off an examination table look good? It really wasn't fair. Considering I'd already ruined any chances of having a civil conversation with the man, I went all in and threw caution to the wind. "I'm not wearing anything under this gown."

He walked towards the door without reacting to my words. Fine, if he wanted to play hardball, I'd play hardball. "Hey, Sammy. If you want someone to teach you how the reverse cowgirl should really be done, give me a call. I know some girls."

There. Not only did I pour gasoline on the situation, I lit a match and tossed it on. It wasn't like I ever had a chance with a man like him anyway. It was better for me if he avoided me indefinitely.

Chief Quinn slammed the door so hard I felt it from across the room. For some reason, my victory only made me feel even worse. Damn it.

I deserved every bit of hatred the man threw my way.

FOUR

Yippee.

IT TOOK two weeks for me to recover enough to escape the hospital, thanks to one baby virus who decided to grow up and become pneumonia. I was stuck with the cough for another week or two, but I could deal with the prescribed bedrest, lots of fluids, medication, and taking it easy.

Those might become my famous last words, as I hadn't expected the NYPD and the CDC to join forces and napalm my apartment. From the outside, there was no evidence anyone had waged war on the interior of my home, but sure enough, everything inside had been reduced to piles of gray ash. While I stood in the doorway trying not to cry, my landlord gave me my formal eviction notice, which claimed I had willfully brought dangerous substances into the building.

Yippee.

Too tired to fight the false accusation, I

accepted it with a nod, folded the slip, and stuffed it into my pocket. At least it would provide evidence I had lived at the building. That might help me get a replacement identification card.

In retrospect, I deserved it. Taking out my bad day and time in a glass coffin on Chief Quinn lowered me to the same basic level as pond scum. I owed him an apology. Hell, I owed him a lot more than an apology. In a stunt worthy of the worst type of asshole, I had made everything worse.

I realized I hadn't had a single visitor or phone call the entire time I'd been in the hospital, and it was no wonder why I didn't have any friends. I'd driven Mary off, burned bridges with my other co-workers by tattling on them, and there was no one else in my life. In a way, it simplified things for me. Since no one cared what happened to me, I didn't have to go to the hassle of sending thank you cards.

I really needed to stop lying to myself. I'd seen the pity in the nurses' eyes when I pretended I didn't care no one came to see me. They had caught me checking the door whenever someone walked by. Whatever goodwill I had earned trying to keep the gorgon dust contained in my apartment I had promptly lost by being a complete bitch.

While I could have made it easy on myself

and gone to the CDC for a temporary identity card I could use to replace my driver's license, I headed for the NY DMV. If I went to the CDC, I'd run the risk of running into someone I knew, particularly from the police department.

The last thing I needed was a run-in with Chief Quinn after what I'd done.

After I visited the DMV to replace my license and the bank to replace my debit card, I'd have to swallow every last bit of my pride, stuff it in a closet, and call my parents. I wondered if they'd talk to me.

I doubted it.

A little after noon, I left my former apartment building and headed for the DMV. The twenty-minute walk cleared my head a little and gave me a chance to prepare for inevitable hell. It took two hours to convince the skeptical clerk my home—and wallet—had been torched with napalm. The eviction notice came in handy, as did the doctors and nurses at the hospital. They helpfully corroborated my story but hunted down what remained of my pride and beat it to death in the process.

At least I walked out with a replacement driver's license in hand. With it, I replaced my bank card with minimal fuss. Too much of a coward to request a balance, I gambled Mary had paid me for my final shift and the rest of my owed hours. I requested two hundred in cash, which the teller gave me without a word.

I almost cried, and it took every bit of my flagging strength to ignore her incredulous stares.

With everything I could do without a home accomplished, I began the tedious task of finding a phone. Why were pay phones so uncommon? I ended up stepping into a hotel and begging the lady behind the desk until she relented and let me use the phone. She kept giving me dirty looks while I dialed my parents' number.

It'd been years since I'd spoken to either one of them, and I didn't even know if they still lived in the same house in New Jersey.

"Hello?" my mother answered.

She sounded so sweet on the phone, the exact opposite of me. Maybe the universe didn't hate me after all. "Hey, Mom."

Silence. Then again, I was probably wrong. I elevated 'don't cry' to the top of my list of things to avoid in the next ten minutes. "Uh, this is going to sound really bad, but the CDC napalmed my apartment. Is there any chance I can stay with you for a few days?" I hesitated. "Please?"

"No." She hung up on me.

I should have known. The universe really did hate me, and so did my parents, and I had earned every bit of their loathing. I placed the phone in its cradle and forced a smile. "Thanks."

I left. Without a credit card, few hotels would let me rent a room for any period of time. If Mary had given me my earnings, I had a hair over six hundred and twenty dollars. What the hell was I supposed to do on six hundred dollars? With that little, I couldn't afford to pay out the first and last deposit. In a month, the first bill for my hospital stay would arrive, I wouldn't be able to pay it, and my battered credit rating would tank completely. While the CDC would likely compensate me for my hospitalization, even before I had quit my job like a spoiled rotten brat, I wouldn't have been able to afford the additional expenses, not without a great deal of overtime.

My mother had been right to reject me. I never left anywhere on a good foot, and I specialized in burning bridges. Instead of asking Mary why she had abandoned me for a ride in Chief Quinn's car, I had lost my temper and quit. If she wanted to go somewhere with Samuel Quinn, that was her choice and none of my business.

I had no right to be jealous or upset over it.

What I had done to Samuel Quinn put me on the list of terrible people who deserved to suffer. How could I be so vindictive, stupid, and selfish? Why couldn't I be a normal person, someone people actually cared about?

Even my own mother didn't want me, and I didn't blame her for it in the slightest. At eighteen, I'd made my stance clear: I had wanted to earn my way in the world without their version of charity, which meant I'd grow up in the job they wanted me to do, carrying on the Gardener name with pride.

I had chosen to pursue certification with the CDC while working at a coffee shop specializing in legalized narcotics. They hated everything pixie dust stood for and the fact I dared to lower myself to working as a barista. They hated magic.

Then again, they had hated me from the day I had been born, so it didn't matter. Nothing I could do would make them happy. That didn't change facts, however.

They'd been right all along. I hadn't been able to afford a college education on my own, and even with certification, I was too poor to transition from my job as a barista to something else. Ten years had gone by, and I ran the treadmill from one day of my life to the next without going anywhere.

Worst of all, I truly had no one to blame but myself.

MY SEARCH for a hotel that accepted cash took me to the worst part of Queens, and by the time I got checked in, my coughs rattled in my chest, promising a world of misery for the foreseeable future. On the bright side, one-twenty got me a room for a week, and it even had a microwave and a can opener. A trip to the bodega down the street stocked me with enough soup to last until I needed to check out or extend my stay, and I bought a few bottles of water to be on the safe side.

Even if it took me two weeks to recover, I had enough time to find a job somewhere. One-twenty for a smoke-stained, dingy hotel room beat the alternative. I'd be miserable, but I could manage.

I choked down a dinner of soup, curled up on the rock hard bed, and cried myself to sleep.

Big mistake.

Sobbing drained the little energy I had left. I'd been warned in the hospital to avoid exertion. I'd been told to get rest, take my medicine, and take it easy. I still had the prescription slips in the back pocket of my jeans. Without my insurance card, it'd cost more than I had to fill the damned things.

I could tough it out. I'd done it before. All I needed was to get a lot of rest. My hike across Queens to get my new driver's license card and debit card hadn't helped me, but I had needed a place to stay. Why couldn't people understand that?

I didn't have anyone to take care of me, and that was that. I probably never would, but I had no one to blame for that but myself. Through a blur of fever and chills, I forced myself to get up and take care of the bare minimum. I drank all my water, thanked God the tub was somewhat new, and even managed to eat my soup like I was supposed to. Every waking moment I spent coughing so much I could barely breathe.

Several times I considered reaching for the phone to call a cab and return to the hospital. That would've been the smart thing to do, but I stayed put and weathered the storm instead.

I considered it an accomplishment I managed to leave my room to stagger back to the bodega, pet the owner's new kitten, and hike back to the hotel burdened with cans of soup, bottles of water, and packs of cough drops. I stopped by the desk and paid to extend my stay. If I didn't feel less like a plague bearer by the end of the week, I'd succumb to the inevitable and call for a cab.

The soup would have tasted a lot better if I had heated it before pouring it down my throat. I plunked a bottle of water on the nightstand, flopped into bed, and passed out.

Hindsight, as always, was perfect, and I

should've just returned to the hospital on my own like a sane person, as I ended up there anyway. Unfortunately, I had no memory of going, which was never a good sign. Another not-so-good sign was my hallucination of Chief Quinn beside my hospital bed wearing a button-up shirt and a pair of jeans he must have stolen from an incubus.

Instead of his normal, clean-shaven jaw, the scruff of a new beard turned him from pristine model to rugged and lethally sexy.

Only my twisted psyche would produce an illusion of my heaven and hell wrapped in one glorious package, present him in clothes I wanted to strip him out of, and leave me to wallow in my misery and guilt over my bountiful stupidity.

Stupid, stupid, stupid me.

My hallucination was a persistent little bugger, sticking around while I contemplated why I might be imagining him in a chair beside me, close enough I could touch him if I could move my arm. It took me a long time to understand they had me hooked up to a ventilator, which explained the whole sexy hallucination thing.

Bummer.

I contemplated trying to say something, but the mask on my face made speaking difficult. Not only did ventilators suck, they blew, too, and made it far too much work to do anything other than stare at the gorgeous imaginary Chief Quinn my twisted little brain had thoughtfully provided for me. I gave up trying to do anything productive and decided to take a nap, hoping for a suit-clad model when I woke up.

I got the dress uniform model instead. Score. He was talking to another cop, one in a regular uniform, and judging from the tone of Chief Quinn's voice, the blurry figure had done something to deserve a scolding. I knew all about needing a scolding—or a spanking. Yes, I definitely needed a spanking from Chief Quinn. Then again, if push came to shove, I'd be happy to be the one doing the spanking.

Imaginary Chief Quinn provided me with a spectacular view of his back, but he ruined it by leaving with the other cop. Far too late, I realized I hadn't tried to apologize.

Damn it.

The next time I woke up, I was free of the ventilator. My subconscious decided fake Chief Quinn needed to be dressed in a… actually, I had no idea what he was wearing, except it resembled a gym uniform of some sort. I didn't approve of it, not one bit, and after a fierce battle with my own tongue, I told him so.

Crap. Why did I keep forgetting to apologize?

It could wait until he came back in better clothes. I promptly returned to my nap so I wouldn't have to subject myself to his wretched attire for another instant.

My stupid subconscious decided I needed to be punished for my rudeness, so she inflicted an endless stream of gym model Chief Quinns on me. At least I recognized one of the jerseys as supporting the Lakers.

Wait a second. The Lakers? Why the hell was a proud member of the NYPD, a chief of police, wearing a Lakers jersey? Unacceptable. "What the hell? Los Angeles? Gym model Chief Quinn sucks. Knicks or bust." Every last one of my words was slurred, and gym model Chief Quinn stopped tormenting the other cop in my room. "Want suit model."

I was whining. I decided I didn't care. Hallucinations couldn't tattle on me anyway.

Gym model Chief Quinn stepped to my bedside and looked down his pretty nose at me. "Do I want to ask?"

Yay! The gym model could talk, and he didn't sound too pissed at me for once. "Ooooh. Never mind. Lakers gym model can talk, and he doesn't hate me."

I thought the occasion was worthy of a happy squeal. The Lakers fan version of Chief Quinn didn't seem quite so enthused. Unsurprising, really. "What are you talking about, Gardener?"

Not only was he talking to me in a civil fashion with a curious tone of voice, he had asked me a question I could answer. "Jeans model Chief Quinn brooded and didn't talk. Angry as usual, because let's face it, you hate me because I'm a terrible person. God help me, the dress uniform model might have lit my panties on fire. Dear God, that view." I giggled, then a thought struck me. "Wait. Am I even wearing panties? Did the dress uniform model really light them on fire? Oh, bother. Bad dress uniform model." I giggled again and tried to focus on the second hallucination my subconscious had so kindly provided. "Right, second hallucination person?"

"You're so high right now, Gardener," the second hallucination replied.

Oh. I knew the second hallucination. "Perky? Yay, it's Perky. Hey, Perky! Perky?"

"This is going to be so, so good. What is it, you crazy woman?"

Confessing embarrassing things couldn't hurt when I was talking to the hallucinations my subconscious provided, right? "I want the suit model or the dress uniform model for Christmas."

"I'll have a talk with Santa about that for you. How does that sound?"

"Huh. Santa's never visited me before. It's probably his fault I turned out so bad. He never gave me any coal. He should've. It's not fair. If you tell Santa, he'll agree I don't deserve the suit model or the dress uniform model," I wailed.

"Good job, Perkins," the Lakers fan version of Chief Quinn muttered. "She was happy for all of ten seconds, and you just had to go and ruin it."

Perky shoved his way to my bedside, pushing the complaining gym model out of his way. "I'll make sure the suit model shows up in time for Christmas, okay? Just please don't cry. Please? I'll beg. If Santa tries to tell me you don't deserve it, I'll kick his sack."

I sniffled. "Promise?"

"I'm going to hell for this, aren't I?" Perky sighed. "Yes, Gardener. I promise. You'll get a suit model Chief Quinn in time for Christmas."

"You're so going to hell," the gym model muttered.

"I should tell you to shut up, but you're the only model who talks to me." It was a stupid thing to cry over, but I did it anyway.

Stupid, inconsiderate subconscious, providing me with equally stupid hallucinations determined to make me cry. Damn them all.

WHILE I WAS FAIRLY certain the satyr nurse and my doctor were real, they interacted with my hallucinations to screw with me. The oversized pixie doctor with a dust complex and a general inability to cope with my immunity was the worst offender, but I understood why. Happy patients healed faster, and most of the Chief Quinn models made me cry within ten minutes. I wanted to blame the drugs Dr. Valleychime kept insisting on dosing me with, but it was my fault.

Every time I had tried to apologize to Chief Quinn, it came out wrong. The last time, I had told him he'd look better naked, and he got so mad at me he left. I had thought he'd blushed, too, but then I had decided I was just seeing things.

To my disappointment, the dress uniform and suit models didn't make an appearance.

The Lakers model showed up with Perky in tow, and I sighed. "Aren't you supposed to be one of New York's finest?"

"I am." Chief Quinn dragged over a seat so he could sit beside my bed. "What do you have against the Lakers?"

"Nothing, except that's a Los Angeles team. We're in New York."

"He's doing it to piss you off, Gardener. He's got his regular clothing in a bag just outside the door." Perky peered at the monitor near the head of the bed. "Jesus. They still have you on the crazy stuff. Do us all a favor and get better already. Sir, please put on something nice for her so she doesn't blame me when she believes Santa hates her."

"No."

It was my turn to sigh. "But Santa does hate me. So does Chief Quinn. It's okay, Perky. This model talks to me." I gave my crappy thin blanket a flick with a finger. "Dr. Valleychime hates me, too."

Chief Quinn stiffened in his seat. "Why?"

"Pixie dust." How could one stupid substance bring me so much misery? "I'm sorry," I mumbled.

There. After countless hallucinations, I'd finally managed to choke out an apology.

Perky cleared his throat. "I think it's because Dr. Valleychime is a pixie doctor specializing in long-term recovery and the mental and emotional well-being of patients in this hospital, sir. He gets sensitive when he can't just flutter his pretty little wings and make most patient satisfaction problems go away. Considering he's packing the good stuff, she's probably stung his pride a little. She's good at that. She's a rose, but she's all thorns."

I couldn't argue with him. "I'm sorry."

Hey, I got out two apologies in one conversation. Maybe there was hope for me after all.

"For once in your life, could you just be quiet, Gardener?"

The Lakers model hated me, too, and I bit my lip so I wouldn't cry again.

My doctor fluttered in through the door, took one look at my imaginary visitors, and sighed. "If you can't stop triggering depressive episodes with my patient, sir, I'm going to have to ask you to leave."

Great. Dr. Valleychime was talking to my hallucinations again just to mess with me.

Chief Quinn snorted.

My doctor glared at the police chief before turning his attention to me. "Do you want me to have him removed, Miss Gardener?"

"I'm pretty sure you can't just make a hallucination disappear, but if you could get him to take his shirt off, I'd be totally okay with that."

At the rate my doctor was sighing, I worried he'd have an aneurism. Lifting his hand, he rubbed his temple. "What did I do to deserve this? Miss Gardener, Chief Quinn is not a hallucination, and neither is Dr. Perkins."

I squinted at Perky. "You're really a doctor? I thought you were some kind of awesome super geek who just happened to know a lot about forensics stuff."

"I can't tell if you hate me or like me, Gardener, and that's really screwing with my perception of reality."

"You don't have a perception of reality.

You're a figment of my overactive and drugged imagination."

Dr. Valleychime tapped on the monitor near my bed, probably to adjust my medications. "They're both quite real. Now, granted, you've had several legitimate episodes involving hallucinations, but this is quite real. Unfortunately, so is that jersey."

My doctor wasn't supposed to try to trick me into believing my hallucinations were real. "I would like to dispute your claim."

"Any disputes you might make won't change reality."

Scowling, I shook my head. "There is zero reason for either one of them to be here. I'm an insufferable bitch, Dr. Valleychime. I have no friends, and there's a very good reason for that. Chief Quinn has at least a hundred good reasons to hate me, and don't get me started on Perky. If murder were legal, I'm sure they would've gotten rid of me by now. They'd do whatever it is manly cops do to call dibs for the right to off me."

"Yet you want Chief Quinn to take his shirt off."

"Hell yeah. Are you blind? Take a good look at him. He's proof God exists and wants to make women happy."

My doctor coughed. "That was incredibly sexist. I'm genuinely astonished."

"Hey, men might appreciate a chance to have him, too," Perky added.

Chief Quinn sighed and covered his face with his hands before running his fingers through his hair, making it stand up every which way. "Can we not discuss this?"

"Why shouldn't men be able to enjoy your masculine beauty, sir?"

"Perkins."

Oh, nice. Chief Quinn could growl, and he sounded amazing when he did it. "If you take your shirt off, we can discuss your virtues and come to an educated decision. It's an important matter we're talking about here."

"Gardener."

The way he growled my name was so much better than the way he growled Perky's.

I wanted to hear him do it again, so I said, "How can we properly discuss your sexiness if you're hiding it behind that jersey?"

"She has a point, sir. We can't properly objectify you if you're still wearing your shirt."

"*Perkins!*"

"As her doctor, I would like to point out that it's my duty to ensure my patient's emotional health and general well-being. Hospital stays of any significant duration can cause psychological strain, and as Miss Gardener doesn't respond to traditional measures, this might be an acceptable alternative."

I beamed at Dr. Valleychime. "I have finally met someone who likes me. It's a miracle."

"Emotional well-being does play a major role in recovery, and Miss Gardener has been a very sick young woman, Chief Quinn. You'd be helping to facilitate a good healing environment for her."

Perky made a sound suspiciously like a giggle. "You heard him, sir. You'd be facilitating her healing."

"This isn't funny, Perkins."

Damn, that growl sure was nice. "Make him do that some more, Perky. That's great."

"She's really into you, sir. I never would have guessed."

"Damn it, Perkins!"

"Come on, sir. It's for her emotional well-being. Just take the jersey off already. It won't kill you."

"Fine. Just shut up." Chief Quinn stood and pulled his jersey over his head, revealing a white t-shirt.

I clapped my hands. "Take it off, take it all off!"

The glare Chief Quinn leveled at me should have burnt me to a crisp, but I somehow managed to survive. "I'm only doing this because it's my fault you're so damned sick."

Wait. Being sick entitled me to a free showing of a half-naked Samuel Quinn?

"Thank you, God. You're still wearing your clothes, Quinn. I've been waiting my whole life for this."

Heaving a sigh, the kind I reserved for when someone tested my patience to the absolute limit, Chief Quinn yanked his shirt over his head. It even ripped a little, and it was the sexiest sound I'd ever heard.

Never again would I be able to think of cops as pudgy-bellied, donut-eating coffee guzzlers. The man must have waged some epic war against fat, because I couldn't spot anything other than lean muscle and the chiseled lines of someone who spent a great deal of time working out and eating healthy.

I was thin, but only because I couldn't afford to eat too much. If he wanted, I bet he could break me in half with his hands and look good doing it.

I would never understand how anyone could even dream of giving him up. He was so, so out of my league it hurt. It took every scrap of my willpower to turn my stare to Perky. "I'd like to report a crime, Officer Perkins."

"I'm amazed. You actually know my real name. Go ahead, Gardener. I'm listening."

"Anyone who looks that good should be a model. An underwear model. In underwear, all the time. You're right. Everyone should get a chance to admire his beauty."

Perky burst out into laughter. "You heard her, sir. I'm going to have to write you up. Everyone should be able to admire you. To not share your beauty with the world is a crime."

"I'm afraid I'm going to have to agree, Chief Quinn. You have been taking exceptionally good care of yourself. If your legs are anywhere near as defined, I may need to use you as a showcase model of what a healthy athlete should look like. Finding such a good specimen is difficult."

Chief Quinn sighed. "Are you done yet?"

Swallowing so I wouldn't drool, I memorized each and every last inch of him, doubting I'd ever get a second chance for such a spectacular view. I wanted to reach out and touch him, to see if those muscles were as hard and strong as they looked.

"If you take your pants off, you might break her, sir."

"*Perkins!*"

Dr. Valleychime chuckled. "Who knew a police chief could be so shy?"

Without bothering to put his clothes back on, Chief Quinn stormed towards the door, gracing me with his equally lovely back. At least this time he didn't slam the door. "Hey, Perky?"

"Yeah?"

"Instead of the suit or dress uniform

model for Christmas, can I have a photograph of him shirtless instead?"

Perky offered me a tissue. "You're drooling, Gardener."

Damn, so I was. Oops.

FIVE

I cursed him in hoarse, raspy whimpers.

AFTER ANOTHER ROUND of pneumonia and a two-day stint in ICU on a ventilator, Dr. Valleychime banned all visitation, which meant Chief Quinn and Perky since there was no one else interested in visiting me. It took several doctors and nurses to determine I suffered from a syndrome associated with my lengthy containment within the glass coffin. The neutralizers hadn't just destroyed the residual gorgon dust in my system; my immune system wasn't responding to vaccinations or developing antibodies, which put me at high risk of contracting something lethal or crippling.

When they moved me from the ICU ward, they put me in an isolation ward typically reserved for people recovering from chemotherapy. After several days of Dr. Valleychime injecting me with substances meant to revitalize the immune system, he called in someone from Texas who specialized in imprinting and rewiring how bodies handled illness and infection.

I wondered where they found a containment suit for a centaur and what sort of diseases a human could catch from a man mixed with a goat. Dr. Tressman seemed like a pleasant enough fellow, and he didn't even mind when my raspy coughing fits interrupted his work. After three or four hours of poking and prodding me, he shook his head and called in Dr. Valleychime.

"You're going to need to call the twins," the specialist announced.

Dr. Valleychime frowned, and then he sighed, a weary, defeated sound. The two talked, using terms I couldn't pronounce let alone spell. Dr. Tressman took pity on me and gave me the news in simple words I could understand: the neutralizer hadn't just wiped out my immune system, it had blown it to bits, and he'd never seen anything like it before. To be safe, they moved me deeper into the ward, and I was treated like a victim of a highly contagious disease. No one came in or out of my room without a suit, which was sprayed down with neutralizer in the doorway.

To purge my body of infections, I was subjected to another round in a glass coffin, a necessity I protested between coughs. We managed to come to a compromise; I'd still go into the glass coffin, I'd still have to wear the mask, but the coffin wouldn't be sealed. They'd even hook me up to an IV if it took more than a few hours for the magic to do its job and kill off the viruses lingering in my body.

I spent eight hours and twenty-three minutes in the glass coffin, and they sent for Professor Yale to handle stage two recovery. I didn't complain when he helped, and he didn't say a word about my inability to sit up. Dr. Valleychime consulted with him, and while my lungs ached and my throat itched from the amount of coughing I'd done, I enjoyed being able to sit up and breathe without the assistance of a machine.

Dr. Valleychime ultimately called in the big guns, faery doctor twins who could do more than just imprint and retrain someone's immune system. In a three hour procedure, they intended to raise mine back from the dead.

They brought in a set of silver and gold chains etched with runes, which they informed me were required for the operation. Like any sane woman, I fought them, but the pair of eight inch tall men won the battle without any help from Dr. Valleychime or Professor Yale, who watched with interest.

It didn't take me long to figure out the chains' purpose. Since the procedure hurt like hell, they kept most of my body immobile while the faery doctors worked. My respiratory system still functioned, so I cursed them until I lost my voice. To add insult to injury, the instant the twin doctors declared they were finished, they gave Professor Yale the go ahead to begin the vaccination process.

I cursed him in hoarse, raspy whimpers while he chuckled and jabbed me with needle after needle.

It took them three weeks to rebuild my immune system. Professor Yale celebrated my recovery by dumping a bucket of gorgon bile over my head and making me clean it up. He also brought some of the CDC's safer samples to confirm my immunities had survived the procedure.

They had.

Not satisfied with the initial results, Professor Yale took me into custody, helped me deal with the massive stack of discharge papers, and escorted me to the CDC's NY headquarters. With demonic glee, he ordered me into a hospital gown, led me to the auditorium and locked me in the containment chamber, where he proceeded to test my immunities while his students watched through a thick pane of safety glass.

At least the CDC would pay for my hospital bills—all of them—in exchange for being put on display like some freak of nature. Granted, I *was* a freak of nature when it came to my immunities, but that wasn't my fault.

"There are no words to express my level of hatred for you, Professor Yale." I glared at the man, who stood with his students in the small auditorium. All in all, there were at least a hundred and fifty people watching me get drenched with various formulas, dried off with the containment chamber's special ventilation system, doused with liquid neutralizer, and dried off again before we repeated the process.

If my immune system kicked the bucket again, I would find a way to make him suffer for an eternity.

"Now that you have seen standard immunities, students, I'm going to show you something rather special. For this demonstration, I will be in the containment chamber with Miss Gardener. While most of our substances can be sprayed into the room with her, the next sample will be given in pill format."

Uh oh. I didn't like the sound of that. Most magical substances only required skin contact to work well, which meant he probably had some hellish mundane poison or irritant he wanted to show off. "Are you going to take it, too?"

"As a matter of fact, yes. I will be the control subject for this demonstration."

I tensed. There was exactly one compound I could think of that he'd be willing to test with me. "Oh no. Hell no. Hell fucking no. Not happening, Professor Yale. You keep that shit away from me."

The old man laughed long and loud. "It's only a D grade sample, Miss Gardener. You'll be fine."

The next time I was volunteered for testing and agreed to put up with it, I'd remember transformative substances carried a hazard rating, which they earned due to their unpredictable nature, risk of permanency, and longevity. Magic worked in mysterious ways, and unlike almost every other class of substance on Earth, transformative substances locked victims into only one shape; after exposure, the CDC maintained a database of names and transformations in case other government agencies required the information.

I became a unicorn, and not the pretty white kind with a sparkling horn and a tendency to fart rainbows.

Contemplating escape didn't help me. Professor Yale moved fast for an old man, and an assistant locked the door behind him before I had a chance to make a run for it. "This is happening, Bailey. You may as well surrender now."

"Damn it." I sighed and held out my hand for the tiny gel capsule. "I don't suppose you'll go first?"

Professor Yale gave me the pill. "If that'll make you happy, sure."

Maybe the students would be too busy laughing at the professor's fluffy bunny ears to notice me. Yeah, right. After I swallowed the pill, within five or ten minutes, I'd be a black and red mottled equine armed with a pointy stick on my head—a very sharp stick with a razor-like edge spiraling from brow to tip.

"The transformative category of hazardous magical substances is among the most dangerous. Until someone has been exposed to a substance, no one knows what they will become. You might become a cat. You might become a rat." Professor Yale popped his pill into his mouth and swallowed. Since he only underwent a partial transformation, it took about twenty seconds for him to sprout his bunny ears. "You might, like me, become a rabbit. Grade D substances trigger minimal alterations in most subjects. Bailey, please demonstrate the rule's exception."

Yippee. I heaved the most dramatic sigh I could manage and swallowed the pill.

Under normal circumstances, I would

have exercised my right to curse up a storm at the discomfort of transformation, but since I had an audience of young men and women about to get an up close and personal look at how a human body could expand, sprout fur, mangle bones and grow new ones, I kept my vocabulary to myself and limited myself to a few pained grunts and involuntary whimpers.

Transformative substances sucked, I hated them, and I seriously considered stabbing Professor Yale with the weapon attached to my forehead. It took me a few minutes after the magic had its way with me to scramble to my hooves, which clattered on the tiled floor. Flattening my ears, I leveled a glare at Professor Yale, who dared to chuckle.

Fortunately, while my head and body were mostly equine in nature, vaguely resembling the love child of a goat and a horse, my specific species of unicorn possessed vocal chords capable of limited English. Anything with two or more syllables gave me trouble, and speaking made my soft, equine mouth ache. I stomped a hoof, which clicked on the floor. "Not fun-ee. Hate you."

Professor Yale grinned. "Class, look very carefully. This will probably be the first—and only—time in your life you will ever see a unicorn of her breed. As a part of your certification, each of you will be exposed to D grade transformative substances to determine your species. Like me, you will probably experience a very minimal alteration, generally harmless in nature. For most situations, there are three grades you need to be aware of: C, B, and A. Exposure to A+ and greater transformative substances will likely result in a permanent transformation or death. D or lower has negligible effects. You can even purchase some limited E grade compounds in novelty stores. Bailey and I each took a pill made from the same batch of compound, which for safety reasons I will not name. No matter which substance Miss Gardener is exposed to, the results are the same, which qualifies her for the safe handling and testing of all A+ graded transformative materials."

He paused for a moment to let his words sink in. "Neutralizer, please."

The ceiling sprayers released a cloud of vapor, and I lifted my head, flared my nostrils, and breathed it in. Professor Yale did the same. From his pocket, he pulled out a meter, which he activated. It squealed, and only when the wretched device stopped making noise did the chamber operators cut off the vapor flow.

Returning the meter to his pocket, Professor Yale gestured to the bloodied scraps of my hospital gown on the tile. "The gown she was wearing didn't survive the transformation process, and her blood was contaminated with the substance. When you're in the field, you need to be aware that contamination can easily spread. All surfaces the victim touched must be neutralized to prevent accidental spread. Any questions?"

On the other side of the glass, many hands went up, and the students eagerly leaned forward.

"Third row, fourth from the left. Ask."

"Why is Miss Gardener black and red? Aren't unicorns supposed to be white?"

I snorted and stared at Professor Yale, hoping he'd let me demonstrate *something* rather than just stand around looking pretty for the amusement and education of a bunch of green recruits. With a faint smile, he nodded.

Twisting around so I faced the glass, I lunged a stride forward, tossed my head back, and stamped my hooves. I gave a swish of my tail and eyed the humans, faery, and other supernatural hiding behind the barrier, safe and sound. Most of the time I hated my dirty little unicorn secret, but the body came with one ability I loved: fire. All the fire, fire for me to breathe, enjoy, and even roll in if I wanted.

I loved fire, and I shared my love with the students, blowing a gout of flame over the glass. Those in the front rows recoiled. A few even screamed, and I enjoyed every moment of it.

"For the record, Miss Gardener classifies as a vanilla human. Transformative substances with an A or greater grading temporarily transfer the abilities of the new form to their victim. This is why these substances are often so dangerous. The higher grade substances come at a great price, including the complete and total loss of personality and identity. In short, should you be exposed to A+ or greater transformative substances, you will irrevocably become a new species. Questions?"

Every hand went up, and Professor Yale picked on a woman. "Yes?"

"Does transforming hurt?"

Since unicorns couldn't shrug, I shook my head before nodding.

"That depends on the individual. Bailey is often quite vocal when subjected to extreme pain. If she isn't cursing, it's typically a tolerable discomfort. However, as I've witnessed her transform numerous times, I'm confident she was sparing your gentle young ears from the profanities that usually spew from her mouth. Today's transformation went better than others."

"Stings a little," I contributed, giving a shake of my mane and relaxing my stance.

Professor Yale pointed at someone in the first row. "Ask your question."

"Can all unicorns talk?"

"No." I stomped a hoof. "Wilds do not. They hunt. Eat. Burn."

Oh yes, did they burn. The desire to snort flame and bask in its heat writhed under my skin and heated me from within. Until the transformation reversed, my favorite place in the world was somewhere with a fire. I turned my head to Professor Yale. "Fire?"

The professor chuckled, stepped forward, and gave my shoulder a pat. "Yes, Bailey. I'll take you somewhere with a nice fire. If you haven't noticed yet, Miss Gardener is keeping to short, easy words, and will often degrade to the simplest methods of communication possible. Unicorn anatomy, while somewhat compatible with human language, makes speaking difficult. It's actually uncomfortable for her to talk. In addition to that, unicorns have a different thought process and base personality, which does blend with Bailey's inherent personality. While at base level she is the same person while human, complete with her memories, she picks up a few elements of a unicorn's temperament. In regards to language, when we were initially evaluating her while she was a unicorn, it took her several weeks of effort to master basic English." Professor Yale pointed at someone in the audience, a young woman who stood up.

"How long will Miss Gardener remain a unicorn?"

"It varies. No matter which grade you're subjected to, duration is dependent on the individual. She might reverse back to human within ten minutes, or she could be stuck for a week. While many people have a more consistent response to transformative substances, hers is widely variable. I will lose my new ears within two hours. The longest time she has remained a unicorn has been eight days. In emergency situations, A grade and weaker substances can be reversed through treatment in a glass coffin. The procedure takes two hours, but it's expensive and risky."

I remembered those eight days far too well. Mary thought it had been funny to use me as a coffee roaster and charged customers a premium for the honor of having a cup made by a fire-breathing unicorn. She often enjoyed my various mishaps with the CDC, finding some way to earn a profit at my expense.

I really hoped the reversal happened sooner than later. Trotting around as a unicorn wouldn't make it easy to find a new job or a place to stay, but at least I could sleep just about anywhere, especially if I stole one of the CDC's horse blankets. Then again, I could also swallow my pride and take a nap in their stable. Wait. Did I even need to ask them for approval? They had turned me into a unicorn in the first place. I'd just invite myself over for a free stay and bite anyone stupid enough to disagree with me.

Professor Yale gestured to someone in the crowd. "Your question?"

"Is it true only virgins can ride unicorns?"

The entire audience cracked up laughing. I wondered if the glass barricade could handle seven hundred pounds of unicorn slamming into it. Maybe if I softened it with a little fire first, I could get through and poke a few holes in the boy.

"I'm sure Miss Gardener would enjoy a midday snack if you're volunteering. No, virginity will not save you from being eaten by a unicorn. Bailey, please show them your claws. Try not to break the glass, as it is very expensive."

I charged the barrier, reared, and pressed my front hooves to the glass, unsheathing my claws and tapping them on the slick surface. I turned my head and exposed my teeth, which were serrated and pointed to better tear meat into chunks I could swallow. As payback for the virgin question, I snorted flame, too. "Dee-lee-ssshh-us human."

The front row cleared out so fast I whinnied my laughter. "Run, tay-stee humans. Run."

To give the kid credit, he didn't flee although his eyes widened.

Professor Yale cracked up laughing behind me. "Would you care to put your virginity to the test, Maverick?"

"No, thank you. I'm good."

"Any other questions?"

The students kept quiet, and quite a few of them retreated to the safety of the doors in the back of the auditorium.

"That concludes today's lesson. Dismissed."

The place cleared out in record time, and I dropped to all fours, letting out another amused whinny. "They run fast, pro-fess-ur."

"That they do. Did you really have to threaten to eat them? I'm going to have whiny students in my office complaining I put their precious little lives in danger." The old man shook his head. "At least there is good news. You're testing out as expected. Whatever gives you your immunity isn't dependent on your immune system. A genetic marker, perhaps? Ah, a mystery for another day."

I shook out my thick coat and gave my mane a toss. "Who knows?"

"Good question. Something to think about later. Are you ready for a trip? We're expected elsewhere. As we had to napalm your apartment, the CDC has made arrangements for temporary housing."

I tossed my head, widening my eyes in astonishment. "Real-ee? Why?"

"Ah, that's right. You probably don't remember what we told you while you were ill. We couldn't neutralize the device with the sprays. It took two rounds of napalm to get it all. As it's partially our fault you lost your residence, management thought it would be appropriate to make arrangements."

Since when did a government-run organization like the CDC do anything outside of their contracts? "Im-poss-ee-bull."

"Get used to the idea. Everyone's very grateful you kept it in your apartment. Had your heating or air conditioning been on, we would have been dealing with a major outbreak. You did everything exactly right. You neutralized the airborne particles, you did your best to contain the source of contagion, and you kept everyone out of the affected zone. It's not often I get to tell anyone this, but well done."

"Thank you." I meant it, too. For Professor Yale, there was no higher praise. When I added his compliment to the fact the CDC was helping me beyond the normal protocols, I was a very happy woman. Unicorn. Whatever.

WHILE THE CDC would have brought in a truck and trailer for me, I decided to hoof it across the city, tailing Professor Yale's little yellow sedan. If I reversed back to human, I'd be better off on the street with him to supervise than in the back of a trailer alone, bouncing around in a bed of flax.

Nothing hurt quite as much as having to pick out hay or flax after transforming, and it often involved a very patient nurse, a pair of tweezers, and a scalpel. I'd much rather gallop ten, twenty, or thirty miles—or more. I'd run my furry ass all the way to the Hamptons to avoid it.

Unfortunately, Professor Yale didn't feel it was necessary to inform me of our destination except to tell me it wasn't in Manhattan. Once we were on the road, I was far too busy dodging cars and pedestrians to care. Within five minutes of leaving the CDC's headquarters, a taxi cut me off, forced me onto the sidewalk among a bunch of annoyed and startled New Yorkers, and blared his horn.

If the cabbie wanted to play, I'd play. I snorted flame at his bumper and gave chase. I caught him staring at me in wide-eyed horror in his rearview mirror as I twisted my way around and jumped over a few cars in my effort to teach him why he should never piss off a fire-breathing unicorn.

I pursued him for two blocks before scorching his bumper, turning tail, and trotting my way back to Professor Yale's car, sending gouts of flame at anyone who had a problem with me going the wrong way in traffic. If the cabbie hadn't tried to run me over, I wouldn't have needed to show him the reality of challenging black and red unicorns.

Professor Yale rolled down his window and stuck his head out of his car. "Don't make me cork your horn, Bailey."

"No touch. Burn." Mmm. Fire. "Fire?"

The first hints of fall encroached on summer's heat, and despite my thick coat, the lower temperature bothered me when I breathed. I wanted to find somewhere nice and warm to curl up and nap. At least running would keep me warm, assuming no other idiot cabbies tried to run me over.

The old man sighed. "It's getting too chilly for you, isn't it?"

"I'll man-age. Little cold." Since he seemed in the mood to talk while driving, I trotted alongside his car and shot glares—and fire—at anyone who dared to complain we took up an entire lane. I even kept right on the line.

If a cop pulled me over, I'd eat him. On second thought, I decided eating one of Chief Quinn's officers wouldn't go over well, so I'd settle with a nibble instead.

"You really are a one-track mind when you're a unicorn. Yes, Bailey. There's a fireplace where we're going, and I was very clear in my instructions there needs to be a fire waiting for you when we arrive. As if I'd forget something that basic."

I snorted, and trails of smoke rose from my nostrils. "Far?"

"Not too far, no. Thirty minutes if traffic doesn't get too bad."

"Where?"

"Just to College Point. Might even make it in twenty if we're lucky."

I flattened my ears. "Queens?" I struggled with the word, my thick equine tongue unwilling to cooperate. "Coll-eeg Point in Queens?"

"Yes, in Queens. You've lived there for how long? You should know where we're going. Pay attention to where you're trotting."

The nice thing about being stuck as a unicorn was the wide assortment of natural weapons at my disposal. The instant we stopped at a light, I shoved my nose into his car and gave him a good look at my teeth. "You try dodg-ing cars."

"I know, I know. I can't help that the cabbies are idiots on even the best of the days and don't like sharing the road with others."

I stomped my hooves to keep warm while waiting for the light to change. In my impatience, I unsheathed my claws and dug them into the asphalt. "Burn them!"

"No, Bailey. You can't burn the cabbies."

"Why not?"

"You can't eat them, either."

"Ab-so-loot-lee no fun, Pro-fess-ur Yale."

"Don't kill the cabbies, Gardener. Don't vandalize their cars, either. And for the love of God, please do not attack any police horses should we meet one on the way. The last thing I need is to have to explain to Chief Quinn why you went after one of his mounted officers again."

I pulled my head out of Professor Yale's car and snorted, grateful the light had changed to green so I wouldn't have to continue the discussion. It wasn't *my* fault the NYPD had decided to have a stallion on the force, and it certainly wasn't my fault I had refused to lose my virginity to some damned horse. One day I would decide to overcome my social ineptitude long enough to find a man—a human man—willing to sleep with me.

Stupid whore horses.

Whatever happened, I couldn't let Chief Samuel Quinn figure out I was a virgin who only knew the finer points of sexuality thanks to the internet, too much time spent in a bar, and having a faery for a boss.

"He start it. I fin-ish it. Bad whore. *Horse*. Bad horse."

Professor Yale laughed. "Whore, horse. Pretty much the same thing when it comes to a stallion. I'll give you some credit. You didn't kill the horse and eat him."

"Should have."

"Next time, just gallop away. You're faster."

No mundane horse had a hope in hell of catching me, that was true. I could even outrun a cheetah, and on a good day, I could maintain better than highway speed for ten minutes, after which I collapsed into a useless, quivering heap. Traffic lights gave me a chance to catch my breath, and even when we hit fifty, I didn't have trouble keeping pace with Professor Yale's car. "Horse need taught less-on."

"I'm sure it did."

"Yes, did."

Another red light halted traffic, and thanks to a bunch of clueless tourists, we ended up waiting two cycles. I sighed at the delay. "We go to an a-part-ment?"

"No, I'm taking you to a proper house. I picked it with your special needs in mind. The owner has a fireplace, a sizable fenced backyard, and everything you need on hand. I even found time to hunt down a fur rug for you."

I pricked my ears forward. The first mistake the CDC had made when I had transformed for the first time involved where I'd sleep. Straw made for terrible bedding for a tired, cranky unicorn capable of lighting things on fire. While flax was better, it still made me sneeze like straw did, and when I sneezed, things had a tendency to burn.

I *really* hadn't liked the sprinkler system, and I'd spent the rest of my first transformation shivering in a miserable, wet, furry ball until the CDC figured out I needed to be kept somewhere toasty warm to minimize the risk to me and everything around me.

Manners mattered, and determined not to alienate one of the few people who seemed to care enough to go out of his way to help me, I said, "Thank you."

"This polite version of you is really starting to creep me out. Stop it. You're welcome."

I decided to shut my mouth before it got me into trouble. Once we reached the outskirts of Queens, traffic lightened enough that I needed to put in real effort to keep pace with Professor Yale. By the time he pulled into a driveway behind an NYPD cruiser, lather dampened my coat, and I blew air in order to catch my breath.

In the garage, I spotted a sickeningly familiar red sports car.

Wait. A police cruiser? Red convertible parked in the garage? Nice house? White picket fence, good part of Queens?

"Oh hell no." In case Professor Yale wasn't

sure how I felt about the situation, I squealed my dismay. While I'd never been to his house, there was only one cop I knew who had a convertible, lived in Queens, and took a cruiser home with him whenever he felt like it: Chief Quinn.

My heaven and hell bundled in one smoking hot package opened the front door, looked at me, and grinned. "Does this mean I get to go for a ride, Yale?"

I gulped. Panic coursed through me, and I wondered how far I'd get before I collapsed in an exhausted heap somewhere. Why was I at Chief Quinn's house? Had Professor Yale coerced the man?

Wait. Chief Quinn wanted to know if he could *what*?

I whipped my head around to stare at Professor Yale. "Big fire?"

I could make a really, really big fire, and while everyone dealt with putting out the flames, I could make it to the next state, no problem. Houses burned nicely. So did trees. I bet I could make the grass ignite, too. And the bushes. And the cars, all three of them. Chief Quinn had helped the CDC torch my place, so turnabout was fair play, wasn't it?

"No, Bailey. Good afternoon, Chief Quinn." Professor Yale stayed in his car, leaning out his open window to wave at the police chief. "Thanks for hosting. She'll be less grumpy after she's been fed and put near a fire. Remember, if the temp gets below eighty for too long, she might try to hibernate, so watch out for that. Drop the temp to seventy at night and bank the coals. In the morning, stoke the fire as hot as you can, put meat in easy reach, and give her about an hour to wake up. When you take her out of the house, don't forget the blanket and the cork."

Chuckling, Chief Quinn leaned against the doorframe. "I remember from the ten other times you explained it. I even have all the brushes you suggested. Come on in, Gardener. You're stuck with me until you reverse back to human at the earliest. Isn't it your lucky day?"

Was the man insane? Had he hit his head on something? Why the hell did he sound so cheerful? I unsheathed my claws and dug them into the asphalt, flattened my ears, and glared at Professor Yale.

The old man ignored me. "Call me if there are any issues, Chief Quinn."

"Will do. Thanks for bringing her over."

"All right, Gardener. Move your ass so I can get back to work."

I snorted but sheathed my claws and stepped to the side so he could back out of the driveway, leaving me alone in front of the brick house with its pristine picket fence, immaculate lawn, and roses in full bloom lining the walkway.

The man who hated me for ruining his marriage had invited me into his home. Me, a fire-breathing unicorn requiring a manual to keep healthy. By tomorrow, if I didn't reverse back to human, I would leave tufts of black and red fur everywhere. I would need someone to help brush out my coat so I wouldn't mat. I would cost him a fortune in firewood and meat.

Even knowing that, he had still invited me in.

"Sor-ree for the truh-bull."

"Come on in, Bailey. It's really no trouble. The competition to host you was fierce, as Perkins and half the station offered their places, but since I was the only one of the lot with a suitable fireplace, I won by default." Chief Quinn stepped into his house and left the door open behind him.

I gaped. Perky had volunteered to host me, too? Who else at the station would actually want to help care for someone as problematic as me, let alone half of them? Impossible. Absolutely impossible.

Aware of Chief Quinn's curious neighbors emerging from their homes to stare at me, I shuffled my way down his driveway to the walkway. The sweet scent of roses got the better of me, and I paused to nibble on a bloom.

"Are you eating my roses?" Chief Quinn blurted.

Oops. I flicked an ear, swallowed the evidence, and feigned innocence. I made it a few more steps before a large red bloom caught my eye. I eyed it, glanced at Chief Quinn, and debated if I could get away with just one more.

"Professor Yale didn't tell me you had a taste for roses. Had I known, I would have bought a bouquet so you wouldn't eat my bushes."

Yep, Chief Quinn liked his roses. What could one more hurt? He had so many of them. It took far more restraint than I liked to leave the big flower alone. Maybe he wouldn't mind if I took a nap on his sidewalk for a while. The run from Manhattan hadn't done me any good. I turned my ears back and swished my tail, annoyed over my aching muscles. My time in the hospital hadn't helped at all, either. When I reached the four steps leading up to the small porch and the front door, I glared at them.

As a unicorn, steps were my archenemies; as often as not, I tripped over my own hooves if I tried to take them any faster than my slowest walk. I lifted my head so I could get a good look into his home. The entry way provided plenty of space with a side table shunted against the white-painted walls as my only obstacle.

Fortunately for me, no one really knew a whole lot about unicorns, especially my species, so when I did something weird, everyone figured it was a part of my new body and the result of transformation.

Wrong.

Unicorns, at least of my breed, normally couldn't teleport, nor could they hitch a lift on the beams of sunlight streaming into Chief Quinn's home. I was different. I had no idea how it worked, but when I had four hooves instead of two feet, a little concentration, a clear path, and some light equalled a fast way to skip the stairs.

When I materialized in front of him, Chief Quinn yelped. "He didn't tell me you could do that!"

I bobbed my head and whinnied, careful to avoid stabbing or slicing anything with my horn. Why did a unicorn's tongue make speaking English such a challenge? "Nice house. Tay-stee roses."

In his preparations to invite me into his home, I suspected Chief Quinn had rearranged his furniture to make room for me. The entry opened to a sitting room with a pair of couches, an armchair, and a coffee table pushed out of the way. In front of a fireplace was a large, black furry rug. Flames crackled in the hearth, and I pricked my ears forward. "Fire!"

"All yours, Bailey. Have fun, just please don't burn my house down, no matter how much I might deserve it."

I angled my head so I could watch him with an eye. "Not your fall-tuh—*fault*—McGee use a bomb with dust. Nay-palm need-ed, Chee-fuh." I struggled to force out his last name but mangled it.

"Just call me Sam. If you try to say my full name in front of the other cops, they might die of laughter. I wasn't kidding about you being stuck with me, either. You'll be coming to work with me. Professor Yale was very clear about that: you won't be left unattended. If you get sick for any reason, we're hauling you back to the hospital."

Chief Quinn wanted me to call him Sam? I cocked an ear back, not sure what I thought about that. When I was honest with myself, I liked the way his last name rolled off my tongue. Come hell or high water, I'd get his name right. Maybe I'd drop the chief, but I'd reserve Sam for something truly important. "I like Quinn."

His name came out closer to queen than Quinn, but it'd do until I found some private time to practice. The last thing I needed was someone catching me while muttering his name. They'd believe I had lowered myself to stalking the police chief.

"I see. Is there anything I can get for you?"

I shook my head.

"Okay. Just shout if there is. I'll be in my office down the hall if you need me." He flicked me a salute and walked away, and I admired the view.

Then I remembered manners were a good thing. "Thank you, Quinn." There. Not Chief Quinn, just Quinn. That was the closest to intimacy I dared to get with a man far too sexy for his own good—or for mine.

SIX

I never needed to come out of the fireplace, right?

MY FIRST ORDER of business involved stuffing my head into the fireplace so I could bask in the flames crackling around my nose and washing over my brow. It took a bit of work to jam my horn up the chimney without damaging anything, but after a few minutes, I was positioned to relax and enjoy the heat. My neck was just long enough I could lie down on the rug without having to rest much of my weight on the hearth's stones.

"When Yale said you liked fire, I didn't think you'd be sticking your head up my chimney. How in the hell did you even fit in there?" From somewhere behind me, Quinn laughed. "That's incredible. When he warned me unicorns were high maintenance, this wasn't what I had in mind."

Could I fit my entire body up the flue? Making an escape through the chimney was beginning to seem like a viable option. In an effort to restore some of my dignity, I replied, "Your fire is nice. I like it."

I never needed to come out of the fireplace, right? At least not until I reversed back to human.

Naked, in Chief Samuel Quinn's house, on a rug, sprawled in front of his fireplace. Naked. The naked part was really important. Unless the magic gave me some warning, which it usually didn't, I'd end up giving him quite the show. With my abysmal luck, not only would he get an eyeful, it would happen in the most embarrassing place possible, like on a busy street in downtown Manhattan. No matter what, I was screwed.

Or not.

Damn.

"So, there's a small problem. The station just called, and they need me to come in. There's a situation. While I'd love to leave you to your enjoyment of my fireplace, you need to come with me."

But I had just gotten comfortable. The fire was perfect, roaring around my head and keeping me so nice and warm. I had found a slice of heaven, and I had to move already? "No," I wailed. "My fire. Mine!"

"I'm really sorry. I'll have to douse it."

Quinn wanted to douse my fire? Fury at the thought of so much wasted wood and flame burst through me, but I squished it back so I wouldn't do something stupid like yell at him. How dare he want to douse my fire? I'd show him the error of his ways. I snorted, sending a shower of sparks up the chimney, and reined in my temper. "Why sor-ree? Not your fault."

Those words cost me, especially since he wanted to take my fire away from me. Still, he was a cop, and he had to go in when called. It really wasn't his fault. "Must work."

I understood work. I had to do too much of it to barely get by.

Quinn sighed. "And then there's the other small problem. I have no idea how I'm getting you to the station. They're supposed to send a truck for scheduled shifts, but I can't wait that long."

"Wait. Mo-ment." I rolled my body so I could get my hooves under me, restrained the instinct to hook my claws into his floor for better balance, and wiggled my head and horn free of the comforting confines of the fireplace. To keep from setting his home on fire extracting myself from the flames, I devoured every last scrap of wood in the hearth, crushing the charred bits between my teeth and ripping the fire-hardened chunks apart with the help of a hoof. I choked and coughed several times in my hurry to swallow. Within minutes, I reduced the fire to nothing more than a few piles of ash and embers.

Bleh, ash. I licked it up anyway to be safe.

"And that would be another thing Yale neglected to mention. I guess I won't have to douse it after all. That just leaves the issue of getting you to the station."

Did Quinn not realize I was a unicorn, thus my own form of transportation? "I can run. Have hooves."

"I was hoping for something a bit faster."

I flattened my ears, tossed my head, and whinnied at the insult. "Out-run you, Chee-fuh *Queen*."

He scowled and crossed his arms over his chest. "You did that on purpose, didn't you?"

"Out-run you, pesky human Chee-fuh *Queeny!*"

"That was even worse. You really think you can outrun me in my cruiser."

Shaking out my mane, I snorted, blowing just enough flame to warn him I meant business. "Yes. Take you. Fass-tur."

During the certification process and evaluation of my species after transformation, I'd carried a few riders. I'd taken another student from Manhattan to the Hamptons and back. In a less-than-legal favor to one of the instructors, I had run her across the bridge to New Jersey so she could speak at a convention after her car broke down.

We had wisely never told Professor Yale about that stunt, as we both valued our lives—and she'd given me extra credit for the favor.

Quinn was heavier than all my past riders, and I blamed his extra inches and his beautiful, beautiful muscles for the extra weight. Still, I could handle him—I hoped.

"You're crazy, you know that, right?"

"You know how to ride, yes?"

"Well, of course. I do mounted patrols sometimes in a pinch, and I teach riding lessons to new recruits when the regular instructors are unavailable."

"You ride. I run. Fass-tur."

Quinn ran his hands through his hair before giving his scalp a good scratching. "You're seriously telling me you think you can beat my cruiser to the station."

"Yes. Stop com-plain-ing. Bri-dle?"

"Yale left me one yesterday."

"Sad-dle?"

"I am not putting a saddle on you. I refuse."

Stubborn human. Why were all humans so stubborn and annoying, especially the pretty ones? "Yes, you will."

"I will not."

"Get sad-dle! Take you. Ten min-nut. Be fass-tur if not argue. Wear un-ee-form, get sad-dle. We go."

"It takes longer than ten minutes to go fifteen miles, Gardener."

"Want to bet?" I'd show him. I'd make it in nine, too, just to spite him.

"No, I don't want to make a bet with you. It can't be done."

"You will. Bet," I demanded. "Bet!" Prancing in place, I bobbed my head and swished the air with my horn.

"Christ, fine. Fine! What bet? I really can't afford to waste time, Gardener."

"When you here in house, no shirt. Feed me best meat by hand. Grapes, too." After all, what girl didn't want a shirtless man feeding her grapes? Unicorn or not, I was going to live the dream. "Keep fire nice, bright, warm. Serve me."

For a chance to have a half-naked Chief Quinn at my mercy, I'd do a lot more than gallop to Manhattan. "You win, you boss me. I give rides. Make fire. Not make fire in house."

With a long-suffering sigh, Quinn stared at me. "If I don't agree, you're going to play with fire in my house to spite me, aren't you?"

Oh, that was a great idea. "Yes!"

"I'll go get the saddle."

QUINN WOULD BE mine to enjoy, and all I had to do was gallop from Queens to Manhattan to have him. As though resigned to his inevitable defeat, he gave me a bowl filled with fresh meat cut into bite-sized cubes while he dealt with my tack. The CDC had custom made my saddle since my body wasn't quite shaped like a horse's. The bridle lacked a bit, which was a good thing, as I would've melted it down and swallowed it to get rid of it.

Metal did terrible things to my digestion.

After he had me saddled up, he went into his house to change, returning within five minutes. The rumpled state of his uniform warned me whatever the situation was, it was bad.

His cheek twitched as he looked me over. "I can't believe I'm doing this."

Swallowing down the last chunk of meat, I gave the bowl a parting lick before straightening and tossing my head. "You ask Pro-fess-ur Yale about ride. You get ride. Com-plain, com-plain, com-plain. You keep time. Me run. You ride. No whine-ing."

Quinn groaned, jammed his toe into the stirrup, and mounted. I grunted as he settled his weight on my back. Yep, the man was made of pure, wonderful, rock-hard muscle. In nine minutes, he'd be all mine.

"Hold tight. I run fast. Ver-ree fast. Fass-tur than car. Red-ee?"

"Fine. Don't you dare break your neck

doing this, you hear me? So help me, I'll kill you myself. I'm timing you, Gardener."

Since losing my rider—my prize—would cost me precious seconds, I eased my way to a canter, unsheathing my claws whenever my hooves couldn't get enough traction on the asphalt. I would give him a block to adapt to my rolling stride before I hit top speed.

While I didn't often drive despite having a license, I knew the routes from Queens to Manhattan well enough. After a moment of thought, I decided Quinn lived close enough to Whitestone to warrant crossing the bridge there before hopping onto the Cross-Bronx long enough to reach Bruckner. Then I'd make my run past Central Park to the police station.

The only issue was getting there without ditching my rider or smacking into a car. Either would ruin my day, although I'd rather break a leg than hurt Quinn. People needed him.

No one needed me.

The thought both depressed and annoyed me, and determined to prove I could be useful to someone, I charged towards the Whitestone bridge. Intersections proved my first obstacle, and I dealt with them by bolting through green lights, treating yellow lights like green ones, and jumping over vehicles when the lights didn't cooperate and stayed red before my arrival.

The first time I disregarded a red light and leaped over oncoming cars, my passenger yelped and clutched at my neck. I loved it so much I did it again at the next light, thundering my way to the bridge in a minute flat, blowing through the tollgate and cutting off several drivers in the process.

"Fucking hell!" Quinn choked out.

Oh, yeah. I loved it. The instant I made it across the span, I dove across traffic, hit the Cross-Bronx, and took the quickest route to the Bruckner. The midday drivers didn't appreciate me weaving through traffic, and the sweet, sweet sound of blaring horns chased us down the expressway. To minimize the risk of clipping a vehicle or losing Quinn, I galloped alongside the median, which gave me all the room I needed to hit my top speed and stay there.

I blew the doors off the slower vehicles, including several patrol cruisers. The wail of a siren warned me at least one had decided to give chase. If he caught me, I'd lose my bet, and Quinn would end up with a legitimate ride to his station. Come hell or high water, I'd deliver him to Manhattan within my ten minute window, and no pesky cop in an annoyingly fast car was going to stop me.

Stretching out my neck, I raced the wind

—and the police—towards Randall's Island, where I'd need to blow through more tolls to reach Manhattan. More sirens shrieked behind me, and traffic parted for the pursuing vehicles.

Why wouldn't they part for *me*? I was giving a police chief a lift. More importantly, I could breathe fire. While tempted to educate the people clogging my road about the superiority of unicorns, I kept my eyes on the prize and charged for the nearest exit.

If I stayed on the expressway, the cops would catch up, and I couldn't allow that to happen.

Ignoring Quinn's cursed complaints and whining, I thundered down the ramp, waited until I was within safe distance of the ground, and leapt to the street below.

Turns out men could squeal with the best of them. Who knew Quinn's voice could go up an entire octave? Lather flew off my coat, and I suspected by the time I reached his station, the man would need a fresh uniform. Cutting down side streets and alleys, I worked my way to the river. To my disgust, the access road and the bridge were deadlocked, and unless I wanted to start leaving hoof prints on car roofs, I needed to pick a different route.

Over the river and through the woods it was, and I dove down the bank, lifting my head to get a better look at the opposite shore. I'd never attempted to take someone with me when I hitched a ride on a sunbeam, but for the chance to have Quinn as mine, I'd take the risk. I slowed to a walk, so if he did get left behind, he wouldn't get hurt landing. Bracing myself for the lurch, I concentrated.

Hopefully, Quinn would forgive me later. I angled towards the water.

Quinn tensed on my back. "No, Gardener. No! Not the—"

I jumped, soaring over the river, picked my mark and willed myself—and my rider—to the far bank. Landing hurt. My hooves slipped on the loose gravel before I recovered enough to scramble away from the shore to the park. Who needed a stinking road anyway? Not me.

Quinn would be mine.

Since I hadn't left my cursing passenger behind, I plowed through the brush into the forested park, dodged trees, and wished I could whinny my laughter at his yelps and general displeasure over my method of crossing the city. Why did people always get so cranky when I gave them exactly what they wanted? Since I couldn't gallop, avoid smacking into something, and talk at the same time, I decided I'd deal with the irritated human later.

I caught a lift on a second ray of sunshine

to Manhattan Island and crossed a few backyards and alleys to reach FDR Drive, sticking to it until I reached the first main street intersecting with Central Park.

From there, it was a cake walk of startled pedestrians and pissy cabbies to head south beyond the park and reach the station full of stunned cops. I staggered to a halt in front of the concrete steps leading to the front doors, shuddering in my effort to catch my breath. "T-time? Time!"

"Eight minutes and forty-seven seconds. Never. Do. That. Ever. Again." Quinn slid off my back, grabbed hold of my bridle, and pulled my head to him. "Are you insane? That's the only explanation." Drawing in a deep breath, the police chief launched into a tirade listing every single traffic law I had broken on my way from Queens to the station. I waited it out, my heartbeat throbbing through my entire body.

Behind Quinn, I witnessed several cops playing an energetic game of Rock-Paper-Scissors, and the loser took several cautious steps forward. "Uh, not to interrupt, Chief Quinn..."

Quinn twisted around. "What is it?"

I liked when the man snapped at someone other than me for a change. The poor sacrificial cop retreated several steps, holding his hands up in surrender. "You're needed inside, sir."

Giving another jerk of my bridle, Quinn glared at me. "This isn't over, Gardener."

I snorted. "I know. I won. Best meats. Yum-ee grapes. All mine."

"Gardener!" Quinn released my bridle, spun, and stomped into the station. I followed in his wake, wobbling my way up the steps.

One of the cops held the door open for me, and I gasped out something he fortunately interpreted as gratitude. "Quinn. Quinn. Sad-dle? Sad-dle heavy, Quinn. Take off? Meat? Wat-ter? Quinn!"

My words made the man twitch. I pursued him all the way to the elevator, chanting my demands. At the parting doors, he turned to face me and palmed my nose. "You are too fat for this elevator, so take the stairs and like it!"

I hated stairs but loved winning, so I called it even and trumpeted my pleasure at my triumph over Chief Samuel Quinn.

Mine.

ACCORDING to the amused cops loitering in the station's lobby, Quinn was on the eighth floor. Did he really expect me to climb eight flights of steps? He would pay dearly for his misguided assumption I would do what he wanted. He was *mine*. I had won the bet, and he wasn't going to be bossing me around anytime soon. In a brief but fierce battle against my quivering muscles, I lifted my hoof, unsheathed a single claw, and tapped the up button. It felt like an eternity until the elevator door swished open so I could stretch my neck and check the max occupancy sign.

Two thousand pounds.

When I got hold of him, I'd take a nibble or two out of him. Death would be too good for him, and I'd enjoy making him squirm. I was not fat! I maybe weighed seven hundred pounds. I could use the elevator. Maybe I'd torch his pants so he had to walk around in the nude. A light nip would remind him he couldn't say mean things to me. With an indignant snort, I stepped inside. Perky and several other cops joined me.

"Purr-key!"

He chuckled. "Gardener. Have yourself a nice run? Which floor you headed to, girl?"

"The one with Chief *Queeny*." I whinnied a laugh. In a perfect world, the name would stick, and I had four candidates to spread my new nickname for the man.

"Eight, then." Perky pressed the button. "I'm headed that way, too. I'm surprised you're here. What brought you this way all dressed up like that?"

"Pro-fess-ur Yale dumped me with Queeny. No time for trail-ur."

"Wait. Chief Quinn was at home? That's—"

"Eight min-nuts and four-tee sev-un secunds away." I really needed to practice talking more in my equine form. "By u-nee-corn."

"Okay, that explains why you're absolutely drenched and look like you were run through a wringer. You'd have to clock in at almost two miles a minute to get here that fast. Damn. I heard you were fast, but that's nuts. You could outrun an interceptor on an empty road at those speeds. Do you have rockets strapped to your ass or something?"

I preened and tossed my head at the compliment. "Sad-dle hev-ee, Purr-key. You take off? Wat-ter?" I hesitated. "Meat?"

After a run like mine, I thought I had earned a little bit of whining and some indulgence—and a drink.

Perky gave my shoulder a slap. "How about some crap coffee and some stale chips?"

Score. "Deal."

The elevator dinged and opened, and I wobbled my way after Perky, who guided me through a maze of desks and chairs. It took a bit of work to ease my way through without knocking anything over. As I passed cops, they offered handfuls of candy and chips. I accepted their offerings and lipped their outstretched hands without taking a single bite of one of Quinn's officers.

At one of the workstations near the end of the line, Perky cleared away enough space for me. "Park your furry butt here for a few minutes, Gardener. I'll get you something to drink and find someone who might be able to free you from that contraption without breaking it."

"Sad-dle, Purr-key. It's called a sad-dle. The one on my face is a bri-dle."

"Contraptions. Wait here."

"Wait-ing," I mumbled, standing where he ordered. While he was gone, I helpfully rearranged his desk and stole his chips, which were stale just like he promised. When I got bored, I dozed, a hind hoof lifted while I used his desk as a pillow.

Someone prodded my nose. "You're drooling on my desk, Gardener."

I snorted, blew several sheets of paper and some envelopes to the floor, raised my head, and blinked at Perky. "Purr-key."

Behind Perky, a freshly groomed Quinn stood, scowling at me. "Hey, lawbreaker. Up for a plea bargain? Admit you're guilty to every last crime you committed getting us here, and I'll let you off easy."

Uh oh. Cranky human was out for blood—mine. "You did not make me swear to follow laws. But I liss-en. Still won bet."

Quinn sighed. "Yes, you won. Here's the deal: someone called in a large-scale gorgon bile mess about five minutes after we got here. The gorgons we have on call are both out of town. Can you deal with it, please?"

How did he expect me to deal with the bile without hands? Roll in it and play in a bonfire? Wait. Could he really be giving me a chance to solve a gorgon bile problem with fire?

Best. Day. Ever.

"Fire? You'll let me solve your gorgon bile problem with fire?" Since I was trying to be more polite, I added, "Please?"

"God save my soul, but yes. You can solve this problem once—and only once—with fire. Only this once."

"Fire!" I squealed. "Purr-key come with me?"

"Feel up for a decontamination job, Perkins?"

"For the record, I hate you both," my new partner replied.

SEVEN

I can not eat that con-crete cake.

WHOEVER HAD DESIGNED 120 Wall Street must have been really hungry. "Big cake. What a waste. I can not eat that con-crete cake, Purr-key."

I also couldn't eat the huge crowd of people who surrounded the building and flooded Wall Street, ensuring we would be unable to reach the entrance without help or magic. I sighed, staring at the glass-fronted revolving doors, something I couldn't maneuver through as a unicorn even if I wanted.

I hoped the two windows flanking the main entrance also doubled as doors, or I'd have to find a different way in—or use even more magic. Sighing again, I twisted my head around to wearily regard my rider.

"They really evacuated the entire building over some gorgon bile?" Perky echoed my sigh. "Lovely."

Unless I wanted to wade my way through

hundreds upon hundreds of people, I'd need to hitch a lift on a sunbeam and take Perky with me. My success with Quinn during the run offered the hope I'd manage the trick without incident. "Call cops there? Make room by door. I can get us there."

"Really? Nice. You have some neat tricks up your sleeve as a unicorn, Gardener. Maybe we should keep some of those transformative pills handy so you'll actually be useful around the station."

"I will eat you, Purr-key."

"No, you won't. I'm stringy and wouldn't taste good." Shifting his weight in the saddle, Perky retrieved his phone and made a call. Within a few minutes, the cops blockading the door moved out of the way. "That good, Gardener?"

"Very. Hold tight, Purr-key. No fall. Would hurt."

"Why am I already regretting my decision to come with you?"

"Purr-key is smart, that is why. You'll be safe with me." I stomped a hoof and picked my mark, bracing for the inevitable surge of motion and vertigo associated with zipping along at the speed of light from a stationary position. Teleporting with a rider was harder than I expected. In the future, I'd try to catch a ride on sunlight from a run. It was less disconcerting.

Perky yelped, groaned, and slumped over, his hands clutching at my neck and mane. His body shuddered, and he gagged.

Apparently, Perky didn't handle teleportation magic nearly as well as Quinn. "No puke on me, Purr-key! That's rude. Bad. I get to deal with enough bile here. Off, off! *No puke on me!*"

"I hate you, Gardener. I hate you so much."

I believed it, but I opted to play along as though he meant it sarcastically, just in case he did. "You know you love me, Purr-key. I let you ride me, a u-nee-corn. I am most con-sid-er-ate. Now, off!"

To my relief, Perky managed to slide off my back without throwing up on me, although there was definitely a greenish cast to his skin. "I'm walking back to the station. No wonder the chief was so irritated. You did that to him, didn't you? That should classify as torture."

The man groaned and leaned against me, panting and swallowing in his effort to keep his stomach under control.

"Poor Purr-key. You stay here, feel better. But you ride back to station. You whine as much as the chief. Gor-gon bile po-tent. Stinky. You stay here and not be sick."

"Chief Quinn will kill me if I let you go in there alone. There will be a murder—mine—

and there will be no need for an investigation. Chief Quinn will hang my body in his office as an example for others. No, Gardener. You're not going in alone."

Why did humans insist on being so insufferably stubborn? I swung my head around in search of the nearest cop. "Chief cry if I go alone. You take Purr-key, I take some-one else? Make every-one happy. I clean bile, your cop watch? Use ex-ting-guish-ur after I make fire?" I paused and sighed. "Yay. Bile."

"Wow, Gardener. I had no idea it was possible to cram so much disgust and sarcasm into two tiny words." Perky straightened and gave my shoulder a solid thumping. "Want us to take those contraptions off you before you go in?"

"No. I wear sad-dle and bri-dle. You need to ride back to station. So. Who goes with me?"

After a brief but intense huddle, two cops were assigned to go into the building with me. Both were armed with a pair of extinguishers, one meant for fires while the other contained pressurized neutralizer. One was a woman, pretty enough I suspected they used her as a spokesperson whenever possible, with her long brown hair tied into a tail.

She stood tall and proud, her chin lifted high, her gaze sweeping the crowds for any sign of trouble before she gave me her full attention. "Ma'am."

I bobbed my head in a greeting. "Off-ee-sur."

The second cop, stuck somewhere in his thirties and probably a candidate for a midlife crisis, stepped back, put his hands on his hips, and looked me over. "You're a horse with a horn. What is with that… fur? I thought women were supposed to groom themselves before leaving for work."

Perky straightened and drew in a breath. Before he could say anything, I swiveled my head around and bumped his chest with my nose.

If anyone was going to put the cop in his place, it'd be me. I concentrated so I could speak clearly. "I am a unicorn." Professor Yale would have applauded my handling of a word with more than two syllables.

The cop didn't seem at all impressed, and the woman shot her partner a glare. "I'm Lieutenant Downing. Please, call me Janet. My partner is John Winfield—a cadet."

Wonderful. A green recruit thought he was better than the one person in the city who stood between him and getting turned into a stone statue. He'd never know how fortunate he was I would never intentionally put someone at risk of exposure to any dangerous substance, no matter how much of an asshole he was. I abandoned my effort to mask my difficulty with speaking English and said, "Here how this work. I go to con-tam-in-ate-ed area. I clean. You stay safe. Do as I say. You no close-er than twen-tee feet. More if able. You watch, bored. Un-der-stand? When fire start, you ex-ting-guish when told. Neu-tra-lize when told."

"Copy," Janet replied, straightening. "If you don't mind me asking, ma'am? What's your certification level?"

Explaining all of my qualifications would make my mouth hurt, so I bumped my nose on Perky's chest again, careful to keep my horn clear of him. "Purr-key?"

Few dared to scratch my chin, but I enjoyed the feel of his fingers digging into my fur. "Miss Gardener is a top-tier specialist, Officer Downing. Chief Quinn calls her in on critical cases as a consultant. Right now, she's the only one in the city capable of handling all classes of gorgon material. She's also certified in the handling of other substances. I've worked with her before. She's very good at her job. She has a perfect record preventing additional exposure."

"What containment gear will you need, Miss Gardener?" Janet frowned, her gaze sweeping over me. "We don't have equipment for centaurs or equines, but I think given ten minutes, we can put something together.

We'd have to wait for someone to bring suits over, though—the hazmat crew isn't even here yet."

There were no hazmat crews at the building yet? Where were they? New York had multiple response teams. In the time it took me to get Perky to Wall Street, one of them should have already arrived.

Perky chuckled. "That's not necessary. Miss Gardener doesn't need equipment to handle gorgon bile. As she's going in without a suit, there are a few ground rules you will both need to follow. Should Bailey tell you to stand on one foot and cluck like a chicken, you will do it. She will be contaminated during the clean up. If you make the wrong move, you will end up being a statue. If you let her do her job, you'll be safe. Cadet, you stick close to your supervisor."

"Yes, sir!" both replied.

After giving me a final scratch and untangling his fingers from my fur, he turned his full attention to Janet. "If anything happens to her, Chief Quinn will be exceptionally unhappy. There are three people qualified to handle large scale incidents like this, and two of them are out of town for an unknown period of time. Her safety is your responsibility."

To her credit, Janet didn't laugh outright at Perky's comment, but her lips curved in amusement. "I think *she* is the one protecting *me,* sir."

"Don't tell her that. It'll go to her head, and we'll never hear the end of it."

While tempted to nip Perky for teasing me, I turned my attention to my job so I could hunt down something to eat and a quiet place for a much-needed nap. "Where bile?"

Janet turned to the building and pointed up. "Twenty-first floor, ma'am. I'll give you the full details inside."

As I had hoped, there were side doors, sparing me from having to bust through the glass revolving doors. Janet held the door for me, but before I could do more than take a single step, the cadet blew by me. The temptation to snort fire at him stirred. Smoke trailed out of my nose.

Perky yanked on a handful of my mane. "Don't. Chief Quinn really will kill me if I let you attack an officer, even a useless cadet with an attitude issue."

"One nip?"

"No, Bailey. Behave. Please."

I sighed. "You stay here, no puke on other cops."

"If you promise not to tell anyone this happened, I'll pay for your dinner tonight."

"Sold. Be back soon. May-be. De-pends on bile."

"Good luck."

I eased my way through the door, lowering my head so my horn wouldn't slice through the door frame. It was a tight squeeze, but I made it into the building's lobby. A short flight of stairs led up to a spacious room, its marble floors broken by columns rising to an arched ceiling. I tossed my head high and leapt up the four steps, landing with my hooves clattering on the tiles. The sound echoed, and the eerie silence unnerved me. "Too quiet."

"It rather is." Janet waited for the door to close before joining me. The cadet glared at me, taking the steps two at a time.

"Where ell-ee-vay-tur?"

"This way." Taking off at a brisk walk, Janet guided me to the elevators. The sheer number of them astonished me. How many people did they cram into the building to need so many elevators? "Here's the situation. Somehow, someone put gorgon bile in the ceiling. We think they used a time-delayed blasting cap and a minor amount of C4 to break the vessel containing it. Headquarters is unwilling to send anyone in hazmat suits in, as they don't know if there are more explosives. I have a camera and a monitor with me, so you'll go in and photograph the scene. Once you get close, I'll evaluate whether it's too dangerous to proceed with clean up."

The evacuation of the building made more sense after hearing the culprit had used explosives in the ceiling to deliver the gorgon bile. I'd seen the tactic used before. A second detonation and more gorgon bile was a possibility.

Someone had done it several years ago, and I'd been the lucky one to get a second dose of bile. Shards of the glass container used had pierced my suit, and I had needed stitches.

"No haz-mat guys when fear of bomb. Un-der-stand. I have done this be-fore."

Janet sucked in a breath. "That was you?"

"Yes. I was the cleaning crew. No problem. I know roo-teen. Even if second dee-vice, I can han-dle."

Only an idiot would attempt to bomb a fire-breathing unicorn. During Professor Yale's experiments, very few incendiary devices bothered me. In the explosive conclusion of my species testing, he had strapped C4 to my back, put me on an ammunitions range, and blown it all up to scare the liver out of every last one of the bomb techs in a joint operation. He had even let me eat the extra C4. Of all the explosives and fuels I'd taken a nibble of as a unicorn, C4 was my second favorite. Napalm came in at the top, but they wouldn't let me have more than a taste to prove it wouldn't hurt me.

Stupid safety supervisors.

"That's very reassuring, Miss Gardener. We evacuated the building in case there were additional explosives, but with a high risk of a copy cat—or the original bomber—we're worried we'll end up with an even worse situation."

Or a bigger bomb, but if she hadn't figured that out yet, I wasn't going to tell her. I worried. I could eat fire and explosives and burp flame, but could I do it fast enough to protect the two cops accompanying me? I had no idea.

With the risk of reversal, no one had been willing to put my abilities to the test, myself included. I liked living.

"Where bile in building?"

Janet pressed the up button on the elevator, and one dinged and opened right away. "It's in an office close to the middle of the building. From our initial investigation, we've determined there are between twelve to twenty victims. The spray radius is at least twenty feet in a cubicle environment. One of the workers who escaped claims they heard a bang before the crash. The victims are still in there."

I stepped into the elevator and used my hoof to hold it open for the two cops. "Many desks? Cu-bee-cle farm?"

"Exactly. At least two of the victims were

exposed to the bile when they tried to help their co-workers."

Ah, good old New Yorkers. In a pinch, they could always be trusted to get the job done—or get killed trying. When disaster struck, they stuck together, for better or worse. It made crowd control interesting for police in serious situations. At least most knew better than to try to handle the truly dangerous substances without certification. "No more after? Twen-tee max?"

"As far as we know. After the evacuation, we cleared the building—even us."

Something wasn't adding up for a gorgon bile removal coupled with a small-scale bomb. While I appreciated the precautions, clearing the floor should have been sufficient until bomb techs could examine the scene. What was I missing? Then again, after the gorgon dust in my apartment, I could understand the police being exceptionally cautious.

A pinch of the dust could turn hundreds of people into statues—and possible carriers —within a few minutes.

It didn't take long for the elevator to reach the twenty-first floor. "Which office?"

Janet pointed to the right down a broad hallway which ended at a glass-fronted office. "It's that office on the end. The contaminated room is adjacent to the reception. We've been informed the interior doors were all left open."

The door leading into the affected suite was ajar, too, and it looked like someone had hit the glass hard enough to crack it. "Come. Stay in hall near re-cep-shun. Will ee-val-u-ate sit-u-ation in-side. Cam-er-uh. You have?"

Janet pulled a small sphere from her pocket, which was attached to a lanyard. "We call this a fish eye. We normally tether it to a line for dropping into holes and pipes to help get a view of rescue op situations we have a tough time reaching. I will have the controller, and I will be able to get a full range of visibility from the sphere."

The cadet snorted. "Never thought I'd see the day a horse could do a man's job, especially when she can't even handle basic English."

Perky had asked me really nicely not to attack other police officers, but would one bite really be that bad? Maybe I could step on the man's toes. Humans didn't really need their toes, did they?

Janet's cheek twitched, and I got the feeling the cadet was known for using 'woman' instead of 'horse' when he tossed that line under normal circumstances. I started with his face and made a show of looking him over, noting his darker complexion, dark brown eyes, and signs of probable South American descent. "Been in America long?"

Cadet John Winfield's eyes bulged. "What? How dare you!"

I snorted and allowed a small trail of flame to billow from my nose.

"Winfield, enough."

Perhaps showing the cadet my serrated teeth broke every etiquette rule in the book, but I did it anyway. "This u-nee-corn eats meats. Breathes fire. You might taste good with ketch-up. Crunchy and tasty, yes?"

"Please don't eat Cadet Winfield, Miss Gardener, even though he deserves it. He's very sorry."

"I am no—"

Janet stomped her foot on his. "He's very sorry, ma'am."

I LEFT Janet and the idiot cadet just outside the doors leading into the office. I carried the camera and a meter with my teeth, both rigged with straps to make them easier for me to handle. In what classified as a miracle in my rather humble opinion, Janet's choice of meter and settings worked best for amateurs with no idea what they were doing.

It'd catch any dangerous substance from

gorgon spittle, which was generally harmless unless someone decided to bathe in it, to phoenix feathers. No one wanted to screw around with a phoenix feather, which could incinerate anything given ten seconds. The damned things had a mind of their own, too. Someone could carry around a pretty little white feather, which to all appearances looked like it came from a pigeon, and then bam. Fire, and lots of it.

Fortunately for society at large, phoenixes disliked cities and guarded their precious feathers as though they were their first-born hatchlings. I'd only seen a feather outside of training once, and it had still been attached to the phoenix, who had agreed to come to the CDC auditorium for a demonstration in exchange for some undisclosed favor.

A phoenix feather or two would come in really handy torching gorgon bile. Of course, the feather would likely torch the entire building in the process, but not even napalm could reach the same temperatures as a phoenix. If the CDC brought in the full bird, 120 Wall Street would be reduced to a big pile of ash within twenty minutes.

I wondered how I'd compare to a phoenix if I let loose and went on a rampage. The thought tempted me, although the presence of the two cops ensured I only considered it for a moment. Still, who didn't like the idea of going full-out pyromaniac for once in a lifetime?

Instead of indulging, I sighed and gave both cops a sour look. "May-be step back more feet. To be safe."

Janet obeyed, dragging her pair of extinguishers with her. The cadet did not. Why was I not surprised? When I got out of the building, I'd give Chief Quinn a piece of my mind for allowing the NYPD to even have such a useless cadet in training. What were they doing at the academy? Twiddling their thumbs and scheming ways to add chaos to an already chaotic—and dangerous—job?

"Meter set to fif-teen feet, Janet?" I asked around a mouthful of lanyards. A girl could hope, right? The meter was set to mass detection; that much I could tell from the screen icons. Maybe my luck would hold for once in my life.

"Yes, ma'am. The CDC recommended the settings. I just did what I was told and confirmed everything with them."

"Good job. Purr-fect." Fifteen feet would give me enough of a range to avoid general contamination and get a good feel for how much the bile had spread in the office. If the initial spatter radius was out twenty-feet, I expected some of the gorgon bile to have gotten on shoes or other materials and been spread around. The worst I'd seen was when one man had stepped into a puddle of it and tracked it thirty feet before it'd gotten through his socks and petrified him.

Maybe I'd get lucky and no one had gone on a long hike with bile all over their feet. I doubted it, but at least I'd know before I stepped in any trace residue.

I squeezed my way through the door and made it two steps before the meter shrieked an angry chorus of warnings, too shrill and piercing to indicate a simple gorgon bile contamination. Lowering my head, I set both devices down on the tiles, unsheathed a claw, and hooked the edge of the meter to flip it over so I could get a look at the back-lit display.

The screen flashed red, indicating a critical contamination. I tapped the diagnostic button and waited for the result. While I expected gorgon bile, and likely the concentrated, A+ grade stuff no one ever wanted to deal with since it stuck to everything and took several rounds of neutralizer—or intense heat—to get rid of, I got something even worse.

Gorgon dust.

Why did I always end up with the gorgon dust cases? Why couldn't it be bile? The meter confirmed the strongest source was at the fringe of its current detection range, but as I initiated a more thorough scan, it picked up a trace source within three feet of me.

Crap.

"Back!" I twisted around and blew a gout of flame at the hallway to drive home my point.

Janet hightailed it to the elevators while Cadet Winfield stood around and gaped at me. How had I gotten the idiot cadet without real training? Why me?

Maybe if he didn't move or breathe, none of the dust would reach him. I returned to my work and glared at the meter, and hoping for a misreading, I tapped away at the device's thick rubber buttons, grateful the CDC had rejected the idea of touch screens, which did not play well with hazmat suits *or* unicorn claws. I did a full reset of the device, a procedure that cost me three minutes, and I reset all the settings before running the test one more time.

Nothing had changed. I still had multiple sources of gorgon dust nearby, and by the rulebooks, standing within three to five feet of a trace source classified as contaminated. I lifted my head and eyed the receptionist's desk, which wasn't close enough to be the nearest source of dust. The gray and brown granite floor tiles gleamed under the office's lights, doing an excellent job of masking the presence of dust.

I snorted and smoke trailed from my nose.

"What are you doing?" Cadet Winfield demanded.

"Do you want to die?"

"You—"

The crack of metal against a hard surface startled me into turning my head towards the hallway. Janet had her billy club out and smacked it against the wall. "That is enough, Cadet Winfield. If you interfere with her work, I will follow protocol to the letter. That involves my gun and your kneecap, followed by a pair of handcuffs and your immediate suspension from the academy. At the scene of a contamination, the certified CDC specialists are the law, and she's working for the public's safety. You are, at most, an observer and assistant."

Maybe I'd let Perky ride in a cruiser and give Janet a lift wherever she wanted to go. I liked when the cops backed me, even if she was twisting the regulations just a tiny bit. Then again, she wasn't, not really—she just didn't know I had a gorgon dust disaster on my hands, er, hooves.

The cop and cadet engaged in a stare off, and I left them to their silent battle while I went to work getting a better feel for the situation. A glass wall separated me from the purported contaminated room, and dark brown fluid streaked the window. If the meter wasn't shrilling its dire warnings over gorgon dust, I would have believed it to be bile. An initial reading of gorgon dust plus a reset reading and full scan showing the same result, without any evidence of bile in the area, meant the liquid was likely the dust.

What *was* the brown gunk? It looked like bile. It looked like every other gorgon bile sample I'd ever seen, so much so if I'd been going in with visuals only, I might have begun clean up without bothering to do a secondary scan. Then again, I always ran the meter just in case there was something else with the bile.

Why me? Why again? Had someone mixed the dust in with a fluid designed to mimic bile? Was the bile-like substance some prank gone disastrously wrong and the dust was from something else? No matter how it had happened, I was stuck. At my range to the contamination, I couldn't leave. By the book, I was contaminated. If the dust was in the fluid, when it dried, the entire building would also be contaminated.

Hundreds upon hundreds of people—maybe even thousands—worked in the building. Anxiety prickled its way through me. With such a heavily ventilated building and no way of knowing if the dust had gotten into the air ducts, I couldn't afford to request help, either.

I had no choice. "Cadet."

"What?"

"Walk back-wards. Slow-lee. Don't dee-sturb air. Go ell-ee-vay-tur. Leave, to ground floor. Dee-mand meter. Call for glass coffins. You will need. You not con-tam-ee-nated, you would be stone, but you may carry res-ee-due."

"*What?*"

"Officer Down-ning?"

"I heard you." The woman remained near the elevators, straightened, and lifted her chin. "How can I help?"

If I got us all out of this alive, I would not only take her on a ride, I would find the best bar around so we could drink ourselves into a stupor. She seemed like the type of person I'd like to take to a bar and get exceptionally drunk with. "This not bile. Is dust. Gor-gon dust. Re-cep-shun con-tam-ee-nated. Leave. Sor-ree. I stay. In con-tam-ee-nated area. Hallway seem safe. For now." While I could try to burn it, I couldn't afford to take any risks, not with so many people in danger. The list of people qualified to demand a na-palming was limited to upper officers in the police, upper management of the CDC, and people with top-level certification at the con-tamination site, like me. I lifted my head and forced my tongue to do my bidding. "I con-demn this building and request napalm. Entire structure. All ducts, all ventilation systems. You call dispatch."

Glass coffins protected humanity, and while there were ones designed for centaurs, they were few and far between and shaped specifically for them. I wouldn't fit.

I would stay. There was no other choice.

Cadet Winfield's eyes bulged, and he crept backwards.

Considering I could stand in fire and like it, maybe I'd survive. I'd even had C4 detonated while strapped to me. It had tickled. What was an entire building being torched with a full load of napalm compared to that? I watched the idiot cadet and decided to pull rank. All things considered, I couldn't allow a loose cannon to put the public at risk. "Officer Down-ning, if he try to leave without scan or ree-fuse glass coffin, you shoot, put him in anyway. Risk to public."

"He won't, not on my watch," she promised.

"I like you, Janet." I did, too. It took real courage to face a leave-someone-behind situation with dignity. "Tell Officer Purr-keens to call Pro-fess-ur Yale to pro-vide sec-un-dare-ee auth-or-is-zay-shun for nay-palm."

"Yes, ma'am."

"Go. Quick."

The cops fled into the elevator.

When I was certain they were gone, I

began hunting for the dust. Picking up the fish-eye camera in my mouth, I began the tedious process of pushing the meter around on the floor in search of the source. Why had I gotten qualified for dangerous material handling? Stupid me. I'd be inside the building when they started flooding napalm in through the top floor, probably pumping all sorts of magic into the gel to ensure it covered every possible surface in the structure.

Even if I survived the fire, if the floors didn't collapse, I'd be astonished. Starting tomorrow, the government would begin planning the rebuilding of the site while a lot of stunned bankers tried to figure out what they'd do without their office space.

If the heat or the building collapse didn't kill me, Quinn would. He'd hunt me down, cut off my horn, and take it as a trophy. At least I wouldn't need another round in the glass coffin when I reversed to human. A round or two of napalm would cook the dust right out of me, assuming I didn't get charred to a crisp.

A little experimentation with the meter confirmed my fears: the dust had made it into the reception. I located a brown splotch of drying fluid on the floor near the receptionist's desk. On closer inspection, I found some other dark spatter marks. How had they gotten there?

I looked up.

A drop of liquid fell on my nose with a splat. Dark stains marked where something leaked in the ceiling. I tried to get a view of my own nose, which didn't work very well. Drawing in a deep breath, I worked to make sense of the smells. The pungent odor of cleaners hung in the air along with the hint of gasoline. Gasoline? No, it wasn't quite gasoline. It reminded me of napalm. Had they already started pumping the gel into the building? I hadn't heard any of the warning sirens.

The authorities liked informing New Yorkers when they were about to put on a show.

Underneath all the other harsher smells, I couldn't detect the earthy, mildewy scent of the gorgon dust. Whatever the fluid was, it masked the presence of the dust far too well.

The lights went out, and utter quiet descended on the building, so deep and still I shivered. A few breaths later, the blare of distant sirens accompanied a bone-deep thrum. The sound of emergency response vehicles drew a snort out of me. What were they hoping to prevent? A fire? With a little help from the CDC and the military, the police and fire department would have no problem shielding the building so the intense heat and cinders wouldn't reach any of the neighboring structures.

I forced my attention back to the stained ceiling. What *was* that stuff? I really needed to practice using my nose as a unicorn if I survived. Short of tasting it, I had no way of identifying it. Whatever it was, the meter wasn't picking it up.

One little taste couldn't make my situation any worse, could it? I already had some of the gunk on my nose. With nothing to lose, I set the camera on the desk, eyed the brown stains, and dragged my tongue over the wood. If someone was recording and it got back to anyone I had deliberately eaten a dangerous substance, I'd be a dead woman walking, but I didn't exactly have a lot to lose.

If I *did* survive, I'd enjoy the arguments. Learning how the fluid worked—or the culprit's goal—might be important later.

I *had* been smelling gasoline. Why on Earth would anyone mix gorgon dust with gasoline, shove it into the ceiling of an office building, and leave it there? Why hadn't it burst into flame when the initial bang happened?

Wait. Gasoline wouldn't be sufficient to neutralize gorgon dust. If it burned, it'd get into the air ducts, spread through the entire building, and potentially affect every single person in the building. While gasoline and other accelerants were used in napalm, modern blends were designed to burn hotter and longer, reaching temperatures capable of destroying gorgon dust.

The possibilities stunned me into staring up at the stained ceiling tiles. Why hadn't anyone reported the smell of gasoline? Had someone mistakenly—or deliberately—reported it as gorgon bile? Gorgon bile smelled far worse than gasoline. A single spark could have blown the whole thing up. Had the fluid been a little more effective at igniting, the dust would have potentially incubated in unwitting victims, priming the city for a petrification endemic. Had the meter not been set to do a bulk scan, I might not have clued in to the irregularities of the brown fluid. I would have breathed a bit of fire in the wrong place and lit the whole building up, sending gorgon dust into the air.

I had come within feet of petrifying both Janet and the cadet and possibly exposing the entire crowd gathered outside of the building, including Perky.

The thrum increased in volume, and the floor shivered beneath my hooves. Everyone in hearing range, probably for several miles, would know something big was about to happen. According to protocol, the tone would continue for five minutes.

In the following silence, aided with magic,

the bomb techs would pump thousands of gallons of napalm into the top story of the building. The thick, gelatinous fluid would ooze its way to the ground floor while bomb techs in hazmat gear would set the charges and prepare to detonate them to ignite the napalm.

A minute following the final check of the explosives, an inferno would rip through the building and incinerate everything inside.

I suspected I'd gain a few minutes due to the sheer amount of napalm required to coat all thirty-four stories of 120 Wall Street and bake it to a crisp. Then again, if they hunted down a replicator or two, they could turn water or gas tankers into napalm in a few minutes without breaking a sweat.

Until they started flooding the building, I'd make the most of my time to find out just how much gorgon dust lurked in the ceiling. With luck, the camera was sending its recording to someone—like Officer Janet Downing—who might make sure the data got to the right people. I'd also hope Chief Quinn *wasn't* the right person.

He'd take my pretty fur coat as a trophy along with my horn. Then he'd give my skinned corpse to Professor Yale for study. My future really wasn't looking all that bright.

Or maybe it was looking too bright.

Sighing, I reared and stabbed my horn into the ceiling, slicing the tile open. In retrospect, I should have known that stabbing a horn capable of cutting metal into a space I couldn't see wouldn't work out well for me. The crack of glass gave me a split-second warning before a flood of fluid dumped onto my head.

I blinked and dropped the camera out of my mouth. It disappeared into the goopy puddle surrounding me. If I got out of this situation somehow, I decided I would quietly accept my scolding as I deserved every last minute of it.

EIGHT

Yummy, yummy C4.

GLASS CONTAINERS FILLED with dust-infused gasoline lurked overhead, and I had two choices: I could waste time trying to pull down tiles, or I could take a bath in the brown fluid and make it easier for the napalm to do its job. Since the gas wasn't doing anything to me as far as I could tell, I decided to take the brute force route. Grateful I could see in the darkness with a little help from the meter's glowing screen, I bucked, slashed with my horn, and tore down every last tile in my effort to spread a swath of toxic destruction around me.

Among the broken glass shards were a network of tangled wires. When I finished making sure all the containers in the reception were broken, I took the time to inspect the setup. Picking up the camera in the off-chance it still worked, I reared and balanced on my hind hooves, craning my neck for a better look into the trashed ceiling.

More of the glass drums hung in the adjacent office space.

Dropping down to all fours, I dealt with the glass wall in the most direct fashion possible: I charged it, lowered my head, and plowed through it horn first. I punched my way into the next room and dropped my hindquarters to avoid crashing into one of the statues. A gaping hole in the ceiling marked where the drums had burst. At least four broken containers hung from the support beams normally hidden behind the tiles. A tangle of wires hung down.

Someone hadn't installed the explosives correctly; blasting caps affixed to wedges of C4 waited for detonation.

Yummy, yummy C4.

After setting the camera down out of the way, I dodged petrified victims, braced my front hooves on one of the drenched desks, lifted my head, and stretched to reach the tasty treat. I snatched the wires in my teeth and yanked. The tangle of cords and explosives separated from the glass drums. Backing up, I kept tugging until the C4, cables, and blasting caps pulled free from the containers.

Something banged in the ceiling, and a cascade of brown fluid splashed to the floor. With a few more yanks, I had fifty feet of bundled wires and balls of explosives. Lowering my head, I stepped on the wires to keep them in place and hunted down every last scrap of explosive, savoring its sharp flavor and the heat it birthed in my belly.

If anyone was actually watching the fish-eye camera feed, they were probably thinking I had lost my mind. Couldn't a unicorn enjoy a special treat in a bad situation?

Once I disposed of all the explosives, I returned to my campaign of destruction, breaking every last one of the drums in the ceiling to ensure they were incinerated when the napalm ignited. With the napalm order, I wouldn't have to worry about the dust surviving long enough to get into the air. The shields they used to protect the neighboring buildings would keep almost every known substance under containment long enough for it to burn to nothing.

Deeper within the office, another room waited.

Someone hadn't been telling the truth when they reported the extent of the contamination. While there were nineteen people in the first room, there were another forty-three statues, most of them seated at their desks, caught completely by surprise when the dust-contaminated fluid had rained down on them.

The dust hadn't taken long to petrify its

victims, seconds rather than bile's customary five minutes.

Had it been gorgon bile, instead of condemning the sixty-two victims and possibly myself to death, I would have been gingerly torching their statues to neutralize the bile and turn its magic inert so no one else would be petrified. In human form, I would have been doing the work with a sponge, a steel bucket, and a lot of water.

Once cleaned, I would have hosed them down with neutralizer to return them to living flesh.

I avoided the victims as best as I could while confirming there were no more unbroken drums in the ceiling. The bomber had managed to detonate them all, leaving no part of the room untouched. If I ever got a hold of the culprit, Chief Quinn would be arresting me for one of the most brutal murders New York had ever seen, and I'd smile through the trial and subsequent jail time.

Retrieving the camera, I set it up so I could drop identification cards in front of it. Bracing for the worst part of my job, I shoved my nose into pockets to gather wallets, chewed through the straps of purses, and took everything to the camera. Bringing the meter closer while it sang a shrill chorus promising death and doom, I planted my front hooves on the table, shredded through leather with my claws and teeth to locate the cards, and did my best to memorize the names of every victim in case the camera wasn't working anymore.

If I lived, and I'd do my best to survive, at least the victims wouldn't be forgotten. There was nothing I could do for them beyond that. Once the napalm hit, the sudden change in temperature would likely shatter their statues. Maybe granite could survive it without melting, but I doubted they were granite; as far as I could tell, they were some dark and glossy stone, possibly obsidian.

The deep warning tone fell silent. A shudder ran through the floor beneath my hooves. It wouldn't take long for them to flood the place if they pulled out all the stops, and considering I had asked Janet to contact Professor Yale, they'd move fast. Professor Yale had one simple rule: if anyone asked him for help, it better be a doomsday scenario. He'd kill anyone who involved him without just cause.

Sixty-two potential carriers and enough gorgon dust to infect Lower Manhattan in its entirety classified as a doomsday scenario to me. Even if I died along with them, the price was small to protect so many people. I could go out in a blaze of glory without a single regret.

If I died and my name was released to the

public, my parents might even be proud of me—or at least satisfied by my demise. Not only would I be dead, I'd get five minutes of fame as a hero, and they'd take full credit for my actions. I turned my head and sank my teeth into the nearest chair, chewing at the upholstery so I wouldn't snort flame and ignite the gasoline.

I forced my attention to my work, determined to survive so I couldn't be used by the two people who hated me the most.

After I finished going through the identification cards, I took the camera and did a second inspection of the affected area. I eyed a sturdy-looking desk far enough away from the statues I wouldn't risk knocking them over. Bracing for a potential collision with the floor, I jumped onto the desk, digging my claws into the metal surface. It held under my weight. From my higher vantage, I stuck my head into the ceiling to examine the glass drums.

How had the culprit gotten them into the office? A janitorial crew could do it over the course of a night or two. But why? Was an epidemic the goal? If so, the culprits had made a lot of assumptions about how decontamination worked. Assuming the cleaners were completely clueless, the neutralizer sprays would revert the newly whelped gorgons to flesh, triggering a petrification spree the likes of which New York had never seen.

From what I could recall, one in a thousand petrified by a gorgon carrier would become a newly whelped gorgon, although they wouldn't be capable of infecting someone. Within days, there would be hundreds—maybe thousands—of new gorgons with no control over their abilities.

Manhattan would become a city of stone within a week.

Any trained and certified crew would use the meters, figure out gorgon dust was responsible, and initiate emergency protocols. Like me, the decontamination crew would end up living sacrifices to prevent the dust from spreading. The police would name them heroes along with the victims lost.

It hit home just how lucky I had been in my apartment. I could have easily been fried to mitigate the risk of the dust spreading. Had my precautions to prevent the dust from escaping made the difference between a stay in a glass coffin and a cremation?

I jumped off the desk and returned to the reception. Had the culprit assumed that the poor bastard stuck with doing the decontamination would be unwilling to issue a napalm order? Did they not know certified handlers could issue the order? I certainly hadn't told anyone the most dangerous element of my side job, which involved signing my own death warrant.

Could my unicorn's inherent affinity with fire spare me from immolation? I'd find out soon enough.

120 Wall Street shuddered again and something gurgled overhead. I turned to face the elevators in time to watch bursts of light surround the metal doors. Thick gray fluid pushed through the gaps. Sparks of gold and silver danced through the substance. Thin pseudopods of the fluid stretched out to coat the walls in a wet sheen.

Showtime.

Still carrying the camera in my mouth, I cantered down the hall in search of the stairwell. More sparkling ooze spilled through a doorway marked with a dark exit sign. The pungent stench of gasoline and other accelerants filled my nose. Had I been human, the first signs of asphyxiation would have begun. Instead, I drooled in the presence of so much fuel. Not only were they pumping napalm into the building, it was magic napalm. Surely magic napalm tasted better than its mundane counterpart. One lick wouldn't change anything, would it?

I dropped the camera and lowered my head, sniffing at one of the outstretched pseudopods. It poked me in the nose. Snapping my teeth, I chomped off the end and went to work chewing on the gel. Heaven tasted a bit peppery with a sharp zing. My tongue warmed, and when I swallowed, heat ignited deep within and chased away all evidence of the cold that had plagued me since my transformation in the CDC headquarters. Its taste reminded me of everything I liked about lying in a nice cheery fireplace.

How could anyone dislike napalm? I took another bite, eager to stoke the warmth inside even hotter. A tingling rush spread through me, and I choked in my hurry to gulp down another swallow.

The napalm rippled around my hooves and tugged at my fur before sweeping towards the camera. I rescued it, but globs of the sparkling gel plopped off my chin onto the device.

Oops.

Maybe it still worked, so I kept it and went back to investigating the twenty-first floor while they finished their preparations to ignite the napalm. I found three stairwells, and all of them were filling with flammable gel. I adjusted my initial estimate of thousands of gallons to hundreds of thousands of gallons. Where were they getting so much napalm?

Probably water.

I hunted down the nearest bathroom, reared, and broke a sink to get to the water pipes. Sure enough, something gurgled in the wall. Bringing my hooves and horn into play, I ruptured the pipe, sending sparkling gel raining into the room. Abandoning the camera, I went on a destructive rampage, trashing sinks and toilets alike.

It didn't take long before I was wading through several inches of the gel. Whinnying my delight, I dropped to the floor and rolled in the napalm. My saddle broke under my weight, and I chewed through the leather cinch to get rid of it. I left the bridle; it'd burn away soon enough.

The gel worked into my fur and warmed my skin, clung to my fur, and burned in my blood. I basked, bathing in it until it covered every inch of my body.

The deep tone blared for a few seconds. The napalm gushing from the broken pipes died away to a trickle. In thirty seconds, the siren would blare again, marking the start of the final thirty seconds of 120 Wall Street's life.

Then my world would burn.

THE MOMENT the charge went off thirteen stories above, 120 Wall Street trembled, but it didn't burn. I waited for the whoosh of igniting napalm, but the seconds ticked by in silence. Fury over having to wait so long to see what would happen surged through me.

No more.

I surged out of my napalm bath onto my hooves, breathed in deep, and charged out of the bathroom. I slipped and slid trying to cut the corner and slammed into the wall. I unsheathed my claws for purchase and lurched into a canter, the fastest I dared to go in the confined space. I blew by the elevators on the way to the stairwell, bounced through the doorway, and scrambled up the steps, tripping several times in my effort to reach the roof as fast as possible.

120 Wall Street needed to burn, and if the bomb techs couldn't pull it off, I would. "Burn, burn, burn!"

I exhaled flame. Droplets of sparkling napalm dripped onto me from above. The gold and silver sparks within flashed, but it didn't ignite.

No. No, no, no. The building would burn. It had to burn. The police and CDC magicians couldn't hold the shield forever. If the napalm drained to the ground floor, it'd eventually evaporate and help the dust spread into the air. It would leak out and rain down onto the city. It would spread.

Perky waited outside. He'd only be among the first to petrify. If the napalm leaked out of the building, he wouldn't live long enough to turn to stone. He would burn, too. If it took too long, if the shield was at risk of failing, others from the station would come to supervise—or try to help.

Quinn would come.

No matter what, I couldn't allow Quinn to get anywhere near the dust. They'd stuff him in a glass coffin. I couldn't bear the thought of Quinn being lowered into unforgiving ground, too much of a risk to be awakened if he breathed in the dust. They'd kill him.

He had magic, strong magic—magic the government would never allow into the hands of a newly whelped gorgon. They'd kill him.

It'd be my fault.

Quinn.

I climbed the stairs, plowing through the goop covering the steps. Placing each hoof with care, I worked my way upward, and the higher I went, the less dense the napalm was. The draining had already begun.

It wouldn't be long until too much napalm filled the ground levels of the building, making the temperature of the twenty-first floor too cool to eradicate the gorgon dust.

A doorway blocked my way. I backed to the end of the landing and slammed my shoulder into the door. It held. I snorted flame, but the napalm didn't light. I retreated and charged again. The door shuddered on its hinges.

My third blow knocked it open, and I staggered into blinding daylight. A rainbow barrier marked the presence of the shield where it curved overhead, encasing the entire structure. Through it, I spotted several helicopters circling, observing, waiting for the moment the napalm lit.

Without me, it wouldn't.

Tossing my head, I trumpeted a challenge and charged across the roof to raise my body temperature. If my regular fire wasn't hot enough to ignite the napalm, I would run until I burst into living flame. I would run until I couldn't take another step as long as it meant the fuel combusted.

I would give my last breath to repay Quinn for his kindness, for welcoming me into his home when he had every reason to cast me aside. I wouldn't fail.

I couldn't fail.

Gouts of red and orange blew from my nostrils with every breath and the napalm coating my fur heated. It lit with a hiss, bathing me in a blanket of flame. The bridle fell away in pieces, the leather incinerating before it could reach the ground. My hooves glowed blue-white, and the fuel they touched caught, leaving flaming hoof prints in my wake. The fire pursued me across the roof.

I could light the napalm. I would win. I slowed to turn so I could cover the entire roof in flame. I trumpeted another call, a promise to the hovering helicopters that victory would be mine. Curtaining heat and flame, a blue, white, and yellow inferno sparking with silver and gold, licked my heels. If the napalm refused to burn the old-fashioned way, I'd help it along floor by floor, top to bottom.

120 Wall Street would burn, no matter what.

IF I SLOWED to a canter for too long, my body lost the ability to ignite the stubborn napalm, so I ran as hard and fast as I could through the building. While the sections I galloped through burned, I didn't trust the fires to reach every floor unaided. Even if 120 Wall Street collapsed around me, I wouldn't stop until I reached the ground.

Columns of flame swirled up the stairwells, and I dove down through the billowing fires. I tumbled down several flights of stairs, squealing my disgust over my difficulty navigating the steps. The structure groaned as more and more of the fuel ignited and the flames spread. The unlit napalm glowed gold and silver, illuminating my path.

When I reached the twenty-first floor, the upper stories shuddered. Chunks of molten steel and broken concrete plummeted through the ceiling around me. I dodged the burning debris, charged the contaminated office, and plowed through the glass without slowing.

My gusting breath ignited the gasoline in the ceiling and the napalm on the floor. A cloud of billowing blue flame engulfed the reception and sucked air in from the adjacent room. The crack-bang of windows shattering cut over the roar of flames. Cool air rushed over me and fanned the fires.

"Burn, burn! Burn, damn you!" I leaped into the next room and pranced, coaxing the inferno to spread, breathing life into it. I needed it hotter and brighter. I surged through to the third contaminated room, turned tail, and returned to the reception.

My breath burned silver-white tinged with the faintest hint of blue. The gorgon dust wouldn't take anymore lives. It wouldn't reach anyone outside. Perky was safe. When 120 Wall Street finished collapsing in on itself, there would be nothing left for the CDC's meters to find. When Quinn came, the public he worked so hard to protect each and every day would be safe.

He'd be safe.

I danced my joy and gave myself over to the flames.

NINE

As soon as the CDC got hold of me,
I was a dead unicorn.

AS LONG AS I LIVED, I never wanted to experience a napalm bender hangover ever again. I'd gotten drunk more than my fair share of times over the years, but none of my other next-morning regrets compared. Even my horn hurt, although I suspected ramming my head through various walls and doors factored into my discomfort. My eyes ached and added to the din in my skull, which was further agitated by the pulsing iridescent shield trapping the smoke and ash until phase two of the napalming process began.

When the CDC determined the fires were out, they'd spray liquified neutralizer over the piles of ash and debris to ensure any trace contaminants were destroyed. Considering how little of 120 Wall Street had survived the napalming, I thought pumping excessive amounts of water into the space I was occupying more than a little unfair.

The shield thrummed, and within several seconds, a cold rain began to fall.

With my ears flopped in misery, I struggled to dig my way deeper into the ash to hide from the neutralizer-infused water. I still wasn't sure how I ended up on top of the debris pile instead of beneath it, but I already regretted not having been buried. At the bottom of the ash, concrete, and steel, I'd stay warm for a little while longer.

I blamed magic. If physics had had anything to do with my situation, I'd already be dead rather than slowly freezing to death. It was the napalm's fault, too. My decision to gobble it down had nothing to do with it. The volume of the spray intensified, and I unsheathed my claws to aid digging into the pile so I could hide from the wet.

My efforts to burrow didn't help, not one bit. I curled into a shivering ball, tucking my hooves as close to my body as I could. Why did they need to spray so much? The dust was dead. The neutralizer was blatant overkill. I had reduced an entire skyscraper to ash. Why did they have to drench the ash and me along with it?

Then again, leveling one of Wall Street's predominant skyscrapers wasn't exactly a good thing. I expected a lengthy lecture on proper napalming techniques. The CDC would probably start with the fact I'd gobbled down napalm like it was candy. Maybe if I pitched my excessive rampage of destruction as reducing the cost of debris removal, they'd look the other way.

Who was I kidding? As soon as the CDC got hold of me, I was a dead unicorn. I missed the magical fire's searing intensity. A final attempt to burrow ended with me tangled in the mess of twisted metal and chunks of concrete somehow left intact.

More neutralizing spray rained down, chilling me until I couldn't even snort smoke. I rested my chin on a steel girder and whimpered. Maybe my napalm binge had something to do with my survival, but did it have to hurt so much? How had I avoided being crushed?

Stupid magic, breaking the laws of physics without being nice enough to prevent the worst hangover of my life from pummeling me. The idea I had survived an inferno only to freeze to death in the final stages of decontamination capped my already miserable day.

As though hearing my thoughts, the universe decided to remind me things could get worse. The man-made rain intensified to a deluge, washing away my blanket of ash.

"Noooo," I whined, uncurling to dig into the debris so I could steal its residual heat.

The remnant chunks of concrete broke apart and washed away, leaving me with the more stubborn metal, which caught on my fur.

Great. Not only was I inflicted with the worst headache I'd ever experienced, I was cold, I was soaked, and I was stuck. Why did the CDC have to go to extremes to make sure the dust was eradicated? I had no doubt the fires had gotten rid of every last speck of it. Then again, I couldn't blame them. The real issue was me; had my flames purged the contamination from my body?

I thought so. For one blissful moment, I had been one with the inferno. I already missed the wild and destructive freedom—and its warmth. The cold numbed me and smothered me until bone-deep lethargy pulled me into miserable darkness.

The crackle of the shield shattering roused me and signaled the end of the cold rain. The respite didn't last long, as someone had the bright idea to spray the ruins with a fire hose. Why? Why would they do that?

If I could have gotten up, I would have hunted the culprit down and stabbed them with my horn before eating them. My fur plastered to me, and I wailed, "Noooo. Watter bad."

The stream cut off, and someone in a white hazmat suit braved the rubble, picking their way towards me, a meter in one hand. I lifted my head and snorted a warning, baring my teeth as a promise of what I'd do to them and their protective gear if they messed with me.

"Scan is clear. I seem to have located an aggressive, oversized drowned rat, sir."

Ah, good old Perky. He always knew the exact thing to say to piss me off. "Rat? Rat? Purr-key, I will eat you! Cold. Fire gone. Bring fire back."

Perky crouched in front of me and shoved the meter in my mouth. "Breathe on the sensor, Gardener. It's on close-range, high-sensitivity. If you've got any dust in your system, it'll detect it."

I clamped my teeth on the device hard enough to keep hold of it, snorting out my nose to remind him I couldn't breathe out of my mouth. I gave it a few licks and spit it out. "No breathe through mouth, idiot Perky. Nose only."

"Ah, right."

I should have known he'd ram the sensor up a nostril. It hurt, and I snorted in my effort to dislodge the obnoxious device. It remained silent.

"You're clean."

"Yippee. No box for me. I'm cold, Purr-key. Cold. Make wat-ter go away. I'm wet."

After hanging the meter from his utility belt, Perky gave my shoulder a pat. "Sir, she's clean. Body temp seems really low, but otherwise, she seems fine. There is one problem. She's tangled in the debris, and I'm not sure I can get her out. Yes, I'm certain she's clean, sir. The napalm must have gotten it all, and if she breathed any in, the high temperatures must have cooked it out of her."

I lifted my head enough I could use Perky's foot as a pillow. "Lit napalm. Did good?"

Perky scratched behind my ears. "You did great, Gardener. Sit tight. We'll get you out of there. I'm not sure how, but we'll figure something out."

IT TOOK A CRANE, a couple of blowtorches, and some elbow grease to extricate me from the rubble. Perky kept me company the entire time, and my whining bore fruit when someone finally took pity on me and brought over a high-powered lamp to help ward away the chill. Full darkness had fallen by the time I staggered onto the sidewalk in front of the destroyed building.

I'd never seen Wall Street so deserted before, and I shivered at the disconcerting sight. Without a reason to delay asking, I mumbled, "Quinn safe?"

While I'd burned the napalm for Perky,

my worries for the police chief had driven me to ensure the whole place toppled in an inferno so intense I questioned if I had existed as anything other than flame while it had burned.

Perky ditched the containment suit in a pile on the road before pointing at the nearest traffic barricade. "He's over there. Last I heard he was screaming something about skinning a crazy, suicidal pyromaniac unicorn."

I spotted a stack of blankets off to the side, and I shuffled to them, lowering my head to grab one in my teeth, turning to hold it out to Perky. Around a mouthful of plush fabric, I said, "Still cold. Want blanket."

With a quiet chuckle, he took it from me, shook it out, and draped it over my back. "Poor thing. You're still shivering. Baths are not good for crazy pyromaniac unicorns, are they?"

"Wat-ter bad," I agreed. "Go? Fire. Sleep. Meat. Not in that order."

"Just promise me you won't pick a fight with Chief Quinn. We've all had a miserable day."

"Yes. Want fire. Cold. Hun-gree. Tired."

"I feel like I should yell at you for being so whiny, but you've earned it. Come on, let's get to the barricade. The CDC promised to send over a trailer so you wouldn't have to hoof it."

I surrendered with a sigh, and we made it half a block before a tall, dark, and handsome figure stormed in our direction.

"*Gardener*!" Quinn stomped up, got in my face, and bellowed, "Are you out of your fucking mind?"

The rage in his voice surprised me so much I recoiled, bumping into Perky and knocking him aside. I flattened my ears. A shiver ran through me, and a bone-deep tension warned me of trouble. Like some living elastic band stretched too tight, I snapped back into my human body, yelping at the blinding surge of pain. My legs buckled, and I pitched forward.

Warm, strong arms wrapped around me, and my face collided with Quinn's chest rather than the sidewalk.

Perky spewed curses. A moment later, he draped the blanket over my shoulders. "Couldn't you have done that an hour ago?"

"I'm sorry. It's not my fault!" Go me. At the rate I was whining and wailing, they'd nickname me Manhattan's Banshee.

Worse, without Quinn's hold on me, I would've oozed to the ground in a limp Bailey puddle. My body refused all my orders, leaving me slumped against the man, my nose pressed against his uniform, forcing me to breathe in his scent. He smelled of smoke and cologne. One moment, I struggled to stand without help. The next, Quinn held me cradled in his arms while Perky tucked the blanket around me.

"Ambulance," Quinn barked. It didn't take Perky long to relay the order using the police chief's radio.

"Not again, damn it. I'm fine. I don't need to go—"

"You were in a burning building, exposed to gorgon dust again, and trapped in debris. Any one of those things warrants a trip to the hospital." Quinn inhaled and launched into a tirade detailing every last one of my sins, beginning with my decision to remain in a condemned building instead of leaving with the two cops assigned to me.

"That's not fair. I was contaminated. I couldn't risk public safety."

"Gardener," he growled.

I scowled and turned my head so I wouldn't have to look at his angry face, which would only serve to remind me I was naked under the blanket, how ridiculously handsome he was even when pissed off, and how I really wouldn't mind if his clothes were incinerated so we were both naked and under a blanket—preferably together.

Damn it, why couldn't I do anything like a normal human being? Even with a skull-splitting headache and aching body, I wanted the man. It wasn't fair.

"You're going to the hospital, and that's final."

Infuriated Quinn was too hot to handle. I clenched my teeth so I wouldn't embarrass myself any further.

THE EMTS AGREED with Chief Quinn, ignored my protests, and took me to the hospital, where I spent the next five hours undergoing tests to confirm I wouldn't fall over dead, turn to stone, or start petrifying people. To add insult to injury, Professor Yale arrived five minutes after I did and insisted on accompanying me through every single part of the examination.

If the old man kept laughing at me, I really would kill him. "Would you please stop?"

"You ate so much napalm you got drunk on it. Of course I'm going to laugh. Who wouldn't?" While he managed to speak the words in his most solemn teaching voice, Professor Yale grinned at me. "Stop complaining and get dressed. I'll even turn around to protect your modesty. You should be happy. Unlike the two cops who went into the building with you, you dodged a trip into a glass coffin. I thought you'd appreciate knowing they were in for six hours just to be cleared and are breezing through recovery. Neither were contaminated, but we weren't about to take any chances."

Even sixty minutes in a glass coffin led to misery and revaccinations, but it beat the alternative. Maybe when my body didn't ache so much, I'd even be happy about it—at least happy for Janet. The cadet could take a one-way trip to his grave for all I cared, and if I never saw the insufferable man again, I'd be content. Grimacing at the pull of sore, stiff muscles, I dug into the bag Professor Yale had brought with him.

Why, exactly, was I holding a pair of black lace panties and matching bra in my hand? I selected my bras for function over form. Could little scraps of cloth held together with lace actually keep my breasts contained? I wasn't even sure what the point of the dainty panties were, but I wore them anyway.

The bra fit a little too well, and no amount of tugging prevented it from giving me the Grand Canyon of cleavage even though my breasts weren't all that large to begin with. Muttering curses, I hoped the lace would actually keep them supported and somewhat contained.

Instead of normal clothes, someone had decided a yellow dress with dinky little straps and barely enough fabric to keep everything covered classified as appropriate attire. I pulled it over my head and discovered it barely fell mid thigh. If I bent over, I'd give everyone a show.

"What the hell is this thing?"

Professor Yale turned around and arched an eyebrow. "I do believe that's called a dress, Bailey. It's a form of attire members of your gender wear. It was also the easiest thing to acquire on short notice with the sizes we had on file in the CDC database."

Right. The CDC kept measurements of all certified employees in case of emergencies, allowing the organization to clothe anyone caught handling situations without being able to pack a bag first. Dresses *were* easier, as fashion designers hadn't quite figured out how to standardize jean sizes.

"I feel indecent, Professor Yale."

"Stop complaining. Just be happy the CDC is footing the bill again. Can you please stop trying to get yourself killed? You're going to give me an ulcer."

"So, did they actually call you for the secondary authorization?"

"Yes."

At least protocols had been followed. It probably wouldn't save me from a lengthy interrogation, but maybe I'd survive without losing my certification. Still, it wouldn't hurt to ask. "I'm dead, aren't I?"

"No."

"Wait. What? Why not? I ordered an entire skyscraper to be napalmed. This isn't like torching a single apartment or something. It was an entire building. I reduced it to rubble." My voice had gone up a full octave, and I cringed. "Sorry."

Professor Yale chuckled. "We have full video evidence of everything that went on in the building. The camera Officer Downing provided was uploading directly to the CDC as well as to her portable monitor. You checked the meter per protocol, reset the meter when you weren't sure if the reading was correct, and took every single precaution to ensure the public's safety. You then did a full examination of the site. While you pulled the trigger quickly on giving a napalming order, there is zero reason for anyone at the CDC to question your judgment."

I pinched myself. It hurt. "Did hell freeze over?"

Shaking his head, Professor Yale grabbed the empty bag, crumpled it up, and tossed it in the garbage can. "No. After the difficulty neutralizing the gorgon dust in your apartment, we decided to go with high-intensity napalm—a new blend, infused with magic to reach higher temperatures. The bomb techs forgot to account for the higher ignition point. We're very impressed—we weren't sure how the hell we were going to get the napalm lit, and you went and did our job for us. That said, was it really necessary to roll around in it while on fire? After the building had collapsed, the reporters captured a few clips of you playing in the debris. They really love the clip of you belching white-hot fire near the end of your drunken rampage. The giggling and chanting of 'napalm' over and over is coming in as a close second favorite. The CDC issued a statement you were chosen for your breed's ability to ensure the new blend of napalm worked. You should be grateful; we kept your name out of the news."

I groaned. "Please tell me you're joking."

"Me? Joke?"

"I was on the news? As a unicorn?"

"Just be grateful the photograph of Chief Quinn carrying you to the ambulance hasn't reached the media. Expect blackmail."

I sucked in a breath and widened my eyes. "Oh, no. You're serious, aren't you?"

"Very. At least you won't have much paperwork to do. I thought you'd appreciate if I handled it for you. All you need to do is review and sign. Even better, I have a check with your name on it. The bad news? There's an official lifetime ban on you eating magically infused napalm without authorization. There will be no drunken revelries without it being cleared by the CDC first."

I sighed. "It's not like I went on a drunken rampage on purpose."

Professor Yale thumped my shoulder. "Ready to get out of here? Chief Quinn is expecting you. At least this time you'll be able to enjoy a more traditional stay. I'm sure you want to sleep off your hangover."

"At Chief Quinn's house."

"Yes."

My life had somehow become very strange. Instead of complaining about it, I accepted the inevitable with a nod. What else could I do? I stared down at the little yellow dress. If I squinted, I was pretty sure I could see my black bra through it. Damn. I was giving the dress a tug to pull the hem down so it was a little closer to a comfortable length when I noticed the hair on my legs.

Crap. I really needed to shave.

TEN

I might start thinking you like the man if you keep acting this way.

AT A LITTLE AFTER eight in the morning, Professor Yale pulled into Quinn's driveway. Armed with a folded check, I got out of the old man's car. The house looked dark and quiet.

The roses lining his walkway caught my eye, and I blushed at the memory of having eaten one as a unicorn. To cover my embarrassment, I leaned down and stared through the window. "I'm going to wake him up, aren't I?"

"No. I called him right before we left the hospital. Go get some sleep. You're so tired you don't even know which end is up anymore. I might start thinking you like the man if you keep acting this way, and you'd regret that later. Have fun at your sleepover party, little girl."

Groaning, I stepped away from Professor

Yale's car and flipped my middle finger at him. "We need to have a long talk about your personal dictionary. It needs adjusted. In what alternate dimension do I have fun with Chief Quinn?"

He laughed. "Take care and get some sleep, Bailey." Backing out of the driveway, he drove away with a departing wave.

"There's nothing fun about being scolded by a police chief at eight in the morning, you know!" I called after him.

The bastard didn't even slow. Sighing, I prepared for the worst and marched to the front door, knocking before I lost my nerve.

A yawning Quinn opened the door, shirtless and in nothing more than a pair of boxers. "Come on in. Sorry I didn't pick you up from the hospital—Yale threatened dismemberment if I got underfoot."

Since when did Quinn, half-naked or otherwise, act so nice? I could do nice, too. I could also talk to the man without slobbering all over him. "I'm so sorry for the trouble."

"Get in the house already, Gardener."

Right. I stepped inside and closed the door behind me. "I have a hangover, so if I say anything stupid, that's why. I'm really sorry." At least I could try to prevent issues *before* they happened for a change.

"Yale already warned me you were paying for getting drunk on napalm. Who knew it'd be like alcohol for a unicorn? Conveniently, I have hangover meds on hand."

"There's medication for hangovers?" Where had those been all my life?

He laughed. "Sure is. It even works, too. Drink a couple glasses of water, take two of those tablets, and you'll be feeling better in no time. Kitchen's this way."

Quinn led me through his home. He had moved his furniture, giving his home a calm, welcoming atmosphere. "You really do have a nice house."

"Consider it yours for however long you need."

Forever would be a good start, but I didn't have the courage to tell him that. No one had ever invited me to make myself at home for any length of time, not in my adult life at least, not even my parents—especially not my parents. I swallowed so I wouldn't cry in front of Quinn.

He wouldn't understand.

"I really appreciate this."

"You're welcome." Quinn filled a glass with water, dropped two orange tablets into it, stirring with a spoon until both tablets dissolved. "Drink this. It'll help."

I set my check on the counter and took the glass. The medicine tasted like oranges, and I guzzled it down before my stomach could rebel. "Did everything work out with the situation yesterday?"

I still had no idea what had happened. While I didn't expect Quinn to tell me, I could fake being a good person with a little effort. People liked when others took an interest in their work—at least, I thought they did.

"I'm of the opinion it was a distraction to keep resources away from the 120 Wall Street incident. Fortunately, we had you on our side, else it would have gotten bad fast."

I almost dropped the glass but set it down before I broke it. "What?"

Quinn pointed at the folded piece of paper. "That's your check?"

"Yeah."

"Haven't looked at it yet, have you?"

Shaking my head, I regarded the payment for a long moment before flicking it with a finger and sending it fluttering across Quinn's counter. "I assumed it was the standard fee for two incidents." I'd be grateful for the extra two thousand dollars when I hunted for an apartment.

"Not quite. Go ahead and take a look. I can't wait to see your face."

I frowned, snatched up the paper, and unfolded the check. After the fifth zero, I forgot how numbers worked. My legs trembled, and I leaned on the counter so I wouldn't melt into a puddle and ruin his nice clean tiles. "What the hell?"

"Yale thought you wouldn't remember the provision in your contract with the CDC allowing the local and federal governments to augment the payment of any certified contractor. The mayor decided to ask the CDC how many lives were likely saved by your actions."

I gasped and dropped my check. "Pen! Pen, pen, pen." Snapping my fingers together, I dredged through my hazy memory for the names of the people I had condemned to death.

Quinn stared at me for a long moment before fetching a pad of paper and a pen from a nearby drawer. Snatching them out of his hand, I scribbled down their names. How could I have forgotten them? Tears stung my eyes over how many had died.

I had helped kill them, and I had forgotten all about them.

Leaning across the counter, Quinn peered at my work. "Ah. It's all right, Bailey. We got the stills of their cards from the footage you recorded. Their families have already been notified. They were celebrated as heroes on the morning news today."

"I killed them, Quinn." I hadn't just killed them. I had rejoiced in my flames, encouraging them to burn brighter and hotter, for Perky—and for Quinn.

Especially for Quinn.

Quinn picked up my check, folded it, and set it in front of me. "When the mayor called the CDC, I was with him. That happened about ten minutes after you lit the place up. We thought you'd gone and kicked the bucket on us." Leaning forward, Quinn stared me in the eyes, close enough I could feel him breathe. "Yale was with us, too. Guess what the mayor asked."

"I have no idea."

"He asked if sixty-three lives compared to the lives and well-being of everyone else in New York City. There were over a thousand people in 120 Wall Street when it was evacuated. If even one percent of those people were infected and became carriers, it would have triggered an epidemic. One newly whelped gorgon can petrify dozens before being isolated, contained, and taught how to control their powers. Someone attacked our city, and *you* stopped them. Not me, not anyone else on the force. You."

There was no way I could tell Quinn why I'd gone on a fiery rampage. If he found out I'd done it because I was scared for him and for Perky, they'd never let me live it down. "I got drunk on napalm and burned down a building. That's hardly commendable."

"You sent my cops out to protect them long before you went on your little bender."

"Little?"

"Okay, intense and rather insane napalm bender. Maybe you got a little carried away, but it worked out."

I blushed and stared down at the check so I wouldn't have to look him in the eyes. "Why?"

Why would anyone attack New York with gorgon dust, something so dangerous it was illegal on a global level and could petrify an entire city in minutes? With the volume I had destroyed, it was entirely possible Lower Manhattan, at the very minimum, would have been turned to stone.

Quinn sighed. "I don't know, but I intend to find out." With a finger, he pinned my check to his counter. "This represents every life you saved yesterday." His expression changed, and fury darkened his eyes and twisted his mouth. "You were willing to kill yourself to make sure that dust stayed contained. You didn't even hesitate. You knew what you faced. You had no way of knowing you'd survive, and you did it anyway."

"Yes." How could one word hurt so much? I'd kept the same dead-end job most of my adult life, breaking the monotony with jobs for the CDC to boost my income enough to barely make a living. I could've done better for myself if I'd just taken my certifications and worked directly for the CDC, but I hadn't wanted to travel the world.

I had wanted to make friends and find someone to love, someone who'd love me back. That hadn't worked out so well for me, but I'd kept trying and failing anyway. I couldn't fool anyone.

Until I figured out how to have friends, I had no hope of finding someone just for me —if that someone existed. The man I wanted stood right in front of me, and all I had ever done was hurt him.

"Why?"

It was so easy to explain, yet the words stuck in my throat. Quinn waited, all his attention focused on me.

"Perky was right outside." I stared at the check, wondering how that much money would change things for me. It had more than five zeros, well over the amount I made in a single year—more than I had made in my entire life. "I knew you'd come. I knew if you came—when you came—the dust might reach you. They'd put you in a glass coffin, and they'd never let you out. I couldn't let that happen."

I'd already ruined his life enough. Maybe it'd set things straight between us, making up for the things I'd done and the hateful words I'd said to him.

"So you would have thrown your life away."

I closed my eyes. "I'm not like you, Quinn. I'm not respected. I'm not liked. I have no one. For someone like me, when I die, that's it. Everyone else moves on. Someone might wonder what happened to the only human stupid enough to work at a faery-run coffee shop. Some might even remember my name was Bailey because they thought it was funny I had the same name as an alcohol often served in coffee. You help people. Me? I mess things up."

"When Yale warned me you had enough self-esteem issues to keep an entire mental hospital busy, I'd really thought he was exaggerating."

Professor Yale had said *what*? One day, I really would kill that old man, and I'd enjoy every moment of it. "He said *what*?"

"I'm going to have to apologize to him later for doubting him. I see where I've been going wrong. I'm obviously going to have to explain this in a way your pea-sized brain can understand."

I stiffened at his insult, opened my eyes, and glared at him. "Hey!"

He closed the distance between us, and I tried to decide whether a handprint would look better on his right cheek or his left one.

His smug smile warned me of trouble, and

I backed up until I bumped into the wall. With a gentle but firm touch, he took hold of my chin, lifted my head, and kissed me.

KISSING SAMUEL QUINN was a little like playing with fire, getting burned, and enjoying it despite the pain—or maybe because of it. I wasn't sure. I wasn't sure of anything except I never wanted him to stop.

I was in so much trouble.

When he pulled away, my heart pounded while I struggled to catch my breath. He stared into my eyes and whispered, "Do you understand now?"

A half-naked Quinn had kissed me in his kitchen, and all I could think about was how I wanted him to do it again. Not only did I want him to do it again, if he didn't, I was seriously considering rubbing up against him until he cooperated in some fashion or another.

Then I remembered he hated me. He hated me so much he had trapped me against his kitchen wall and kissed me. What was wrong with him? Or me. Or both of us, together. There was definitely something wrong with us.

There was definitely something wrong about how much I liked his mouth on mine.

"But you hate me." There. I managed to get the right words out instead of blabbering about how I'd really like him to keep me trapped against the wall so he could do whatever he wanted. I really wouldn't mind a single bit. "Those pictures I took!"

Why was I stupid enough to mention the man's ex-wife when I might be able to get him to kiss me again?

Stupid, stupid me.

"Yes, I hate you so much I want to strip you out of that little dress and make you like it." He growled, and I longed for him to make the sound again. "That dress on you should be classified as criminal. There's a crime being committed in my kitchen, and I'm pretty sure it's my job as a law enforcement officer to uphold the law and stop crime."

A hundred and one thoughts crashed through my head, and three in particular stood out to me: yes, please, and I was a virgin.

"I'm a virgin," I blurted.

Crap.

It turned out it wasn't actually possible to die from embarrassment, although I was sure I came close. Why couldn't I have said "Yes, please!" instead? Then I'd have a decent chance of taking my virginity out back, clubbing it in the head, and leaving it to die in a ditch while I did things with New York's prime stud, single-because-of-me Chief Quinn, who I had dreamed about far too often. Instead, I guaranteed myself a lifetime of mockery the instant anyone found out.

"It seems I was right. There are definitely multiple crimes being committed in my kitchen. That also explains your offer to introduce me to some of your questionable friends."

I whimpered at the reminder of what I'd said to him. "I never should have said that."

Something about the way Quinn smiled warned me he had the upper hand and knew it. "I have you figured out, Bailey Gardener. You have no idea how to tell me how badly you want me, so you say the first stupid thing to pop into your head, hoping I won't guess the truth."

Oh my God. I had to be dreaming, hallucinating, or dead. Maybe I had died and gone to heaven, a heaven where Chief Samuel Quinn wanted to kiss me and fully intended to end my days of being a virgin, ripping my dress off in the process. There had to be a rational explanation for the situation.

"Am I dead, drugged, or dreaming?"

Quinn sighed, leaned forward, and banged his head into the wall before sighing again. "Obviously, this is going to be even more difficult than I thought. This explains so much. How can one woman be so incredibly dense?"

"Now you're just being mean."

"I'm going to put this as simply as possible so there are absolutely no misunderstandings. I am absolutely furious you tried to get yourself killed. I want to bend you over my knee and spank you until you swear never to do that again."

"Yes, please."

Crap. Why couldn't my mouth stop blurting whatever the hell first came to mind?

He straightened, stared down at me, and blinked several times. The realization I'd just asked him to spank me sank in, and we stared at each other for a long time in utter silence.

I wanted him. I wanted him so much my entire body ached.

A slow, wicked smile spread across his lips. "Well, then. Since you asked so nicely, how could I possibly refuse?"

ELEVEN

How haven't I tired you out yet?

I DIDN'T LOSE my virginity. 'Lose' implied I wanted it back, cared it was gone, or would otherwise miss it. I liked to think we took it out back, clubbed it to death, lit it on fire so it'd never bother me again, and gave it a nice funeral. But now I had a new problem, a very big one: Quinn.

With one taste of him, I never wanted to let him go—or let him let me go, as the case currently was. He trapped me against him, cuddled close, and kept nibbling on the back of my neck. He had exhausted me, made me feel way too much, and somehow left me wanting more.

Unfortunately, I had a second problem: I needed to pee.

Where was the bathroom, and how was I supposed to reach it when every muscle in my body protested even the thought of moving? I ached in places I hadn't known I could. Worse, I wanted more. I wanted Quinn over and over again.

But first, I really needed to pee. "Quinn?"

"Mmmm?" He really needed to stop nibbling on me. If he didn't, I'd never want to leave his bed. "How haven't I tired you out yet?"

Determined to say something other than 'let me up or I'll pee on you,' I replied, "Where's your bathroom?"

"But I like it when you're dirty."

Nice. I liked it when he was dirty, too, and he liked showing me just how wonderfully sinful he could be.

Screw it. "Let me up or I'll pee on you."

Quinn laughed and pointed at a closed door. "Through there."

It would be a lot easier to escape his warm bed if he let me go. I wiggled free, shivering at the way his hand skimmed over my skin, and made a strategic retreat to the bathroom. Marble floors, a huge tub with jets, and a separate shower promised I'd spend some of the best moments of my life in Quinn's home.

That was it. If he wanted me to leave, he'd have to kick me out, and I'd fight tooth, claw, hoof, and horn to stay. "I'm never leaving," I declared before closing the door.

Point to me. I didn't slam it like I often did when overly excited or pissed.

He chuckled, a sensual, rumbling sound.

Police Chief Samuel Quinn wouldn't be laughing when I made myself at home in his tub and made good on my promise never to leave. I took the quickest shower possible before preparing for the nicest soak of my life. In one of the three big cabinets, I found a bottle of sea-scented bubbles and a staggering number of body washes.

Later, when I finally drifted down from the heavens and crash landed back on Earth, everything would go wrong. I'd find out I was in a hospital again or dead, the usual result of doing the right thing at great risk, having helped a lot of people—and Quinn—because I could rather than for a paycheck.

Alternatively, maybe the universe was rewarding me for a job well done and sent payment in the form of Quinn. Was he the naked model? Maybe he was a gift from Santa, because I sure as hell couldn't figure out why the man would want *me* of all people.

And holy shit, had he wanted me.

I could die happy, and I eased my way into the warm water with an ecstatic sigh. Life, for the moment, was absolutely perfect. I wanted to kiss whomever had invented bathtubs with jets in them, as the rush of water not only made the bubbles better but also worked the stiffness out of my muscles.

A phone rang, evidence I was somehow in

a very real world. Quinn cursed in the bedroom and answered, "It better be an emergency, otherwise, the answer is no. Gardener's taking a bath, and there's no way in hell I'm bothering her unless it's really important. What is it?"

Quinn had just sealed his fate, which he would learn soon enough. By defending my bubble bath, he signaled the end of his reign as a free man.

Damn it, that had to be the predatory unicorn in me still talking.

Then again, maybe it wasn't. Could anyone blame me for wanting to stay in heaven after having found it? Maybe I'd, in some horrible fashion, done Quinn a favor by taking those photos of his ex-wife. Maybe if I pitched the argument in the right way, I'd believe it for a little while.

I submerged to my chin and snorted so the bubbles wouldn't go up my nose.

Quinn made a frustrated noise in the other room. "I may require a manual. How long should I leave Gardener in the tub before it's safe? What? What the hell do you mean there's no manual? You're the one who wants me to come into work tonight. That's not at all reasonable. Under the assumption I can coax her out of her hard-earned bath, we'll come to the station. Probably around ten, since we'll need dinner first."

There was a long moment of silence, and Quinn gave one of those little growls that made me hold my breath so I could better listen while my toes curled. "No, I'm not leaving her home alone. She can sleep on my couch at the station, supervised. Those are doctor's orders—she's to be supervised in case exposure to so much neutralizer compromised her immune system again. She's coming in with me, and that's final."

Quinn hung up, and at the rate he was grumbling and growling, he'd lose his voice in short order.

I thought long and hard about what I'd overheard. Obviously, I'd need to address the whole leaving the house at all issue. Wait. He planned to be at the station by ten? After *dinner*? What time was it?

The last time I had checked a clock, it had been eight in the morning. How long had we been occupied in his bed?

And elsewhere in his home. *Everywhere* in his home. I thought about that long and hard.

No wonder I was sore.

Quinn knocked on the door. "Bailey? We need to go to the station in a few hours."

"What time is it?"

"Just before seven."

"At night?" Somehow, I avoided squealing the word.

"Unfortunately." Quinn opened the door

and peeked inside. "Please tell me you're not a vegetarian. For some odd reason, my fridge is loaded with meat."

"Cook it up, bring it in, and serve me while at least half-naked. I seem to recall winning a certain bet. And don't you forget my grapes, Mr. Samuel Quinn."

I really liked his wicked smile, which made him look like he would pounce and have his way with me given half a chance. "Your wish is my command."

It no longer mattered if I was suffering from drug-induced hallucinations, had discovered heaven in the afterlife, or even if reality had turned in my favor for a change. For the moment, everything was perfect, and that was good enough for me.

I WENT from better than fine to sniffling and sneezing before we left for the station. After a short but fierce argument, which ended with me against the wall, trapped by Quinn's warm body, he won the battle by shutting me up with his mouth on mine, but I won the war. Convincing him I'd die of shame if I went back to the hospital again classified as underhanded, but so was him using his weapon-grade lips against me.

"I really should be taking you to the doctor," he murmured in my ear.

"I should be taking you back to bed, but no, I have to go to work with you. When I'm so sick I can't fight with you over it, then you can take me to the hospital. Until then, I'm fine." While I thought I'd be better than fine curled up on his bed, wrapped up in his blanket, using his pillow, he refused to leave me in his home unattended.

Since Quinn had ripped the sundress in his hurry to get it off me, I wore pajamas. Leaving for the station at nine at night justified my choice. Since he wasn't letting me stay in his house alone, I'd stolen his blanket off his bed and stuffed it in a bag along with a pair of jeans, white t-shirt, and a black leather coat so I'd have something to wear when I went shopping for a new wardrobe.

"We don't have time to go back to bed again."

"I can dream, can't I? It's not my fault they hosed me down. It's their fault I caught a cold."

"Bailey."

"What?"

"Just shut up and get your ass in the convertible."

"But I can't. I'm trapped."

He chuckled, dropped another kiss on my

lips, and pulled away. "Don't touch any buttons, you. You're a disaster waiting to happen, and I like that car. If you start pressing buttons, I'm certain you'll find a way to break it."

"That's me. Bailey, the walking catastrophe." I sighed, snatched the bag of clothes and pilfered blanket, and dragged it to his car. While I could have put my ill-gotten gains in the two seater's trunk, I crammed it between my feet to prove I could make everything fit despite his doubts. "Hah. I told you I'd fit. Hey, wait a minute. I'm the one who's supposed to be bossing you around."

"We're not in the house anymore, so deal with it, Gardener."

True, the garage technically wasn't in the house. "So I guess I can't get you to start stripping out of your uniform in the car?"

"Not a chance."

"Damn, Quinn. You're mean."

"No. If I were mean, I'd be taking you to the hospital instead of to the station, where I'm sure you'll give every on-duty officer your cold. I really should take you to see your doctor. It's right on the way."

"Please don't."

"Then you better buckle up, shut up, and sleep quietly on my couch while I keep a close eye on you."

I snorted. "You're not going to be

watching me. You're going to be sleeping on your desk while drooling on your paperwork, Chief."

"You're worth it."

I blushed. His statement, spoken with a smug smile, made me wonder just how long he'd been interested in me. Why? Why couldn't I work up the nerve to ask him how he could possibly like me enough to want to sleep with me, especially after I had photographed his wife with another man? Guilt gnawed away at me, and I shifted on the leather seat.

"Put your seatbelt on, Bailey. Cop, remember? There's no way I'm leaving my driveway if you aren't buckled in."

Ah, right. Wearing my seatbelt would help, wouldn't it? I buckled in and sighed. "Even after…?"

Maybe he'd be able to read my mind so I wouldn't have to ask him. I could say demeaning things about myself all day long, but when it came to apologizing or asking important questions, I failed in a spectacular fashion.

"You're something else. Did it ever occur to you that maybe you did me a huge favor? I knew long before I had solid proof. Audrey was a lot of things, but she wasn't discreet, nor was she very good at covering her tracks.

Just so we're clear, I'll be very blunt: she was sneaking in home pregnancy tests when we hadn't been sleeping together often—if at all. Exhibit one: she made no effort to hide her period. Exhibit two: she developed a habit of doing a pregnancy test four or five days after her trysts. At least she had the brains to sleep around *outside* my house rather than inside. I had other suspicions, too. No, I was more than happy about getting out of that relationship, and you provided all the proof I needed."

I had a feeling Audrey had taken someone for a ride in Quinn's backyard. Yick. Central Park was bad enough, but out where the neighbors might spot her? "Wow. Why bring me into it?"

"I figured if I had the Calamity Queen's help, I'd catch her in the worst way possible. That way, I'd get through the divorce without her trying to pull any of her crazy shit. It worked, mostly. I didn't anticipate her brother getting hold of gorgon dust and a cellphone bomb. I'm so sorry you got involved in that mess."

Were there people seriously calling me the Calamity Queen? "Please tell me no one actually calls me the Calamity Queen."

"I plead the Fifth."

I groaned. "Maybe it's true, but that's terrible, Quinn. Anyway, it's better he did the dust and bomb against me. I'm immune. You're not."

"I'm still sorry you got involved in their crazy shit."

Crazy was one way to put it. The dust and bomb was one level of crazy. My desire to jump Quinn in his own car before we ever made it to the station bordered on insane. Then again, crazy *was* my reaction to him. I'd have enough trouble keeping my hands to myself on the drive to Manhattan. Just the thought of possibly going three months without finding my way into his bed frustrated me. Why would Audrey even consider abstaining? "All right. I give. How the hell did she keep her hands off you for so long?"

"I'm still trying to figure out how you kept your hands off me for so long. Years, even. Do you really think of me as various models?"

"God, no!" I sucked in a breath. "Wait. That really happened?"

"Yes, Bailey. Yes, it did. You really hated my Lakers jersey, too—so much you demanded I strip out of it. Perkins wouldn't stop laughing. He even caught a video of you on the strong painkillers. From what we've pieced together, we suspect you were hallucinating. Your hospital room was apparently occupied by a bunch of spiders. Most women scream when they see spiders.

You? No, you were in tears begging us to bring them flies so they wouldn't starve to death."

I had no memory of any spiders, real or hallucinatory. "I did no such thing."

"You did. We have video evidence, Bailey. I'm not above using it as blackmail. While I'd like your promise you'll sleep with me again, I'll negotiate to keep the videos a secret."

If Quinn wanted to play, I'd play—and I'd love every second of it. "I'm going to need to see proof of this video's existence before I agree to anything." If he couldn't figure out I had every intention of learning the art of seduction with him as my test subject, he deserved to squirm. "You could be making that up just to get me to sleep with you again. You're going to have to do better than that, Chief Quinn."

"For such a recently deflowered virgin with a reputation for being a thorn bush without a single rose, it didn't take you long to figure out how to use your feminine wiles against me."

"Deflowered? The historic romance section just called. They're looking for their lost stud."

"When you're good, you're good, and I'm good. I can't help it I'm so good I'm timeless."

Why me? "If thinking that helps you sleep at night…"

"I think I'll be enjoying something a lot better in my near future."

Yes, please. I thanked the universe so it wouldn't kick my ass for being ungrateful. Then again, maybe I was just having a really great dream, one where I had a cold and someone willing to pamper me and feed me tidbits of grilled steak and grapes in his tub to make me feel better. "Keep dreaming, Quinn."

I MADE it all the way to Quinn's office, where I collapsed onto his couch and didn't budge for at least eight hours. I had a faint recollection of people trying to talk to me on the way in, although I couldn't remember who or why. Quinn's blanket smelled like him, and I woke to him talking on the phone with someone, his tone warning me the caller tested every last bit of his patience. Since listening in was rude, I pulled his blanket over my head and burrowed under the throw pillow.

It felt like an eternity before he finally hung up. "Rise and shine, Gardener. You're going to love this."

I was going to love murdering whoever was behind me having to get off the couch. "I'm going to love what? Actually, there is no chance I will love anything. I will kill whoever just called, and when I'm done tossing them out the window by their entrails, I'll light them on fire. Go away. I'm going back to bed."

"Defenestrate."

"What?"

"Defenestrate and disembowel. Those are the words you want. You're going to disembowel Yale and defenestrate his corpse. If you're going to kill someone, at least take the time to do it properly."

"That was Professor Yale?"

"It sure was."

The identity of the caller confirmed I didn't want to know what was going on. "I'm sleeping. Good night."

"It's morning, and in the past ten minutes, there have been six gorgon bile reports, two incidents involving harpies, a phoenix sighting, and a swarm of pixies on a sugar high. Yale called me to get you to deal with the bile."

"Ask the phoenix to deal with the bile." I shivered. "It *is* bile, right?"

"While tempting to find someone brave enough—and stupid enough—to approach a phoenix and ask it to deal with a group of drunk gorgons, I suspect it wouldn't work out too well for the city. Turns out the gorgons went to a bar, got hammered, and tried to walk home afterwards. They made it about a mile before they decided to sit down and play with their own vomit. These specific gorgons are registered as living in New Jersey."

"They were trying to walk to New Jersey?"

"From Lower Manhattan. They used to be very drunk, now they're very hungover."

"If you ask really nicely, maybe the CDC will take pity on you and take care of everything except your pixie problem."

"They are."

I rolled over and pulled his blanket tighter around me. "I'm going back to sleep, Quinn."

"Would you believe that the CDC suggested I contact some woman named Bailey Gardener to make sure the gorgons headed home without further incident and decontaminate the sidewalk and bar?" Quinn chuckled.

I peeked out from beneath the blanket and pillow. "I hate you."

The police chief propped his feet up on his desk and smirked at me. "I told them I might know someone named Bailey Gardener. You were looking for a new job anyway, right? I'm pretty sure cleaning up gorgon bile is your favorite thing on Earth."

"I would rather deal with the pixies."

"Oh? Are you volunteering? That could be arranged—after you check out the bile situation." Quinn reached for his phone and pressed a few buttons. "Calems, bring your partner to my office. I have a job for you."

"You're really going to make me deal with more bile, aren't you?"

"I'd send Perkins with you so he'd have a real reason to throw up, but it's his day off. Have fun, Gardener. Try not to napalm anything this time."

"I hate you so, so much."

TWELVE

If Officer Fluffy barked at me, I'd sock him in the snout.

OFFICER CALEMS'S partner was a werewolf, and he herded me out of Quinn's office with snarls and bared teeth. Only threats of mutiny and grand theft police cruiser bought me enough time to change into too tight jeans, a white shirt, and my new black leather jacket. One of the on-duty cops stuck in the station doing paperwork stole my pajamas and gave me my wallet in exchange.

Damn it. The werewolf with two-inch long fangs driving me away from Quinn was bad enough, but I had left my wallet in his office? I hated mornings. Why couldn't I be back in bed? I'd settle for Quinn's couch in his office, warm, cozy, and safe.

The werewolf growled at me, and I turned to face him. Werewolves qualified to work on the police force had three forms: human, wolf, and a blend of both. Officer O'Daniel was in his blended form and wore a special uniform designed for his hybrid body. He showed me his teeth again.

I curled my lip and showed him mine. "Go ahead. Push me, fluffy. I'll eat you."

If people were expecting a nice, coherent me before I had time to wake up and drink some coffee, they were out of their minds. And so help me, if Officer Fluffy barked at me, I'd sock him in the snout so hard he'd yip his way back to Quinn with his tail tucked between his legs.

Werewolves. Ugh. At least O'Daniel seemed tame enough; I made it all the way to the garage without having to pick a fight with him, one he'd probably win considering he was waist high on all fours and probably more than six feet when he stood upright.

At least he kept his nose to himself and didn't try to mark his territory. Once I could talk without growling worse than he did, I'd ask him why he was running around on all fours with a furry coat.

"Your tailoring bill must be atrocious." I glared at the cruiser, sighed, and crawled into the back, shutting the door before the werewolf got any crazy ideas about joining me and using my lap as a pillow.

Both cops shot dirty looks my way before getting in the car. Yep, O'Daniel was easily six and a half feet tall if not pushing seven.

I really needed to stop my mouth from blurting whatever it felt like. "What? I haven't had coffee yet."

"Heard you had a smart mouth, Gardener," the werewolf growled at me.

I liked Quinn's snarls a lot better. Yep, I had it bad. Did infatuation classify as a dangerous disease? It needed to be; my common sense had already abandoned ship, and at the rate I was going, my self-respect and dignity would soon follow. "I can finally die happy. Word of my infamous smart mouth has spread. My work on this Earth is done."

Officer Calems snickered, slid behind the wheel, and started the cruiser's engine. "No wonder you drive the chief crazy. You can't help it, can you? I'm genuinely surprised he hasn't gagged you yet. It's so refreshing to see someone get on his nerves. Reminds us all he's actually human."

Great. I had a reputation for pissing Quinn off? Wait. That was a good thing. It dawned on me I couldn't let anyone suspect there was anything going on between us. He'd never live it down, choosing to sleep with the crazy, scarred CDC chick. "Does he even know how to use his handcuffs? I thought they were decorations he used to convince people he's actually a cop."

"How is it possible for someone like you to have top-level certification?" Calems shook his head and backed the car out of its spot, and I remembered I needed to wear a seatbelt without anyone reminding me. Go me, acting like an adult for a change.

I decided the truth worked best since no one would believe it anyway. "Once upon a time, a woman went to a bar, got drunker than a skunk, forgot to take birth control, and got knocked up. Nine months later, yours truly was born, and the woman's random hookup coerced her into marrying him using me as blackmail material."

Ah, I loved the sound of stunned silence.

"Okay, only part of that is true. He didn't coerce her into marrying him. Dear old Dad comes from a stuffy traditionalist family who doesn't believe in abortion *or* adoption, so to avoid losing his inheritance or smearing the family name in the dirt, they claim it was love at first sight while they pretend the worst mistake of their lives was never born."

Nope, I wasn't bitter, not at all. I'd have to work on that. If I was going to use them as a shield, I'd have to at least try to sound cheerful about it.

"That… doesn't explain how you ended up working for the CDC as a specialist."

Since when had I gone from overpaid janitor to a specialist? "Since abortion or adoption Simply Wasn't Done, I became known as the family disease, the ruiner of lives. It was great fun, especially when they took me to every single meet and greet of magical beings. They thought they'd solve their problem if they left me unattended near the gorgons' tent, hoping they could pretend I was an actual statue and not petrified. Nope, no such luck for them. Too bad!"

There. I sounded a lot happier about the whole thing. Who knew I could actually sound so chipper?

"I can't tell if you're yanking my chain, and that's really freaking me out, Gardener."

I added Calems to my short list of people I actually liked. "They found me playing jumprope with the whelps and a few statues; a couple of humans had had the bright idea of trying to make a profit by kidnapping a few young gorgons. So, not only was I the unwanted daughter, I didn't uphold the Gardener pure vanilla family values to their satisfaction. What sort of freak is immune to gorgons, anyway?"

Yep, I was totally bitter about the whole thing.

"Whoa. You're really immune to gorgons? Not just their bile or dust?"

"Oh, piece of advice. Don't let a gorgon bite you. It hurts like hell. That venom's just plain nasty. Since I don't petrify, I itch, and it makes me really, really pissy."

"Good to know. Do I want to know the

rest of this story? Why am I certain there's a rest of this story?"

I chuckled. "That's because you're smart. And you do. You so do."

"All right. Hit us with it."

"I did it out of pure spite. They said it wasn't proper. When that didn't work, they told me I wasn't smart enough. When *that* didn't work, they swore I'd never amount to anything. That was when they told me if I was so sure I could do it, to get out and go do it, but to never bother them again. Top of my class, top-level certification later, I showed them."

I sure had, and the one time I had made the mistake of asking them for anything, I still hadn't been good enough for them. Why had I even tried? I blamed the fever.

"That's impressive and terrifying. I could have sworn you worked as a barista."

"Used to. I quit."

I frowned. Wait. Why *had* Mary gone with Quinn and left me alone on that nightmare all-day solo shift? Damn it, I was supposed to be mad at him over that, not sleeping with him. Hmm. Maybe I could still sleep with him while pissed off? The idea would need to undergo a great deal of testing.

"If you're looking for work, the coffee at the station sucks."

Since reaching between the seats wasn't

possible thanks to the cage that kept criminals away from the cops, I forced my best smile. "You wish, Calems."

A MILE long trail of vomit lined with statues promised a lousy day of hard work was ahead of me. I suspected karma was somehow at play. Since I had glimpsed the heavens through Quinn and his sinful touch, I just had to get kicked out and suffer through hell. "Is it premeditated murder if I kill those gorgons after I finish cleaning up their mess?"

I had completed four years of education so I could hand scrub a sidewalk with neutralizer while drunk gorgons rolled around in their own vomit. My cheek twitched. Why did gorgons have to look so damned close to humans? Except for the gray-green cast and snakes for hair, they came as close to human as the truly magical species got. With some makeup and a good hat, some even passed as human until they made eye contact.

"Yes, Gardener. You lost your chance for a basic manslaughter charge about five minutes ago," Calems replied.

Officer O'Daniel wagged his tail while his tongue lolled out of his mouth.

I sighed. "Stay with the car, wear sunglasses, don't get bit, and try to look cool or something. Please tell me the CDC sent some supplies until they could send a truck."

"In the trunk."

"Yippee. Let me out so I can get this over with."

Calems laughed, freed me from the backseat, and wouldn't stop chortling, especially when I wailed my dismay at the contents of his trunk. While I'd love to get my hands on the shotgun, he slapped my fingers and pointed at the five-pound bag of high-grade neutralizer.

If the CDC thought a single bag would be sufficient to deal with a quartet of gorgons who were smearing their mess all over the sidewalk with their bare hands, they were nuttier than I was for agreeing to handle the clean up.

To make matters worse, one of the gorgons was a *male,* which meant one thing: it was gorgon breeding season. The males didn't come out of hiding unless they were looking for a human surrogate to help them reproduce with their females. For a single male to be out with three females meant trouble and a lot of it. The females would be looking for human women willing to engage in the strangest lesbian sex known to Earth. If everything went well, which it usually didn't, the surrogate would then turn her attentions to the gorgon male and engage in the second strangest sex act involving humans.

After the surrogate mother was treated for petrification, the tiny fertilized gorgon eggs were retrieved so the gorgons could nest with them. Then the woman was paid a filthy amount of money for serving as a breeding vessel for the gorgons.

The male caught sight of me and looked me over head to toe. A lecherous smile crossed his lips. His snakes, while fewer in number, closely resembled real ones in size. I didn't recognize the species, although I would have bet everything I owned they were venomous—more so than usual.

Yippee. I went from unlucky virgin unable to find a willing man to having too many, and my latest suitor could pump me so full of venom I wouldn't know which end was up after a few minutes. "No, I will not service you or your ladies. If you're looking for a surrogate, call the CDC."

"No fun," he hissed, flicking his forked tongue out at me. "You should. Pay well. Three mates, all mine. Good times. You have nice big hips, good breasts. Curves. You would help us produce beautiful whelps."

I did the math: a mile long trail of nasty bile, a trio of females, an aroused male, and at least fifty human statues of pedestrians too stupid to get out of the way or really unlucky.

The gorgons must have struck out at the bar, which probably meant everyone at the bar had gotten petrified and needed my help, too.

Oh boy.

"Hey, tiger. How many did you stone at the bar?"

He hissed at me again. "They weren't interested. Good offer, yes? Be the mother of my children and I won't petrify you."

Yippee. The gorgon was really trying to coerce me into having sex with all three of his brides with him as the grand finale. A regular woman would've ended up petrified once, twice, or three times depending on the skills of the mating gorgons.

With three females all wanting a surrogate, I expected the 'lucky' woman would end up petrified at least three times.

"You should be interested. You look so sturdy."

"Sturdy? Really? That's your line? I look sturdy? Give me a break. How many did you petrify?"

"Only one or two. Come on. We'll have fun, little lady."

I sighed. "Sorry, not interested."

For a drunk he moved really fast, and his spittle splashed onto my cheek. His rancid, alcohol-tainted breath washed over my face. He ditched his sunglasses and stared me in the eyes, and every last snake on his head rose up and hissed with him. A tingle spread through me.

Any other human would have begun petrifying, their muscles stiffening. A determined gorgon ready to breed would have approximately five minutes to get their business done before their victim was no longer able to serve as a surrogate without reversing the petrification first.

Hell no. Infuriated he had tried to petrify me so he could turn me into a play date for him and his brood, I kneed him in the groin and proceeded to feed him a knuckle sandwich. "Excuse me? Let's try this again, pumpkin. I said no. Do you know what the word 'no' means? It means I'm not fucking interested, asshole! Don't you know what the penalty is for deliberating attempting to petrify a civilian? Oh, wait. I'm not technically a civilian. I'm certified by the CDC, you scum sucker. If you thought petrifying a civilian could land you in trouble, wait until you see what happens when you assault a CDC rep."

On his way down, the bastard's snakes pierced their fangs through my shirt and jeans. That would hurt later. It'd hurt a lot. If I were really unlucky, I might even pass out on the sidewalk from the venom.

"I'll kill you, little girl."

Oh hell no. "Now you're threatening to kill me?" If he wanted to start with that shit, I had a bag of neutralizer with his name on it. I ripped it open and dumped the entire thing on his head. "How about this? I don't think so."

The male gorgon shrieked and writhed on the ground at my feet. The neutralizer wouldn't kill him—it wouldn't even hurt him for long, much to my disappointment. He'd feel it in the morning, though, and that would have to do. "Listen up, dipshit. If you don't want to spend your entire breeding season behind bars in solitary confinement, you're going to haul your ass to that sidewalk, you're going to tell your girlfriends to stop playing with their own puke, and you're going to clean this mess up. No games, no more funny business, and if you even *think* about trying to breed with me, I'm going to start braiding your snakes together with tiny pink bows as a reminder you need to ask really nicely for a willing woman to help you out. Keyword: willing."

He bit through my jeans and sank his fangs into my calf.

"You did not just bite me."

Snake fangs really hurt, and the male decided to start gnawing on me. If he wanted a fight, I'd give him a fight. I grabbed a handful of his serpents, yanked his head up, and stepped on his face with my free foot. "Eat this, bitch!"

IT TOOK a werewolf and two cops, all dressed in hazmat suits, to pull me off the gorgon. In any other situation, a CDC representative yanking a burlap sack over a sentient's head would have counted as excessive force. I snarled curses at the idiot male. "You tried to use me as breeding stock, you son of a bitch!"

Officer O'Daniel pinned my arms to my side, and with a grunt, picked me up and backed away so I couldn't keep kicking the shit out of the gorgon at my feet. At least the three females cooperated, donning sunglasses and hiding their snakes under heavy shawls to prevent accidental petrification.

Calems stepped between me and the gorgon male. "All right, Gardener. Don't kill him."

Ignoring my protests and threats of violence, the werewolf carried me over to the waiting CDC truck and growled, "Spray."

Instead of a spraying neutralizer, I got a bucket of pink, thick fluid dumped over my head. The werewolf released me and hopped around like an excited puppy. "Me next. Me next!"

Damned werewolves. While they could be excellent cops, sometimes their second nature reduced them to excited two-year olds on a sugar high, and I'd never met one who didn't love a spray down with neutralizer more than life itself.

"You may as well or he won't be happy," I muttered. Dripping neutralizer, I raided the truck for a proper sprayer, steel brushes, a mop, and a bucket so I could start cleaning the damned sidewalk. "If that gorgon even thinks about touching me again, I'm shoving this nozzle right up his ass and pulling the trigger. Do I look like a baby factory to you?"

No one answered, a wise decision all things considered. Still fuming, I headed to the contaminated sidewalk and unleashed a torrent of pink foam, got on my heads and knees, and blew off steam scraping drying bile off the concrete. Everyone else watched from a safe distance, and I wasn't sure if they were avoiding me or worried about accidental petrification.

At least they made themselves useful and brought fresh buckets of water to make my job a little easier. It took me five hours to reach the bar, and when I peeked inside, I groaned at the collection of naked statues arranged in compromising positions. A bat-winged male was tangled with three human women.

How lovely. The gorgons had teamed up with an incubus. Who the hell knew what would happen in nine months? The CDC would have its hands full, that was sure, and the reporters would have a field day with the headlines.

By the time the evening news aired, ‘Come here often?’ would be the new inside joke at the bar. I really needed to burn my certification. Damn it. The CDC had already done that for me, and yet I was still doing their dirty work. What the hell did a girl have to do to lead a normal life?

I sighed, turned around, and banged my head into the door.

Unfortunately, the damned werewolf stopped me before I could pummel myself into blissful unconsciousness.

THE TRICK to dealing with a petrified orgy usually involved one sacrificial lamb in a hazmat suit, several sprayers, and backup—non-human backup lacking a reproductive system.

Unfortunately, the sacrificial lamb—me, in this case—didn’t get a hazmat suit. At least I had left my wallet with Calems, where it would be safe and sound.

I ordered everyone to stay at least twenty feet away from the bar’s entrance; even petrified, the incubus was doing *something* to the place. Fortunately for me, my pride, and my dignity, I’d been living in a state of sexual frustration my entire adult life. I could handle some discomfort. The incubus had nothing on what Quinn did to me, and I could handle close quarters with him without humping his leg.

I could escape the bar without losing my grip. I couldn't say the same for anyone outside or the patrons in the bar when the neutralizer reversed the incubus's petrification, but *I* would be fine. How bad could it be? Every CDC representative tangoed with an incubus at least once in their careers. I'd escaped three incidents without losing my virginity.

What was once more?

I prayed Quinn would forgive me if I rubbed myself all over him or humped his leg the instant I saw him. It'd be a battle. How could I lose? I doubted I could. Quinn just had to look at me to light my panties on fire. Add in the influence of an incubus, and I'd be the happiest woman on Earth.

If I blamed the incubus, would anyone really care? Quinn might, which popped my bubble of wishful thinking. I sighed. No matter what, I wouldn't jump Quinn until I got him somewhere at least semi-private. He wouldn't mind if I jumped him somewhere discreet.

Muttering a curse, I went all in and requested an angel. Angels could turn a petrified orgy into something a little easier to manage. So much divinity in one place would suppress the sexual urges of an incubus long enough to get the victims separated, herd them out of the bar, and get them clothed.

I had no idea what I'd do about the incubus, but I'd figure that out *after* I hosed everyone down and reversed the petrification.

In a miracle of the highest order, the CDC sent two angels. In typical angel fashion, they manifested outside the bar in a column of golden light within five minutes of my call. On the surface, they looked human—almost. They had two legs, two arms, and a chest connecting all the pieces together. Feathered wings of white with bands of gold and sky blue sprouted from their shoulders. Neither one of them wore a single stitch of clothes, but they didn't need them.

With nothing to cover, what was the point of clothing?

One day, maybe if the seas parted and the skies burned, I might get used to an angel's lack of a head.

"Hi. I'm Bailey. I'm certified with the CDC. Have you been briefed?"

"They said you have an incubus problem." I couldn't tell which one spoke. How could they speak without a mouth? If they didn't eat, how did they not fall over dead?

I suspected immortals enjoyed toying with humanity just because they could. Angels could pull a far better teleportation trick than I could. I was willing to bet they could manifest a head with eyes, nose, mouth, and even hair if they felt like it. Instead of voicing my opinion, I replied, "You could say that. A quartet of gorgons hunting for a human surrogate joined forces with an incubus, so I have a bar full of petrified people, more gorgon bile to clean up than I care to think about, and an incubus in the middle of a foursome. When the reversal of petrification begins, it's going to get rather rowdy. I'd like to start spraying the area down and save the incubus and his girlfriends for last. Unless you're immune to petrification, if you could stay by the door until hell breaks loose, I'd appreciate it."

"Wise. We can help you once hell breaks loose, so do not worry. We will leave the details to you."

I got the feeling the angels wouldn't notice a gorgon even if it tried to gnaw on their ankles. "Thanks. I appreciate the help."

Look at me, capable of mastering the art of being polite to people in the face of gorgon bile. Since pissing off an angel or two would end my existence on Earth, and probably elsewhere, too, I grabbed the nearest sprayer, yanked out the pin, and went to work. I went the deluge route, soaking the whole bar down, ceiling included, and hoped I neutralized the bile and other gorgon fluids in the place long enough to get the naked revelers outside for a proper decontamination.

I didn't envy the people stuck with the paperwork—or the paternity tests that were required.

Did Quinn even like kids? Would he mind an entire herd of miniature people? I was game for entire herds of miniature people.

Stupid incubus. Stupid ovaries. Stupid ovaries in the presence of a tripped-out incubus.

The closer I got to the incubus, the stronger his influence grew, until I was dripping with sweat. I really wished Quinn would walk through the door so I could solve every last one of my life's problems with sex—a lot of hot, kinky sex. I stormed to the door, dumped the first empty extinguisher onto the sidewalk, grabbed the next one, and somehow kept my tongue under strict control so I wouldn't start cursing in front of a pair of angels.

The bastards were probably having a field day watching me dodge the patrons slowly reversing from petrification. Their poses as statues had been bad enough, but as they returned to living flesh, they resumed their orgy right where they had left off, and they weren't quiet about it, either.

Jesus Christ in a bucket, couldn't they at least keep it down? With my face burning bright red, I ditched the second empty canister, grabbed the third one, and unleashed the pink foam on the incubus and his trio of eager ladies.

Being within ten feet of a petrified incubus made me want to abandon ship, hunt Quinn down, and drag him into an alley. The instant stone began reverting to flesh, desire seared through me, so intense I panted as my body warmed and ached.

I shook, and my first step back began with a whimper and ended with a breathy gasp. The little bit of distance helped, and I made it a second step.

There would be no pouncing and jumping the incubus. I would head right for the door without a single side trip. I wouldn't jump the angels, either. I'd save the sexual assault for the only sober, uninfluenced man capable of putting up with me for any length of time.

I really hoped Quinn would forgive me when I got my hands on him.

"Should be clear," I whispered.

I didn't moan. I refused to acknowledge the sound that came from my throat had any resemblance to a moan. As far as I was concerned, the first one hadn't slip out, and neither had the second.

If I ever ended up in an incubus-infested bar again, I'd remember to ask for earplugs, some sedatives, and maybe some sort of suppressant for my ovaries. Did they sell such a thing? If it didn't exist, someone needed to invent it, fast.

Most importantly, if I ever ended up in an incubus-infested bar again, I'd remember I wasn't immune to angel song. Two angels singing in chorus had me on my knees by the end of the first note. By the start of the second, I couldn't even remember my own name. My body went cold and numb, and on the third note, the heavens descended and bashed me over the head.

An angel brought me back to Earth with a slap across the face so hard I yelped. I blinked at the headless, winged figure, who clutched a handful of my shirt in an iron-strong grip. A six inch layer of pink goop coated the entire bar. Yippee. Someone must have brought in a tanker of neutralizer while leaving me with a duet of angels. One of them must have kept me from drowning in the thick gunk.

"Other humans are flighty birds, squawking their dismay you are in here and not out there. They complain. It is not our fault our song so moves you. Please convince your fellow humans you have not been struck down."

My throbbing head disagreed with them; if they hadn't struck me down, they'd done something. Smited? Smote? Ah, hell. At least I hadn't drowned during the hosing. I hung limp in the angel's hand, turning my head enough to get a look at the pink disaster around me. The bar wouldn't be the same, and it wouldn't surprise me if the place shimmered for years to come. "Incubus?"

"Calmed. Asleep. The humans took him away. We use their meter as they instructed, it kept quiet, but still they fear."

I giggled, forced my hand to move, and gestured to where the angel's head should have been. "It's the whole no-head thing. Don't worry about it. You're so awe-inspiring they can't handle your awesome incubus-smiting ways." Oh, yippee. I sounded drunk. Great. "Maybe a halo. A halo might help."

On the grand scale of things, I'd never been so wrong in my life. I was so wrong the angels had to slap the sin out of me to knock the sense back into my skull. "Pretty stars," I slurred.

At least I came away with an understanding of why mortals couldn't go to heaven until after death. I'm pretty sure I caught a glimpse of it, and I hid from the memory like a turtle withdrawing into its shell at the first sign of trouble. I couldn't tell if it was good or bad, but *something* about it made my skin crawl.

"I was wrong," I informed the angels. "No halos."

Both of them laughed, the sound tinkling in my head, as delicate as crystal chimes in the wind. "You only died a little. This is good."

Angels had a morbid sense of humor. Who knew? "How long was I out?"

"Dying only a little takes a little time. The sun set a little while ago. We told the upset, complaining humans outside you needed a little time to stop dying a little."

I groaned. Why did I have the sinking feeling time meant absolutely nothing to an immortal? Right. If the sun was down, at least three or four hours had gone by. "And the bar patrons?"

"They are calm. Happy, even. Incubus magic does that to humans. We have conferred with the humans overseeing things, and we offered to glimpse a little into their futures. Incubus magic brings many young, but human young. Incubus magic did not help the gorgons procreate. The rest falls under the dominion of humans and is not for us to decide."

"Oh boy." I shook my head to clear it and forced myself to sit up.

"You should take a little time. Get up in little time, so you do not die a little again. That would be inconvenient."

"Dying usually is. And no offense, but I'm done with this whole dying thing already."

The angels laughed, and one of them touched their long, slender finger to my nose. "Amusing human. Such entertainment over such a little time."

Next time I asked for an angel, I hoped someone reminded me angels made bad things happen to me. I staggered to my feet with the help of a fallen chair and slogged to the door, swallowing my curses so the angels wouldn't actually smite me.

Two police cruisers and a shiny red convertible waited in front of the bar. "Oh boy."

Quinn leaned against his car talking to four officers, and when he caught sight of me, he crossed his arms over his chest. "Enjoy your nap? Are you aware you'rc dripping pink slime all over the place? You look like the victim of a glitter factory explosion."

Behind me, the angels laughed. If they never stopped making the sound, I'd be happy. I could listen to them all day long and never tire of it. "The strong little human only died a little, see?"

They stepped around me and vanished in a flash of golden light, and when darkness fell, the goop crumbled to a shimmery powder and piled around my feet. My clothes remained wet, but at least I no longer left puddles on the sidewalk.

"Oh, it's Chief Quinn. Hi, Chief Quinn. I got my ass smited by a pair of angels, and I asked for it."

Quinn didn't look impressed. "I think you mean smote. Next time, when you request angels, leave the scene before they start singing."

"Didn't you hear them, Chief Quinn? I only died a little." Maybe pulling the tiger's tail wasn't so great of an idea, especially since he did a full body twitch when I said the word died. "I found out it's gorgon mating season."

"So I've been told."

Uh oh. Quinn kept his tone calm and collected, his expression neutral, and save for his crossed arms and the occasional twitch, his body remained relaxed. His utter control did unfair things to me, including reminding me how nice he looked without a single stitch of clothes on. Crap.

Inappropriate or not, I undressed the man with my eyes, looking him over from his face all the way down to his polished shoes.

Yep. Had he strolled into the incubus-infested bar, I would've jumped him and started ripping his clothes off. What I would have done to—with—him wasn't legal in any state.

Damn, damn, damn. I loved everything about the man, even—especially—when he was pissed at me for doing something stupid.

I was in way too deep.

I straightened, stared him in the eyes, and stated, "I am not sorry I beat the shit out of the gorgon. I'm okay with it if you need to arrest me." Since I was cooperating, I even held my hands out. "I'll even let you handcuff me without putting up a fight."

One of the cops choked, probably so he wouldn't laugh. Me and my big, stupid mouth. Why couldn't I say something serious without mangling it or turning it into something far worse than I actually meant?

Quinn cleared his throat, and the cop quieted. "The attempted assault was caught on both body cams with full audio. You're not going to be arrested, and you won't even need to show up in court."

"He tried to petrify me!"

"So I saw."

I lifted my chin. "O'Daniel wouldn't let me kill him. I think that's unfair. That gorgon was working with an incubus."

"I'm aware, seeing as that's the reason you requested an angel in the first place."

"I got smited, Chief Quinn. Smote. Whatever. Angels sang, the lights went out." I was whining, but hadn't I earned at least a little whining?

"Then you got the dumbass idea to request a halo. That was not one of your brighter moments."

Yippee. If I got really lucky, Quinn would dress me down in front of his four cops for at least an hour. "I didn't do it on purpose. I'm sorry. How long have I been bathing in neutralizer?"

If I'd been in it for more than an hour, I'd be going right back to the hospital for vaccinations. Again.

Quinn put on an infuriatingly sexy show of checking his watch, humming while he considered the time. "Seventeen minutes. I should have let you stew in there for sixty-one minutes, Gardener. I was so, so tempted to let you stew in there for sixty-one minutes. Do you know what would have happened if I had?"

I lowered my head and accepted my scolding with the little dignity I had left, reminding myself he did it to all his cops who did something stupid. "I would have needed vaccinations, Chief Quinn."

Giving the correct answer earned me a round of applause. "The tanker left about five minutes before you staggered out of the bar like a drunk. The angels suggested we leave you in the neutralizer for fifteen minutes just to be safe since you had finished dying a little."

"Right." Quinn wasn't going to let go of the whole dying a little thing, was he? Then again, I couldn't blame him for it. If he'd been the one who had died a little, I wouldn't have been so calm or collected. "I'm soaking wet and have no other clothes, Chief Quinn."

Sighing, Quinn shook his head. "Get in the damned car, Gardener."

THIRTEEN

Angels are assholes.

ANGELS WERE SNEAKY BASTARDS. The instant I slid into Quinn's convertible, my whole body started tingling and the smoldering heat of the incubus's influence rushed through me. The chiming laughter of angels rang in my ears.

First they smited me, then they dumped me in Quinn's car, revved *my* engine, tossed in an extra side order of lust, and laughed about it. It took all my willpower to keep from squirming on the leather seat. I bit my lip, buckled my seat belt, and waited for him to start the car and get on the road. "Hey, Quinn?"

"What?"

"Angels are assholes."

"Oh?"

The tinkling laughter intensified before dissipating like fog in the morning light. "Angels like you, don't they?"

He snorted. "What gives you that idea?"

"I think they want me to have sex with you right now." I really wanted to unbuckle my seatbelt, crawl to his side of the car, and start ripping off his clothes. Maybe I'd even let him pull over first. "I'll take anything. Something. Please."

"Hallelujah and amen. Thank you, God."

Great. The angels had a convert. "It's the incubus's fault, Quinn. And they're laughing about it. The angels lulled me into a false sense of security, put me in your car, and then flipped the sex switch."

"The angels flipped the sex switch, huh? So I guess this means you don't want to go out for a nice dinner and do some clothes shopping before I take you home? I was also thinking we might sit down and have a long talk about us. We probably should have talked sooner, but I can't help it I'm just a man. When a beautiful woman tells me she's a virgin and wants me to spank her, I obey."

"That should classify as cruel and unusual punishment. I hate you so much right now."

Worse, I loved hating him. Damn it, the man confused me and made me like it.

"That's only because you want me to throw you onto my bed and have my way with you. I'm not against making love with you all night long. I'm sure I'll enjoy it."

"Yes, please." I bit my lip. "Sneaky angels."

Quinn laughed. "Angels have a very odd culture. They're probably thanking you for having done a good deed. They're also telepaths and can read minds. Since incubi are really, really good at stirring human desires, the angels likely knew everything you were thinking in there and who you were thinking about. Did I mention they're telepaths and mind readers? So, without a doubt, they knew what *I* was thinking, too. It involved me being very, very cranky you were anywhere near an incubus. Angels are jerks and enjoy screwing around with me. The good news is you'll survive until I get you home."

"What's the bad news? That tells me there's bad news. Hasn't there been enough bad news?"

"I have to get rid of my ex-wife before I can toss you onto my bed and have my way with you. Audrey's probably camped out on my front step and won't go away until I talk to her. She's a pain in the ass like that."

I scowled. Quinn's ex-wife was at his house? Unacceptable. "I guess I'd get arrested if I got rid of her, wouldn't I?"

"I have a trick up my sleeve that should get rid of her, so don't worry. It shouldn't delay us for long."

Alarm bells went off in my head, which distracted me from my desire to have *my* way with Quinn as soon as possible. While still tempted to beg him to pull into the nearest dark alley, I swallowed and asked, "What are you going to do?"

"When she asks what you're doing at my house, I'm going to tell her the truth. I'm going to tell her you're living with me. I'm going to do this while I admire you in those jeans you're wearing. If she doesn't get the hint, I'm going to start running my hands all over you before I toss you over my shoulder and carry you into my house. Then I'm going to slam the door, lock it, and we're going to make so much noise that she gets uncomfortable and leaves."

How had I gone from hopeless and doomed to stay a virgin to having one of the hottest men in Manhattan wanting to throw me over his shoulder and carry me into his house to establish his territory? My poor ovaries couldn't handle much more before they combusted.

Just like that, the angels had made a second convert. Thank you, God. "Did the incubus influence you, too? Because that's hot, Quinn. That's 'pull the damned car over' hot."

"Bailey, if the incubus had influenced me, we'd still be in the bar having sex with an audience. It'd be on the morning news. Actually, they'd have to censor the whole thing because us together is so amazing no one would be able to handle watching it."

I spent a very long minute trying to imagine what would have happened in the bar. "I'm strangely disappointed right now."

"Of course you are. You want me. I'm impressed you haven't tried to seduce me while I'm driving. You have a freakish amount of self-control."

"Your house has an ex-wife infestation. It might end up condemned. We should go find a hotel. I haven't had a chance to be a girlfriend before, and I don't want to be a convict before I become a girlfriend."

"You're going to have to help me out with this one, Bailey. I have no idea what you're talking about."

"If your ex-wife comes between you, me, and a bed, I will kill her."

"I followed that part. It's the convict before girlfriend part I'm having trouble with."

I frowned. "You just explained it. What don't you understand? I don't want to be a convict before I have a chance to be a girlfriend."

"Bailey."

"What?"

"I don't do casual hookups or one-night stands. I present the evidence you were, until yesterday, a twenty-nine year old virgin as proof you don't either. You're the first woman I've been with since I divorced. You're a damned beautiful girl, and since I find friendship—even a weird one with lots of yelling and bickering—mandatory for a relationship, I think it's safe to say you're my girlfriend. Granted, I really should have talked to you about this *first,* but you had to open your mouth and beg me to spank you." His voice turned husky. "I enjoyed every moment I spent making love to you in every room of my house."

I had seen my face in the mirror enough times to know I had little scars all over my cheeks and nose. Even before a bomb had gone off in my face, I didn't think I was pretty, let alone beautiful. "Oh."

He shot me a grin. "You found my weakness and exploited it. Well done."

I needed him, and I needed him now. "There's a really seedy hotel less than two miles from your house. We could go there."

"I know. How do I know? I was home when the call came in you'd been found there in critical condition. For the record, that was when I decided I needed to take extra measures to get your attention."

I should have known. Crap. I scrunched my shoulders and slouched in my seat. "I really was going to call a cab and take myself to the hospital."

"You know what? Screw it. Let's go to a

hotel. I don't do seedy ones, though. Audrey can stalk my empty house for all I care. I've got better things to do right now. You, for the record."

Yes, yes, yes! *Score.*

"WE'RE STAYING AT THE PLAZA?"

A smug Quinn flashed me a grin, turned the car around, and headed towards Central Park. "I don't do seedy hotels, it's close to work, and they have really nice beds. They'll also have dinner ready not long after we arrive. I hope you like steak and potatoes, because I'm going to be feeding it to you piece by piece."

"You have my attention."

"All I'd have to do to have your attention right now is unbutton my shirt."

"I can help you with that."

"You can wait ten minutes."

Could I? Maybe, but I didn't want to. I settled with staring at him, and he chuckled, a low, throaty sound I wanted to hear again. I sat on my hands. Undressing him before we got to the hotel wouldn't help very much, no matter how badly I wanted to. "Someone like me doesn't belong at the Plaza, you know."

Quinn snorted. "Are you referring to your matted, pink, and glittery hair, your pink-stained shirt, or the fact your jeans should be classified as a felony?"

"What's wrong with my jeans?"

"Nothing. That's the problem. I'm going to have to peel you out of them. It'll be like unwrapping a present, but a stubborn one prone to wiggling."

"You're doing this on purpose, aren't you?"

"Me? Tease the incubus-influenced woman I intend to keep thoroughly occupied in our hotel room starting in about ten minutes? Never."

"You could just pull into an alley, damn it!"

"Is this whole alley fetish a sign of your desperation, or are you actually interested in making out in an alley?"

Damn it. I scowled, pulled my hands out from under me, crossed my arms over my chest, and stared out the window. "You drive too slow."

"Taking my woman to a hotel so we can stay up all night isn't a legitimate excuse to run my sirens. You'll survive for ten minutes. I suppose I should scold those angels for not waiting until we were somewhere a bit more private before dropping their magic. That was a little underhanded of them. Are you being rewarded or punished? Maybe you were right, and I'm the one being rewarded while you're being punished. I can live with that."

I needed to think long and hard about what I liked so much about Samuel Quinn. Everything, which was my default answer, had to be incorrect. "You're an asshole."

"But I'm an asshole who is really good in bed and willing to prove it to you all night long."

Once again, he won, and the smug bastard knew it, too. I surrendered with a whimper, slouched in the seat, and decided my goal in life was to keep from squirming, whimpering, or moaning until we reached the hotel room.

It took Quinn six minutes to reach the Plaza, and the instant I got out of his car, he tossed me over his shoulder, secured a hold on my legs, and carried me inside. The valet did his best but ultimately laughed his head off. Quinn strutted into the lobby, whistling a happy little tune.

I snatched handfuls of Quinn's shirt so I wouldn't succumb to the temptation to grab something enticing but rather inappropriate. I added groping to my list of things I wouldn't do until we reached our room.

"Chief Quinn. Your room is ready. Your other requests should be prepared within the next twenty minutes."

I peeked around Quinn's side. The man behind the large desk smiled; good hotels always had smiling employees, even when one of the guests was spreading pink, glittery dust all over the marble floor.

"Excellent. Thank you. Hey, Bailey? Grab my wallet, would you?"

It wasn't inappropriate if he asked me to do it, right? I didn't need to be asked twice. I slid my hand into his back pocket to retrieve his wallet. Maybe I shouldn't have squeezed him in the process, but if he wanted a miracle, he needed to ask an angel. I slipped his wallet into his hand. "Here."

At the front doors, the busboy and the second valet were laughing so hard I was worried there'd be bodies. With my luck, they were taking pictures, so I smiled and waved. Maybe the real miracle was my restraint.

I didn't leave a pink handprint on Quinn's ass.

Quinn carried me to the elevator and waited until we were in our room to put me down. The first thing to go would be his shirt. I almost had him out of it when his phone rang.

"Break it," I suggested, contemplating tearing off the stubborn button thwarting me. "Violently."

Instead of obeying, he answered, "Chief Quinn speaking." There was a short pause, then he chuckled. "No. I decided I wasn't up for her shit tonight, so I ran away. I meant to call in I wasn't going home." After another pause, Quinn laughed again. "Huh. I suppose you could classify it as a kidnapping. Hey, Gardener. It's apparently kidnapping if I take people wherever I want. You okay with being kidnapped?"

How was I supposed to get him naked without the caller learning I intended to drag the police chief to bed and keep him there? "I beat the shit out of a male gorgon today. You don't stand a chance, Mr. Police Chief. Tell them I kidnapped you. That should confuse them. Hey. Where are your handcuffs? I better make it look real. I guess if I stuffed you under the bed, housecleaning would eventually find you, huh? Pity."

I started patting him down, taking everything out of his pockets in search of his handcuffs. With handcuffs, I had limitless options on what I could do with Quinn.

Why *were* his handcuffs stuffed down his pants, anyway?

Quinn smirked. "Did you hear that? Good. Since Audrey's brother did try to kill her, call in someone to check over my house, and ask the CDC if they'd send an investigator as a personal favor to me—I'll pay their fee out of pocket. If the rep can be an incubus who hasn't gotten laid for a very, very long time, even better. I wouldn't mind if she was kept busy for a few months. What? I can't request an incubus? That's not fair. How about a succubus?"

I could hear someone laughing on the other end of the line, and I worried he would choke to death if he didn't stop soon.

"You really don't have to laugh that hard."

If I broke the phone, would he forgive me? "Quinn, stop playing with the phone."

He ignored me. "I'm hiding at the Plaza. The angels finally let Bailey out of the bar. When she found out Audrey was at my place, she started screaming something about that woman getting between her, a bath, and some sleep, there would be bodies. I was concerned my body might be one of them. Since she was primed to kill my ex-wife, I thought a hotel might be a wise decision. She—"

I'd have to dig the handcuffs out of his pants later. Yanking the phone out of Quinn's hand, I said, "Hello? Hi. Please don't listen to him. He's so tired he has no idea what he's talking about. He's going to bed."

With me. All night long.

With the phone against my ear, I recognized Perky's strangled laughter. "Oh. It's Perky. Hey, Perky."

"Hey yourself, Gardener. Last news on the wire was you went and got yourself killed by a pair of angels."

"Only a little bit. Chief Quinn really needs to get some sleep."

With me. Now. All night long.

"You don't seem very dead to me. Not even a little bit. The chief was pretty cranky you'd gone and gotten yourself killed."

"It was only a little bit!"

"Do we need to rescue you? Because honestly, the thought of you two sharing the same house has us worried. The same hotel room..."

"If I kill Chief Quinn, I promise you'll be the first person I call."

Quinn grinned at me. When someone knocked at the door, he headed across the room, buttoning his shirt back up and making himself as presentable as he could with pink handprints all over him.

Maybe it would have been a little awkward if I'd already gotten him to bed. Had calling in advance for room service really been necessary? I scowled.

Perky chuckled. "That's considerate of you."

"Not to be rude, Perky, but a gorgon wanted to use me as breeding stock, and he didn't want to take no for an answer. Reverse cowgirl bitch is at Chief Quinn's house and came between me, a bath, and some sleep."

With Quinn. While that part was extremely important, Perky didn't need to know my plans for the rest of the night. "If anyone else delays me, I will make what I did to the gorgon look polite in comparison."

I learned a very important lesson: men could laugh so hard they cried. "I'm so sorry that happened, Gardener. You were magnificent. The ladies at the station adore you. The asshole deserved the pummeling. That said, you need to take self-defense courses. Amanda teaches one on Monday and Thursday nights. I may have enrolled you. Get some sleep and have a good night." Perky hung up. I stared at Quinn's phone for a long moment before setting it aside.

Quinn set two covered dishes on the room's table. "Now that dinner has arrived, I think you should pick up where you left off. I seem to have undone your hard work. Unless you want to eat dinner first?"

"Screw dinner." I pounced. If he wanted a shirt with all of its buttons intact, he shouldn't have put it back on.

"Excellent."

AT SOME POINT, Quinn got out of bed long enough to call housekeeping and hand over our abused and battered clothes so they could be saved or replaced. His request amused the hotel employee, who promised to take care of everything.

I wanted him to come back to bed and feed me more morsels of steak and potatoes. "Come back to bed, Quinn."

"Are you sure you're not part succubus?"

"No, but I'm thinking you're possibly an incubus in disguise. Come back to bed. Please?"

He laughed. "It's seven in the morning, Bailey. Aren't you tired yet?"

"No." I patted the pillow beside me. "You still have to feed me the rest of my dinner."

"It's seven in the morning."

"Breakfast, then. Feed me. I'm hungry."

"And whose fault is that?"

"Yours, obviously."

Quinn slid under the covers, pulled me close, and held me. "And you thought I was crazy for reserving two nights. It's ten minutes to work if traffic cooperates. That means we have extra time together. It was careful planning. I think I'll have a cruiser pick us up when it's time to go in. That'll save at least five minutes."

"What time do you need to be at work?"

"If we go to sleep now, we'll get a few hours."

I wrinkled my nose, wiggled free, and sat up so I could finish my dinner. "So I guess we really should get some sleep, then."

"Probably wise. Feeling better now?"

"Yes. I'm not sure if I should hunt down

those angels and that incubus and hit them or thank them."

"I'm feeling pretty thankful right now."

Quinn's phone rang, and I grabbed it first. If they wanted him, they needed to go through me. The police chief frowned at me, and I flipped him my middle finger before I answered, "Chief Quinn is asleep right now. Do I need to wake him?"

Some lies were so worth telling. Quinn shook his head and rolled his eyes.

"Yes, please," a woman replied. Maybe the mysterious self-defense teaching Amanda?

"One moment, please, Officer…?"

"Hitchenson. Amanda Hitchenson. Good work with that gorgon yesterday, Miss Gardener."

"Thank you. Perky told me he was enrolling me in your class?" I gave Quinn a kick, and the police chief grunted. "Quinn, your phone was ringing. I answered it for you. There's a nice lady named Officer Hitchenson wanting to speak with you."

He groaned and reached for his phone. "Thanks, Gardener. I'm awake, Amanda. What's wrong?"

After several moments, Quinn's eyes widened. "She's a *what*? No, no. I heard you the first time. Okay. Did you find out why? When? I don't really care how."

The silence stretched on, and Quinn

rubbed his temple with his free hand while listening to Amanda. When he finally hung up after a few incredulous words and a strained goodbye, he threw his phone across the room. It bounced off the bathroom door and splashed into the toilet.

"Wow. Nice aim. You're going to need a new phone there, Chief." Hoping to rescue the device, I scrambled out of bed and peered into the toilet bowl. The phone's display was dark and cracked. "You killed it."

"My deranged ex-wife decided to snort gorgon dust, became one, and is, and I quote, 'She's looking to breed and picked Gardener to be the mother.' She petrified three police officers and was recorded making a promise you would like making babies with her. It doesn't appear the officers contracted the gorgon virus, fortunately."

I returned to the bedroom and gaped at Quinn. "Excuse me. What?"

"My ex-wife wants to have babies with my girlfriend."

All right. I could handle the discussion like a mature adult. I would not laugh. I would not, under any circumstance, laugh. I wouldn't giggle, either. "That is not something I hear every day. I think I need a new life. Have you thought about running away? Once I cash the check in my wallet, I think I can get us anywhere. Ever been to Hawaii?"

I would not laugh, I would not laugh, I would not laugh. I really wanted to laugh.

Quinn's sigh broke me, and choking on a giggle, I ran into the bathroom and fished his phone out of the toilet. I set it on the vanity and washed my hands so the running water would cover my mirth.

"Hawaii is too easy to reach. Someone might find us. It's not *that* funny, but you're welcome to come laugh in my face if you want. I'm not the one she wants to sleep with. She wants to have babies with *you*."

I collapsed against the sink and giggled until I cried. "I'm so sorry. Panama?"

"Also easy to reach."

"Timbuktu?"

"That's a bit more remote. I'll think about it."

It took me several minutes to regain any semblance of control. "Quinn, your ex-wife wants to have babies with me, your girlfriend. Me, your girlfriend."

"You make it sound really bad when you say it that way, Bailey."

I straightened, wrapped Quinn's broken phone in a towel, and brought it from the bathroom, presenting it to him. "I think it needs a funeral."

"You even gave it a funerary shroud." Quinn unwrapped his phone, sighed, and set it and the towel on the nightstand. "That's the second one this month."

"What happened to the other one?"

"It had an accident."

"A Quinn-created accident?"

"That phone's death was entirely your fault. If you hadn't almost died in a shitty hotel, I wouldn't have thrown my phone."

"You need to stop throwing your phones, Quinn. That's a bad habit." I sat on the edge of the bed at his feet and gave his leg a slap. "There's only one question left."

"I'm not sure I want to know what this question is."

"Who would be the father?"

"I was right. I didn't want to know what the question was. In fact, I don't want my now-a-gorgon ex-wife anywhere near you, my girlfriend. I definitely don't want *two* gorgons near you, my girlfriend."

There was only one way it could possibly get any worse, which meant I needed to tell him. "Unless she wants you to be the male gorgon."

"Bailey Gardener, that is the most fucked up thing I have ever heard you say. Worse, she was crazy *before* she became a gorgon, so you might be right."

Since I'd already taken one dive into horrible, disgusting yet hilarious waters, what was one more? "Since I'm immune to gorgons, if you become a gorgon, would you still need a female gorgon, or could we make all your little gorgon babies without help?"

I was a terrible person for laughing, thus earning being kicked off the bed. I hit the carpet and rolled, clutching my sides.

"You just had to go there, didn't you? You really had to go there."

"I-it's important," I choked out.

So much for not laughing.

"Becoming Audrey's gorgon plaything is not on my list of things to do before I die. However, if you're offering to become the mother of my little babies, I'm definitely interested in hearing your offer. How much practice do you think we need? Do I have to marry you before we practice some more? It's important."

I laughed so hard I cried. "I'm not sure I could handle you as a gorgon. Gorgons have breeding seasons and become sex fiends. I'm not sure it would be possible to contain you if you have an enhanced sex drive. This is a very serious issue, Samuel Quinn."

"I'm so glad you find this situation so funny."

I howled my laughter. "I can't help it your ex-wife wants to have babies with your girlfriend. And I thought *I* had the worst luck."

"You're never going to let this go, are you?"

"Depends. Will I have to compete with a gorgon harem to keep you? If so, damned straight I'm never going to let this go."

"Are you going to kill me if I tell you that I find your jealousy very attractive?"

"Oh, good. Then you'll be turned on when I get around to scolding you for running off with my ex-boss." I giggled, got to my knees, and peered over the edge of the tall bed. "That really did piss me off. She left me on the worst day shift ever."

"Ironically, I was asking her for relationship advice."

My brain slammed on the brakes. My train of thought plummeted right off a cliff. "You *what*?" Was Quinn trying to kill me with laughter? "What sort of idiot asks a faery high on pixie dust for relationship advice?"

"I never said she was high on pixie dust."

"Quinn, she's a faery. She owns a pixie dust shop. She's always high on pixie dust. That's a given."

"Fine. Yes, I did."

Could I actually laugh to death? If I could, I would find out soon enough at the rate I was going. "How did that work out for you?"

"I should be mad you're laughing so hard over this."

"You asked a faery high on pixie dust for relationship advice. Expecting me not to laugh is unreasonable."

Quinn sighed. “The worst part about this? You’re right. To answer your question, I got a twenty-minute lecture on the qualities of the best coffees in the city. Then she told me I’d have better luck if I slept with a cactus instead.”

Poor, poor Quinn. I winced. “Ouch.”

“She then suggested I should sit on the cactus so I might fully enjoy the experience, as that was the perfect reflection of her opinion regarding my relationship choices.”

While Mary could be an epic-level bitch, the type to abandon an employee on a busy day, I never would have dreamed she would come up with something quite so rude and say it to Quinn’s face. “Wow. That was harsh.”

“She also laughed for five whole minutes. I know because I timed it.”

I needed to know, even if Quinn got mad at me for asking. “What relationship advice did you ask her for?”

“I asked, and I quote, ‘Do you think it’s possible to convince Bailey to go on a date with me?’”

That explained a lot. Oh, boy, did it explain a lot. “I think you might have had an easier time with the cactus, Quinn. I’ve never been on a date in my life.”

Quinn laughed. “You kept running away every time I tried to talk to you. That’s not my fault. Do you have any idea how much I spent on coffees just for a chance to see you? I needed the light hit of dust to get over my daily dose of rejection."

"That is so sad. Pathetic, even."

The Plaza had nice, fluffy pillows, and Quinn introduced my face to one. "It gets better. I almost asked her what it would take to get you to sleep with me instead. If I had, I'm not sure she would have survived. I would have killed her. She would have died from laughing at me."

"That's really desperate. And coming from me, that's pretty pathetic." I took the pillow before he could smack me with it again. "Really pathetic."

"Look at it from my shoes! If I had known I'd end up falling in love with the woman I hired to prove my wife was cheating on me, I would have just complained about Audrey's infidelity to an incubus and waited for the sex tapes to show up. I had no idea you'd actually catch her in the act in Central Park. And you were right. Her technique was atrocious."

"Wow." I needed a lot of time to process his words. I got stuck on 'falling in love' and the rest slipped in one ear and right out the other. It took me several tries to comprehend everything else he had said. "That should be on a warning label for women across the world: cheat at own risk. Scorned men may jumpstart your career in adult entertainment. Bonus: you'll debut with an incubus."

"I don't share. Maybe I should have warned you about that *before* sleeping with you. I don't handle a few other things well, but I really can't tolerate cheating."

"Does watching me kick a gorgon's ass count as something you don't handle well?"

"Are you kidding? God, no. That was the hottest thing I've seen a woman do in a long time, and that's saying a lot. As soon as I realized you were handling the problem on your own, that is. I think that shaved ten years off my life. No. We're good there. If anyone tries to touch you, I'll pay bail if necessary, just kick their ass so hard they never forget it."

"He tried to use me as breeding stock, Quinn. Me!"

"I'm pretty sure everyone within a mile heard you. You were fantastic. I thought you were going to cut his balls off and feed them to him for a while there."

"Didn't have a knife."

"That's a pity. He deserved it. He's lucky I hadn't been there, because I'd be in jail right now. They would have been picking up body parts blocks away if I had gotten my hands on him."

"You being in jail would make certain things very difficult. I think I can afford your bail now at least. I'd pay your bail bill."

"And you call me insatiable."

"It's your fault. You're Manhattan's Most Wanted Bachelor."

"One day people will realize a divorced man can't be a bachelor."

"You know what, Quinn? I'm done talking for right now. Shut up and kiss me."

FOURTEEN

We have one question.

SLEEP WAS a luxury Quinn could apparently live without. I couldn't. While I thought I'd be safe sleeping the day away in the Plaza, he disagreed.

Long before I had even dreamed of sleeping with Quinn, we had fought. How had we gone from hating each other to… us? After I got some sleep, I'd be able to make sense of it. Our first real fight as a couple ended with my frustrated tears. Why couldn't I go back to bed? Instead, as the loser of the discussion, I got dressed in new clothes the hotel magically made appear since mine were ruined with pink neutralizer stains. Quinn ignored my sniffled complaints and herded me to the lobby, where he proceeded to manhandle me into the back of a waiting cruiser.

To ensure I couldn't escape, he slid in beside me. "Anything critical on the wire?"

Quinn blocked my route of escape by

closing the door. Damn it.

"The CDC called Washington for support regarding our gorgon problem. They also called trying to get hold of you, Gardener. They're expecting a call back."

Oh. I knew the cop from her voice. Amanda seemed like the type of woman Quinn would actually pursue, down-to-Earth, wearing a uniform, and pretty enough to model if she wanted. I was a crow to her swan, but she grinned at me as though it never occurred to her we were in two totally different leagues.

"Yippee."

Quinn jabbed me with his elbow. "Anything else?"

"The CDC did a full sweep of your house. It's clean."

"Good."

"We have one question, however." Amanda sounded far too amused for my comfort, which meant trouble for *someone*.

If Quinn kept frowning so much, I would worry for the safety of everyone in the cruiser, especially after the death of his phone. "What?"

"We never took you for the lace lingerie type, Gardener. What *were* they doing in the chief's bedroom anyway?"

Oh no. Had I actually left the black lace bra and panties in his room? "I was trying to kill him in a way that wouldn't get me convicted."

Amanda clucked her tongue. "Try dangling them from the rearview mirror of his car. That might have better results. It seems your plan didn't work."

She and her partner laughed.

"I see dead cops," I snarled, reaching for the cage dividing the front and back seats. My fingers brushed the metal grate before Quinn got his arms wrapped around me and pulled me back.

"Gardener's a little cranky today. She had a long day yesterday beating up a gorgon and may need a few more hours of sleep."

"A little cranky? Are you sure you're safe back there, sir?"

"I'm sure I'll survive until we get to the station. Relax, Gardener. You can nap in my office or in the break room. Hey, Vanderhorn. Ask the station to dig out a pack of the transformation pills—D grade should suffice. If any gorgons get any bright ideas, I think I'd enjoy watching them play with a napalm junkie."

Still laughing, Amanda's partner relayed Quinn's orders.

There was only one thing I could say. "I hate you so much, Chief Quinn."

He smiled as though I had given him the best gift in the whole wide world. "I know."

UNTIL MY FIRST sip of police station coffee, I hadn't considered myself a coffee snob. "What is this sludge? Am I drinking sewage? Who made this? What decade was this made in?"

Perky leaned against the doorway into the break room and pointed at Quinn. "He did. It's the station rule. Whoever walks into the break room when there's only one cup left has to make the new pot. You were stealing my stale chips while he was making the coffee."

How had stale chips become a part of my diet, anyway? I leveled my best glare at Quinn. "The angels couldn't kill me, so you're trying to finish me off, aren't you?"

"Think you can do better?"

Every single cop turned and stared at the police chief. I arched a brow. "Raise your hand if you think the barista with more than ten years of experience making you dipshits coffee can do better than Chief Quinn."

Perky raised his hand. "This dipshit thinks Gardener made the best coffee in Manhattan. I cried when you stopped making coffee I could buy."

"Who are you and what have you done with Perky?"

"It's the truth. Even Chief Quinn liked

your coffee so much he had to have it at least three times a week or he complained."

"Perkins!"

"I'm only telling the truth, sir. The woman's a coffee goddess."

"Don't you have work to do, Perkins?"

Perky made a show of checking his watch. "Oh, look at that. I have some reports to file. Please be the first person to walk into the break room when there's only one cup left, Gardener. Please."

Since killing a law enforcement officer would land me in jail, I turned my wrath in the direction of the coffee maker. "You bought that at a discount store for less than ten bucks, didn't you?"

Taking a sip of his coffee, Quinn gave the white plastic machine a pat. "Don't you be mean to Suzy. She treats us real good."

Several cops in the main room whimpered, and I suspected a few of them cried. How could I be mean to so many heartbroken adults at one time? Even I couldn't do it. It was worse than kicking a puppy.

"I'm going to need a ride to the bank and a trip to a restaurant supply store." I guzzled down my cup of crap coffee, shuddered, and left the break room. "I'm also going to need a strong man willing to sacrifice his body for the sake of good coffee. Volunteers?"

Every cop in the place, even the women,

raised their hands with the exception of one cranky-looking Chief Quinn.

"What do you think you're doing, Gardener?"

"I'm kidnapping at least one cop, possibly more, so I can have good coffee. Some cheap bastard put the world's worst coffee machine in this place, and I will not stand for it. Leave me alone, Chief Quinn. You have committed crimes against coffee in this station. Don't you have work to do?"

"You need to call the CDC, remember? There's nothing wrong with Suzy."

"As soon as I'm back, I'm going to take Suzy to your office and dismantle her piece by piece while you cry and beg for me to spare the machine. Guess what? It isn't going to work. She dies. Today."

"You're not killing Suzy."

"Suzy dies. She will be replaced by a stainless steel beauty of a machine, one that doesn't make charred, disgusting sludge instead of coffee. And you'll like it. You will end up on your knees begging me to make you coffee."

The cops cracked up laughing.

"You still need to call the CDC."

I stepped to the nearest desk, which was occupied by an older gentleman. The amused cop raised both hands and rolled his chair away. "Press nine to call out, Gardener."

Did everyone in the station know my name? Probably. I peeked at his nameplate. "Thanks, Officer Nilman."

It took me five minutes to navigate my way through the CDC's menu so I could speak to a real person. When the receptionist answered, I said, "This is Bailey Gardener. I'm returning a missed call."

"Hold."

So much for speaking to a real person. I tapped my foot and parked my ass on the edge of Nilman's desk. "Yippee. I'm on hold."

Satisfied I was doing what I was told, Quinn headed for his office. The instant his back faced me, I flipped my middle finger at him.

"I can see you in the mirror, Gardener." Quinn lifted his mug and gestured to a mirror mounted in the corner over the sea of desks. "Nice try, though. And here I thought you preferred to flip me off where I could see you do it. Subtlety is not your forte."

The line clicked and robbed me of my chance to talk back to the police chief. "You have reached the office of Marshal Clemmends. Please hold."

Oh boy. What had I done to deserve being transferred to the head honcho's office? The man worked in Washington, I'd never met him in my life, and I doubted I wanted to. I'd been to Washington exactly once, and about ten minutes after I got there, I had found a liquor store, went to my hotel room, and got so drunk I couldn't remember why I had gone in the first place.

The hangover ranked second only to my napalm bender.

"Good afternoon, Miss Gardener. Thank you for returning my call."

Was I actually talking to Clemmends, or was I speaking to one of his minions? Since I didn't know, I replied with, "Sir."

"It has come to my attention you publicly assaulted a gorgon prince."

"Gorgons have princes?"

Good job, mouth. One day, my mouth and I were going to sit down and have a very long talk about what should and shouldn't be said.

"Yes, Miss Gardener. According to our records, the local clan has two of them, and you assaulted the older one."

Nice. If I was going to cause an inter-species problem, at least I went all in and beat the shit out of the oldest prince of the gorgons. "That's going to look so cool on my gravestone. Look, sir. If the motherfucker hadn't tried to assault me first, I wouldn't have beaten him. Do you know what rape is? Rape is when one being tries to force itself on another being. Since rape—mine included, thank you very much—is a felony, self-defense is completely legal. If he hadn't tried to rape me, I wouldn't have needed to beat the shit out of him. He should be fucking grateful I hadn't been armed with a knife, because I would have cut off his limp dick and fed it to him. I am not breeding stock. So, fuck off, sir."

I slammed the phone down on its cradle. "The nerve!"

Was clapping over my tirade really necessary? The cops sure seemed to think so. My face flushed.

"You just hung up on your boss, didn't you?" Nilman rolled his chair back to his desk and grabbed his badge, wallet, and keys from a basket beside me. "I'm off duty in ten minutes. I can take you to the bank and drive you around. You might want to recruit some extra muscle, though. I'm a weak, little old man as these young whippersnappers like telling me at least once a week."

A door banged open, and Quinn leaned out of his office. "Gardener, did you hang up on the head of the CDC?"

"I am not breeding stock!" Maybe I shouldn't have let my voice turn shrill, but it was *his* fault I was so tired. If anyone expected calm and collected from me, they had obviously never met me.

"Gardener."

"I don't care if he was a prince."

Quinn sighed. "Gardener."

"I'd beat him up again."

"Just come answer the phone, Gardener."

"Damn it." Wasn't hanging up at the end of a screaming fit a sufficient reason to fire me? I'd have to try a little harder. Lifting my chin, I marched into Quinn's office, picked up the phone, and barked, "What part of 'fuck off' didn't compute? Let's try this: take my certification and shove it up your ass."

I hung up.

Quinn leaned in his doorway and smiled at me. "You're so cranky when you're tired. Why don't I give you my credit card? Then you can go shopping all you want without risking the murder of a poor bank teller."

Bristling, I glared at him. "I have my check."

"I know you do." Stepping into his office, he headed for his desk. "You can pay off anything you charge today after you go to the bank. It'll just cut out a step in your outing. If you take Nilman, I won't worry. He's a one-man army and not even a swarm of gorgons would try him."

"Good to know. What's his trick?"

"Last time he got petrified, it took over an hour for him to even start stiffening up. He's not immune, but he's resistant. He gets really offended when gorgons try to petrify him, too. He's also one of the best shots in Manhattan and carries the maximum amount of ammunition I'll let him get away with."

Quinn's phone rang, and he sighed, circled to his chair, and answered, "Chief Quinn speaking. Hello again, Mr. Clemmends. Yes, Miss Gardener is still here. No, she hasn't burned down the station yet. I'm not sure where you got that idea, sir. One moment." He sighed. "Gardener, he's really, really sorry he implied you weren't within your rights to defend yourself from sexual assault. Would you please speak with him?"

"Stop sounding so damned reasonable. I don't want to talk to him. I just want a half-decent cup of coffee." I snatched the phone out of his hand. "What?"

"He's offering you six million dollars if you agree to be the surrogate mother for his children."

My mouth dropped open. The slimy, disgusting menace was offering me *what*? I stared at Quinn, lowered the phone, and whispered, "Quinn, he's offering me six million to help him spawn his whelps."

"No." With a scowl so fierce I expected him to flip his desk in a fit of rage, he got up and closed his office door. "No. Absolutely not. No fucking way in fucking hell. No."

"I was thinking the same." I returned the phone to my ear. "No, sir. I will not."

Clemmends sighed. "He wants a tough,

beautiful virgin, and he is of the opinion you are the only one even close to acceptable for serving as the surrogate mother of his children. Due to your immunities, you are the ideal candidate."

I looked up to the ceiling, thanked God my mouth had begged Quinn to spank me, thus evicting me from the pool of eligible virgins forever and ever and ever. "Quinn, the asshole gorgon prince wants a beautiful virgin."

"Why are you relaying this conversation to Chief Quinn?"

I held the phone out to Quinn. "He wants to know why I'm relaying all this to you. Do you want to tell him?"

With a grin that turned my knees to jelly, Quinn slid onto his chair and propped his feet up on his desk. "And ruin such a wonderful chance for you to run your mouth? I couldn't. Please, Gardener. Tell him anything you want."

"Anything I want?"

"Anything you want. My office is soundproofed."

Hallelujah and amen. Of course, the bastard head of the CDC didn't need to know Quinn was the reason I was no longer a virgin, but I'd make do. "Sir, while the offer of six million is more than generous, I'm not a virgin."

Quinn grinned and sipped his coffee.

"Your file—"

"Is so very, very wrong. In bed. On the counter. On the floor. If it's found in a house and can support the weight of a wilting lily like me and a big, handsome, muscular man, I've probably had sex on it."

I dodged Quinn's spray of coffee and smirked while he choked out, "Gardener!"

"You said I could say whatever I wanted. Sir, you can write whatever you want, but make sure the phrase 'definitely not a virgin' is in there. Not a virgin. I'm very happy not being a virgin, thank you. If that prince wants me to beat the shit out of him again, can he wait until next week? Say, on Tuesday? I think I take my first self-defense course on Monday. For the record, Chief Quinn's ex-wife wants me to have her babies, too. The answer is no, no, no, and no. I am not going to serve as a gorgon harem mistress and help them spawn their little whelps. Absolutely not happening."

"I now understand why you informed Chief Quinn of the situation. How about this? I'll pass on a polite refusal and inform him that while you are single, you're not a virgin."

"I'm not single, either, sir."

"Your file indicates you're a loner, Miss Gardener. There are no relationships of any sort listed, no emergency contacts, nothing."

"I'm not single. I just haven't figured out how to get the bastard to marry me yet."

Quinn slid off his chair and ended up on the floor, coughing and wheezing.

And laughing. The man was definitely laughing between the coughing and wheezing fits. I sighed. "Chief Quinn, will you stop laughing, please? I'm on the phone. You told me to say whatever I wanted."

"This could simplify matters for us. Do you have proof of a relationship I can provide for His Highness?"

"I need proof? Since when was no an insufficient answer?"

"The CDC needs to provide evidence a potential surrogate among our employees isn't eligible. It's a rather annoying law."

"I'm not technically an employee. I'm a contractor. I'm still saying no. That's also ridiculous. I'm not serving as a surrogate, period. Not for him, and definitely not for one of his gorgon friends, either. There's only one man I'll even consider having children with, sir. End of story. I'm unwilling."

Quinn coughed another laugh out. I grabbed the nearest available object, a hardback reference book, and dropped it on him. A satisfying thump heralded a grunt and a groan.

"Proof of a relationship and confirmation of your..."

"Very active and happy sex life?" I provided, unable to stop from smiling. Since I was certain my words pleased Quinn, I dropped another book on him.

"Yes, that. If you can provide verification, the CDC can ensure no one will bother you in the future."

"How the hell am I supposed to provide verification? Should I corner my man and record it or something? Should I have sex in a public place with him? Haven't you heard about privacy, sir? Is this so-called gorgon prince a pervert who just wants a chance to watch? If he wants pornography, tell him to get it off the internet."

Quinn sounded like he was dying on the floor, so I dropped a third book on him. When that didn't stop him from laughing, I grabbed a three-inch binder, which seemed to do the trick. "I'm not a broodmare to be put up for sale to the most fashionable stud. What sort of *legal* verification would work? Because I promise you, some dimwit rapist prince isn't having anyone poke at me to confirm my virginity. Are we understood?"

"A marriage license would be sufficient to prove an engagement, *if* you can find a man willing to sign one. They last a period of six months before they expire. I'm sure if you have an actual boyfriend, this wouldn't prove too problematic for you to acquire."

Wow. The head of the CDC had a set of brass balls on him, that was for certain. "Let me get this straight. I'm going to be sexually harassed by someone of another species unless I coerce someone into signing a marriage certificate."

"Essentially, yes. In your file, you are described as an argumentative and difficult individual. Your performance record is top notch. Our records also indicate you're currently unemployed. I can offer you a lucrative position."

"That position better not be as a surrogate, Mr. Clemmends."

"Bring me proof of your non-single marital status and we'll discuss the proposal for your employment, Miss Gardener." He hung up on me. The bastard had hung up on me. I listened to the dial tone for a solid minute before I returned the phone to its cradle.

An amused, unharmed Quinn got to his knees beside his desk. "You're speechless. Such a rare moment. I need to really enjoy this."

"I have to prove I'm not a virgin and that my marital status is not eternally single, Quinn. How the hell am I supposed to prove I'm not a virgin?"

"We could—"

"Don't even think about it, buddy."

He grinned at me, gathered the dropped

books, and set them on his desk. "It's easy. I'll ask an angel or an incubus to confirm. Preferably an angel. An incubus would take one look at you and want to experience you for himself. I don't share. As for the other part, I have an idea." Picking up his phone, Quinn dialed a number. "Commissioner? It's Sam. I need the day off—and possibly part of tomorrow—to deal with the psycho ex-wife, another gorgon issue, and some personal business. I also broke my phone again, so I need to pick up a new one. I'll give you a call on it later today."

"You're a terrible police chief, Quinn," I muttered.

"Yes, there's a woman in my office. No, she isn't one of my cops. Okay. Fine." Quinn offered me the phone. "He wants to talk to you."

Puzzled, I took the phone and perched on the edge of Quinn's desk. "Hello?"

A man with a deep voice chuckled. "You must be the mysterious Bailey Gardener."

"Yes, sir."

"I saw a picture of you with your hand in Sam's back pocket this morning. At, if I'm not mistaken, the Plaza. I have another picture of him carrying you like a princess in his arms in front of 120 Wall Street. I was wondering when I'd get to speak with you."

Oh boy. "It's really not my fault this time,

sir."

The commissioner laughed. "Call me Jack, dear. I've already been informed of your gorgon problems, especially the one you discouraged yesterday."

"Yippee." I sighed.

"If you're going to do anything nefarious with Sam that may have long-lasting repercussions, I recommend Virginia. It's closer than Ohio and enjoys the same lax laws." Jack hung up.

"People keep hanging up on me, Quinn."

He took the phone out of my hand and returned it to its cradle. "It's okay."

"He recommends Virginia for anything nefarious we might be planning. I wasn't aware we were planning anything nefarious, Quinn."

Laughing, Quinn grabbed his coat and headed for the door. "Move your ass, woman. We're going on a drive."

"We are?"

"Yes. Move it." Yanking open his office door, he stuck his head out into the main room. "Perkins, call Longville in. I'm leaving for the day. I need two volunteers going off shift to come with me."

"I'm in," Perky replied. "Calling Longville now."

Nilman stood. "I already volunteered, sir."

"Get your stuff. We leave in five."

FIFTEEN

Why are you wearing my clothes, Quinn?

QUINN LEFT me at Perky's desk long enough to change his clothes. When he returned, he had stolen my outfit. I looked down at my white top, leather jacket, and jeans the Plaza had delivered to replace my ruined clothes.

Ah-ha. Mystery solved. *Quinn* had been the one behind the clothes.

The sneaky bastard was probably responsible for the dress and lace lingerie, too. Sneaky, sneaky, sneaky. I'd have to reward him for his cunning later.

But first, I needed to rib the devious police chief. "Why are you wearing my clothes, Quinn?"

"You looked so good in yours I had to see if I could compare."

And the round went to him. Spluttering, I turned to Perky and pointed at the smug police chief. "I think he's defective. Has he ever seen my face, Perky?" I tapped my cheek to point out my scars. "Ain't nothing pretty about this package."

Perky laughed. "The scars look like cute little freckles, and you're surprisingly pretty when you smile. That said, I'm going to have to side with you on this one. Chief, you don't have to do anything to be pretty."

In Quinn's sigh, I heard the worn patience of a man near the end of his rope. One or two more yanks wouldn't hurt anything, right? I flashed the cops my best smile. "He's so much sexier in that jacket than I am. How much do you think I'd get for him if I put him up for auction?"

Perky's laugh promised trouble for someone. "You'd get a lot more for him if you got him out of his jacket and dumped some water all over him."

"You're right. I would."

"Gardener."

I needed more of that growl. "People are going to ask if I'm your ugly sister or something. Then the men are going to start hitting on me so their sisters might get a chance to have you."

"Gardener!"

Score. "That's punishment for that travesty you named Suzy in the break room. Who uses such a cheap pathetic coffee maker in such a nice place?"

"Hear, hear!" the cops cheered. Then, a chaotic chorus of catcalls filled the station.

"Down with Suzy!"

"Can we keep the barista full time?"

"Hey, Gardener! You can come home with me anytime."

I blinked since the last comment had come from one of the women. "You just want me for my coffee, don't you."

"Don't forget to bring the dust. Your dust is the best."

With my certifications, I *could* contact a supplier and put in a few orders for dust. Happy cops made for a happy city, right? Maybe if I got Quinn happy enough, he'd keep me happy.

"I don't like that look on your face, Gardener. You're scheming something."

Damn it. "I don't know what you're talking about, Chief Quinn. We need to go to the bank and deal with Suzy. Now."

Quinn sighed. "Is your SUV here today, Perkins?"

"For the honor of watching Gardener kill Suzy so we can have good coffee, I would love to drive you around in my SUV, Chief Quinn."

"Why do I feel like you all like Gardener more than you like me?" Quinn shot a glare at me, and if it weren't for his mouth twitching in an effort not to grin, I might've been worried.

"She's going to make us coffee, Chief." Perky widened his eyes and swooned against Nilman.

Nilman shoved Perky upright. "He's right, sir. You make us coffee, but we've been considering asking the CDC to give it a hazard rating."

I smiled, skipped my way to the elevator, and pressed the down button. "Bailey Gardener, Goddess of Coffee."

"Calamity Queen," Quinn muttered.

Kicking would be a lot more effective if the man stopped dodging me. "Stay still, you."

"No."

"Bah."

In the downstairs garage, we piled into Perky's black SUV, and Quinn sat in the back with me. "Take us to the bank, first. Gardener needs to deposit a check."

I gave Perky directions to the nearest branch. It took twenty minutes and a call to the CDC to confirm I really was a newly fledged millionaire for the bank to deposit my check. The reality of the situation shocked me even more than the teller, who could see my pitiful balances over the course of my entire adult life. Updating my home address to Quinn's place took an extra fifteen minutes, and I ultimately needed to wave him over so he could present his badge and his driver's license to convince the teller I was staying at his place until further notice. He even promised to submit better proof of residency later.

Within ten minutes, I bet the rumor mill would get hold of the news and go wild with it.

Worse, the woman drooled over Quinn, and I barely escaped the bank without trying to kill her.

"You're so jealous," he whispered in my ear on our way out. "Come on. Teach me the errors of my coffee-making ways instead of trying to murder a swooning bank teller."

"I thought we were going on a drive."

"We'll get to that part eventually. First, I need to buy the good will of my officers, so when I do return to the station, they don't stage a mutiny."

"You should buy them some snacks, too. They keep feeding me stale chips. That can't be healthy."

"You're trying to bankrupt me, aren't you? First you threaten to kill Suzy, now you want me to buy snacks for the station? It's a fifteen story building. That's a lot of law enforcement personnel."

"Maybe if you were a better police chief, you wouldn't have to bribe your officers to like you."

"You might be right." Quinn herded me into Perky's SUV. "Chauffeur, take us to a store that sells good coffee machines. The Calamity Queen herself has declared it."

"Shut up, Chief Queeny."

I SUFFERED from a case of sticker shock so severe Quinn took the terminal out of my hand, swiped my bank card, and held the device for me while his hand covered the display. "Just tap in your pin, Gardener. Ignore the number I'm covering with my hand. The number is a lie. You can actually afford the money you're spending. You reassured me twenty times you intend to spend this money so you can murder my precious Suzy. You even called the bank to make sure the transaction would clear."

My pin. Right. I had one of those. If I hit the little black and yellow buttons on the device in the right order, it became my pin. I pressed the buttons. The machine made a happy pinging sound. The police chief took over, pressing a few more buttons on the terminal before handing it to the cashier.

A whimper escaped me.

How could a coffee maker be so expensive? Why had I purchased fifteen of them? I turned to Perky and made a choked sound in my throat. "What have I done?"

"I'm concerned, Chief. I think you broke her."

"It's not my fault she has a problem with Suzy."

"I just spent five thousand dollars on a coffee maker. Why didn't you stop me, Perky?" I swallowed. Why had I spent so much on one coffee maker? No, on fifteen of them, one for each floor of the police station.

Quinn slipped his hands into my coat and retrieved my wallet, slipped my bank card back inside, and returned my wallet to its proper place. "Fifteen of them."

"I just spent five thousand dollars on a coffee maker."

"You're so tired. Yes, you spent a lot of money on coffee makers. The entire station will idolize you now. You'll visit, and your worshippers will line up and feed you stale chips and bow before you." Placing his hands on my shoulders, Quinn turned me around and marched me out of the restaurant supply store. "Suzy really was doing fine. She has served faithfully for years."

"Suzy dies."

"You really have it out for my poor Suzy."

"The bitch dies. Her coffee's terrible, and you pay too much attention to her. My coffee's better. Deal with it."

"But I'm going to miss Suzy."

"I'll shove Suzy so far up your ass you'll need an operation to get her out. So help me, if she's still there the next time I go to the station..."

We left the store and headed to Perky's SUV, which was parked right outside the building. While I fumed, Perky and Nilman cracked up laughing.

"Just get in the damned car, Gardener."

I yanked open the door and scrambled inside. "What have I done? I just spent five thousand dollars on a coffee maker."

Perky twisted around in his seat, reached back, and gave my knee a slap. "It's okay, Gardener. I know you're not used to performing charitable acts. You did a good deed, and I promise it won't kill you."

Did buying coffee makers for sad cops count as a charitable act? "Are you sure?"

"Yes," everyone chorused.

Quinn grabbed my seatbelt and buckled me in. "One more stop, Perky. I need to swing by the Plaza and get something out of my car. Then we're going for a drive."

"What about your phone? You threw your phone in the toilet." Oh, I sounded all slurry. Damn it. I really was tired.

"I better get some coffee first, Chief. We might lose Gardener if we don't get some java down her throat."

"Might be wise. Three stops, then. Coffee, Plaza, replacement cell phone. Nilman, you're on coffee duty. If you run in, Perkins can drive around the block. You need the exercise."

The old man laughed. "What do you take in yours, Gardener?"

"Make mine blacker than my soul."

Quinn snorted. "Don't ask for the impossible."

NOT EVEN A TRIPLE espresso saved me. The instant Quinn tucked his blanket around me, it was lights out. The scent of coffee right under my nose roused me, and with a wordless growl, I untangled myself enough to make a grab for the cup. It warmed my hand and promised good things to come.

Coffee made everything better.

I could even forgive Perky for chuckling and sounding far too happy for anyone's good. "We're here."

Where was here? Did I care? Mmm. Coffee. I sipped at it, and a happy sigh escaped me.

Someone with a good coffee machine and some skill had made my coffee, so black I needed to drink it before it dissolved through the cup and made its escape. "What time is it?"

"Three in the morning. We got stuck in traffic leaving New York, leaving New Jersey, again in Baltimore, and one last time in Washington. I tried telling the chief taking the 95 was a dumbass move, but he insisted. Since I had talked back—and was right—the chief thought I'd be the best one to wake you. I'm not sure if he thinks you like me or if I'm just expendable. He's inside, and thanks to a little bit of powdered joy, he's in a really good mood. I may have spiked his coffee with some pixie dust I bought from Mary. If he hasn't figured it out, don't tell him."

Why would Mary sell a cop pixie dust? Was she insane? Was she trying to get arrested? I sighed and took another sip of my coffee. Nope, turned out coffee didn't have magical properties capable of restoring sanity to the world. Bummer. "Mary sold you dust. What grade, Perky?"

"C. The tiny vial sealed in red wax scares me, especially since she put it in my pants. I got groped by a faery. If my wife finds out, she's going to kill me." Perky pulled out a vial I recognized as containing A+++ pixie dust. "I'm pretty sure having this in my pants is a felony of some sort."

I sighed, as he was correct about the felony part. The thick coating of wax would probably keep the vial from breaking if someone dropped it. At least Mary—or whoever had packaged it—had treated the batch like the hazardous material it was. While pixie dust of any grade wouldn't actually hurt someone, it took days for the highest grade stuff to wear off, and anyone dosed could be talked into doing anything with a smile.

"Give me that, you idiot. Did she really give that to you?" I secured my grip on my coffee with one hand and snatched the vial with the other. "You were right. Having this *is* a felony. Do you know what would happen if I dosed you with this?"

"I'd be the happiest man on Earth, and I wouldn't be exaggerating."

"You'd be my slave, too. You'd be so happy you'd do whatever anyone wanted and not even think twice about it."

"But I'd be happy, Gardener. Would you deny me my happiness?"

"Yes." To make certain he didn't get any ideas, I stuffed the tiny vial into my bra. If Quinn wanted to find some happiness down my shirt, I'd consider having a fortunate accident occur. "Since C grade doesn't actually require a special license, we'll pretend you didn't have this vial, Perky."

"Despite appearances, I'm actually a good cop. I was issued a temporary permit. She can't stock it in her shop without you, so she requested someone to dispose of it. The CDC gave me a permit since I'm the closest thing they had to a reasonable adult at the station. I've been sitting on that for weeks waiting for a chance to give it to you in private. I figured you wouldn't want anyone knowing you were packing the good stuff."

"Did the CDC tell you what they wanted me to do with this vial?"

"No, they didn't. I figured the certified specialist would know what to do with it."

"Great. I'll have to call in and ask. Wonderful. Haven't they caused me enough problems for one week? I'm still surprised they gave you a permit. You really have them fooled, don't you?"

Perky laughed. "I know. It's like they think I'm a cop with a doctorate for some reason. So weird."

If Mary had unloaded the A+++ vial, what had happened to the A++ one? Some instinct, the same one that had warned me Chief Quinn was walking trouble the first time I'd seen him, blared silent alarms. "What happened to the A++ vial?"

"What A++ vial?"

"The one Mary had in stock."

"I have no idea. She gave me this one plus some C for the station. She even had a permit to sell the C grade vial. She gave me a really good price on it, too. Maybe she used the

A++ dust? She was pretty happy when I saw her."

Why me? I'd have to investigate eventually, which meant I'd be sent to her shop, which meant I'd have to deal with the disaster surrounding my terminated employment in person. Unlike Mary, I wouldn't be cruising on a high to get through the discussion. "Please tell me you scanned the vials to confirm their grades."

"Yes, Mom." Perky snorted and got out of the SUV. "Now that you've had your coffee, can we go inside? I'm sure Chief Quinn is causing trouble for someone without adult supervision, and Nilman likes encouraging him."

"Where *are* we, anyway?"

"Richmond, Virginia. It had the nearest courthouse to the state line serving nocturnals."

I really needed to hunt Quinn down and figure out why we couldn't have gotten the preliminary documentation from a New York courthouse. Why would anyone, including the police commissioner, suggest Virginia or Ohio? "Why are we here again?"

Next time, I needed to ask more questions before I got into an SUV with anyone. How had I ended up so far from home? What had I been thinking? Oh, right. I hadn't been thinking. I'd been too tired to think.

"Why are you asking me?"

"Because I have no idea what's going on. I haven't had enough coffee yet." To demonstrate the truth of my words, I took another sip of coffee. Then another. I guzzled it down and set the empty cup in the holder. "I haven't had enough coffee yet," I repeated.

Snickering, Perky opened the door and untangled me from Quinn's blanket. "You're still tired, aren't you? Poor girl. You've had a tough week."

"I will kill you, Perky. I will smile while I do it."

"No, you won't. You like me too much to kill me."

I sighed because it was true. "How much dust did you give him?"

"The last I saw him, he was smiling ear to ear. I may have heard him giggle."

"God. You got him that high? He only needs a light dose. I'm surrounded by idiots!"

Perky laughed. "You better go rescue him, then."

"I really will kill you, Perky, and I really will smile while I do it. Why the hell did you drive us all the way here? We could have gotten a stupid bogus license anywhere, even in New York. Damn it!"

"You were so much nicer after Chief Quinn tucked you in and you were sleeping like a little baby. Well, except for when you had that nightmare, screamed, and startled me so much I may have driven the SUV right off the road into a ditch. Fortunately, it was a shallow ditch. My SUV didn't mind too much."

"You drove your car off the road."

"You slept right through it, too. Fortunately, you only screamed once and whimpered a few times before settling down."

Great. Now everyone would be questioning my sanity. "You'd have nightmares, too, if you had the week I've had."

"Gardener, I'd be dead."

I grimaced. "While that might be true, you didn't have to say it."

"If you say no, he'll cry."

Full stop. Startled, I stared at him. If I said no? If I said no to what? To who? "What?"

"If you say no, Chief Quinn will cry."

With one mystery solved, I tried to deduce what I might say no about. Sex? There was no way in hell I could see myself saying no to sex with him. Well, unless I was dying of the plague or something. That would make some sense. Or in public. I couldn't imagine Quinn wanting to have sex in public. He seemed like the type to enjoy his privacy. "Say that again. Slowly, just to make certain I heard you correctly."

"If you say no, Chief Quinn will cry."

Did anyone think I'd say no to a marriage

license so no one would bother me about being a surrogate? I'd enjoy my claim to Quinn for the next six months. "Explain it in smaller words I can understand."

"Wow, Gardener. I used monosyllabic words. How the hell am I supposed to use smaller words? Most of them max out at three letters. You know what? Forget I said anything. I'll just sit back and enjoy the show."

What show? All I needed was a stupid piece of paper proving the existence of a man idiotic enough to marry me. What did Perky think was going to happen?

Crazy cops.

"I need more coffee for this."

"Fortunately for you, Chief Quinn anticipated your special needs and bought you a second one." Perky pointed at a cup in the front seat holders. "Take it for the road."

Miracles could happen. I grabbed the cup and slid out of the SUV, stifling a yawn. "Thank you, coffee gods."

"You're welcome."

The problem with going to a courthouse in the middle of the night involved the nocturnals the system served. Every city had at least one courthouse open from dusk to dawn with full judicial services catering to those unable to venture out into the sunlight. Vampires and the various incorporeal supernatural came to mind, but a lot of people took advantage of the late hours to take care of paperwork.

To make matters worse, vampires often served as the late-night staff, allowing them to participate in bloodless hunts. Without fail, they'd have at least one vampire and an entire coven of lawyers waiting to prey on hapless idiots expecting the night court to be simpler than the day court.

On a bad night, the place would be infested with incubi and succubi, vampires, ghouls, and other undead nasties needing to navigate the murky waters of government paperwork. On the really bad nights, hell broke loose on Earth in a very literal sense.

And then there were nights when my mother and father stood in the courthouse lobby and engaged in a glaring match with Quinn while an angel, an incubus, Nilman, several vampires, and an amused human couple watched. Hell no. Hell no.

No, no, no. Absolutely not.

Someone must have spiked my coffee with a hallucinogen. There was no other explanation.

"And we're done here." I almost managed to turn around to walk out, but Perky linked his arm with mine and dragged me deeper into the building. "Hey!"

My protest caught everyone's attention,

and Quinn's cheek twitched. "Gardener, are you actually related to these people?"

I turned to Perky, casting a desperate look at the doors. "How long has he been in here?"

"Twenty minutes."

I gulped. Had he been talking to my parents for the entire time? Why were they in Richmond? What had lured them out? How? Why? A thousand questions without a single nice answer hammered through my head. "If we could forget this ever happened, that'd be great. I think I left something in the car, Perky."

Perky tightened his grip on my arm. "Drink your coffee. Everything'll be fine."

Drinking my coffee sounded like a good idea. Would I find a hidden stash of alcohol at the bottom of my cup? Miracles could happen. There *was* an angel in the room after all.

Quinn cleared his throat. "We need a copy of your birth certificate."

"They try their best to forget I was born. You do realize I could have expedited one, right?" Did we need a copy of my birth certificate to get a bogus marriage license? Damn it. Stupid government bureaucracy. If my parents had brought the certificate with them, I had ways of getting it out of their hands. Beating them to death in a courthouse full of witnesses wouldn't work. I would need something equally violent but more private.

Did Richmond have a river or lake? Maybe a deep pond? Drowning them seemed like a good idea.

Sighing, Quinn shook his head. "I thought it would be faster to check with the CDC's HR department, get their number, and ask for it nicely. I'm sorry. I had no idea they were such—"

The angel clapped its hand over Quinn's mouth. "You will be polite, little one. Those words you intend to speak are not polite."

Okay. I could act like an adult, or I could get smacked down by an angel. I could act like an adult. I could speak to my parents without screaming, yelling, or breaking down into an anxious, crying mess. Holding out my hand, I said, "Birth certificate, please."

Look at me, all sorts of polite.

Everyone stared at me like I had grown a second head. My mother scowled and turned away. My father also scowled, but at least he had the basic decency to look me in the eyes when he did it.

Okay, then. If asking nicely wasn't going to work, I had a second plan, and all I had to do was dig the vial out of my bra to implement it. "I have enough pixie dust on me to turn this into a very public party you'll never forget. I'm probably the only person in a hundred miles licensed to do this. If you don't want my grandparents finding out you went on a pixie dust bender in a courthouse, I suggest you hand over my birth certificate. Please."

I could be polite while issuing threats, too. I needed to give myself a gold star for my skills at being a real adult.

The angel's laughter tinkled in my head. "How refreshing. She's so serious."

Stretching his velvety black wings, the incubus joined in, his chuckles making my toes curl in my shoes. I could threaten my parents while snuggling up to Quinn, couldn't I?

The angel reached out and slapped the incubus upside his head. "No. You're being bad."

My desire to rub all over Quinn evaporated. Damn it. I couldn't tell if I was disappointed or annoyed over the incubus manipulating me.

The incubus giggled. "Pixie dust benders are the best. Can you blame me? I'm allowed to do so much when everyone's high. I even brought my camera."

Sure enough, the incubus held a camera with his tail, and the red flashing light informed me he was already recording the scene. I spent several moments admiring his steady grip on the device.

One of the vampires cleared his throat. He wore the black robes of a state-licensed judge. "Miss, are you actually licensed for the handling and distribution of pixie dust?"

I gave Perky my coffee so I could dig out my CDC card for the judge to look over. He read over my long list of permit codes and chuckled. "Very nice, Miss Gardener. Should you decide to turn my courthouse into a rave, do handle your substances with the appropriate amount of caution—and send someone for me. Some things simply can't be missed."

My mother whirled around and her eyes widened. "You wouldn't dare!"

Damn, she had a piercing voice. I rubbed my ear against my shoulder while returning my identification card to my wallet. What had possessed me to call her when I had been ill?

Quinn grunted and shot the angel a glare. With a shake of its wings and shoulders, the angel made a disapproving clucking noise. "No, little one. That is not a polite thing to say. I'm sure this can be handled without Miss Gardener resorting to her secret stash of pixie dust, especially as I believe she has special plans for that vial. It would be a pity to ruin her plans, wouldn't it?"

Crap. Angels were mind readers, and it must have been picking my brain when I had been outside. My entire body flushed. Tricky, sneaky angel.

The angel's laughter sounded in my head, and I got the feeling I was the only one to hear its chiming amusement.

"Mr. Gardener, Mrs. Gardener. All they need is the birth certificate. It is in your possession. I can hear you thinking about it."

"You filthy, headless blight," my mother hissed through clenched teeth.

I took my coffee back from Perky, drank it down, and launched the empty cup in the direction of the nearest trash bin ten feet away. It bounced off the rim, teetered, and fell inside. With my hands free, I turned to Quinn's officer and used his shoulder to hide my face. "She just called an angel a blight, Perky. We're going to get smited."

I didn't want to be smited again. Smitings hurt.

"I think you mean smote." Perky patted my back. "It's okay, Gardener. Some people are just too stupid to live. We're very grateful this pair lived long enough for you to be born."

The angel's amusement rang out, the sound so full of warmth and joy my entire body relaxed against Perky. Without his help, I would have melted to the floor and been happy about it. "No, little one. You can't strangle your friend." The angel turned to the human woman standing off to the side. "Darling, how ever did you manage to birth such a troublesome child?"

She laughed and flipped her dark hair over her shoulder with a smug smile. Yep. I'd seen that smug smile plenty of times on Quinn's face. "Careful planning, Dad."

Wait, what? Dad?

I stared at the angel. If angels had eyes, I'm certain it would have been staring back. Wait. Him? Did angels have gender? How could an it be a dad? How could a human have an angel for a dad?

Nothing made sense anymore.

"Please just give me my birth certificate." There. I could become a bastion of sanity in a world gone mad.

"Wow, Gardener. You have really aced this being polite thing. Who are you? What have you done with my favorite coffee-making bitch?"

"Perky, I will kill you."

The angel needed to stop laughing. It—his—laughter made me go all weak in the knees. "She loves you too much to kill you, Mr. Perkins, so don't worry much. She'll just make you suffer for a while."

Damned angel, blabbing my darkest secrets. Perky wasn't supposed to know I liked him too much to kill him. No wonder Quinn kept telling me angels were jerks.

"Yes," the angel agreed.

My mother inhaled, and I closed my eyes, leaned against Perky, and braced for the worst. It came when she said, "And to think we were hoping you'd finally gone and gotten yourself killed. No. I don't see why we should do anything for you. You caused this mess all on your own. Deal with your own problems."

I'd heard variations of the same thing over and over again, but it still hurt. What had I done so wrong? Why were their shortcomings my fault?

The angel's laughter stopped, and the world seemed an even darker place for its loss. Perky rubbed my back and whispered in my ear, "Please don't cry. Chief Quinn loses his shit when you cry, and I don't want to witness a murder today."

The angel coughed, an accomplishment for an immortal lacking a throat. "Your Honor, fellow singers of the night, you might wish to turn around for a moment."

I peeked through my lashes. The vampires cleared out so fast they forgot to take their clothes with them.

With another stretch of his black wings, the incubus chuckled. "This is so much fun."

The angel smacked the incubus with a white, blue, and golden wing. "Mr. Gardener, Mrs. Gardener, let us try this one more time. You will give my future granddaughter-in-law her papers. You will do so now, without complaint. If you wish for me to be a blight on this Earth…"

I sucked in a breath, shoved away from Perky, and squealed, "Not the halo! Or the singing. Or the smiting. But please, please, *not the halo!*"

Quinn cracked up laughing, lifted his hand, and peeled the angel's fingers away from his mouth. "Maybe you should step outside for this, Gardener. Perkins, why don't you go with her and maybe cover her ears. If she faints, try to catch her, would you?"

"You just want to watch, don't you?" Perky accused.

"Yes."

By the book, I was supposed to walk away from dangerous individuals to avoid drawing unwanted attention. If the angel wanted to chase me, could I really get away in time anyway? I ran all the way to Perky's SUV and hid under Quinn's blanket so I wouldn't have to witness when the angel smited my parents, no matter how much they deserved it.

Smote. Whatever.

SIXTEEN

If that bothers you, wait until she calls the incubus 'Father.'

THE SUV'S DOOR OPENED, and Quinn laughed, a soft, gentle sound. "You can come out now. The smiting is all over. I have your documents, and those devil spawn are gone. I'm really, really sorry. I meant to get rid of them before Perkins got you moving."

I wrapped the blanket tighter around me. "You called my parents. Hadn't I told you they were assholes?"

"You hadn't. I'd heard rumors about them, but I had no idea they were anywhere near as bad as I'd been told. They're the absolute worst. My parents are infinitely superior, and they want to meet you." Quinn tugged at the blanket. "If you don't come out, I just thought you should know I'm manly enough to carry you inside, blanket and all."

"That woman called the angel her dad, Quinn. I didn't think angels had gender."

"If that bothers you, wait until she calls the incubus 'Father.'"

"Wait. What? Both of them? Is she adopted or something?"

"No, she's really their daughter. When an angel falls in love with a human enough to have children, they need to ask an incubus or succubus for help. Since my grandfather loved my human grandmother, I ended up with an extra grandfather. Yes, it's as weird as it sounds."

"You're part angel."

"And part incubus, too."

Well, that explained a few things. "But you look human."

"On paper, I'm about as human as it gets, although I have a magic rating that exceeds the norms a little."

Holy hell. Quinn really was my heaven and hell rolled together into one sexy package. "That couple in there. They're your parents?"

"I'm so sorry. I wasn't expecting them, either. I walked in and they were waiting for me, looking smug. They're really, really good at that."

The angel manifested in the seat beside me. "It really is safe to come out now."

I screamed, launched out of the SUV, and ended up trapped in Quinn's arms, half tangled in his blanket. "Y-y-you demonic angel! You did that on purpose."

"Yes, I did. She is so much fun, little one."

Quinn sighed and rested his forehead against me. "I told you angels were jerks."

"I like her, little one. Marry her before she gets away. I didn't go through so much trouble to watch you squander such a nice opportunity." The angel disappeared in a column of golden light, and I clung to Quinn in case it—he—returned.

"Did he just say marry?"

"He may have."

"Me, marry you?"

"You know, thinking about it, that would be nice. Then, if a gorgon even looks at you funny, I can assault him, too. No court would convict me for protecting my wife. I like it. Did you know that's how gorgons solve disputes over lovers? With violence. Lots of violence. Lots of violence I'd be legally allowed to participate in. I like it."

Had Quinn hit his head? Had the angel smited him, too? I worried. "Uh, Quinn?"

"What?"

"You're supposed to hate me when we're not busy having amazing sex. I'm pretty sure that's our relationship. We hate each other with moments when we lose all reason and end up in bed together."

Quinn sighed. "Okay. I see we're going to have to address this. Yes, Bailey. I hate you so much I need to marry you so our mutual hatred can last the rest of our lives. I heard you, you know. I very clearly heard you. You said, 'I just haven't figured out how to get the bastard to marry me.' I'm calling you out. This is how you get the bastard to marry you. You walk him into that courthouse—in handcuffs, if you really want—and march him in front of that vampire judge. Then the bastard is forced to marry you. If you *really* want, ask for a gun. I'm sure someone has one you can borrow for a few minutes. Then the bastard will be forced to marry you at gunpoint. Aren't I helpful?"

Crap. I had said that. Me and my big mouth got me in so much trouble. "Did I really say that?"

"You did. Be responsible, Bailey Gardener. You said it, so you have to marry me. Here. Now. It would make me really happy."

My mind went blank. Quinn really wanted to marry *me*? He must have hit his head in the courthouse when the angel had smited my parents and done the scary angel halo thing. I didn't believe it, not for an instant, but I couldn't bring myself to call him out on it. "Do I get a real wedding later?"

Stupid mouth. Was there such a thing as a fake wedding? Well, there *were* bogus marriage certificates used to keep amorous gorgons away. Maybe a fake wedding was a little like one of those. Would I still get to sleep with Quinn if we had a fake wedding?

"Do you want one?"

Good question. Did I want a real wedding? I tried to imagine myself walking down an aisle in a white dress, and my brain promptly fizzled and went blank. To cover my complete inability to handle feminine issues, including the possibility of having a real wedding, I blurted, "I might!"

"If you want a real wedding, we'll have a real wedding."

Since that hadn't been the answer I expected, I floundered again. "Here? Now? Us? Are you serious?"

"Here. Now. I need you to be mine. I never want to let a single gorgon even look at you again without being able to beat the living shit out of him and make him regret he ever saw you."

Okay. Wow. Clearly Quinn needed to be educated on the reality of the situation. "But me? Why me? Look at me. I wasn't pretty before a bomb went off in my face. I'm no model. Until earlier today, I scraped pennies to get by, and I didn't exactly do a stellar job of it, either. You could have any woman in the world. All you'd have to do is smile at her, waggle your finger, and ask. You're *that* sexy."

"There's only one woman I want, Bailey.

You. When I'm an asshole, you tell me so. I'd say you're afraid of nothing, but my grandfather scared you so much you ran and hid under my blanket. You're brave, and that scares the shit out of me. When I watched that damned building burn, I was devastated. I had sent you in there, and I thought I'd never see you again. But then there you were, a sodden, shivering mess trapped in the rubble and so miserable, but you were alive. I wanted to take you home, lock you up, and never let you out again so I could keep you safe."

"That's crazy." It was, too.

He made it sound like he actually loved me.

"You do that to me. You drive me crazy, and I love every minute of it. If I had known a woman like you existed, I never would have settled for someone like Audrey in the first place."

There were so many things wrong with our situation I barely knew where to start addressing them. I went with the easiest one first. "But I'm a bitch, Quinn. I've never exactly been nice to you."

"You're joking, right? Have you looked at me? An egotistical asshole like me needs a bitch like you. You're blunt. You're honest. You're prickly as hell. You're a lot of things, but you're not weak. I don't scare you one bit.

When I fuck up, you let me know. You don't back down. You don't let me step on you. Hell, maybe if we stay together long enough, we'll just be two people with tough jobs trying to make the world a better place."

"Quinn, the romance section called. They're looking for their lost stud again."

He laughed. "Just shut up, stop complaining, and marry me."

I had been right all along. I was in way too deep. "Well, then. Since you asked so nicely, how could I possibly refuse?"

AN ANGEL and an incubus in the same courtroom seemed like the start of a bad joke to me. Once I added the vampire judge, two cops serving as witnesses, and a crowd of mismatched supernatural, I ended up with a wedding.

My wedding.

A gorgon with coral snakes for hair sat in the front row talking with Quinn's father. The gorgon's lack of sunglasses or a veil covering his head puzzled me. Why wasn't anyone a statue yet? The mysterious absence of petrified victims kept me staring at him longer than was socially acceptable. Quinn caught me gawking and chuckled, nudging me with his elbow.

I ignored him. If he wanted me to be polite, he needed to do something about the centaur in the center row; she was playing with the gorgon's coral snakes, cooing at them and kissing each one in turn. I was pretty sure she had named them and was determined to whisper sweet nothings to them all.

I suspected her genes had somehow contributed to Quinn's existence, as I struggled to accept someone so beautiful existed in the world and shared the same air I breathed. She also had Quinn's dark hair and rich brown eyes. A rational explanation surfaced, and I turned to Quinn, tugging on his sleeve. "Quinn?"

"Yes?"

"I think your grandfather smited me. I'm actually in the hospital dying. Again. I need to stop doing that."

"Yes, you do. You're not hallucinating. You're watching my grandparents harass my father. It's their biggest joy in life."

Okay, I could handle an incubus and angel getting together with a human and somehow producing Quinn's mother. I tried to imagine how a gorgon and a centaur produced a human. I couldn't.

I returned to safer waters. "I'd like to point out that no one has been petrified yet. This concerns me."

"Hey, Grandfather. Bailey is having trouble coming to terms with the fact you haven't petrified anyone yet. I think it might be screwing around with her perception of reality. Don't you keep a ready stock of stoner bait around?"

I pinched the bridge of my nose and sighed. Too often, those bored, high, or on some sort of drug sought out a gorgon to experience petrification. Some liked it so much they became gorgon groupies, nicknamed stoner bait by the law enforcement officers tasked with keeping such incidents to a minimum.

Why was Quinn encouraging the gorgon with lethally venomous serpents on his head to petrify someone?

"You should have brought her to visit us earlier, then. I'm sure you'll figure out some way to handle the problem you created with your neglect."

Quinn sighed. "Why am I not surprised?"

"Because your father raised you almost right. Not quite, but almost."

Tugging on Quinn's sleeve to recapture his attention, I whispered, "A gorgon and a centaur having a child together really equals a human?"

"Yes, surprisingly. Hey, old man. What are we waiting for, anyway?"

My future grandfather-in-law, the gorgon,

chuckled. "Your aunts. Not even the judge is willing to risk their wrath. Your great-grandparents wanted to come, too, but they're busy skinning my brother for daring to whelp a menace to society. If you're lucky, they'll show up a bit later."

"You have a big family, Quinn."

He smiled at me and leaned over to kiss my forehead. "You'll get used to it. I did. They had to tie me down and subject me to the whole lot of them until I went into psychological shock and accepted them, but you'll get used to it. I might have a dirty secret. It's really bad, and I'm really, really sorry. I hope you'll still marry me once I tell you."

Uh oh. "Oh boy. All right. Just say it. It can't get any weirder than this."

"You beat the shit out of my first cousin once removed, and he offered you six million dollars to become his harem queen, which is another way of saying his wife. I'm pretty sure this means I get to beat him up, Grandfather." Quinn sighed. "I'm going to get my ass kicked by my great uncle over this, and he doesn't fight fair."

"I was wrong. It got weirder." Running away wouldn't help. Somehow, I had found the freakiest but sexiest man alive. Marrying him fit my crazy life well. So his great uncle might be a gorgon king, and his first cousin once removed was a perverted prince who'd gotten influenced by an incubus during gorgon mating season. I could handle the situation like an adult.

I wouldn't laugh. Oh, how I wanted to laugh. I wanted to laugh so hard I cried. Then I would return to Perky's SUV and curl up with Quinn's blanket while sucking my thumb.

Sometimes, the only way to deal with adult reality was to indulge in a good thumb sucking while wrapped in a nice blanket.

"I would have told you sooner, but I was too busy fantasizing about murdering my cousin. Then I remembered my woman beat the shit out of my cousin, and everything seemed okay at that point."

"My grandson is easily distracted," the gorgon informed me. "You'll get used to it one day, I'm certain."

I drew in a deep, cleansing breath. "All right. Your grandfather whelped a gorgon king. What does that make you?"

"Technically, I suppose I'm a gorgon prince since Dad's from my grandfather's first whelping. We're just humans, though, much to his disappointment."

Quinn's grandmother kicked out a hind hoof and thumped the bench behind her. "You are a prince, young man. I have the papers to prove it. You are *my* son's child. You are a gorgon prince, and don't you forget it.

The only reason those in New York City don't know to grovel at your feet is because your mother asked me really, really nicely. Your father is just as much of a king as my bratty brother-in-law." The centaur grabbed a handful of coral snakes and tugged. "Can we get a refund on him, dear? Really, allowing one of his whelp to humiliate himself in public like that. I really should let our little Sam beat the shit out of him."

My husband-to-be sighed, and I began to understand why he was so patient. "Mom, please tell me my great-grandparents aren't coming, too."

My future mother-in-law checked her phone. "They should be here in five minutes."

Quinn stiffened beside me, and his eyes widened. "Your Honor, can we start? I need to be out of here with my wife within four minutes and thirty seconds."

Maybe things would seem a little more normal if I sat with the gorgon. Since he couldn't petrify me, maybe I could get one of his snakes to bite me. I sat, clasped my hands in front of me, and pretended I belonged among the menagerie. "If I have to clean up after you tonight, I will turn into a unicorn and fry your ass."

Okay, I hadn't meant to say that, but for once, I agreed with my big, stupid mouth.

"I love how she's so serious about this."

Quinn's angelic grandfather laughed. "She's so charming, little one. Wherever did you find her?"

"You don't find the Calamity Queen. She finds you."

I could always trust Quinn to be a smart ass. I sighed. "A coffee shop. I made him the best cup of coffee he has ever had in his life, and when he annoyed me, I spiked it with pixie dust so he could remove the stick he had shoved up his ass. Then he asked me to prove his ex-wife was a cheating whore, which I did. Then I got my full certification with the CDC, and the universe repaid me by smiting my ass and making him my contact within the NYPD."

Quinn snorted. "She wants to kill Suzy."

"Violently. I'll like it."

"Of course you will. You're pure evil."

"Why do you want to marry me again?"

The incubus snickered. "Lifetime supply of the best sex he'll ever have."

It didn't surprise me at all when Quinn smiled his smug smile and shrugged. "I can't argue with that."

What had I gotten myself into?

QUINN'S GREAT-GRANDPARENTS weren't human, either, and I grew numb to the insanity required for Quinn to have been born. "Let me guess. Your great-grandmother is a sphinx. Your great-grandfather is… a… okay, I give up. What is he?"

While humanoid in the sense the man had two legs and two arms, he had a dog's head with an elegant, long snout, jet black with a crest of thick golden fur.

"His name's Anubis. And yes, before you ask, when you mix Anubis and the Sphinx—not a sphinx, *the* Sphinx, you get a human—my grandmother on my mother's side, to be exact. If we're really unlucky, Grandmother will show up, too. Considering she's been dead for at least fifty years, things get awkward when she comes to visit."

Anubis shot a glare at Quinn and sat beside his mother. "Not today, you insolent puppy. She's busy bullying some ingrates. I'm really intrigued I got invited this time, my darling dear. I was having fun watching my daughter bully the ingrates, but I didn't want to miss this."

Quinn's mother chuckled. "His bellyaching caught his grandfathers' attention. Turns out she only died a little when his cousins showed off their halos. She's a tough one. I like her. She's not at all like that other woman."

An opportunity to nail Quinn so hard his family would talk about it for years didn't present itself every day. "That other woman wants me to have her babies."

With a low, whimpered groan, Quinn sank onto the bench beside me, leaned over, and buried his face in his hands. "You had to go there."

"It's not *my* fault your ex-wife was stalking your house looking for me so I could have her babies. It's definitely not my fault you irresponsibly married the psycho."

"Truer words were never spoken," Quinn's angelic grandfather murmured.

"I'm still lost over how this turned from getting a bogus marriage license so your cousin would go away to a family reunion with a wedding."

Half the hands in the room went up. In perfect harmony, most of Quinn's family announced, "It was my idea."

Indignant protests rang out. It took ten seconds for a brawl to start, and I retreated to the witness stand so I wouldn't be caught in a supernatural fray. Quinn followed, sighing and shaking his head.

Only the angel escaped the chaos. "Call me Sylvester, dear. It gets tiresome listening to you think of me as 'the angel' all the time. Ah, Your Honor. I do believe it is time we married the children so they can run away and be happy together."

The vampire sighed. "My poor courtroom.

All right, kids. You want the pretty, romantic version, or do you want to sign and bolt?"

"Bolt, please," I begged. Quinn glared at me. "I'll sign first!"

"You better, or I'll chase you down and drag you back here."

The judge sighed. "Are you two even capable of being romantic? I *finally* get a wedding, and it's a circus."

"Your Honor, it's a miracle there's someone willing to marry me. I need him to sign the papers before he changes his mind. Hey, Sylvester? Is there a way to make sure he doesn't get away?"

"Sex every day makes an incubus stay."

In retrospect, it made a lot of sense. What *didn't* make sense was how Audrey had been capable of cheating on him. "Audrey must have been defective. I don't understand how it was possible for her to even think about wanting to cheat on him. He walks in the room, and all I can think about is not rubbing all over him and making an idiot out of myself."

Silence.

Crap. My mouth had gone and done it again. I sighed.

My future grandfather-in-law patted my head and smoothed my hair. "He's part angel, little one. Bad seeds bear no fruit, and that woman had turned rotten. You suit him. All roses start out as nothing but thorns, but given time, their flowers are the most beautiful of all. It is the nature of humans to err. It is also the nature of humans to persist. Of course, I *am* an angel. I can—and do—cheat a little. I foresee you driving each other crazy until the end of days. I look forward to it very much. You will bring me much entertainment over a long time. Go ahead and sign your paper, children. Seal your fate."

"Angels are scary, Quinn."

"I know." He smiled at me. "Once we sign, we can bolt."

"Give me a pen."

Papers rustled, and the vampire slapped a sheet of paper on the broad sill separating us from him. "Once you sign, you're married, blah, blah, blah. Till death do you part and some crap about the State of Virginia. Sign here." The judge held out a pen.

"We should use that on a card, Quinn. 'Blah, blah, blah, till death do we part and some other crap.' It's brilliant." I snatched the pen. "Don't we need some witnesses watching us sign this damned thing?" I checked to make certain I was actually signing a marriage certificate before I scribbled my name on the appropriate line.

"I'm witnessing, and no one doubts an angel." Sylvester stepped towards the brawl, reached out, and snagged the nearest body.

He ended up with the gorgon. “I need you to sign this so the children can be married.”

Quinn took the pen and signed before making room for his grandfathers. Sylvester signed first. Instead of signing with the pen, the gorgon smeared his bloodied thumb over the page. It turned into a stone tablet.

“There. It is written in stone. Can’t be undone now. Deal with it.”

“He did that on purpose,” I blurted.

“It’s not a party without at least one petrification.” Sylvester, an angel and my new grandfather-in-law, shrugged. “I can’t argue. It *is* written in stone now. I guess I’ll give you your wedding present.”

He grabbed our left wrists. With an indignant, startled squawk, the vampire vanished.

Quinn sucked in a breath. “Shit. No, no, not the—”

Damned angels and their stupid Bailey-smiting halos.

I DIDN’T DIE, not even a little. All of heaven’s pretty stars danced and twinkled before my eyes, however. I sprawled over Quinn, who sighed his worn-out, patience-tested sigh. “You suck, Grandpa.”

Sylvester laughed and vanished in a column of golden light.

"Angels are jerks," I slurred.

"Told you."

"I can't bolt like this, Quinn. I don't think I can even crawl right now. I got smited at my own wedding." I giggled. "We started our marriage with a bang."

"And my wife's first act as a married woman is to pun me. I haven't even gotten a kiss yet."

I was a wife. Huh. How *had* that happened? "I'm going to need a few minutes on this one. I wasn't even used to being someone's girlfriend yet. I don't know how to be a wife."

"Tip: have sex with me, and only me, often."

"And there's the rest of my life, having sex with a sinfully hot man. However will I cope?"

"I'm sure you'll figure something out. Now that we're married, shall we get a non-petrified copy to take to Clemmends? Actually, two extra copies. I'm going to need to shove the first one down his throat. Then I'm going to have to actually look at the laws regarding surrogates and figure out how we got played, because I'm pretty sure we got played, Bailey."

"You can't attack the head of the CDC. He might have a real job for me."

"I'm not sure I can obey that order. What

if I want to? I need to protest his bullshit bogus bureaucracy."

"Aren't you supposed to be thanking him? He's why we're here. I'm on top of you, married to you, while your relatives brawl in a courthouse."

Quinn scowled. "Can I thank him at the same time I shove the certificate down his throat?"

"I don't think that's how it works, Quinn."

Listening to him sigh in frustration made me unreasonably happy. "Can you walk yet?"

"If it means escaping without having to be the one to clean up this war zone, I can manage." I needed the help of the witness stand to get to my feet, but I pulled it off, huffing my triumph. Quinn hopped up without any sign the angelic smiting had affected him. He dusted his clothes off, and I spotted a shining, golden tattoo circling his wrist. I pointed at it. "What the hell is that?"

Quinn lifted his left arm, and his gaze locked onto his wrist. His eyes widened. "He didn't."

"He didn't what?"

"Damn it. Grandpa either doesn't trust us, doesn't trust my idiot cousin, or just wanted to be a jerk and remind us our marriage is written in stone—permanently. There's good news: I'd like to watch someone who isn't me try to get into your pants. These things will be entertaining should that happen."

I checked my wrist, and sure enough, I had one, too. "What are these things?" I couldn't tell if writing or meaningless patterns circled my wrist. "It's a tattoo. An angel smited me and slapped a tattoo onto my wrist. Oh! Is this the mystical ball and chain I keep hearing about? It's prettier than I expected. Wait. If a woman starts pawing all over you..."

"She'll get zapped."

"Someone invented woman repellent." I hugged my wrist to my chest. "And to think I thought I'd be spending the rest of my life beating off the competition."

"And now I'm thinking Grandpa may have realized your self-esteem issues are actually coupled with jealousy-induced anxiety."

I scowled at him. "Have you checked your reflection in the mirror? I'm pretty sure there's a disproportionate number of men who'd sleep with you given half a chance. You're not allowed to give those men a chance, either."

Hanging his head, he sighed. "This is all my grandfather's fault."

"Which one? Because seriously, Quinn, there are three realistic options. Four if you count your great-grandfather. For a non-human, Anubis is pretty handsome. I'm also pretty sure your centaur grandmother played a significant role in your sexiness factor. She's gorgeous."

Quinn sighed again, louder and longer. "Anubis is packing divinity. Of course he's handsome. Just be glad my great-grandmother showed up looking like a cat. She's the one who taught the succubi their tricks. Let's get out of here before it gets anymore awkward—and trust me, it will."

"You know what? I'm not going to ask. Let's bail before the cops show up."

With a quiet laugh, Quinn grabbed hold of my hand. "You learn fast."

I pointed at the brawl, snorted, and headed for the wall, dodging the writhing mass of bodies on my way out the door, pausing long enough to snag Perky and Nilman so they wouldn't be left to face the terrors of Quinn's family.

SEVENTEEN

How could a piece of technology thwart me?

I STOLE the keys from Perky because I could, but I drove because everyone else passed out the instant they got inside his SUV. Nilman managed to get his seatbelt buckled before he started snoring from his prized spot in the front passenger seat. The other two barely made it all the way into their seats before they decided they had no more interest in being conscious.

Stealing Quinn's new phone out of his pocket, I scowled at the device's locked screen. How could a piece of technology thwart me? All I wanted was a single picture for blackmail.

A flash of gold warned me of the angel's arrival, and my new grandfather-in-law manifested behind me, reached over my shoulder, and tapped the screen. "You need a phone of your own. And yes, I agree. This blackmail opportunity is too good to pass up."

Sylvester vanished.

Damned angels. I wrinkled my nose, decided I appreciated the chance to capture pictures of all three peaceful sleepers, and took several photos before buckling Quinn and Perky in. I covered them both with the blanket, took one final picture of them together, and hit the road.

It was a good thing Nilman had taken the front seat; had Quinn been seated there, I doubted we would have reached Washington. The urge to pull over and drag my new husband off to somewhere private to prove I could be a good wife bordered on the excessive and insane.

It took a gargantuan amount of effort and patience to drive the two hours to Washington without making a pitstop for wicked, kinky purposes. The effort involved in dragging Quinn somewhere no one would spot us discouraged my plotting. After an epic battle with morning rush hour traffic, I pulled up to the CDC headquarter's guarded gate. My CDC card and a brief introduction of my sleeping passengers got me into the visitors' lot, where I parked and killed the engine.

A slow smile spread over my lips, and I twisted around in my seat to watch my new husband sleep. Growing up without any real friends, I'd never had a sleepover party or been around many people napping before. He looked so defenseless and peaceful.

One little scream wouldn't scare too many years off his life. It would, however, let me enjoy some pandemonium while the three men figured out where they were, what had happened, and who was screaming. I drew in a deep breath and pretended I had a promising career as an extra in a horror flick.

Their startled cries and attempts to get up only to be thwarted by their seatbelts amused me so much. "We're here," I announced in my best sing-song voice.

Quinn glared at me, and I couldn't tell if the gleam in his eyes was the fires of hell about to incinerate me or a lot of lust. I hoped for the latter but expected the former. "You bitch."

Oh, how I loved that growl. I beamed at him. "Good morning."

While he made scowling sexy, the narrowing of his eyes promised retribution in some form later. "It's too early in the morning for you to be in such a good mood without sex being involved."

Perky and Nilman choked. The older cop turned his head and coughed.

It took a great deal of effort, but I swallowed my laughter. "Quinn."

"What?"

"You're embarrassing the cops."

"Cops? What cops? I don't see any cops here. I see two hitchhikers and my beautiful wife." Quinn stifled a yawn and looked Perky and Nilman over. "We didn't leave you at the courthouse?"

Perky smacked the back of my husband's head. "Mrs. Quinn, can you control him? It's too early in the morning to put up with him being a smart ass when I'm not being paid for it."

Maybe I should have left them sleeping in the SUV while I dealt with the CDC. "Just get out of the damned car so we can head back to New York sometime today. And Quinn, you may not kill anyone with our wedding certificate. Actually, don't kill anyone at all."

"If they hurt you, I'm killing them."

Oh boy. We hadn't been married for even a day, and we were going to need to have a long talk about when—if—killing someone was appropriate. "Don't kill anyone. I mean it."

"Why not?"

Losing my temper and breaking my own rule by killing Quinn wouldn't help anything, and I needed to keep him around for a long time. I sighed. "Perky, explain this to him in small words he can easily understand."

"She wants you for your body. You should be grateful she's willing to put up with you.

That said, I don't want a new boss. If we make it out of here without excessive violence, I won't tell anyone at the station you married Gardener during a courtroom brawl."

I frowned and leveled a glare at Perky. "Is there a reason my enslavement of Chief Quinn needs to be kept a secret? Am I a closet wife or something? I'm pretty sure I should be offended."

"No. I'm concerned everyone at the station will die of shock if you spring the news on them without warning. I was prepared since I saw you two in the hospital. Nilman almost choked to death on his coffee when your husband told him we were headed to Virginia so you two could get married. We need to acclimate the others to the idea." Flashing a grin at me, Perky freed himself from his seatbelt and the blanket.

Nilman chuckled. "It was pretty obvious once I stopped to think about it."

Shaking my head over the trio of police officers, I got out of Perky's SUV and tossed him his keys. "I'm going to be clear on something right now, Mr. Chief of Police Quinn. Suzy still dies. I will not tolerate any competition or bad coffee. We clear?"

Quinn scowled. "Crystal. Fine, no more bad coffee. Poor Suzy."

I chuckled, and to soften the blow to his

poor abused pride, I said, “Hey. Do you have any transformative pills on you? I’m thinking I’ll go up as a unicorn and light his hair on fire.”

“No, Bailey. If I can’t assault him, neither can you.”

“Damn.”

IT TOOK some snarling at the receptionist to get an appointment with Marshal Clemmends, and she made us wait for an hour and a half to see him. I spent it drinking coffee and cursing under my breath while Quinn, Perky, and Nilman used their phones to work. As far as I could tell, Quinn issued the orders, Perky hunted down information, and Nilman relayed messages. If I hadn’t known better, I would have thought they were at their desks rather than inside the CDC’s cafeteria.

An hour into the wait, I decided they’d probably forgive me for sneaking off to deal with Clemmends on my own—maybe. If Quinn had been paying a little more attention to me, he would’ve noticed me slipping away. I tiptoed my way to the elevators and finished the rest of my wait in the reception.

The secretary glared at me when she thought I wasn’t watching. Her phone rang, and she answered in a murmur. When she hung up, she sighed. "He'll see you now."

I considered myself lucky she bothered to gesture to the huge oak door leading into the man's office. While I understood I had probably made her life difficult demanding to see him, Clemmends had caused the whole situation in the first place. I got up, lifted my chin, and let myself inside.

For some reason, I had expected a fat slob of a man. Instead, I got a thin, older man in a classic suit seated behind a sleek black desk. He had company, and I grimaced when I recognized two of the three gorgons.

Yippee. Quinn wouldn't get mad at me if I beat up his cousin a second time, would he? While I thought about it, I turned my attention to my new grandfather-in-law, noting he was the only gorgon who wasn't wearing sunglasses. "Oh, look. It's the old man."

My stupid mouth was going to get me in trouble again.

Every last one of his coral snakes hissed at me. I hissed back. Quinn's grandfather relaxed and chuckled, and his snakes settled and quieted. "Good morning, Bailey. How was the drive?"

"The babies fell asleep the instant they got into the car and didn't budge until we got here. I left them in the cafeteria doing cop stuff. You?"

"Uneventful. This is my brother, Barnabus. The whelp is Darrel. He'd apologize for his crude behavior, but I'm afraid he won't be saying anything at all today. I petrified his tongue for daring to be rude and smearing the family name."

I still didn't know my grandfather-in-law's name, but at least I knew the name of the gorgon king. Sweet. Maybe I'd survive the meeting. "Pleased to meet you, Your Majesty."

Was Your Majesty the appropriate title? No one seemed offended, so I added a tally to my score of being polite like a good adult.

"Miss," Barnabus greeted. "I appreciate you coming here today."

Signing the papers in the courthouse moved me from Miss to Mrs.; I frowned, glancing at Quinn's grandfather. "You didn't tell them, did you?"

"And ruin your chance to tell them yourself? I wouldn't dream of it."

Who knew I could like a gorgon so much? "You're so sweet."

His coral snakes cooed at me, and my grandfather-in-law winked. "Don't tell them that. I have them fooled."

Okay, maybe the sweetness was a bit much. "I will still kill you if you make me clean up after you."

"Miss Gardener!" Clemmends bellowed, rising from his seat and slapping his hands against his desk. "You are in the presence of gorgon royalty. Remember your place."

I was going to have so, so much fun with Clemmends. If he didn't cry by the time I finished with him, I'd be disappointed. Stepping to his desk, I dug out my folded marriage certificate, made a show of opening it, and slammed it on his desk. "Mrs. Quinn. I'm pretty sure this stunt robbed me of dating, a proper proposal, and a nice wedding. While I have nothing against a good brawl, I didn't even have a chance to get a wedding dress."

Being tired and cranky made it easy to fake watery eyes. I even got my lip to tremble. "Sir."

Clemmends sat down and tried to pick up the marriage certificate. Straightening, I lifted my hand so he could read it. His brow furrowed. "Quinn? You don't mean Chief Quinn."

All three gorgons turned their glares on the head of the CDC, and I considered it a miracle he didn't end up petrified. A few of my grandfather-in-law's snakes hissed their displeasure.

"Yes, Chief Quinn. Once he finished laughing and could get off the floor of his office, he grabbed me, tossed me into an SUV, and carted me to Virginia. He refused to allow me out of the courthouse until I married him. He didn't think a mere license was sufficient to convince you I was off-limits."

"You married Chief Quinn."

I really couldn't blame the man for his incredulous tone and doubtful expression. After a trip to Virginia, two hours driving to Washington, and waiting in a cafeteria for an hour, my white shirt had turned gray, my jacket had new scuffs and leather wrinkles, and my jeans needed a good washing. "Is it that hard to believe?"

It was, but I fully intended to be a bitch to the man after having to endure his stupid phone call at the station.

"Yes. It's on file you have a terrible relationship. Actually, it's on file you have a terrible relationship with everyone, but Chief Quinn is able to make you do your job with minimal struggle."

I turned to my grandfather-in-law. "Can I really say whatever I want?"

He chuckled. "Be my guest."

"You might want to cover the whelp's virgin ears. I'm not sure if gorgon kings have delicate sensibilities, but if they do, maybe your brother better cover his ears, too."

Barnabus cleared his throat and hid his mouth behind his hand. "Excuse me. By all means. I'm sure my son could use the education. While it would be tragic if he didn't survive the experience, I would enjoy whelping more children to replace him."

Ouch. I almost felt bad for the gorgon prince—almost.

I smiled at Clemmends. "My relationship with Chief Quinn is so terrible we've had sex in every room of his home. Absolutely miserable, our relationship. Oh dear. I forgot to ask Sylvester to confirm I am most certainly not a virgin." With a dramatic sigh, I fluttered my lashes at my grandfather-in-law. "Quinn must have gotten his charm from you."

My grandfather-in-law chuckled. "You're such a gem. I'm sorry, Barnabus. Little Samuel has been after her for years. Once I found out about her altercation with your whelp, I may have called in a few favors." Every one of his coral snakes rose from his head and turned to Quinn's cousin. "As for you. You made a very poor choice. If I ever catch wind of you even thinking of forcing a woman, I will castrate you myself. Being my nephew will not save you. Once your tongue softens, you will apologize to your cousin and his bride in a sincere fashion. Give them a wedding gift while you're at it. You're fortunate he wasn't present. A courting prince is well within his rights to safeguard his future bride, and I'm sure he wouldn't have had any problem with petrifying you and bashing your statue into tiny fragments."

It would take some time to get used to anyone referring to me as someone's bride, let alone as someone's wife. How *had* that happened? I'm not sure I would ever understand the nature of miracles, which was what I thought had been required to have someone like me marry someone like Quinn.

Quinn's cousin cringed and stared at the floor.

Later, I'd have to ask who would be doing the petrifying and how Quinn would go about bashing his cousin's statue to pieces.

"Excuse me?" Clemmends choked, cleared his throat, and shot looks at my grandfather-in-law and his brother. "A courting prince? Did I hear you correctly?"

Clemmends didn't realize my Quinn was related to the three gorgons in his office? My grandfather-in-law had even referred to the prince as Quinn's cousin.

Idiot.

With a slow, sly smirk, my grandfather-in-law sank onto on one of the room's three guest chairs and propped his feet up on Clemmends's desk. "Gorgon society is complex, but I'll focus on the local gorgons. We have two kings and two princes born of the same line. My brother is a gorgon king. My eldest human son is also a gorgon king. I gave my rank to my eldest male offspring, as is proper. I have whelped many girls, and they are the pride of my life. My son's eldest child is Samuel Quinn, and as his father is a king, he is a prince. While there are other gorgon clans in the area, only ours has the right to rule."

Clemmends paled and his Adam's apple bobbed.

I was missing something. While I specialized in cleaning up after gorgons, learning about their familial structure hadn't been a priority for me. "Right to rule? Why's that?"

"It's a what, not a why, dear. It's a type of magic, and it's why I am not wearing sunglasses. My brother wears his only because he loses his temper far easier than I do. It's also why our snakes are uncovered. Our control over our powers is superior. Many other gorgons petrify with a look, as their abilities are always active. We choose when we petrify someone. That is evidence of our right to rule. I have it. My brother has it."

I didn't need to do the math; if Quinn ever became a gorgon, he'd have it, too. Would dust even work on someone who carried gorgon genes already? I couldn't remember anything about the CDC testing the possibility.

I hadn't even known gorgons could have human children.

The head of the CDC blanched. "Chief Quinn is gorgon spawn?"

Every single snake in the room hissed, and Quinn's cousin's expression turned so terrible I suspected his sunglasses were the only thing keeping Clemmends from petrifying. I filed 'spawn' away as an insult.

"My grandson is the child of two humans. By the CDC's own rules, he's quite human, I promise you. He will not accidentally petrify anyone."

My eyes widened at the subtle inflection in my grandfather-in-law's voice. Could Quinn petrify someone as a human?

"I see."

"Bailey, dear heart, do show Mr. Clemmends your bracelet."

My bracelet? Oh, the tattoo. I'd forgotten about the thing, and I obeyed, shoving back my coat sleeve to reveal the golden pattern, which still glowed with a faint light, although it had dimmed. "It's really pretty. I didn't get a chance to thank Sylvester."

"Don't you worry your lovely head about that. Angels love weddings. I give it a day at most before his common sense dribbles out of his ears and he has eloping regrets."

"He doesn't have ears."

"Oh, he does. If you want to see a great reaction, give his shoulder a slap one day. You might luck out and launch him into orbit."

I could handle an angel's lack of a head. I could handle their ears being on their shoulders. I could. I'd gotten better at being a polite adult. "That's good to know."

My grandfather-in-law smirked at me before turning to the head of the CDC. "Mr. Clemmends, I witnessed the signing of their marriage certificate. Samuel's other grandfather bound them together until the end of days, and they both carry the evidence of their binding on their left wrists. Now, please explain to me why you thought, for even a second, it was acceptable to attempt to coerce someone into an agreement to serve as a surrogate?"

I took a discreet step to the side to get out of the biting range of the hissing, swaying coral snakes, and Barnabus joined me, whispering in my ear, "I'm just the scapegoat. On behalf of my side of the family, I'm very sorry you got dragged into this. My whelp's idiocy is inexcusable."

"Let's review," I muttered. "I really had no idea how I'd get my husband to marry me—or even keep me as his girlfriend at the minimum. I'm hopeless. I should be thanking someone for this mess, but if I get too close to your whelp, I might be tempted to try to kill him again. He tried to petrify me!"

"Tried?" Barnabus straightened, and both of his eyebrows rose. "He didn't succeed?"

"Freak bit me, too. I *hate* when gorgons bite me. It hurts like hell."

"You're really immune. Full immunity?"

"I'm really immune. That's why I get the worst jobs in the city."

The gorgon king made a thoughtful noise in his throat. "Even to dust?"

I wrinkled my nose at the mention of the substance. "I'm immune even to dust."

"It seems Prince Samuel picked an extraordinary woman indeed. I'm impressed, and that doesn't happen often. You should escape while you can. Once my brother begins to rant, he doesn't stop for a long while. Welcome to the family."

"Thank you." I backed away and fled while I could, easing the door open enough I could slip out of the office and make my escape.

I MADE it to the ground floor before I realized I'd forgotten to ask about the CDC's proposal for employment. While I could use a job, in a way, I was grateful I hadn't stuck around. The idea of working for someone who viewed me as a thing with monetary value left a sour taste in my mouth. If I'd been treated like a person rather than a commodity, I never would have needed to marry Quinn in the first place, although I had zero regrets about having done it.

We'd figure it out, and I suspected

Sylvester was onto something with his comment about the best sex of my—and Quinn's—life. Mary's belief in the bright side of things worked sometimes. Quinn drove me crazy in all the right *and* wrong ways. The longer I was with him, the more time I wanted to spend with him, in and out of bed.

Quinn, Perky, and Nilman were where I'd left them. The three had their heads together, staring at Perky's phone. One of them giggled. "Not to interrupt your play time, but we can leave now. I delivered the papers. No one was assaulted."

"Sneaky," my husband muttered. Then he giggled. My eyes widened.

Why was Quinn giggling? What *were* they looking at on Perky's phone? I frowned, circled their table, and peeked over Quinn's shoulder. A video of a kitten playing with a scrap of paper enthralled the three men. Narrowing my eyes, I twisted around to get a good look at the cafeteria, homing in on the cafe portion. A stamp featuring a pixie marked the upper left corner of the sign.

"I leave for half an hour, and you three get high on pixie dust?"

A chorus of giggles answered me, even from the older cop. My husband flashed me his best smile. "You slipped off while I was working. You only have yourself to blame."

I eliminated a light dusting of C-grade

dust as the culprit; it put Quinn in a better mood but didn't change his base personality. A full dose of C-grade made him more likely to smile and take it easy on those around him. I had found the change disconcerting enough I hadn't wanted to give him B or better.

"You shouldn't have been paying so much attention to your phone, then." Would Quinn turn out to be one of those who people were determined to make everyone around him as happy as he was? If B or better turned him into a giggling, kitten adoring mess, what *would* A+++ do to him? My curiosity would lead us to a dark—and sexy—place. I'd need a lot of neutralizer before I experimented with felony-level drug administration on my husband. "Can we go home?"

Quinn leaned back in his chair so his head rested against my stomach. "Yes, we can leave. Up for driving the rest of the way? We can work if you're driving."

Oh boy. Three cops high on pixie dust trying to do serious work would likely lead to hilarity at the station later. Hilarity I hoped I would get to watch. "Seems fair since I slept on the way to Richmond. I might stink the station out if I don't get a shower, though."

The smoldering look my husband shot me made me want to drag him somewhere semi-private. "I can help—"

Nilman jabbed Quinn in the ribs with his elbow. "No, sir. You can't help her."

"But—"

Perky joined in, slapping Quinn upside the head. "No."

Kitten video forgotten, the three degenerated to elbow jabs, finger pointing, and kicks under the table, giggling the entire time. I opened my mouth, snapped my teeth together with a clack, and waited. Waiting didn't change anything. I suspected they had rules to their odd brawl. They remained seated, their faces were off-limits, and they seemed intent on some goal.

It took me a few minutes to determine they were trying to tickle each other and failing miserably at it.

I checked their coffee cups to discover them empty. Leaving the men to their play fight, I disposed of the cups, headed for the cafe, and dug out my CDC identification card, holding it out to the young woman at the counter. "I'm the responsible adult driving the three idiot cops home. What grade did they take?"

The barista chuckled, looked over my card, and handed it back to me. "A+, ma'am. A gentleman was in here earlier and paid for their coffee, asking me to dust their drinks."

Considering one of Quinn's grandfathers

was upstairs, I had my suspicions. "Did the gentleman happen to lack a head?"

She grinned, put her finger to her lips, and nodded.

Damned angels. "Thanks. I'll make sure they make it home without menacing someone."

"They've been very well behaved."

I cast a doubtful look at the three men engaged in a tickle battle. "Well, they're very happy now, that's for sure."

"The pretty one was very anxious after you left. He needed a little liquid joy."

Good old pixie dust, controller of depression, easer of anxiety, tester of patience. "Good to know. Thanks. Have yourself a good day."

I returned to the table and sighed. "Come on, then. I need to get you three to work." Would the dust wear off in time? If it didn't, what would I tell the other cops at the station? The complaints would come in early and often. A slightly happy Quinn unnerved me. A giggling one skewed my perception of reality and stirred all sorts of bad thoughts. If I ditched Perky and Nilman, I'd regret it sometime after I got Quinn somewhere alone.

They ignored me. I made a mental note to suggest the CDC classify A+ pixie dust as a controlled substance rather than a devilishly expensive one. Then again, I knew how much Sylvester had paid to make my life interesting.

"Worth it," the angel murmured in my ear.

Too startled to scream, I whirled around. "You!"

"Indeed."

"Why would you do this to me?" I pointed at the three men who were oblivious an angel had just popped into existence nearby.

"How could I watch my precious grandson mope when you left without him? He needed to stop whining, so I bought them coffee. I may have whispered a few suggestions to his friend to convince him they really needed a refill of coffee while they waited."

"You poured several hundred dollars worth of pixie dust down their throats to stop Quinn from whining?"

"Consider it part of my wedding gift to you."

"Your wedding gift is giving me three punch drunk men to babysit?"

"One of them will provide you with certain amusements in due time. He was sulking. I couldn't just let him sulk while you dealt with business."

"That really doesn't explain why Perky and Nilman are so, so happy right now."

"My little grandson needed someone to play with."

"I left them alone for *maybe* an hour. They would have survived." I sighed, hung my head, and willed myself to have patience.

"A man shouldn't be sad on his wedding day."

"I'll remember this, Sylvester," I promised.

"You are so entertaining." The angel fled in a burst of golden light, probably to avoid my wrath. Sneaky, wicked angel.

Unless I intervened, I doubted the three cops would leave the cafeteria, happy to play like children while being amused by the smallest things. "All right, you three. It's time to go."

Quinn flashed his panty-igniting smile in my direction. "Hi, beautiful."

Okay. Maybe I could find a few minutes to drag him into a stairwell first. No one would notice, except the security guys monitoring the cameras. Damn it. "If you don't get in the car, I can't take you home, Quinn."

While pixie dust could short circuit someone in a hurry, it didn't completely remove their ability to reason and connect the dots. Quinn moved fast when he wanted to and was halfway to the door before I realized he had left his phone and wallet on the table. I gathered his belongings while Perky cracked up laughing.

"I think he wants to go home for some reason. I wonder why that might be."

Men. "In reality, he's going to work so he can pester everyone at the station."

"That's funny."

"You're going to work, too."

"Work sounds like fun. Let's go to work, Nilman!"

The pair jumped to their feet and hurried after Quinn, leaving their phones and wallets behind, too. I sighed, gathered their things, and checked the seats and floor for anything else they had dropped during their playful excitement.

Maybe I wouldn't give Quinn the good stuff after all. I considered hunting down some neutralizer to restore the men to sanity. I sighed and gave up. Who was I to ruin their harmless fun?

EIGHTEEN

If someone doesn't bring me neutralizer in the next five minutes, there will be bodies stashed in the nearest stairwell.

IF QUINN, Perky, and Nilman sang another note of a children's song, I would become a serial killer and a widow at the same time. Easing the SUV into a parking spot at the station, I killed the engine and regarded my passengers with narrowed eyes. Of the three, Nilman seemed the most sober. I turned my glare to him. "So help me, if someone doesn't bring me neutralizer in the next five minutes, there will be bodies stashed in the nearest stairwell."

The older cop smiled at me. "Look at them, Gardener. They're so happy. How could you take their happiness away? It's so rare."

Nilman was happy, too, but instead of reminding him of that, I turned around in my seat and banged my head into the steering wheel. "Get the hell out of the car."

It took a lot of work to herd the three smiling men to the eighth floor. *Everyone* wanted something from Quinn, who was quite happy to volunteer to help with even the smallest task. After five stops on the way to the elevator, my husband had given himself at least five hours of work.

I hoped it was work he actually needed to do. Under the influence of A+ pixie dust, he'd enjoy doing anything anyone threw his way. At least it wouldn't compromise his ability to realize someone was giving him an order he *shouldn't* comply with. It would impair his base ability to refuse requests, but it wouldn't force him to act against his nature.

If angels had necks, I would have wrung Sylvester's with my hands and enjoyed every minute of it. Immortals wouldn't die from a mere strangulation. I could indulge for hours without any harm done. I'd enjoy it.

On the eighth floor, Quinn's cops gaped at us while I herded my trio of miscreants to their desks and locked my new husband in his office. Turning and pressing my back to the door, I glared at the cops. "Get. Me. Neutralizer."

Everyone stared at me in dead silence, doing a fair imitation of statues. Great. They probably thought I had lost my mind.

"Three choices: I kill you all, I swear never to make any of you a single cup of coffee as long as I live, or you get me neutralizer right now."

My threats needed work. People weren't supposed to laugh when I issued them. I sighed. "*Please*."

Amanda stepped away from her desk, grinning so wide her face had to hurt. "How much do you need?"

"A spoonful in a cup of coffee each should work. Make it an espresso."

The woman laughed. "We don't know how to use the machine."

Screaming my frustration, I pointed at the nearest cop, one of the younger men. "You. Do not let Chief Quinn out of his office." I picked two other victims and pointed at them in turn. "Keep those other two at their desks. Pretend they're little kids. Give them candy or something."

The three saluted, and my first volunteer replied, "Yes, ma'am!"

In retrospect, giving the cops a good coffee machine without teaching them how to use it classified as cruel and unusual punishment. I could kill multiple birds with a single stone. "All right. The rest of you, fall in. Time to learn how to make coffee."

A few whoops answered me, and with a herd of eager cops in tow, I descended on their new machine. Suzy sat on the counter with a half-filled pot. I hissed at it.

Suzy's time would end soon enough—after I restored Quinn, Perky, and Nilman to sanity.

"Pay attention, but I'll be here to teach you how the whole thing works after I sober the three idiots up."

The break room couldn't fit everyone, although they made a valiant effort to cram as many bodies into the space as possible. Armed with three espressos spiked with neutralizer, I delivered them to my intended targets. It didn't take much to convince them to drink. Within five minutes, the neutralizer would do its job and counter the worst of their pixie-dust high. I turned to the rest of the cops. "Chief Quinn never gets A or higher grade pixie dust again. Ever."

I'd think long and hard about using a tiny bit of the dust stashed in my bra in the safety of his home with neutralizer on hand. If I gave him a hit of the truly good stuff, I could make sure no one learned of it.

When I was certain they drank down every last drop of their coffee, I turned to their volunteered babysitters. "Watch them until they stop giggling."

In a way, I envied the high threesome. Why couldn't I benefit from a small hit of instant joy? I sighed and headed back to the break room. "Just this once, I will make you all a cup of coffee, but in exchange, you need to teach everyone else in the building how to use the machine."

My plan to spread the love of coffee would have worked a lot better if someone hadn't opened their big mouth and spread the word I was on the eighth floor teaching people how to get a good fix of java.

SINCE PIXIE DUST didn't come bundled with a low, ten minutes after I got the espresso into them, Quinn, Perky, and Nilman went to work as though nothing had happened, still in a good mood, but otherwise oblivious to their high. While tired, they dove into their jobs with the same cheerful determination as someone dosed with a mild hit of C-grade dust.

It would do.

Five hours of dealing with an endless stream of cops eager to have a good cup of coffee convinced me I definitely never wanted to work as a barista ever again. As soon as the tides shifted and the cops no longer needed my help to play with the coffee machine, I headed for Quinn's office. It took another twenty minutes of waiting before he got off the phone. I let myself into his office. "Do you still have the room at the Plaza?"

"Indeed we do. I decided to reserve it for a week before we left for Virginia."

I came to a decision, and it involved the vial hiding in my cleavage. "I dealt with six hours of listening to you sing about beer on a wall and wheels on a bus. You owe me, Quinn."

A sly smile creased my husband's lips. "Okay. I'll ask someone to drive us to the hotel."

"I need a favor."

"Oh?"

"I'm going to need a vial of neutralizer." When I dosed him with the good pixie dust, I needed to get him down from the high after I finished making him the happiest of men.

"All right. What quality?"

"Best you have."

"Why? Should I be worried?"

"I'm going to commit a felony tonight while making you the happiest man on Earth." Consent was important. I didn't know anyone who would reject such an offer, but with Quinn, I never knew.

His eyes widened. "Oh."

"The neutralizer, Chief Quinn."

When motivated, he moved fast. Within five minutes, I had a mason jar filled with pink powder. He also brought an unlabeled pill bottle with him. "D grade transformative. I thought it might be useful for you. There are a hundred pills in the bottle. Try not to abuse your unicorn privileges too much."

I took the jar and bottle, set them on Quinn's desk, and snatched a tissue from the box. Fishing out some of the pills, I wrapped them up. After a brief search, I located plastic bags in a drawer. Later I'd find a better way to keep them close at hand. The pills joined the vial in my bra. "You filed the papers to give me these properly?"

"Of course. What do you take me for?"

"A man hoping I'll need an entire mason jar of neutralizer."

"Can you blame me?"

"Yes. Let's get out of here. Between the drive and teaching your cops how to make coffee, you really owe me. March, Chief Quinn. It's time for you to pay up."

I loved the way he smiled at me.

EVERYTHING WENT ACCORDING to plan until Quinn decided he wanted to make plans of his own. I left him in the lobby talking to the concierge about something he promised I'd like a lot if I gave him five minutes alone to complete his scheming. The playful gleam in his eye intrigued me enough I agreed and headed up to our room.

I'd use the few extra minutes preparing the pixie dust for his consumption. I'd also change into one of the bathrobes so he'd have a soft, fluffy package to unwrap. Smiling at the thought, I swiped the key card for our room and opened the door. A pop startled me, bright blue powder puffed in my face, and within three breaths, someone turned all the lights out.

The world was blurred around me, and I had the faint sense of people nearby—and something not quite human, too. A feeling of wrongness clung to me, but every time I realized something was amiss, something soft and warm sucked me back into the darkness.

When I finally clawed my way free of the smothering, comfortable lethargy, spurred by the sense of something not being quite right, my ears rang and my entire body hurt. I groaned.

Ouch, ouch, ouch.

Why couldn't I go an entire week without someone or something cleaning my clock? I blamed Quinn. The closer I got to sharing a bed with him, the worse my circumstances became. Then again, I wouldn't change anything. He was worth it. However, we needed to have a long talk about his cursed luck.

"She's awake, Mistress." A man giggled

from somewhere disconcertingly close to me. "Can I play with her now? Please? I've been good."

Oh hell no. No, no, no. The only man I wanted playing with me was Quinn, and he wasn't Quinn; his voice was too deep. My attention turned from my aching body to the man who wanted to play with me. I wanted to tense, but my muscles hurt enough I remained limp.

Would Sylvester's fancy golden tattoo bracelet work? Where was I? What had happened? I remembered a pop followed by a big, black nothing.

Not good.

A soft, feminine voice laughed, and I recognized the sound. Yippee. I needed to have a long talk with Quinn about his ex-wife. Of course, if I had my way, we'd be having the discussion over Audrey's corpse. It counted as self-defense if I killed her while escaping, right? I cracked open an eye.

As a human, Audrey had been pretty, a good match for Quinn in appearances. Becoming a gorgon had changed her, giving her skin a gray-green cast, narrowing her face, and giving her cheekbones a sharp edge. Her smile revealed a pair of fangs, and a writhing mass of black snakes coiled around her head.

If the kings and princes of the gorgon world had venomous snakes for hair, Audrey appeared harmless although uglier than sin. She didn't wear sunglasses or a shroud, which made me wonder. I thought I remembered someone mentioning some gorgons were so weak they could easily learn to control their powers, petrifying their victims only when their emotions were heightened, including during sex—or when they bit someone. Was the male her gorgon lover? That would also explain the lack of a shroud. Peeking through my lashes, I checked.

Nope. I recognized the incubus, although the last time I'd seen him, he'd been tangled with three human women in a bar. Wonderful. Why wasn't the incubus a statue? Was Audrey really that impotent, or had she somehow learned to control her gaze, petrifying her victims only when she wanted rather than by accident?

If she had become a gorgon through exposure to gorgon dust, she should have been able to petrify even other gorgons.

The incubus knelt beside me, his tail lashing from side to side while his wings quivered. He stared at Audrey with wide eyes. "Please, Mistress? Can I play with our harem queen now? I've been waiting, just like you wanted. She's awake."

I bit my lip so I wouldn't groan from a mix of pain and disgust. Since they knew I was awake anyway, I forced my eyes open all the way and took a good look around. Musty, threadbare blankets, check. Abandoned warehouse-like building, check. An incubus reduced to an adoring teenager in lust, check. Evil ex-wife gloating over me, check.

I wiggled my hands and feet, and with a little experimentation, I determined they hadn't tied me up or removed my clothes. A quick glance down my cleavage revealed the pixie dust vial and the pills remained where I'd stashed them. The number of felonies I could commit within ten minutes would enter the double digits. Would I get off with a light or suspended sentence if I committed them escaping a gorgon and an incubus working together? Self-defense went a long way as justifiable motive, but would the law bend enough in my favor?

Quinn would still love me if I broke more laws, right? I could afford bail at least.

Yippee.

"Give her a few minutes, darling. She's still sleepy. Be gentle when you play with her. Soon she'll be our harem queen, but we need to wait a little while longer." Audrey leaned over and kissed the incubus's cheek. "You've been so good."

The incubus pulled the gorgon into his embrace, covered her with his wings, and did things to her that made her moan. I shuddered. Ew, no. No, no, no.

In the future, I'd remember there were worst fates than catching people in compromising positions when I worked my magic. Then again, my magic could still be biting me in the ass in the form of Quinn's ex-wife being obsessed with me having her babies.

When the pair separated, the incubus relaxed. Audrey straightened her clothes.

"Yes, Mistress. Soon." The incubus smiled with wide-eyed innocence, which creeped me out considering the creature specialized in having sex with anything that moved.

Audrey's attention turned to me. "It's been a while, Bailey. I'm pleased you handled my dust so well. We'll make beautiful children together. I knew you'd be perfect." Like her incubus, she smiled, but instead of child-like innocence, I preferred to think of her expression as the purest form of bat-shit crazy. "Aren't you grateful? You'll get to be a mother. I've heard how no one else wants you. No friends. No family who cares for you. I'll take care of you, and so will Lexington. You saved me from a terrible marriage. Until you, I wasn't free. Now I am."

Wow. What was she on? First, she gave her brother a bomb loaded with gorgon dust. Second, she viewed marriage to Quinn as terrible. Sure, Quinn and I hadn't gotten along so well from the start, but that was as much my fault as his, and even when we'd been busy dodging each other, I'd lusted for him.

Quinn's officers respected him because he was a genuinely good person who worked hard for the sake of others. Everything I knew about Quinn pointed in the same direction.

Him being part angel didn't hurt his case, either.

I swallowed, and it took a little effort to make my dry mouth and tongue cooperate enough to speak. "You gave your brother the cell phone with the gorgon dust in it."

"Yes. I asked him to talk to you and give you the phone. He didn't find out what he had given you until later. It's a pity he didn't approve of my plans. He would have made a good sire for my sisters' children. He refused. Poor Magnus. All he would have had to do was take in a single breath of my dust. He could have shared eternity with me and my sisters. Why did he refuse?"

Tears welled up in the gorgon's eyes and fell down her gray-green cheeks. Had she actually killed her own brother? The woman needed a permanent stay at a mental institution. I decided informing her I was the new Mrs. Quinn would be a really, really bad idea. I'd also use my newfound skills at being a polite adult to avoid her wrath. "I'm sorry."

I even spoke the truth. No one deserved to

be murdered for refusing to become a gorgon's reproduction toy, and from my understanding of the situation, Magnus McGee hadn't had a good death.

She had left him the way I had found her with her college stud, and no one deserved that.

Audrey wiped her tears away and smiled at me. "We got off to a poor start. I'm Audrey McGee. You're a very special woman. I've been watching you for months."

Okay, that was creepy. "You've been watching me?"

"I needed to protect you from that vile man after he coerced you into sharing a room with him. If I left you alone with him, he would have worked his evil magic on you and lured you to his bed."

The crazy ex-wife's insanity rating went up another level. I needed to remain polite. Laughing hysterically at her assumptions wouldn't do me any good. "That would be tragic."

Crap. Mouthing off to my kidnapper was *not* polite or wise.

"Yes, it would be."

Wow. How had she not noticed my use of sarcasm? My mouthing off skills needed work. "Right."

She smiled, showing off her snake-like fangs. "Your virgin body will bring our children into the world. I can't allow him to taint you."

The incubus's expression changed, but he remained quiet. He knew. He knew I wasn't a virgin anymore. Instead of telling Audrey, he stretched his wings and wrapped them around his body.

"Why me?" I whispered.

"No one will be able to oppose our children. My powers and your immunity will give them everything they need to thrive. Through them, we will rule the world."

Next time, I wouldn't ask stupid questions. Stupid questions had stupid answers, and it took every scrap of my self-restraint to keep from bursting out into helpless laughter. She thought she could rule the world with *my* contribution of genes? Did she not know of Quinn's relatives?

I couldn't think of a single thing to say. Audrey seemed to interpret my silence as agreement. She straightened, waved, and left, strolling to a door across the empty warehouse.

The incubus turned to me and unfurled his wings. "Time to play," he cooed.

Oh crap.

NINETEEN

The incubus wanted to play poker.

THE INCUBUS PULLED a deck of cards out of his pants, and I gaped at him while he shuffled. My stunned silence lasted until he cleared space between us and started dealing. At first I thought he meant for us to play Blackjack, but then he started dropping cards in the river.

By play, he had meant *cards*? Not just cards, poker.

The incubus wanted to play poker with me. He seemed to have missed the memo that it was a betting game, but I went along with it anyway, at a complete loss of what else to do. Play to an incubus always involved sex.

Why were we playing poker?

After the second hand, the absurdity of my situation hit home along with a skull-splitting headache. The incubus exhibited a few of the classic symptoms of high-grade pixie-dust intoxication, including suppressed willpower and child-like tendencies, but I was worried something else was influencing the incubus.

An incubus high on pixie dust sought out lovers, and anyone would do. They lost control of their powers, influencing everyone in their maximum range. Most incubi were banned from having pixie dust, and the ones who got it enjoyed it under very controlled situations.

A+++ pixie dust would create complete and total chaos centered around the incubus, and I'd get a full blast of it. If I could transform into a unicorn, maybe I'd escape without having to put Sylvester's bracelet to the test. I gulped. Would the angelic magic work on an incubus so high he'd touch the heavens?

If I stuck around too long, I'd find out what it'd be like to have an incubus's full attention, which would be even harder to resist. No matter what, I needed to get out of the warehouse and as far away as possible.

"Hey. Can I leave now?"

The incubus looked up from his cards. "Oh no, my beloved harem queen. The mistress would get mad at me."

Right, of course. I should have known. I resisted the urge to roll my eyes, stare at the ceiling, and pray for patience. I ended up praying for patience but didn't expect an answer. If I couldn't leave without having to fight an incubus, maybe I could get some information out of him. "So, how long have you been with your mistress?"

"Oh, I don't know how long. I'm blessed. She wants me to father her children."

What kind of children was Audrey expecting to have? If an angel, an incubus, and a human made a human, *the* Sphinx and Anubis made a human, a gorgon and a centaur made a human, I suspected a gorgon and an incubus using me as their surrogate would also produce a human—or a lot of humans born from gorgon eggs.

Hell no. Over my dead body. Since there was no way in hell I'd be involved in such a sick threesome, committing felonies was my only option. I'd start with the illegal handling of pixie dust. I'd add to that with the very illegal intentional overdosing of transformative substances. At least I'd be able to write that one off; I'd be taking the pills instead of forcing them on someone, but I could lose my certification over it. Bonus.

I *could* try to get a pill or two down the incubus's throat and hope they cancelled his seductive powers, but I doubted they would work. A higher grade might, but D grade pills wouldn't do much to him. I'd be better off overdosing myself and seeing what happened. Maybe I'd shift faster, maybe I'd flare and burn hotter than normal. I had no idea what would actually happen.

Some risks were worth taking.

Once I busted out of the warehouse, I'd make my escape. If Audrey tried to stop me, I'd put an end to her idiocy.

First, I needed to make sure the incubus wasn't packing anything other than his sex drive and desire to spread the love. "How about we play a spicier game?"

I captured his undivided attention. "What game, my queen?"

The real idiot was me for even suggesting a game of strip poker to an incubus. I hoped Quinn would forgive me. "How about strip poker?"

Heat built in my body, the kind I only wanted to be from Quinn's hands on me. I clenched my teeth and ignored the stirring of my desires. I would not do any sort of dance with an incubus. I just needed to get him naked to make sure he wasn't carrying any weapons. If he had weapons, I might be able to get hold of one.

I would not succumb to a damned incubus, no matter what.

"That's my favorite type of poker," he purred, soft and seductive.

I bet it was. "Deal the cards."

He did, and I concentrated on winning every hand. Fortunately for me, incubi lived to lose at games like strip poker, and within five hands, I had him down to his socks.

Holy hell. No wonder women jumped at a chance to be with an incubus. The creature's sculpted beauty went from head to toe, and he wasn't at all shy about giving me a show to stoke my interest in him.

Yep, Quinn had definitely gotten more than his fair share of genes from his incubus grandfather. I'd thank God for that later—after I escaped. Of course, Quinn wouldn't be happy with me for working up an incubus and trusting a shiny gold tattoo to keep me out of trouble long enough to make my break. Then I'd have to stay out of trouble until I reversed to human shape, hunted Quinn down, and found relief in his bed.

He wouldn't mind that part of my plan, right? He'd understand. I didn't want the incubus. I just needed to dose him long enough I could rescue myself. At least the actual orgy I'd trigger when I dosed the incubus with the good pixie dust wouldn't count as a felony; if anyone charged me with anything, I'd get off with a misdemeanor.

I lost the next hand on purpose, breaking a pair of aces and hoping he could beat my pair of fours. He won, and I made a show of taking off my sock. I wrinkled my nose at its stench and flicked my wrist. I hadn't meant to be seductive, but the incubus's eyes flashed anyway.

"You're going to make me work to see you in your full glory, aren't you?" he purred. "I can't wait to taste you."

Hell no. My body squealed a different tune, but I fought to ignore the temptation. With me letting him win, it didn't take long for me to lose my shirt. In a show of shyness, I turned my back to the incubus.

He slid his hand beneath the material and ran his fingertips along the curve of my spine, helping me remove my shirt. The instant it was over my head, I shucked the fabric off my arms, dipped my hand into my bra, and pulled out the vial and baggie of pills.

I should have known the incubus would undo the clasp of my bra. Crap, crap, crap. In my panic, I tore into the plastic bag, and popped all the pills I grabbed at once. While I choked them down, I ripped off the red wax sealing the vial, flipped off the cap with my thumb, and showered the entire contents over me and the incubus.

I'd only needed a little.

Crap, crap, crap.

WHILE I'D TAKEN transformative pills of all grades, I'd never taken more than one at a time. The incubus's lust blasted through me and waged a brutal, messy war with my body's need to change shapes.

The pills won. Their magic tore through me and began the transformation process moments after I swallowed them. I screamed as all my bones shattered at the same time. A convulsion ripped through me, and my body contorted as my limbs lengthened and combusted into living flame.

I burned, and the musty bedding ignited.

While I cursed and thrashed in the throes of shapeshifting, the incubus moaned, a sound of pure lust and need. Panic seized me, and before my body finished changing shape, I surged to my hooves.

I belonged to Quinn. Quinn belonged to me. I wouldn't allow a smoldering, moaning incubus to take him from me. The creature tempted me; he could stoke my flames higher and bring pleasure and release.

I bolted across the warehouse, lowered my head, and charged the steel door. Either I'd bust out or I'd break my neck, but I wouldn't fall to the incubus. I belonged to Quinn until my last breath.

Right before impact, I closed my eyes. *Thwack.*

The door won.

Ouch.

Not only had the door won, my horn slid

into the metal until my forehead slammed into the steel. My hindquarters dipped, and my hind hooves cracked into the door. Somehow, I didn't break my neck although I wasn't convinced I hadn't cracked my skull open.

Ouch, ouch, ouch.

My neck and spine throbbed from my introduction to the door. With a shudder, I unsheathed my claws and situated my hooves beneath me. Once upright, I pulled.

My horn refused to budge. The hinges groaned, and metal shrieked. Step by step, I backed up. Instead of pulling free, I popped the door off its hinges and out of its frame. I flattened my ears and snorted my displeasure at my unwanted adornment.

How the hell was I supposed to escape the warehouse with a door stuck to my head?

Behind me, the incubus moaned, spreading lust through me, my body demanding I surrender to him. I needed him, my desire so strong I ached.

No, no, no. I would not give myself to a high incubus whose name wasn't 'Quinn.' I wouldn't give myself to the incubus, no matter how much pleasure he offered. Crap. Not a good thought, not a good thought at all. I needed out before I discovered how an incubus made love to a unicorn. It probably involved shapeshifting and becoming the world's sexiest stallion.

I turned my furry ass around, used the door as a shield, and backed through the doorway.

Clang.

Crap.

Of course I'd get the door stuck in its frame. At least I had a nice metal barrier keeping the incubus from touching me. If he touched me, I'd lose. If the bracelet didn't work, I'd be in a lot of trouble.

"Come to me, beloved harem queen," he purred, and my lust and desire intensified.

"In-cu-bus go play with miss-tress. Miss-tress. Miss-tress wants you. Bad. Wants you bad."

I wanted him bad. It took every tattered bit of my willpower to keep from whimpering or moaning. I burned, and the stench of heating metal filled my nose. I tried to step back, but the door remained lodged in its frame and stuck to my horn. Jerking my head back shifted my improvised shield.

"Come to me. I'll enjoy you first, then I'll enjoy you both together. You'll enjoy it, I promise."

Not good. Not good at all—or really good, if I wanted a wild fling with a walking, talking sex machine.

I only needed one man: Quinn. Quinn, Quinn, Quinn. Married-to-me, heaven and hell rolled together in one delicious package

Quinn. I snorted, and flame blossomed over the door.

"Why do you deny yourself? You know you want me." The sound of the incubus's voice drew closer.

I did. I wanted him so much it hurt. I also wanted to bash his face in with the door lodged on my horn. I gathered my muscles, gave in to the need to get closer to him, and lunged forward, claws unsheathed so I could shove the door across the warehouse's concrete floor.

I hit the incubus at full speed, and the impact knocked me off my hooves and dislodged the door from my horn. I fell in a tangle of arms, legs, and incubus wings; his tail slithered over my fur and ignited lust deep within.

A squeal burst out of me. Oh God, I needed more. Not fair. Not fair at all.

My body demanded I stay while the rest of me flailed in incoherent panic. If I didn't get out of the building, I'd end up rubbing all over the wrong man. Incubus. Whatever.

I stabbed him with my horn, mauled him with my claws, and turned his moans into screams. His hold on me weakened enough I could get to my hooves and bolt for the door. I kicked my hind hooves and flashed my claws at him in warning of what I'd do if he tried to impede my escape.

Running like a bat out of hell, I hit the asphalt outside so fast my claws sparked and embers flew from my fur. I surged across the empty parking lot towards the road.

Quinn, Quinn, Quinn.

I chanted his name to keep from turning around and begging the incubus to forgive me for clawing him and kicking him and stabbing him before pleading for him to take me on the warehouse floor to make up for my violence.

If I'd been paying a little more attention to where I was running rather than fantasizing about throwing myself on the nearest male, preferably Quinn, I wouldn't have collided with a transport. I bounced off its grill, got tossed like I weighed nothing, and smacked to the sidewalk on my side. I rolled, tucking my hooves close to my body so I wouldn't break a leg. Gouts of flame flared from my coat. The concrete sizzled and melted beneath me.

Lesson learned: getting sideswiped by a transport cured incubus-inspired lust. It also hurt like hell. The transport's brakes squealed.

Great. Now the truck driver would end up having the night of their life. I staggered to my hooves. Maybe they'd leave before the incubus recovered. I doubted it. Shaking out my coat, I limped away from the warehouse and the road. I'd already avoided one sexy incubus bullet, and I wanted to get the hell out of Dodge while I still could.

"Sor-ree, truck dri-ver. Have fun. Please. Much fun, long time."

No court would convict me, right? Well, at least not for running away from the sex-crazed incubus. Fleeing the site of an accident would get me into trouble. So would pouring an entire vial of the best pixie dust in the world on an incubus.

The truck driver would get a hit of the pixie dust the instant the incubus went on the hunt for a partner and discovered them near the warehouse. They wouldn't be responsible, nor would they have to spend a fortune on the high. They would also have one hell of a story to tell later.

Maybe Mary had been right all along. Looking on the bright side helped.

THE INCUBUS'S influence returned after I staggered away from the transport, and it took two long, dark blocks of abandoned warehouses for it to fade away. I spent at least an hour shivering in an alley before the heat of my lust ebbed enough I was willing to face anyone of any species.

Most women and men would consider me

crazy, especially since unexpected dalliances with an incubus or succubus didn't count as cheating. Maybe Sylvester's magical ball and chain had helped me get away. I'd probably never know.

All that mattered was I *had* gotten away without rubbing all over the incubus. I even felt a little guilt over hitting him with a door, slicing into him with my claws, and stabbing him with my horn. It wasn't *his* fault I happened to have pixie dust tucked in my cleavage. It wasn't his fault Audrey hadn't been smart enough to search me for potential weapons.

The temperature dropped. My shivers strengthened to full-body shaking. I shifted my weight from hoof to hoof in an effort to warm myself. The cold air bit my nose, and the musky stench of live gorgons tainted the wind. Audrey's mention of sisters worried me. If they had a full hive of three to seven females, their smell would permeate the air within a mile of their lair.

An abandoned warehouse district was a sensible site for their home. The neighbors wouldn't complain, and they'd have all the space they needed for raising their whelps without accidentally petrifying someone. I doubted they had a male, needing to rely on an incubus—and me—for their breeding purposes. I shuddered.

One determined female could spawn enough whelps to establish a full clan—*if* she had a male of the right species. What would tossing an incubus into the mix do? I wasn't sure I wanted to know. No, I knew I didn't want to know.

I wanted to go home.

If I was lucky, Audrey would find a willing surrogate. Then she and her sisters could keep their pet incubus busy for months to come. I wondered how she had managed to avoid petrifying him. Was she simply that weak, or was there something else to it?

Quinn's cousin had left chaos in his wake in the bar, and from what I gathered, he hadn't been involved with the incubus in the first place but was merely another victim of lust.

Screw it. I'd worry about it later. I needed to find somewhere warm and cozy to take a nap. After a nap, I'd deal with my gorgon problem. Warm places to sleep made everything better. I trudged out of the alley, my legs quivering beneath me. Sirens wailed in the distance and drew closer. I pricked my ears forward.

Sirens meant vehicles. Vehicles meant engines and cops. Cops meant jail. Car engines were warm, and so were jails.

Score.

I followed the sounds. The flash of red

and blue lights splashing onto the empty warehouses led me back to the transport. Four cruisers surrounded the vehicle I'd crashed into. I could smell the heat and gasoline, and with a happy purr, I rubbed against the nearest car in my effort to steal its warmth. I was vaguely aware of cops gaping at me. They weren't from the NYPD, and disappointment surged through me. Their uniforms weren't quite right, and a quick glance confirmed the cars weren't the right model and design, either.

The engine wasn't warm enough. With a low, desperate moan for its elusive heat, I circled the cruiser. The driver's side window was down, so I shoved my head and horn inside, careful not to stab anyone or anything. I ignored the driver's startled protests and lipped at the climate controls. Once I had the heat blasting, I closed my eyes and basked in the warmth.

WHILE MY ABILITY TO become a unicorn embarrassed me as often as not, I enjoyed the advantages of my big, furry ass. When I didn't want to move, no natural force on Earth could move me. The cops tried and failed, and I lipped at the vents in a wordless plea for more heat. When the woman I had trapped realized she could open the door and squeeze out, I shifted to the side enough to give her space without losing the little warmth I had managed to steal from the vehicle. I still shivered but breathing in the heated air helped.

"There's a unicorn in my car," the woman blurted.

I couldn't blame her for her incredulous tone. If I were her, I'd be pretty surprised, too.

"An injured one from the looks of it. I'm pretty sure that's blood all over its legs. I'm getting the feeling our driver didn't hit a deer," a man replied. A moment later, a hand touched my shoulder. It hurt. I flattened my ears and snorted.

I was too cold to blow smoke and too sleepy to kick him. The cop would survive his familiarity without a nip—as long as he kept his hands to acceptable places. I'd stomp on him if he tried any funny business.

"Seems friendly enough. Who the hell do we call about a unicorn?"

"Do we even need to call someone?" the woman asked. "It's not like we charge deer for running out in front of cars, so why would we prosecute a unicorn? I mean, it's basically a deer with a fancy horn."

"The incubus probably startled it into running across the street. The timing is about right."

I liked these cops, providing me with such a useful—and true—alibi. "C-c-cold," I whined. Nuzzling the vent didn't make it blow hotter air, much to my disappointment.

"Melissa? The unicorn can talk, and it's apparently cold."

Silence.

"Okay." The woman sighed. "I'll go get the shock blanket out of the trunk."

Within a few moments, the cruiser shook and she slammed the trunk closed. I closed my eyes and stomped a hoof, contemplating taking a nap. The cops wouldn't mind too much, would they? They had cop things to do with the transport. A short nap wouldn't hurt anything.

One of the cops tossed the blanket across my back, and while it didn't cover much of me, it helped. I mumbled a thanks, lifted a hind hoof, and yawned.

"It's trying to talk, Melissa."

"What's it saying?"

"Not sure. It's mumbling."

"I'll go ask Fredrick. Maybe he can put that fancy degree he likes bragging about to good use for once in his life," Officer Melissa grumbled.

A few startled curses announced the arrival of more cops.

"Jesus Christ! That's a cindercorn. Where the hell did it come from?"

Cool. My breed had a nifty nickname. I liked it. I liked cinders, too. Yummy, delicious warm cinders.

"So, what do we do with it?"

"For starters, pray it doesn't eat you. Call animal control, tell them we have an exotic, pyromaniac carnivore we need captured and taken out."

I didn't like the sound of that at all. "No, don't take me out. Out cold. Cold, cold, cold. Want fire. Be good for fire? Fire? Please? Fire?"

"And I never would have guessed they could talk."

"Cold," I insisted.

"All right. The cindercorn is apparently cold and has its head stuck in your car. I've got nothing, Mel. Did you really put a blanket on it?"

"It was cold. What else were we supposed to do? Is this cindercorn a risk?"

"You hear about 120 Wall Street?"

"Who hasn't?"

"That was the work of a cindercorn."

Silence. I would have preened but posturing took too much effort.

"I'm sure it'll be fine. Just don't piss it off. Maybe it'll get bored and wander off?"

"How did the NYPD deal with their cindercorn problem?"

"Theirs wasn't a problem, for starters—

they didn't have a wild animal. I'm not sure about the details, but I think it was one of their agents maybe? Anyway, I think they used blowtorches and a spotlight or heat lamp."

Officer Melissa sighed. "Hell, why not? We've had an incubus on a high tonight already. A cindercorn needing a heat lamp is nothing compared to that."

No kidding.

TWENTY

You can eat this nice steak instead of my hand.

A HEAT LAMP lured me out of the cruiser. With a contented sigh, I curled around it and went to sleep. A stronger source of heat roused me, and I lifted my head seeking it. A bright point of fire caught my eye. I staggered to my feet to get closer to it. A cop dangled a raw, bloody piece of steak in front of a blow-torch, and the scent of searing meat woke my hunger. I pursued the man to a horse trailer, snapping my teeth at the treat.

"That's right, come on in. I got some nice warm blankets for you in here, and you can eat this nice steak instead of my hand," he murmured, his tone soothing.

My desire for the steak got me into the trailer, and while I flattened my ears, I re-sisted the temptation to nip him. I took the steak gently with my teeth and held it in my mouth while hunting for a spot to set it down so I could rip chunks off it. I spotted a generator near the back of the trailer and plopped the steak on it, lifted my hoof, and pinned the meat so I could devour it.

Two braver cops strapped a horse blanket on me and added heated blankets on top of it. I licked the generator clean, my head nodding as the warmth seeped into me.

Instead of jail, the cops took me to a stable with an indoor arena. Large, overhead lamps heated the air, and a ring of heat lamps warmed a circle of sand. I waited long enough for an amused cop to strip the blankets off me before I charged the circle, hopped over a lamp, and went to work digging a hole so I could bury myself in the sand.

Perfect.

The cops needed a gold star or whatever they got when they did a good job. Tucking my hooves close to my body and resting my nose near my belly, I basked in the heat and returned to the serious business of dozing off. I cracked open an eye whenever anyone approached. Most of them were curious cops, and they stayed outside of my ring of heat lamps.

The two men in suits worried me. I lifted my head, turned my ears back, and bared my teeth in warning. Neither showed sign of leaving, and they stared at me. I stared back.

One of the cops joined the duo.

"You're definitely correct, Officer Andrews. That is definitely a blazer—a cindercorn, as you call it."

A second cop trudged across the sand and joined the group. "Did I miss anything?"

"No, sir. We've determined she's a female, but this is the first time she's been responsive or interested in us."

I assumed the new cop was a higher rank than the first to warrant the sir, so I focused my attention on him. "That's probably a good thing. Rumor has it the males are meaner."

Officer Andrews shrugged.

I snorted, and smoke trailed from my nostrils. "No proof. No close stud-ee. All stud-ee know is u-nee-corn eat meat, burn, like fire. Warm-er now. Thank you."

The humans stared at me in slack-jaw shock.

Was my talking *that* startling?

The higher-ranked cop sighed, lifted his hand, and pinched the bridge of his nose. "All right. There's only one talking, fire-breathing unicorn I know of, and she was kidnapped from New York last week. Eight days ago."

"Last week?" I squealed, lurching to my hooves and whinnying my alarm. "So long? Eight days? Where? Where?"

How could it have been so long? My mind blanked as I struggled to account for so many days.

"We're in Vermont."

I paced in a circle, whinnied again, and bucked so the world could witness my fury. "Ver-mont!"

Snorting smoke, I pawed at the sand and trembled with rage. I expected to lose a day or two due to the sedative, but the realization I'd been gone for eight days horrified me. What had happened to Quinn?

Was Quinn all right?

Officer Andrews gaped at me while the other cop pulled his cell from his pocket, dialed a number, and held it to his ear. "Request a copy of the Quinn file from the NYPD. We might have a hit. Can you confirm the key points about the woman taken from Chief Quinn's suite? In particular, I want to know if there was any evidence of A+ transformative substances—"

"D," I corrected. "D grade pills, may-be ten? May-be more? No re-mem-ber count, new stash. A+++ vial pixie dust, may-be broke. I cer-tee-fied with CDC."

There. I covered my furry ass. Maybe I wouldn't go to jail after all.

"It seems I'm being corrected. D grade trans, a possible vial of pixie dust, A+++. That does explain a lot. Yes, the unicorn is talking to us and appears to be coherent. When she was brought to the stable, she was rather lethargic. She bordered on non-responsive when she stuck her head in one of my cruisers."

I pricked my ears forward and stood still. "You chee-fuh of po-leese?"

"One moment, the unicorn is asking me a question. Yes, I'm the chief."

With a squeal, I tossed my head and stomped my hoof. "You bring me my chief, yes? Bring!"

"And now she's whinnying at me and demanding her chief. I'm assuming she means Chief Quinn, as she was in his hotel room."

Did they not know Quinn belonged to me? "Bring me Quinn. Mine. *Mine*. Bring. Bring my hus-band. Bring!"

Again, the men gawked at me. The chief recovered first and cleared his throat. "When you're getting information from the Quinn file, could you please inquire on Chief Quinn's marital status? In particular, could you ask if he is married to a unicorn?"

"You idiot. I human. Change back later. Call CDC. Pro-fess-ur Yale teach you proper care of u-nee-corn. You bring me my chief. Mine. No share. Mine."

The chief chuckled. "I'm being scolded by a unicorn, and she just called me an idiot."

"If you bring me my chief, I no call you idiot." I thought it was a reasonable offer, but if he was going to start cooperating, I'd give him some helpful advice on the proper care of a unicorn. "You bring me meat, I no call you idiot. You bring me nay-palm snack, I like you a lot. Cee-four? I like gas-oh-leen. Yes, bring me food. Hun-gree."

"I can't even make this shit up, but the unicorn is asking for meat, napalm, C4, and gasoline."

Satisfied the police chief understood my demands, I curled up in my hole, showed them my sharp, pointy teeth, and waited for them to cooperate.

DUE TO ITS STABLE NATURE, the cops opted to feed me treats of C4 rolled into little balls, as anyone could handle the clay-like substance without risking accidental detonation. I doubted it would blow even if they dropped a piece directly onto the heat lamps. A CDC rep oversaw the explosives; I guessed he had brought about five delicious pounds.

They used it as bribes to ensure my cooperation. One pound doled out in marble-sized pieces bought three vets enough time to do a head-to-hoof examination.

It took another pound to convince me to allow them to shave off my fur so they could give me fifty-seven stitches. I ended up losing more than half my fur to remove bloodied mats. I resembled a poodle, and I wailed my dismay. A third pound of C4 bought four dog groomers enough time to finish the job so I looked like a nice poodle rather than a scraggly one.

I voiced my anguish as low, quiet moans between offerings of C4.

Without my precious fur to protect me, I froze whenever I strayed from the heat lamps.

"Cruel," I accused, huddling as close as I could to the lamps without knocking them over.

The police chief, a middle-aged man who went by the name of Hollands, sighed. "You were covered in blood and needed stitches. You're lucky you didn't break your legs along with your ribs.

Chief Hollands sounded a lot like my Quinn when he was irritated. "My chief. Where is he?"

"He's on his way, Mrs. Quinn. He should be here soon."

I pawed at the sand, arranged it around my hole to my liking, and curled inside. "Move lamp closer, please? Cold."

With the help of Officer Andrews, Chief Hollands moved the lamps closer until I had a blazing red shield cocooning me. "Your friend Professor Yale told me you'd have problems in this weather. He suggested we keep you talking until Chief Quinn arrives. If you go back to sleep, we will have a very difficult time waking you until we can get the temperature up—and shy of lighting a bonfire in here, he seems to think we won't be able to get you warm enough using our lamps."

If the cop wanted me to talk, I could talk. I nosed the sand over my hooves and legs to keep them warm. "Audrey McGee did this. Turn me into poodle. Don't want to be a poodle."

"Yes, we're aware of Audrey McGee's involvement in your kidnapping. She was spotted nearby the Plaza. I'm unable to share details with you at this point, but if you could fill me in on what you remember, it would be helpful."

"She work with in-cu-bus. He seemed drugged. In-cu-bus not in con-trol of fac-ul-tees."

"Take it from the top. Begin in the Plaza, please."

"Quinn's cops bring us to Plaza. He talk to front desk. I go to room. I open door. Hear pop. Blue pow-dur in face. Lights go out. Woke in warehouse with gor-gon and in-cu-bus. Pan-eeked, ate pills. Vial may-be leak during pan-eek. I run. No want to be gor-gon bay-bee fac-tor-ee. I run. Hit trans-port. Sor-ree. I pay fix? I run. No see trans-port."

"The transport was equipped with a

moose grill. It won. The grill will need replaced, but the transport was otherwise undamaged. The driver, a single woman in her early twenties, has expressed her appreciation over the situation."

Well, at least someone had enjoyed my nightmare. I sighed. "Trans-port won. I sad."

"Would another steak help?"

I lifted my head. "I like steak."

Chief Hollands tossed me a raw t-bone, which I caught. It took a bit of work and several snorts to clean my foreleg of sand so I could use it to hold my snack while I gnawed through the bone and gulped down the meat.

"If you're anywhere near as high maintenance as a human, I'm amazed there's a man alive capable of handling you."

"She's worth it."

I squealed, dropped my half-eaten steak, launched out of my hole, and whirled so I could charge across the arena, skidding to a halt in front of Quinn. I rammed my head against his chest, careful to keep my horn away from him. "Quinn."

Huffing and pawing at the sand, I pressed as close as I could, staggering him back several steps. Quinn wrapped his arms around my head and neck, holding me close. "You look like a poodle. What have you done to my wife? Why does she look like a poodle? Damn it, Bailey. I've been worried sick."

I nuzzled his chest and lipped at his uniform. "Quinn."

Chief Hollands crossed the arena. "Hello, Chief Quinn. I'm Chief Hollands, Vermont State Police. Your wife needed stitches and has cracked and possibly broken a few ribs. Blood had matted her fur, so it was shaved. She had an unfortunate encounter with a transport. It's a pleasure to meet you. I've heard a lot about you."

"Quinn, Quinn. I escape all by my-self, but I run in front of trans-port. I stupid. Sor-ree. Room went pop. Lights go out. Sor-ree. But I escape all by my-self?"

Quinn stroked my neck before lifting my head. After dropping a kiss on my nose, he smiled at me. "You sound so tired. You have nothing to be sorry about. Audrey does, and she'll pay for taking you away from me."

I longed for my human body so I could rub up against Quinn and hold him close. I settled for draping my neck and head over his shoulder and holding him against my chest, careful to avoid stepping on him with my hooves. "Quinn."

"How many of your pills did you eat, Bailey?"

I turned my ears back and lipped at the back of Quinn's shirt. "All. I pan-eek, sor-ree. Ate all. I may-be break A+++ pixie dust vial, too. And beat in-cu-bus with a door, and stab him, and claw him. No want in-cu-bus, only you."

"You're incredible. Did you really think I'd be angry with you about anything that may have happened?"

Yes, I had. I did. I couldn't bring myself to say a word, so I chewed a hole in his uniform.

"Are you eating my uniform?"

I grabbed a new piece and gave a tug. It ripped. I swallowed the evidence. "Nooooo."

"You're eating my uniform. Bailey, you're ridiculous. My uniform is not food." Quinn laughed and patted my neck. "You didn't hit the incubus hard enough. When I get you home, I'm going to ask Amanda to give you private self-defense lessons. Are you all right?"

"All right now. You here."

A flash of gold light alarmed me into lifting my head. I spotted Sylvester on the far end of the arena, and he teleported closer. I squealed, pulled free of Quinn's hold, and bolted across the arena. "Devil angel!"

With his laughter chiming in my head, Quinn's grandfather stalked me across the sand. "We must take you home safe, little granddaughter. Don't run away. I must check on your health for my little grandson's sake."

"No, you smite me." I flattened my ears and backed away.

My traitor husband doubled over laughing. "He's not going to hurt you, Bailey. He came with me from New York. He insisted. Grandfather Xavier is taking care of some other matters."

"Which one Xavier?"

Quinn sighed. "I didn't introduce you by name, did I?"

"No." I kept backing away from Sylvester, displaying my teeth for the angel to admire. "You no smite me. Bad angel."

"I'm afraid to ask what's going on," Chief Hollands admitted.

"Bailey is very sensitive to angels. Their song, their light, their halos—you name it, she's weak to it. Bailey, he isn't going to hurt you, I promise."

I didn't believe him for a single instant. I stomped my hoof and kept retreating from his grandfather.

"And Xavier?"

"An incubus. Grandfather Archambault Quinn's also here; he's a former gorgon king. He's off to grill one of the clan who lives in the area to see what he can find out about Audrey's hive."

"And he's your grandfather."

"Father's side. My grandmother is my grandfather's harem queen—his formal surrogate. They're married. She's a centaur."

Chief Hollands stared, his mouth hanging open.

"Me feel same way, too, when I learned. No feel bad. His family? Is insane. This bad devil angel is from his mother's side. Very bad devil angel. Bad. No smite me!"

Sylvester laughed and cornered me despite my protests.

"No smite me."

"You'll live, I promise."

Damned angels.

I CAME BACK to my senses as a human, wrapped in a blanket and cradled in Quinn's arms. The soft murmur of voices included his, and I spent a while listening to him.

After a few minutes of listening to him discuss cross-jurisdiction procedures and personal interest in a case, I decided it was too much work to make sense of the conversation. I blinked and winced at the throb in my head, which forced my to squint through my lashes. We were in an office on a couch, and I decided I liked my spot situated across Quinn's lap with my head nestled against his chest. Snuggling closer, I made myself more comfortable and stifled a yawn.

"Quinn?"

The discussion halted. "Hey, Bailey."

"The angels keep smiting me. It's not fair." Although I slurred, I got the words out. My effort to grab Quinn's shirt was thwarted by the blanket, which smelled like him and his cologne. I could get used to being held, but I missed the use of my hands. How could I rub his chest and reassure myself he was whole and healthy without the use of my hands?

"I'm sorry he smote you, but it's hard to hold you while you're a unicorn. Grandfather offered to help. We discussed it on the way, and we thought it was wise to get you back into your human form as quickly as possible. Unfortunately, he needed to use his halo. With it, he was able to force you back into your proper body. You spent fifty minutes after that in a neutralizer bath. I refused to let them put you in a glass coffin. We vaccinated you to be safe, though. No one at the CDC knew what would happen with an overdose of those pills, so we may have gone overboard purging your system of it. Next time, take one. Not twelve, one."

Since I couldn't free my hands, I rubbed my cheek against Quinn's chest. "I'm sorry. I panicked. I didn't want to be an incubus's date."

He scowled at me, but the corners of his mouth twitched. "Hey."

Smiling, I pulled up my knees to get closer to him. He hooked his arm under my legs and shifted me on his lap so my head rested beneath his chin.

"I only want you." I wanted to tell him I loved him, but the words stuck in my throat. He had come for me, and he had brought his insane grandfathers with him. Audrey had been wrong.

Someone wanted me. Quinn wanted me. Quinn wanted me enough he sent his angel grandfather chasing after me so I could be human so he could hold me. I wasn't alone.

Audrey was wrong.

Quinn kissed my hair. "I can live with that. How are you feeling?"

"I think you gave me a headache talking about procedures. Do all police chiefs have couches in their offices? Oh. You're Chief Hollands, right?" My struggle to sit up ended when Quinn wrapped his arms around me and pinned me to his chest.

Okay. I could live with being trapped in his arms, no problem. If I never had to move, I could live with that, too.

"Yes, I'm Chief Hollands. Your husband and I were just reviewing the situation and trying to come to an agreement over which departments would handle which parts of the investigation. I think we've agreed the Vermont State Police will handle the primary investigation with the cooperation of the NYPD. I don't think your husband's very happy with this."

"Of course not. He's a control freak and a busy body."

My mouth kept getting me into trouble. Quinn's laughter rumbled in his chest. "I can't say she's wrong."

"Tell me what happened. I'm missing eight days." I hated the waver in my voice.

Quinn squeezed me, dropping another kiss on top of my head. "It's all right, Bailey. Nothing is your fault. If anyone's to blame, it's me. I should have been with you."

"Oh, yes. You should have been with me so you could be easy pickings. Door went pop, lights went out. Your lights would have gone out, too."

Quinn sighed. "Damon, you have your notepad ready? I'm not going to want to go over this twice tonight."

"Notepad and recorder are ready. Give me the whole story so we can put an end to this bullshit."

The thought of two police chiefs cursing and acting like bad boys made me giggle. "Today on *Cops*…"

"Bailey, you're ridiculous. You comfortable?"

"Never better. Talk, talk. I want to know what happened."

Eight days had gone by in a blink from my perspective, and I couldn't imagine what those days had been like for Quinn. I could guess; judging from the way he held me, he had no interest in letting me go anytime soon. If I got my hands on Audrey, I'd wring her scrawny little neck before popping a transformative pill and trampling her into a fine paste so she'd be easy to scrape off the concrete and dispose of so no one would ever find her.

"All right. It began several years ago."

Chief Hollands cleared his throat. "How many years ago?"

Quinn sighed again. As the one used to asking the questions, I suspected he loathed the scrutiny he faced, forced to detail every moment with his unfaithful wife. "Six as of October. I have a rather mixed heritage, part of which is angelic. As a result, I'm incapable of remaining with a disloyal partner. I've been assured by my grandfather there are exceptions. Being influenced by an incubus is one of them. I'm incapable of remaining with an *intentionally* disloyal partner."

"Intent matters."

"Exactly. Due to my heritage, I knew Audrey was unfaithful. We'd been married for a little over three years when she started cheating on me, and it went on for a few months before I decided I needed to get out of the relationship. At this point, I'd known Bailey more by reputation than anything else. I first heard of her while she was studying for her CDC certification and knew she had a knack for finding things—or people. She often found them with disastrous consequences to the involved parties, something that had factored into my decision ask for her help. Of course, since the consequences often had legal ramifications, I knew more about her tendency to stir up trouble than she probably liked. I contacted her, gave her a camera, and asked her to check into Audrey's activities."

I scowled at the memories. Quinn had been, as always, devastatingly handsome, adored by just about everyone, and so out of my league it hurt. How had my league changed to be his league? However it had happened, I wasn't letting him get away. "Audrey was stupid. She thanked me for getting her out of a so-called terrible relationship."

Quinn shrugged. "I guess I asked her for the one thing she couldn't give me."

"Her loyalty? Seriously? She needed to bang every guy on the block when she was married to the hottest man in Manhattan?"

"Your wife apparently adores you, Chief Quinn."

My husband sighed. "You know the most eligible bachelor lists? Someone thought it would be funny to name me Manhattan's Most Wanted Bachelor, playing off the fact

I'm a cop. I married to escape the title, and the instant I divorced, I made the list again."

"It's true," I confirmed. "I'm pretty sure he has a rap sheet full of incinerated panties. He walks by and panties spontaneously combust."

Quinn laughed. "Bailey!"

"What? It's true."

"Anyway, let's just say Bailey and I had a tumultuous relationship at best. With the photos she took, I convinced Audrey to divorce without a fight, and due to her infidelity, the settlement favored me so she wasn't entitled to a full fifty percent—she didn't ask for it, either. She asked for a lump sum, which I paid her without argument. The judge decided it was a fair enough settlement. That was that. We went our separate ways. Bailey had gotten her full certifications by that point. Afterwards, I made a point of contacting the CDC and requesting that I serve as her primary contact for the NYPD. I figured her skills at ferreting things out might come in useful. After my divorce was finalized, I made a point of getting coffee at the shop she worked at most mornings before going on duty."

How could things have changed so much? I'd gone from loathing his stops into the cafe to snuggled in his blanket on his lap. "Cream, no sugar, and light on the dust."

"The dust helped me get through my daily dose of rejection."

Chief Hollands's eyebrows rose. "And this continued for how long?"

"I ended up in her shop at least three times a week on average, more when I could manage. This pattern continued until this summer. I admired Bailey's tenacity and wanted to get to know her better, but I couldn't figure out how to approach her. So, I asked her boss for a few minutes of her time. I was with Mary for thirty minutes before I went to work. Mary disappeared for the rest of the day, and none of Bailey's co-workers showed up for their shift. That was when the recent trouble started."

Trouble was a mild way to put it; I considered the circumstances leading up to marrying Quinn a string of catastrophes. "I guess it's my turn. Magnus McGee, Audrey's brother, came into the shop and asked me to find someone. It happens sometimes. Someone hears how I'm good at finding things people don't want found, so they come to me. I usually tell them no. He offered me a substantial amount of money to do the job, gave me a cell phone, and claimed it had the data about the person he wanted me to find. He also claimed he would call me on it, but he never did. I put the phone in my pocket and forgot about it until I got home that night.

Since he hadn't given me the passcode, I wasted a few hours experimenting to unlock the device. Turns out entering the right passcode detonated the bomb inside, which contained gorgon dust. I locked down my apartment and decontaminated it the best I could with the supplies I had. I always keep the excess neutralizer in case I need it."

Quinn tightened his hold on me, and startled, I canted my head so I could stare up at him. "Quinn?"

"My turn." He fell quiet, his expression distant. "Mary called me the next morning. She had reviewed the store's security cameras and had spotted McGee on the footage giving Bailey something, and she thought something was wrong—she said Bailey looked uncomfortable but took the object anyway. Mary knew McGee was my ex-wife's brother, so she thought I needed to know. Call it a gut instinct, but I interpreted that as evidence something was wrong. Of course, I had assumed McGee had been attempting to blackmail Bailey."

Blackmail would have been so much better than a bomb laced with gorgon dust. "I'd like to see someone try to blackmail *me*." If I courted disaster when I used my magic, if someone attempted to blackmail me, I'd actually enjoy using my magic to create havoc.

"While it might be entertaining to watch,

I'd rather avoid you being blackmailed. Anyway, I went over to Bailey's place during a long lunch break. She didn't live far from my house, although her place was in one of the less savory parts of Queens. When I got there, she refused to open the door. She ordered me to seal her in while she tried to clean up the gorgon dust."

"Mrs. Quinn, you're qualified to handle even impotent dust?"

Right. I'd have to explain my qualifications for everything to make sense. Sighing, I leaned my head against Quinn's chest, and he shifted his hold on me and rubbed my back. I stayed quiet for a few moments to enjoy his attention. "The dust wasn't impotent. It was the real deal—and the strong stuff. Probably the strongest I've ever seen. I'm immune, Chief Hollands."

"Damned good thing, too," Quinn muttered. "After she finished bossing me around, she tried to tell me McGee had given her the phone, but he had put a geas on her. She collapsed. Since my jurisdiction is Manhattan Island, I lost some time calling in for backup and requesting cross-jurisdiction authorization to handle the scene. The CDC helped, as they were aware we had a somewhat functional working relationship—an accomplishment when she's involved."

"Hey," I protested.

"Sorry, Bailey. It's not my fault you have a reputation." With a throaty chuckle, Quinn lowered his head and pressed his lips to my cheek. "I can't say I mind no one else was wise enough to try to get your attention."

Chief Hollands cleared his throat. "So the CDC helped you push through a cross-jurisdiction authorization. What happened next?"

"I called in a few people from my station, people who were qualified to handle meters and had basic certifications with the CDC, trained to use custom hazmat suits, and had glass coffin conditioning. Once we were all in dust-rated suits, we broke into her apartment. Fortunately for us, she's good at her job and had contained the dust source in plastic. She had managed to neutralize the free-floating particles." Quinn drew in a long breath. "I put her in a glass coffin myself."

Silence.

"I've spent more time in a glass coffin than I care to think about," I complained. "To add insult to injury, they banged the door into my head breaking into my apartment. Because they hadn't managed to finish me off by banging the door into my head, they stuffed me in the stupid box for four days." I wiggled in the blanket and did my best to pout at Quinn. "You helped them napalm my apartment."

"It was all part of my clever scheme to force you to live with me."

"You're so full of shit, Mr. Police Chief Quinn."

Quinn sighed. "All right. It didn't actually occur to me that you really needed to live with me until after you were discharged, decided you were going to stay in the seediest damned roach motel you could find, contracted pneumonia, and almost died. I may have been the one to suggest the CDC retest all your immunities, knowing of your unique reaction to transformative substances, but Professor Yale picked my house because of my fireplace and space sufficient for a unicorn. It's in the file the NYPD has on you."

"You sneaky bastard."

"I'm sorry to interrupt, but can we backtrack for a moment? I'm not sure I follow. You napalmed your wife's apartment?"

"We weren't a couple then, but yes. Her measures to neutralize the gorgon dust weren't able to decontaminate the bomb. While we were able to get her into a glass coffin without spreading the contamination, we had to napalm the interior of her apartment twice; the first round hadn't managed to completely destroy the cell phone and dust inside. It was a lower-grade napalm. The second round we used a higher-intensity napalm. We suspected the same dust batch was used at 120 Wall Street, which is why the CDC agreed with Bailey's initial verdict to napalm the entire structure. It was dumb luck Bailey was a unicorn. With the level of gorgon dust contamination, there was no realistic way to get her out. She knew it. The CDC knew it, too. Any other CDC agent would have been immolated. That was the second-worst moment of my life."

I wondered what the first was, but I wasn't brave enough to ask. "Sorry," I mumbled.

Shaking his head, Quinn adjusted his hold on me and flicked my nose with a finger. "You did the right thing, and while I don't like it, we both know it."

"Please elaborate on the circumstances surrounding the contamination."

I echoed Quinn's sigh and detailed how the glass containers had been set up in the ceiling, wired with C4. It took me almost half an hour to describe how the trap had been set up, my speculations on what would have happened if the CDC had attempted standard decontamination, and what I feared would have happened if the napalm hadn't lit.

At first, I considered leaving out the part about my napalm bender, but I grumbled a few curses and confessed I'd been so drunk I couldn't actually remember much after I had finished igniting the twenty-first floor.

Quinn chuckled. "I'll confess, after I could breathe again once I realized Bailey had survived, watching her completely skunked on napalm was one of the funniest things I've seen in my life. Her antics lasted almost two hours. She played in the debris, putting on a show for the reporters and giving New Yorkers some of the best news clips of the year. Fortunately, we were able to keep her name out of the papers by telling everyone we intentionally brought in a magical species capable of igniting the high-intensity napalm."

"Oh. Quinn. Audrey told me her brother had refused to breathe in any of the dust and provide her sisters with children. She gave him the bomb and the dust. He had no idea what he had. She told me she had killed him. She could have been the one behind the Wall Street incident. She's a little crazy, Quinn."

"A little?"

"What else did McGee tell you?"

"Not much. I wasn't with her long. She left me with her pet incubus. From what I could tell, she wanted him to be the father. It was the same one from the bar, Quinn. He wasn't quite right in the head, either. He acted like a little kid unless sex was involved."

Quinn frowned. "How much do you remember from the eight days you were gone?"

"Nothing. I woke up, Audrey talked to me

for a few minutes, then she left me with the incubus—he wanted to play poker." Grimacing, I confessed my sins and my very inappropriate handling of the pixie dust, although I did make a point of emphasizing I only meant to use a small amount rather than the entire vial.

"Do you have any memories you think were a dream? That's a rather common symptom of sedation." Chief Hollands drummed his fingers on his desk. "Is there any chance you were assaulted while you were under sedation?"

Quinn tensed and squeezed me so tightly I squeaked. "There's no chance she was assaulted. I would have known." Loosening his hold, he lifted his left arm, revealing his golden tattoo. "When the incubus influenced her, I was aware of her panic—and her serious case of lust."

Crap. "Quinn—"

He covered my mouth with his hand. "Shh, Bailey. You did nothing wrong. Damon, our bracelets didn't discharge, so I knew the incubus hadn't managed to catch her in his trap. Bailey, I'll keep telling you this until you believe it: you did nothing wrong. Incubi can influence just about anyone. Grandfather told me afterwards we can get feedback from the bracelets if there might be a situation requiring it. The bracelets take energy from both of us to discharge. The tattoos were winding up to strike, but you escaped the situation on your own. Also, Grandfather assured me the bracelets would work even when we're unconscious. No one touched you."

I deserved a prize. Who else managed to escape an incubus's influence so many times? "Hah. That incubus must be pissed. That's the second time I've gotten away from him. Look at me, escaping from an incubus without doing anything indecent. Isn't there a prize for that? You should give me a prize, Quinn. I deserve one."

A startled laugh burst out of Quinn. "So you do. I will think of something appropriate."

Yes, please.

Chief Hollands looked through a folder on his desk and tapped a sheet. "Samuel, do you think the bar incident was a deliberate attempt to lure Bailey to the site?"

Shaking his head, Quinn sighed. "No, I don't. My grandfather spoke to my cousin, who had been at the bar. The incubus had arrived before he did and was just starting to pick out a few lovers for himself. He got caught up in the incubus's power. There was no evidence it was anything other than a coincidence. Anyway, Audrey had gone to my house."

"Ah, that reminds me. She wanted to remove me from your evil clutches so you wouldn't steal my virginity. That was very important to her, Quinn. I got the vibe the incubus knew I wasn't a virgin, but he didn't say anything to her about it. She didn't want me tainted by your evil ways."

Quinn's smug smile made an appearance. "I see."

Chief Hollands sighed. "How often did your ex-wife contact you?

"Every couple of months she'd show up to ask a question about paperwork. She was never the most organized person. I'd give her a copy of the paper she needed. She'd leave. The last time she was at my house, however, she *was* after Bailey—the night of the bar incident. As soon as I found out Audrey was at my house, Bailey and I decided to go to the Plaza instead."

"Why?"

I snorted. "It probably had something to do with my threats of killing the whore if she got between me and taking Quinn into his bedroom. I may have still been under the influence of the incubus."

With a chuckle, Quinn hugged me. "Bailey likes to run her mouth, but I wasn't going to risk it, not after she had been around an incubus. She's very determined, and she probably would have started a fight with my ex-wife, all things considered."

"You two have had an eventful few weeks. I have the report on McGee's visit to your home, which includes notations about her new status as a gorgon. According to this, none of the petrified individuals were infected with the gorgon virus, fortunately. It's unknown if she's an actual carrier or merely became a gorgon after her exposure to gorgon dust. Do either of you know?"

"No," we replied.

"Are there any other details you think might be important?"

"I already mentioned it was the same incubus, right?"

Both men nodded.

"To confirm, the male gorgon from the bar incident *is* one of your relatives, Chief Quinn?"

"Yes. He's been educated about the error of his ways, and my grandfathers questioned him about the incident."

I stifled a yawn and leaned against Quinn. "You know, we're really bad at this taking everything from the top thing. We're all over the place. I'm starting to lose track of what happened, and I lived it. Hey, Quinn? Can we use one of those fancy murder boards they have on television? I think we should. It'll be fun. I've never gotten to use a murder board before."

"How about a white board and some markers?" Chief Hollands suggested.

"That doesn't seem as fun as those digital things they have on television, Chief Hollands."

"Reality is often disappointing."

"Bummer."

"Still, it's a good idea we pool our information, lay it out, and take it from the top. Let's break for an hour and come back to it. I'm sure you'll enjoy a chance to stretch your legs, get changed, and get some fresh air, Mrs. Quinn."

Clothes *would* be useful, although I didn't mind cuddling up to Quinn at all. "Sounds good."

If it meant having a real chance to get rid of Quinn's ex-wife so she never bothered us again, I'd talk my throat bloody to see it happen. Quinn was mine, and I wasn't going to let a psycho gorgon ex-wife separate us.

TWENTY-ONE

Are you sure you're not an angel in disguise?

AN HOUR GAVE me enough time to take a quick shower at the station. I dressed in a pair of brand new yoga pants and a black t-shirt too big for me. It smelled like Quinn's cologne, and I decided possession was nine tenths of the law, so if he wanted it back, he'd have to strip me out of it.

I really hoped he wanted it back soon.

When one of the Vermont State Police offered to pick up a late dinner for us, I got the feeling Quinn didn't approve of my choice of the greasiest fast food money could buy. The cop found my request amusing, and when Quinn ordered rabbit food, the man laughed.

I ended up with a huge burger, fries that had taken a bath in a grease vat and were salted into oblivion, and a milkshake. "Are you sure you're not an angel in disguise? Because this looks like heaven." The cop chuckled and dipped into a bow. "Thank you so much."

Quinn claimed his salad, set it on the table, and pulled out his wallet, but the cop waved him off. "I mugged the actual angel downstairs for cash already. Chief's orders."

"I like these cops, Quinn. They mug angels to pay for my dinner. Can we kidnap a few of them? I'm sure we could fit a few extra desks on the eighth floor somewhere."

"Run while you can," Quinn suggested.

Still laughing, the cop obeyed, leaving Quinn and I alone in the break room. The late hour gave the place an empty vibe, although there were a few cops out in the main area hard at work. I sat, unwrapped Quinn's blanket, and draped it over the back of my chair so I wouldn't ruin it with grease, ketchup, and mustard.

"That isn't healthy."

Yep, he didn't approve of my glorious burger one bit. I stared into Quinn's eyes and took a big bite, making a point of exaggerating my sounds of enjoyment while I chewed and swallowed. Then to drive the point home, I licked my fingers and smacked my lips. "You're just jealous because you can't have any, especially my fries. Those are mine."

"If I wanted fries, I would have gotten fries."

I gave his salad a dubious look. "I'm not

sure that's healthy, either. How can such delicate fare sustain a big manly man like you?"

Chuckling, Quinn pointed at his dressing. "I'm using dressing. It lost its right to call itself healthy the instant I decided to slather it in liquid calories. Anyway, I had a big breakfast."

"Was it a healthy breakfast?"

"It involved bacon."

"Bacon's healthy. I approve." I set my burger aside and popped a few fries in my mouth, keeping one for when Quinn tried to claim bacon wasn't actually healthy. The instant he opened his mouth, I shoved the fry inside, cupped his chin with my hand, and helped him chew. "It's delicious, isn't it? Yummy, yummy, delicious grease."

He swallowed, opened his mouth, and I crammed several more fries in. "Chew or choke, Quinn."

After three more fry assaults, he covered his mouth with his hand. "You're being ridiculous again. They didn't feed you napalm, did they?"

I sulked over my thwarted attempt to feed him fries and popped the ammunition into my mouth. Once I swallowed so I wouldn't choke, I giggled. "I got them to give me some C4."

"Are you drunk?"

If I was, I didn't care. "No idea. I'm feeling

pretty good, though, all things considered. If my ribs are cracked, they don't hurt much, my headache's mostly gone, and the stitches aren't bothering me at all. I thought they would fall out when I transformed. I thought the cuts would have closed up, too."

"That's Grandfather's doing. He said something about keeping your insides where they belonged, and after that, I stopped asking questions and decided to be grateful."

"I'm pretty sure he was exaggerating, Quinn. I was never at risk of spilling my guts."

Quinn's expression soured. "You were hurt."

I loved his growl so much. "It's my fault I ran in front of a transport. I earned my stitches. Hey, you should be proud of me. Before I ran out into traffic, I smacked an incubus with a door, then I mauled him a bit. I also went straight to the cops, too."

"You stuck your head in a cruiser because you were cold."

"It still counts."

"I really don't think that counts. You could have gone up to them, told them you'd been kidnapped, given them my name, and *then* stuck your head into the cruiser to warm up."

Of course he'd use logic against me. "Says the man who lugged his blanket all the way from New York."

He smiled at me. "You like my blanket, which is why you're still snuggling with it."

Busted. "That's cheating, Mr. Samuel Quinn."

"I'm known to do underhanded deeds to secure my victory. No more joking around. This next part is going to be long, tiring, and very frustrating. I thought I'd warn you before it begins. We'll have to go over the same thing many times. We'll discuss a lot of possibilities, most of them will be wrong or a dead end, and it'll make you cranky."

"I come cranky by default. I thought you knew this already."

"Crankier, then. We need to try to figure out Audrey's goals so we can get ahead of her, especially if she's capable of crafting gorgon dust."

I grimaced. "Or is working with someone who can."

"Yes."

While it didn't matter in the grand scheme of things, I couldn't force my thoughts away from the fact Quinn had brought his blanket with him. "You really brought your blanket from New York because I like it?"

Smiling, he reached across the table and flicked my forehead. "Yes, of course."

I didn't understand how something as insignificant as a blanket could hurt so much. I didn't deserve him bringing me anything.

Why? Every emotion I had packed away over the years escaped from their prison and converged in a single spot within my chest.

Quinn stood, circled the table, and crouched beside my chair. "Bailey, it's okay."

It wasn't until he lifted his hands and brushed his thumbs across my cheeks I realized I was actually crying. It'd been so long since I'd cried without being sick or drugged the fact I could startled me. I swallowed to suppress them, but the tears came harder and faster.

I didn't deserve it. I didn't deserve him.

"Bailey, don't cry. I thought you'd enjoy having the blanket. What's wrong?"

"I didn't do anything to deserve—"

My traitor mouth betrayed me, confessing my dark, dirty secret all on its own. I opened my mouth to force out an apology, to somehow take the words back, but Quinn sighed and pressed his fingertips to my lips. "You don't have to do anything to deserve something like that. I brought it for you because I thought it'd make you happy and you'd like it. I love you."

Maybe his words would have made other women scream for joy or lose their minds, but not me. I cried harder. Quinn dislodged his blanket from the back of my chair and wrapped it around me, kissed my forehead, and sighed. "You've been told all your life you don't deserve anything, haven't you? It makes me want to beat those assholes who dare to call themselves your parents."

I shook my head to deny it, but Quinn cupped my cheek in his hand. "You're just going to have to get used to it, because I'm never going to stop. When I think you need something to help you feel better, I'm going to bring you our blanket. I'm going to try to make your problems disappear, though I'm starting to think I might be striving for the impossible. How am I supposed to keep the Calamity Queen out of trouble?"

A choked laugh escaped me. "You don't."

"I'm doomed. I suppose I'll just have to happily suffer. I mean it. You better get used to it, because I really won't stop. When you're stuck as a unicorn, I'll bring you roses when I can't convince the CDC to give me C4. I draw the line at magic-infused napalm, though. You might talk me into gasoline with a few additives so it has a gel-like texture and higher ignition point, but we won't call it napalm. I'm pretty sure I can come up with plenty of other little things you'll like."

"But—"

Quinn covered my mouth with his hand. "I'll do it because I want to. I like seeing you smile while you're snuggling in my blanket. When I get you home, I'll take you to the station and let you cuff me to a chair so you can force me to watch while you beat Suzy to death."

If his goal was to stop me from crying, he was failing miserably. I sniffled and pulled his hand from my mouth. "Really, Quinn? Home-made napalm? Are you sure you're a cop?"

He smiled, reached across the table, and grabbed a napkin so he could wipe my cheeks. "I'm a bad one. I ditched work the instant I got the call you were here. I may have forgotten to tell anyone why I was leaving. If I'm fired, I might have to mooch off you for a while."

The realization he *could* mooch off me startled me so much I stared at him with wide eyes. I liked the thought of him at my mercy. "Underwear model."

Quinn's eyebrows rose. "You want me to model underwear?"

"I'd make a fortune to pay for your mooching." Swallowing and rubbing my eyes, I cleared my throat and tried to pretend I wasn't a sniffling, crying mess. "Why do I need to handcuff you while I beat Suzy to death?"

"It's more fun that way. Everyone in the station will love it. You can gather your loyal fans and have them watch Suzy's murder while I howl over the injustice of it all."

A weak laugh bubbled up and escaped between my unsuccessful attempts to quit blubbering. "I don't have loyal fans."

"You have an entire station full of them. Not only did you get them a good coffee maker, you taught them how to use it. That's automatic heroine status among us cops. I'm sure you'll get used to it."

"Now you're the one being ridiculous."

"If it makes you stop crying, I'll be ridiculous and take my shirt off."

"You without your shirt is never ridiculous." While there was a box of tissues on the counter, I grabbed a napkin and blew my nose. "I'm sorry I ate part of your uniform."

Quinn laughed. "It gives me a good excuse to order some new ones. Go to the bathroom and wash your face. I love you, but you are not one of those women who does the crying with grace thing. You might scare the on-duty cops."

I cringed because he was right. On a good day, I only splotched bright red in uneven patches, making me look like I'd been on the losing end of a nasty fight. On a bad one, I scared babies. "I hate you because you're right."

"No, you love me because I'm honest."

I did, but instead of admitting it, I stuck my tongue out at him.

DESPITE QUINN'S warning preparing me for the discussion, the investigation did wear away at my nerves. My patience frayed, and the snarky, cranky elements of my personality rose to the surface, forcing me to bite my tongue several times so I wouldn't snap at someone—or hiss like one of Grandfather Quinn's snakes.

If I hunted the gorgon down and asked him really nicely, would he bite someone for me? I could have antivenin nearby along with some neutralizer. That counted as considerate, right?

I sighed. I understood why the two chiefs needed information about me and my lifestyle, but it shamed me to reveal my difficulties with getting by. Some people called it making a living. I called it barely surviving.

Quinn's teasing over my greasy burger ended the instant he got his hands on my financials. With narrowed eyes, he flipped through the pages. "I think we can eliminate wealth as a motivation: Audrey likes her money like she enjoys her men."

I snorted. "Plentiful and easily spent?"

Crap. There went my mouth again, blabbing whatever it felt like. My face flushed from embarrassment.

"Close enough." Quinn sighed. "I had no idea it was possible to live in New York on this income, Bailey."

The heat in my cheeks intensified. I needed to swallow so I could speak. "I managed. If you need help with your budget, I'm your woman."

There. Somehow, my pride survived almost intact. Everyone appreciated good budgeting skills.

"Next time I beat my head against the wall working on the law enforcement budget, I'll take you up on that. Whenever I call in accountants, they start to cry. They're always complaining about how I want to do too much with too little. It's not *my* fault the city doesn't want to give me more funding."

I wondered if my foot would taste terrible if I actually stuck it in my mouth. "I'll take your word on that."

Quinn tossed my financials into the box of papers representing my life. "It has to be your immunities she's after. Nothing else makes sense."

Chief Hollands glared at the pair of whiteboards taking up precious space in his office. One focused on me while the other concentrated on Quinn and Audrey's failed relationship. "Sam, when did you learn about Bailey's immunities?"

Quinn grabbed the red marker, which we were using to denote first encounters or occurrences, and made a notation on my whiteboard. "I knew she had immunities from her file, but I didn't believe it until five years ago. A bomber rigged an explosive device to glass containers and detonated them. They contained gorgon bile. When I called the CDC for cleanup, they sent her—it was her first solo job. The CDC tries to keep newly certified consultants and agents partnered for a year before sending them out on their own. Her task was to clean the site, purify the petrified victims, and apply the neutralizer. Per protocol, she was handling the bile while wearing a hazmat suit. Unfortunately, my team, the CDC's bomb squad, and the NYPD's auxiliary squad missed a device. It detonated, and several glass shards pierced her suit. Instead of petrifying, she cursed a storm, ripped her suit off, pulled a chunk of glass out of her arm, and started tearing down ceiling tiles. Five destructive minutes later, she had pulled down broken jars and one more device. Her solution to an active bomb was to grab the C4 and rip off the attached wires."

The glare Quinn shot my way promised he still harbored a serious case of cranky over my handling of the bomb. I hadn't known some devices were designed to explode if fiddled with. "It worked."

Quinn sighed.

Chief Hollands also sighed, bowed his head, and rubbed his temples. "That poor crime scene. That's one way to wreck evidence."

"The only thing she didn't break was the intact container. She handled that with care, neutralized its exterior, and very carefully placed it in the hall. She gave us the dirtiest look, called us a few names I'm unwilling to repeat, and went back to work."

"I called them overpaid, talentless man whor—"

Quinn lunged at me and clapped his hand over my mouth. "Please don't. Please."

I peeled his fingers away from my face. "I'll let you off the hook this once. You won't have to go to a strip club and learn how to lap dance properly. Or—"

Or he could kiss me and shut me up that way. With a satisfied murmur, I enjoyed my prize for having nettled him.

Chief Hollands cleared his throat. "Please continue. What happened after she cleaned the bile container?"

The man would have to pay for ending such a nice reward. I licked my lips and sighed. "I got gorgon bile in my hair. Do you know how hard it is to clean gorgon bile out of hair?"

The police chief's expression told me he didn't want to know. Too bad. "It involves a five pound bag of neutralizer, a comb, and careful brushing. If you get the neutralizer wet first, it'll clump in the bile. Then you have to wait until it dries. If you apply it as a powder, the bile will crumble. So you apply, brush, apply, brush, and keep repeating until you're down to spaghetti-like strands. Then you have to shower it out using a shampoo infused with neutralizer. Your hair glitters and shines for a week but becomes really, really soft."

"You also needed stitches but decided to clean the rest of the site first. Then you attempted to leave without getting stitches." Quinn glared at me.

I glared back. "You yelled at me the entire time they were stitching me up. I was the one who was supposed to be yelling at *you*. You didn't make sure all the bombs were gone."

"I tried telling you the NYPD bomb squad is actually part of the CDC, but you didn't care. Anyway, maybe I was worried. You have no self-preservation skills."

"Unless she's running away from me," Sylvester murmured, his melodic voice a whisper in my ear.

I shrieked, launched off the couch, and ran for the door only to be trapped in Quinn's arms. Spinning me around, he pulled me to him and held me close.

Any other time, I would have been too embarrassed to cling to him so I wouldn't ooze to the floor in a quivering heap. "He's going to be the death of me, Quinn."

With a soft laugh, he rubbed my back. "I see you've returned, Grandfather. Was there any reason you tried to scare my wife to death?"

"A two-hour bicker fest over your failings, of which there are many, wouldn't be a productive use of your time. She would win, you would sulk, and more time would be wasted while we waited for you to find the nearest hotel you could tolerate—a thirty minute drive each way, for the record. You'd then spend the next few hours keeping each other close company, resulting in this conversation being suspended until tomorrow midday. I thought I would pop over and remind you of the day you met your lovely wife. Thus, you will lose far less time and be much happier as a result. I do need to go home now, since I've been on the mortal coil for too long. Xavier's coming with me, but your other grandfather is still here. Have fun, children."

Quinn's grandfather vanished in a flash of silvery light.

"He usually comes and goes in golden light," I observed with a worried frown.

"Gold is when he's nearby." Quinn turned me around and guided me to the couch, shoving until I sat down. "For him, that could be anywhere on Earth. Silver's for when he's leaving or entering the high heavens. Angels are powerful, but they are often limited while on Earth, and Grandfather's been around more than usual—and used more power than usual, too. He'll be back eventually. If we're lucky, maybe he'll stay gone for a few years."

"Keep dreaming," Quinn's other grandfather declared from the doorway.

Quinn sat on my lap, which prevented me from entering orbit at the gorgon's arrival. Although he was heavy, I appreciated his warmth, and the hole in the back of his uniform amused me—and was an excellent place to slip my hand inside his shirt and stroke his skin. He leaned into my touch.

The gorgon cleared his throat, probably trying to catch my attention. Did he think I cared with such a wonderful, beautiful man in front of me wanting me to touch him? Nonsense.

"We need to leash you, girl."

I peeked around Quinn at the gorgon; his snakes cooed at me, and he'd come within easy reach. I scratched one of the coral snakes under its chin. "You might be right."

Quinn chuckled. "If you're leashed to me, I'm okay with it."

Why wasn't I surprised? "I'm going to make Suzy's death as horrific as possible for that comment, Quinn."

Chief Hollands's eyes narrowed, and he frowned. "Suzy?"

"My coffee maker."

"Ah. Why is your coffee maker going to die at the hands of your wife?"

"My wife is a coffee snob."

"Your wife thinks you have a stick up your ass again and you need a dose of pixie dust to be tolerable company."

I blinked. Wait. When I had first met Quinn, I had thought he was an uptight ass; beautiful, infuriatingly sexy, and unfortunately married, but a snobbish ass. Dosing him with pixie dust had been my way of getting rid of the lust-inducing nuisance.

Did pixie dust affect him like it did other incubi?

I trailed my fingers along the length of his spine before pulling my hand out of his clothes. "Hey, Quinn?"

"What?"

"Does pixie dust make you a sex fiend?"

Everyone in the room choked and spluttered. Quinn stood, turned around, leaned over me, and rewarded me with a kiss. "Is there a reason you're asking me this, my beautiful?"

He stole my breath. He needed to stop doing that. I needed to breathe. I also needed another kiss, but he pulled away. Later, once my heart stopped racing, I'd deal with him calling me beautiful. "I may have spiked a few of your coffees with pixie dust while you were still married to Audrey."

He froze, sucked in a breath, and widened his eyes. "Oh."

"You were being an uptight ass, and Mary kept pinches of pixie dust on hand for spiking drinks to keep irate customers from flipping out. It's like a quarter of the amount we use in a light dusting—just enough to take a bit of the edge off." I bit my lip. "It's legal."

"I know."

"It's important information," I stuttered. How much dust would I need to turn him into my personal living, breathing sex machine? "It really is."

"The answer is yes."

I now had proof God loved me and wanted me to be happy. Nice. "So for the past five or six years I've been sending you to work as a tortured, sex-deprived sex fiend."

Quinn sighed. "You're far too happy about this, Bailey."

I smiled. "Of course. I'm very happy about this."

"She won that round, little Samuel. Just accept it. I think I see what she's trying to imply, however. If Bailey drugged you with pixie dust, your behavior would have changed, especially if your relationship wasn't as, ah, intimate as some might think.

Audrey may have linked Bailey to your whetted appetite, thus giving her the impression Bailey was more than she seemed."

"Demon between the sheets," my mouth contributed.

Quinn turned scarlet. "Bailey!"

I was not sorry. "Oops."

"She's not wrong. Pardon us, Chief Hollands. My grandson has a bit of incubus in him from his mother's side of the family."

While I expected some sort of reaction, did Chief Hollands really need to dissolve into helpless laughter? Men. "It's not that funny."

Quinn walked across the room and banged his forehead into the wall. "Damn it. I managed to hide my heritage for a long time, too."

I stared at Quinn's back as I realized he had never been at risk of being encased in a glass coffin and buried. Gorgon dust could petrify even gorgons, but there was no evidence it did anything other than inconvenience anyone with gorgon blood. I had worried for nothing.

Well, shit.

Still, I needed to know for certain. "Hey, old man. If I dumped your grandson in a vat of gorgon dust, what would happen?"

"You'd piss him off."

Damn it. The answer didn't help at all; I'd

be pissed off, too—I'd be alive, stink of gorgon, and want to kill whoever had dumped me in, but I'd be fine. Would Quinn? I needed to know. "After he's been petrified?"

"You'd piss him off," my grandfather-in-law repeated.

Grandfather Quinn needed to have his pretty snakes braided and tied off with pretty little bows. "Let me rephrase this: I've been terrified that if Quinn was exposed to dust, they would lock him in a glass coffin and bury him due to his magic rating. *What would happen*?"

Quinn sighed and banged his head into the wall a few more times.

"He wouldn't be buried. First of all, the Quinn family wouldn't allow it."

With a low groan, Quinn bumped his head into the wall again. "I'm very cautious around dust and bile. Don't worry, Bailey."

"I torched a skyscraper for you!"

Ouch. Even to my ears, my voice turned painfully shrill.

Quinn turned to face me and sighed. "I'm sorry. I had no idea that was bothering you. There's a reason I'm cautious around bile sites."

If he could be reasonable, so could I. I wouldn't yell nor would I shriek again. "Okay. Can you tell me this reason?"

With a soft clearing of his throat, Quinn's

grandfather shut the door to Chief Hollands's office. "He is his father's son, that's why. While he's technically human, he does have an exceptionally high magic rating."

Quinn shook his head. "I'll tell her."

"Then do it."

Quinn approached and sat beside me on the couch. He took hold of my hand and rubbed his thumb against my palm and traced my fingers. "It's a matter of gorgon biology. In most circumstances, bile won't petrify another gorgon. Their dust, on the other hand, can petrify many gorgons—most, in fact. Gorgon kings and their scions are only petrified by the dust created from a stronger gorgon."

"So it'd be difficult to petrify a gorgon king—and princes, like you."

"Right."

I clacked my teeth together to bite back my growing irritation. "Did the pixie dust bring out your incubus tendencies?"

"Yes."

I pointed at the whiteboards. "On the timeline, put when you remember coming to Mary's shop for coffee and I served you. Does it line up?"

"Before we continue," Chief Hollands lifted his hand and waited for silence. When he had it, he continued, "I'm not sure I understand why this is relevant, Mrs. Quinn."

Oh, right. I was interrogating and filleting my own husband. Crap. "He's a demon between the sheets *without* pixie dust. On it, he must be like a god. If they were only together when I was dosing him…"

The chief snapped his fingers. "Sex addict."

Quinn groaned. "You're really going to make me detail this, aren't you?"

"It's important information." At the very least, I'd make sure I wasn't messing up and driving him away. Of course, I had already pushed my luck with him as it was. "That, plus if I ever see the bitch again, I can tell her I don't need any damned pixie dust to rile you up. Then I'll shove her own snakes down her throat and punch her in the mouth until she swallows her teeth."

With a soft laugh, he shook his head. "There you go running your mouth again. Should I fetch you a shovel so it's easier to dig the hole you're trying to bury yourself in?"

"Quinn!"

"All right, all right. I'll detail my lackluster sexual exploits with my ex-wife. For the record, I think this is ridiculous." Hopping to his feet, Quinn went to work, and to my surprise, he pulled out his phone to reference it.

"You note when you have sex?"

Crap. I clapped my hands over my blabbering mouth.

"No, I noted when I saw you, actually."

Stunned, I lowered my hands. "What? Why would you do that?"

"I record where I go and interesting people I meet. You disliked me from the start. It's odd for women to dislike me. I cheated and checked the facial recognition database to find out who you were and saw you were a promising CDC student. That made you interesting. Honestly, though, you made good coffee, and that was more important."

"I should have known you bothered me because I made you coffee."

"You made the bed, sweetheart. You know what they say about that." After flashing his sexiest smirk at me, Quinn filled in the dates and times of his encounters with me that led up to Audrey's first infidelity. "That should be all of them."

Chief Hollands pointed at a two-month gap prior to Audrey cheating on him. "Were you together during this period of time?"

"Not often."

"Why not?"

"I had a lot of work. Audrey knew my job was time consuming when we got married. She liked my wealth and looks, but she didn't bring a whole lot to the marriage for me. She did help me dodge the bachelorettes, which is what I needed from her at the time. I did not anticipate my general lack of interest in her as a woman."

"You are incredibly young to be a police chief." Chief Hollands snatched up a folder and flipped it open. "Thirty. That must be a record."

Quinn flinched. "Manhattan has ten police chiefs spread across the island, and all of us have the same magic rating. I enrolled at the police academy at eighteen, three years before the legal enrollment age because of an exception due to my rating. My predecessor was murdered. I was the only one in the force with the required rating, so I got the job. I had six months of field experience. Since the reporters liked me, I got recruited to do the majority of the talking and ended up with blanket jurisdiction over the entirety of Manhattan Island.

"With no experience."

"I said the same thing, trust me. I even tried quitting once. The commissioner laughed at me."

While I had wondered why Quinn had looked so young for a police chief, I had assumed he had been promoted due to some stunning act of heroism or something equally impressive. I tried to imagine him as a cadet, and instead I got the memory of the dipshit I'd gone into 120 Wall Street with. Yuck. "If you don't come home at acceptable intervals,

I will come to the station, steal your car, and start breaking laws so you're forced to chase me down and put me in cuffs."

Oh, shit. Stupid mouth. I groaned and leaned forward, bowing my head and running my hands through my hair.

"Bailey probably doesn't mean it. She just forgets to think before she speaks when she's embarrassed over something." Quinn chuckled. "She's also the jealous type."

"Quinn," I groaned.

Chief Hollands clapped his hands. "All right, back on subject. Sam, is there any chance Audrey McGee might have associated your heightened interest with Bailey?"

Quinn froze and his eyes widened. "Excuse me for a moment."

In four long strides, he left the room, closing the door behind him with a soft click. Through the room's window, I watched him straighten. He spewed curses so loudly I could hear him through the wall. The cops in the main room jumped.

I grimaced. "I'm going to take that as a yes."

IT TOOK Quinn's grandfather almost twenty minutes to calm my husband down. A whispered suggestion brought Quinn's tirade to a halt, and he let out a breath in a gusty sigh. "Fine. I'll go."

A few minutes later, he left with an off-duty cop to go to a gym down the street. It amazed me the former gorgon king had managed to soothe the raging police chief *and* convince him to leave the station without me.

"That was amazing. How did you do that? I need to know so I can use it against him. What did you tell him?"

"I merely suggested he might lash out at you by accident. He's been wound tight since you were taken. An hour in the gym should take the edge off and soothe his frayed nerves. His father is the same way."

I saw so many problems with the idea of him going out unsupervised I wasn't sure where to begin. When Quinn decided to do something, he did it. The man took stubborn pride and determination to the extreme. I thought of everything he had done to lure me to him without me suspecting a thing.

I shook off the feeling Quinn had just hoodwinked us all and turned to Chief Hollands. "Can you shine some light on his little freakout there?"

"It's a typical reaction when a husband or father figures out he may be to blame for something that happened to someone he loves. Don't worry about it, Mrs. Quinn. He likely realized there was something he had said or done that may have suggested to Audrey McGee you were somehow responsible for his behavioral changes. He may also be trying to come to terms with being the one questioned instead of the one doing the questioning."

I turned to Quinn's grandfather and waited.

"That sounds about right to me. Don't look so alarmed, Bailey. The only one in any danger is Audrey. If their paths cross, I wouldn't be surprised if he decided to deal with her himself. He's well within his rights to kill her for her crimes without a trial or jury. Gorgon laws trump human laws in cases like this. The kidnapping and attempted coercion of a prince's bride is punishable by death. He'll feel better about the situation if he deals with Audrey himself."

A man capable of becoming a predominant police chief with only six months of field experience could do just about anything. One off-duty cop didn't stand a chance against Quinn. Worse, I expected the off-duty cop would be happy to do anything to please him.

Most people did.

A headache brewed behind my eyes. "You really don't think he's not going to do something stupid like ditch his cop babysitter? I can see it now. He gets nice and sweaty doing whatever it is manly men do in the gym and pretends to take a shower so he can slip out the back and do what he wants. Are we talking about the same person here? The one I know, Mr. Police Chief Samuel Quinn, does not tolerate people who are a threat to his peace of mind or his people. I could see him doing something like ditch his babysitter so he can resolve this problem in the most expeditious way possible, especially since it's legal for him to do so."

Over the years I had seen him tear strips off his cops for taking unnecessary risks only to go and do the incredibly stupid and risky thing he had just scolded his officers for doing. Him entering my apartment to activate the glass coffin came to mind. It wouldn't have cost him anything except his peace of mind to request someone from the CDC do the work.

"I find that unlikely," Chief Hollands replied with a scornful sniff.

"Oh, no. I think it's absolutely likely. Probable, in fact. His new wife was taken from him on their wedding night," my grandfather-in-law countered. "He left her in a station full of capable cops and me. Most importantly, he waited for his other grandfathers—yes, the angel *and* the incubus—to leave before blowing his lid. Want to make any bets? I'll win."

I sighed. Quinn could take care of himself, couldn't he? If he wanted to do something about his ex-wife, I couldn't really stop him—I wanted her out of the picture, too. Too many lives had been lost for her to be allowed to run loose. Bad luck had put me in the line of fire more than once, and I viewed it as a miracle I had survived to tell the tale.

Maybe a better wife would have trusted her husband more. Then again, I had met his family. They were nuts, all of them. They had started a brawl in a courtroom and viewed it as good entertainment. Not even an angel had wanted to break that party up. Quinn would be fine, wouldn't he?

I massaged the bridge of my nose and willed my headache to fade. It didn't obey. "I'm going to have to go rescue him, aren't I?"

"He's only going up against a handful of gorgons, Bailey. That's hardly reason for concern."

Right. Quinn's entire family was utterly insane. I should have known his gorgon grandfather wouldn't think there was any reason for concern. "You know what? I don't care. I don't want to know. Let's assume the idiot decides to run off and cause trouble. Where would the trouble be found and can I get in on it?"

Chief Hollands groaned and hung his head. Quinn's grandfather grinned and dug a glass bottle out of his pocket, giving it a shake so the pills inside rattled. "I happen to have transformative pills with me. Who am I to say no to a fire-breathing unicorn? In gorgon culture, it is perfectly acceptable for a young prince's bride to go and correct her wayward male for failing to do as told. I see no reason you couldn't make an appearance and encourage him to return a little faster."

I no longer knew whether I hated or loved gorgons. Damn it. "How about a canister of neutralizer and some handcuffs instead? I'll hide behind the gorgon king and watch—and help if he really can't handle it on his own."

"Former king."

"So you're not up to par with a human prince? How disappointing." I shrugged. "Oh, well. I had to try. Chief Hollands, assuming Quinn gets himself into trouble, is it legal in Vermont to use restricted substances to put an end to a serious gorgon infestation?"

"If the handler is certified, yes, it is legal."

I smiled. So many substances, so little time. I could bring absolute chaos to the gorgon hive with five minutes, a phoenix feather, and some magical napalm. "How nice. I have an idea."

TWENTY-TWO

What are you attempting to do? Single-handedly raise the birthrate in Vermont?

THE CDC REFUSED to give me napalm, not even the non-magical variety. I scowled, drummed my fingers on Chief Hollands's desk, and wondered how else I might incinerate a batch of gorgon dust without napalm. Well, I already knew, but it involved me getting close and personal with the dust and breathing it in since someone in a hazmat suit couldn't handle a phoenix feather.

Immune or not, I'd end up in a glass coffin again if I didn't handle the situation perfectly. "Can you get me the phoenix feather at least?"

The CDC representative on the other end of the line sighed, and she didn't sound happy with my request at all. "I can authorize you to have a phoenix feather for the purpose of dust removal."

"And a glass coffin somewhere in the general vicinity should it be required."

The woman clacked her teeth. "Yes."

If the idea of a phoenix feather bothered her, the rest of my list would drive her to the brink of insanity. With a little effort, I bet I could push her right over the edge. "I have some other items I'll need."

"What?"

"Pixie dust, the highest grade you'll give me, and if possible, a succubus and an incubus."

"You want pixie dust, a succubus, and an incubus. What are you attempting to do? Single-handedly raise the birthrate in Vermont?"

Nice. So few CDC representatives had any sense of humor at all. How refreshing. "I also would like a vial of ambrosia, your best sedative, a jar of honey, two hundred empty gel pill capsules, and three eyedroppers rated for both substances."

"You want ambrosia." The disbelief in her tone almost made me laugh—almost. No sane person asked for the essence of a god. No one wanted the stuff, not unless they were the descendent of a god. For mortals untouched by divinity, ambrosia did one of three things: it killed fast, it killed slow, or it killed spectacularly. A single taste—not even a drop—killed. Most died within a few seconds. The unlucky ones lasted longer, a few minutes to a full hour.

The spectacular deaths worried every

trained CDC member. Gods entered the world as they pleased. To the relief of everyone, they didn't visit often. Earth bored them. Humans bored them. Everything about our little lives, our magic, and our sciences bored them.

It still shocked me Anubis had stuck around long enough to meet the Sphinx, convince her she wanted him, and make a child together on Earth. It astonished me he had cared enough to come to a courthouse to brawl while I married Quinn.

"You want ambrosia," the CDC representative repeated.

I really needed to stop woolgathering and start browbeating the woman on the phone so I could hurry and hunt down my wayward husband. "A full vial of ambrosia and the sedative, a jar of honey, and three eyedroppers. Don't forget the two hundred gel capsules, either."

"To hunt gorgons."

"Yes, to hunt gorgons. How else am I supposed to hunt gorgons and destroy their dust if you won't give me napalm?"

"You intend to kill gorgons with it? Do you have a warrant?"

She should have asked me about a warrant when I first told her I needed the materials to hunt gorgons. Were my requests *that* shocking? I sighed. "Hey, old man. Can you tell this

CDC representative about the gorgon rights and laws crap I know nothing about?" I offered Quinn's grandfather the phone.

"I have a name."

Did he? Huh. "I bet you do. It might even be a nice one. I bet Miss CDC Representative would love to hear your name."

The gorgon and his snakes hissed at me, but he took the phone. "I am Former King Archambault Quinn. I am a gorgon, and the guilty have interfered with a gorgon prince's bride on their wedding night. This is a grave insult, one covered by gorgon law, condemning the hive to death. Give her all she desires." He listened for a moment. "I appreciate that, Miss Milson. I'm sure you'll have no trouble handling any problems."

Without waiting for an answer, Quinn's grandfather gave me the phone back. "Since you can't provide the incubus or succubus for reasons I can understand, how about the phoenix feather, the ambrosia, the sedative, and the other materials I requested?"

The CDC rep made whimpering strangled noises. "What are you trying to do? Cause a disaster?"

After I retrieved Quinn and dealt with the gorgons, their dust, and made certain Audrey McGee never bothered anyone ever again, I needed to have a talk with someone at the CDC about their supply representatives. Miss

Milson had no appreciation for the dangers of gorgon dust. "No. I'm going to wipe out a gorgon hive believed to be manufacturing gorgon dust. Since nobody trusts me with napalm, I have to get creative. You *could* just provide a tanker truck of the best napalm manufactured—the high intensity stuff—and a few strong men to operate the machinery. Then I wouldn't need to get creative."

"You're banned from having napalm of any rating."

"Then I need to get creative. Can you have everything I requested within an hour?"

"Heaven help us all, but yes. There are no willing succubus or incubus available, so I will procure the rest of your supplies *after* I contact headquarters for authorization."

I grimaced at the thought of having to deal with Marshal Clemmends again. "If it greases the wheels, tell Mr. Clemmends Archambault Quinn is involved."

If using my grandfather-in-law's reputation smoothed the way for me, I had no problem dropping names. The gorgon and his snakes watched me; I reached over and stroked the nearest coral snake under its chin.

"I'll make certain upper management is aware there's a reasonable adult with you."

"Excellent. Thank you." Hanging up, I smirked at the receiver before rubbing my hands together. "I have waited my entire adult life for a chance like this. Also, that representative seems to think you're adult supervision. You obviously have her fooled."

A bunch of worried cops and an annoyed gorgon stared at me. I smiled and waited. The standoff lasted at least ten minutes.

Quinn's grandfather sighed. "Very well. I'll bite. What are you planning?"

"Probably not what you think. I told you I have bad luck, right?"

"You didn't need to tell anyone you have bad luck, dear. We know. Anyone who has met you knows."

Yep, Quinn had definitely gotten his smart mouth from at least one of his grandfathers. "There's a reason for it, and it involves magic. While I'd love to kill Audrey and her brood with the ambrosia, that's not happening. Too dangerous for anyone nearby." I shrugged. "What I'm going to do is something a lot worse and bordering on the idiotic."

I had kept my vanilla human status for a long time. If Quinn could live a relatively normal life, if my magic helped me find him and put an end to Audrey, I could deal with the consequences of changing my status. Meeting the rest of Quinn's family reassured me my magic rating wouldn't bother him too much.

"I find that answer rather worrying."

"I lie sometimes." There. That was a good

start to my confession, although no one seemed impressed with my statement.

"Just explain what you're planning."

"I lied when I told people I find things through luck or research. I use magic. Bad things usually happen when I use it, so I try to avoid it. I can also do a few other tricks I don't think other unicorns can."

Quinn's grandfather sighed. "You're a closet caster, then. A practitioner."

"Oh, no. I'm the real deal. Ask Quinn or Perky. I caught a sunbeam while they were both riding me. I didn't leave them behind." Smiling at the memory, I relaxed despite the scrutiny of the men surrounding me. "I was so proud of that. Perky almost threw up on me."

Every last one of my grandfather-in-law's snakes reared back. "You caught a *what*?"

"I hitched a lift on a sunbeam. I like it because it's fast. Only works when there's strong enough light and I'm a unicorn, but there you have it. No, I'm not a practitioner. I'm a hack, though. The last time I did this seriously, I found Audrey McGee in Central Park riding a college stud. That's really not something anyone should ever see. Let's just say that soured me on using my magic."

"Just tell me what you're planning, Bailey."

I wrinkled my nose at the gorgon. "I'm going to locate the gorgon dust stash, incinerate it, find Audrey, beat the shit out of her, toss her into the flames, shovel her ashes into a bucket, take her out in the woods, dig a deep hole, and bury her where no one will ever find her. Since the only being capable of burning dust so it's impotent without napalm is a phoenix, I'm going to have to take the playing with fire route, hope I piss one off enough it rises from its feather, and bribe it with ambrosia so it won't kill me."

"This is even worse than I feared. How do you intend to piss one off? Why would you?" Quinn's grandfather shuddered.

No one in their right mind pissed off a phoenix on purpose, so I didn't blame him for his reaction. Ambrosia might buy me enough time to convince the angry bird it should help me rather than burn me to a crisp and eat me. "Just trust me."

"Only three words worry me more," the gorgon muttered.

"Oh?"

"Hold my beer."

I snickered.

TWO HOURS after Quinn should have returned, worry cramped my stomach. I hated waiting, but I couldn't do anything until the CDC arrived with everything I needed. The glass coffin delayed things; there wasn't one in the area, so they had to fly one—and a technician—in from New York.

I got sick twice, although I blamed the overdosing on transformative pills and my stint as a unicorn rather than my concern for my missing husband. At least no one questioned me both times I had retreated to the bathroom.

At the two-and-a-half hour mark, a CDC representative arrived at the station in a covered pickup truck. He brought everything I had asked for with the exception of the incubus or succubus. None on staff were willing to take on a gorgon hive, and I couldn't blame them in the slightest. At least the rep had tried, which went beyond my expectations.

Shivering in the cool evening air, I regarded the contents of the truck with an arched brow and a frown. "Is there a reason there are two baby blankets in a glass box back here? I may not be a math whiz, but I'm pretty sure two baby blankets means two phoenix feathers."

The CDC rep circled the truck and leaned against the tailgate, grabbing hold of the case's rope handles. "Yes, there are two feathers. The fathers of the children requested their blankets remain together, and the set was all we had available."

I tensed. "And the mothers?"

With a soft sigh and shake of his head, he replied, "They were killed in a car accident. The women were best friends, and their due dates were within a week of each other."

Oh no. I swallowed back the lump in my throat, staring at the box and the blankets it held. The blankets of unborn children were the only thing on Earth capable of quieting a phoenix feather and subduing its flames. Anyone holding such a blanket could handle the feathers without risk of being burned.

When the mother of an unborn child went into labor, a new blanket replaced the old one, and it was returned to the family. Expecting parents sent their blankets to the CDC hoping to give their unborn child luck in life. For parents stricken with grief and loss, sending their lost child's blanket gave them a sense of hope and closure.

When a phoenix rose from the ashes of one of its feathers, it would take its blanket with it, using it to create its nest, keeping it as its own. Many believed the spirit of the unborn child became part of the phoenix and gave the bird its new life. I didn't know what I believed, but I would never blame anyone for hoping for such a happy ending.

"And the phoenixes?"

"Both are dead. They were, in their last life, a mated pair."

I gulped. Despite folklore, phoenixes didn't often resurrect automatically. Sometimes it took days, months, or years before one rose from one of its lingering feathers—or the last of its feathers was destroyed, forcing its rebirth. A mated pair of phoenixes died bringing a hatchling into the world, leaving behind a single feather each when they immolated to create an egg.

"Are you *trying* to create a disaster?" I blurted.

One newly risen phoenix was bad enough. I couldn't imagine what two would do.

"It would have taken at least eight hours to bring in a feather from a still-living bird. We only have five of them. Three are in Europe, one is in Africa, and the other is in California. Considering the nature of the problem, upper management thought it was wise to risk the potential resurrection of two phoenixes. You demonstrated you understood the perils of using a feather when you requested everything needed to control one or two of the birds should they rise."

Feathers from still-living birds only lit everything around them on fire, nature's most potent flamethrowers, making them much safer to use than the feathers of a dead bird.

Would a hundred ambrosia pills be enough to bribe two phoenixes? I sucked in a breath through clenched teeth. Two fathers had given the CDC their grief, their love, and their hopes for their lost children. Who was I to deny them? Quinn was going to kill me when he found out.

My agreement to take two dead phoenix feathers into the field would infuriate him, especially when he found out I knew exactly what I was getting myself into. With one mistake, I'd be incinerated. They'd likely devour my ashes, too, using me as fuel for their first molting.

Maybe I could avoid telling him that part. Mr. Police Chief wouldn't know the logistics of using a phoenix feather, would he?

"If it makes you feel better, Mr. Clemmends said if you can handle the Quinn family, two phoenixes shouldn't be any problem at all."

Yep, Marshal Clemmends was pissed about me marrying Quinn and unleashing the hounds of gorgon war on him. "How nice of him."

"It's quite the compliment, really. Mr. Clemmends doesn't trust most people with phoenix feathers *or* ambrosia, and he's given me authorization to give you both. He did ask me to inquire about your request for the pixie dust and the sedative."

"It might be best if you don't ask."

"Should I be concerned?"

"You're giving me two dead phoenix feathers from different birds. Why are you worried about pixie dust and sedatives?"

"I'm Kevin. I think we're going to get along just fine."

"Bailey. What grade is my pixie dust?"

"A."

I could work with that. A grade pixie dust wouldn't circumvent someone's will, but it would buy me time. "And the sedatives?"

"You'll like this. It's the good stuff. You're not certified for it, but I convinced Mr. Clemmends a temporary exemption would be prudent, especially as it should be handled in the same way ambrosia is, which you are trained for. Your request for honey made me suspect you wanted to disguise sedative capsules as ambrosia, likely to give to the phoenixes to calm them down and make them docile."

"You're right. I think we are going to get along just fine."

"It's ungraded, but only because it comes in one potency. Those who take it will become docile, although they remain mostly coherent. It will not induce unconsciousness, but it induces certain numbing properties. It was developed for use in surgery, but it wears off too fast and leaves the subject aware of their surroundings. It's restricted, since when combined with other substances, it may circumvent someone's ability to make their own decisions."

"Does it leave people susceptible to suggestion, like higher grades of pixie dust?"

"Let's just say the development of this substance was banned beyond this level due to its potential. In this form, it will make subjects pliable yet maintain coherency. It's ideal for hostage situations—if you're the one holding the hostages."

If I were a better person, I probably would have considered subduing the gorgon hive rather than indulging in first-degree murder. "I'll be careful with it."

"I thought you would. I've also been informed of your immunity to gorgon dust and have been given instructions on how I should use the glass coffin if you require it. We've determined forty-eight hours followed with an immediate dosage of transformative plus a special containment chamber with a bucketful of our best napalm should resolve any potential issues should you be contaminated."

"You could just skip straight to the napalm."

"We are considering it, depending on how Chief Quinn handles your treatment in a glass coffin. There will be a two-hour minimum if you're contaminated."

While I didn't like it, I could live with the arrangement. "All right. Let's get this stuff inside so I can get to work on my preparations."

I took custody of the phoenix feathers, which required two hands. The box didn't weigh a whole lot, but if I dropped it and the glass broke, I'd die. With my luck, I'd die, and both phoenixes would make an appearance, incinerating anything within ten to twenty feet—or more—when they rose from their feather. If they weren't contained—or moved—within ten minutes, they'd go through their first molting, which would give them the ability to fly and ignite anything.

Quinn's grandfather met me inside the doors. "You look like you swallowed a lemon."

"The CDC sent two feathers."

"I'm guessing that's why there is a pink bundle and a blue bundle in that box."

"They're from dead phoenixes."

The gorgon's expression remained blank, guaranteeing he hadn't studied phoenix lore. "And?"

"Gorgon king school didn't include a course on what might happen if you use the feather of a dead phoenix? Tsk, tsk. It's simple. You might get the whole bird." I grinned at my grandfather-in-law.

He blanched. "Do you have to sound so cheerful about it?"

"Yes. Yes, I do. I'm bringing phoenixes to a gorgon fight."

"God help us all."

I HATED WORKING WITH AMBROSIA. Like other lethal substances, I came with a natural resistance to the stuff, which made me one of a handful of people certified to handle it outside a CDC containment vault. No one knew what would happen if I ingested ambrosia, and no one was willing to experiment to find out. The furthest anyone had gone was to dab a minor amount on my fingertip with a protective coating of neutralizer on my palm and arm. I glowed a lovely golden hue when exposed, and not even the neutralizer blocked the reaction.

That had terrified the piss out of all the observing scientists and researchers, as they realized their precious pink, sparkly compound was no match for the essence of a god. After two minutes, the glow had spread all the way to my shoulder, had turned my hair blonde, and had done *something* to me, something I felt in my head and my chest but couldn't describe beyond an itchy feeling and pressure.

Angels kicked my ass and frightened me, but ambrosia made angels seem insignificant in comparison.

In the interest of preserving his precious

status as a vanilla human, my father had done a lot of research on my mother's side of the family. I had no doubt he would have found a way to kill me if he had uncovered anyone questionable during his research. He'd gone back four hundred years before he had hit a stone wall.

Considering magic hadn't been widespread then, limited to the rumor of witches and mythology, my father deemed me pure enough I wouldn't utterly disgrace the family name. Hiding the murder of a baby in a family unwilling to use birth control wouldn't have ended well for him, and he knew it.

How had I survived my childhood?

Sighing, I went to work filling the gel capsules with blunt needles attached to syringes. Kevin had brought a hundred slot tray to make my work easier and simplify the filling process. Wearing latex gloves and a dust mask, I filled the smaller half of the capsules with the golden fluid first. Then I began the tedious process of using tweezers to fit the larger halves on top. The second part of the tray would flood the chamber with enough heat to meld the two halves together and prevent leakage.

It took me almost an hour to fill the capsules with both substances and put them in their appropriate bottles. I put the ambrosia in a red bottle to give a very visual cue I carried death in my pocket.

Somehow, I managed to avoid contaminating anything, although such close proximity to the ambrosia left me with a mild headache.

"Are you finished turning the break room into a death trap?" My grandfather-in-law leaned in the doorway, watching me slip both bottles into my pockets.

"Whoever made yoga pants with pockets needs a raise."

"Is the room contaminated, Bailey?"

I sighed. "Bring a little ambrosia into a police station and everyone freaks out. I didn't spill any, so don't worry. I'll spray the place down to be cautious, but everything's clean. I've been careful. I'll even do a full scan to be sure. It'll take ten or twenty minutes for the place to clear out."

"You have a tan, and you're glowing."

Was I? I lifted my arm and scowled at it. Sure enough, I'd developed a golden-brown tan with a faint gleam. "Oh, look. I'm shiny. Neat."

Unless I turned into a living lightbulb, I wasn't going to worry. The ambrosia would bleed through most containers. Indirect contact wouldn't hurt anyone. Just to be certain, I checked the meter Kevin had left with me, set it for a close-range blanket scan, and watched the results, stifling a yawn.

It confirmed ambient ambrosia in the area and a single strong source. Had I spilled any, there would have been a second strong source detected.

"I'm concerned."

"You encouraged Quinn to run off. If you hadn't, I wouldn't be handling dangerous substances right now." I peeled off the gloves and set them inside the emptied tray, covered it, and set it aside. Mixing a strong batch of neutralizer spray, I spritzed the entire room and coated the tray in a layer so thick I couldn't see inside due to the pink, glittery fluid coating it. "There. Give it ten or twenty minutes and the residual essence should be gone."

A faint golden radiance illuminated the glass box containing the baby blankets. Oops. At least the phoenix feathers wouldn't be affected by it; the birds loved ambrosia, and my stash might convince them to help me rather than fry me to a crisp. The sedatives might help, too, if push came to shove—and I lived long enough to trick them into eating a few along with the ambrosia capsules.

"It is rather concerning he isn't answering his phone."

I glared at him. "It's just a handful of

horny gorgons—including one who hates him. How bad could it be?"

"You must drive my poor grandson crazy. Your sarcasm has been refined through extensive use, I see."

"If you hadn't let him go wandering off, I wouldn't need to be sarcastic, now would I? Anyway, I need a map, some chalk, and a pot of ink. After that, I'm going to need a vehicle."

"The car and map I can understand, but why the chalk and ink?"

"You'll see. Just trust me."

"I'm concerned."

Sighing, I shook my head and headed for Chief Hollands's office. The man eyed the glass box warily. "This scaly pest has a list of things I'm going to need. If you could help him, I'd really appreciate it."

"Of course."

"I'd stay out of the break room for twenty minutes unless you want to glow for a while."

"I'll keep that in mind."

"Thanks for the help." I turned to my grandfather-in-law. "Remember: chalk, map, ink, car."

"Would you care to elaborate what you're going to do with all those things?"

I was beginning to understand how Quinn had become so infuriating. It had to be a part of his genetic makeup, just like his devastatingly good looks. "You're the one who thought it was a good idea for Quinn to go to the gym. Therefore, you're the one who has to get the things I need to find him—and that poor cop. I bet he kidnapped that poor cop sent out with him."

"No, I suspect he suggested the young man should go home and enjoy the rest of the night with his wife. I told Chief Hollands his cop was probably influenced and to let it be."

"Influenced? How?"

"Little Samuel *is* part incubus, dear. He just doesn't draw on that part of his heritage unless necessary."

My eyes widened. "He can do that? Without pixie dust?"

"He prefers to handle matters with his own skills rather than rely on, and I quote, 'a cheap trick.' He makes things more difficult on himself than necessary. If I could—"

"I don't want to know."

"But—"

"No."

"If—"

"I have pixie dust, phoenix feathers, ambrosia, and sedatives. You and your snakes don't scare me. Go ahead and continue that sentence, old man. I could be sleeping in some nice hotel room right now, but no. I have to chase my idiot husband who got the idea into his pea-sized brain he needed to handle a horny gorgon hive on his own."

"You mean eradicate."

I was so tempted to find out what pixie dust would do to the gorgon. "He's not stupid enough to cheat on me. Remember, magical ball and chain? I'd know."

"He's also incapable of it."

"Not stupid enough, incapable—whatever. He wouldn't. End of story."

"You're very trusting."

"You're very lucky I'm holding phoenix feathers right now, or you'd be sporting coral snake braids, old man. Quinn's a stubborn ass, but he's not like that. Just help me find a damned map, ink, chalk, and a car already."

Quinn's grandfather sighed. "Gorgons are patriarchal."

"Bullshit. You're whipped by a centaur, and we both know it. You're not dumb enough to cross her, and you're not dumb enough to cross me, either. Do you want to know why? Please tell me you do, just so I can tell you."

He scowled, and his snakes hissed at me. "Why?"

"You adore me because I don't put up with your shit. Now, go fetch my things so I can find Quinn."

"God help us all."

"You keep saying that."

Had I been anyone else, I would've been petrified. The gorgon's magic made my eyeballs itch. He grunted, hissed at me, and stormed off. "Fine."

"Thank you," I called after him. See? I could be a polite, well-adjusted adult when I wanted.

TWENTY-THREE

This is almost entirely your fault.

AN AUDIENCE of two curious cops, Chief Hollands, Kevin, who turned out to be a CDC evaluator in addition to a supplier and general busybody, and my grandfather-in-law observed me open the map and spread it out over the hood of Kevin's pickup. I pinned it in place with the vial of ink, grabbed the box of chalk, and went to work crushing it against the asphalt. Dust coated my hand in a thick layer of white.

I hated the feel of chalk on my skin.

Sighing, I glared at my filthy palm. First, I needed to find Audrey's gorgon dust cache and destroy it. After, I would hunt Quinn down and give him a very stern reminder we would work together when insanely dangerous stuff was involved.

With a little luck of the good variety, I wouldn't find Quinn at the cache.

How the hell was I supposed to concentrate with so many people watching me? I ground my teeth together, unstoppered the ink vial, and leveled at glare at Quinn's grandfather. "This is almost entirely your fault."

"Oh? Who am I sharing the blame with now?"

"My stupid husband!" I thumped my palm on the hood of Kevin's truck, and the CDC rep winced at my rough handling of his vehicle. "Oh, lighten up. Your big manly truck isn't going to be damaged from a little love tap like that."

"But it's my baby."

"Men," I snarled.

"Ah, I understand. This is what my beloved queen speaks of so often. Us men and our ability to infuriate the fairer sex. One day she might remember I'm not a human."

"Don't hold your breath waiting," I muttered.

"You are nervous, little one. Why are you so nervous?"

I pointed at Kevin. "He's going to take one look at this and turn me into a research subject."

Maybe wailing over it was a little out of line, but I couldn't stop myself.

"I can't tell if you're being serious or not," Kevin confessed.

"Don't mind her, Kevin. She's had a difficult few weeks, and she's been poked and prodded enough during her evaluations. It's fine, little one. First, you are a part of the Quinn family now, so the CDC will refrain from any invasive research. Won't they?"

Lifting both of his hands, Kevin nodded. "Don't look at me. I'm just the nice guy with the truck."

"Just get on with it," my grandfather-in-law ordered.

I sighed, placed my palm on the center of the map, and closed my eyes. The ambrosia, pixie dust, sedative, and pair of phoenix feathers ensured I'd face trouble no matter what happened. If there *was* a large stash of gorgon dust, phoenix fire might be the only thing capable of destroying it without the CDC bringing out the same sort of crew required for 120 Wall Street's demolition. Without napalm, I couldn't do it as a unicorn—even with it, I wasn't sure I'd try again. One napalm bender was enough for my lifetime.

No matter how I approached the situation, I could easily die trying to get rid of any substantial amount of dust.

Why did I always have to be the one making difficult choices? I didn't want to be the one hunting down dust and destroying it, but I was doing it anyway. I clenched my teeth and concentrated on what I needed.

I needed to eliminate Audrey's cache of gorgon dust, if it existed. If she was manufacturing it, the operation needed to be destroyed. My palm tingled, and the chalk residue slithered over my hand.

Someone gasped.

I drew in a deep breath, held it until my lungs burned and body trembled from the need for air, and exhaled in a slow, gentle sigh.

When I opened my eyes, I focused on the map. Blue flames licked at the edges and washed over my arm without burning me. While the map burned, the fire didn't consume the paper. Some would call my magic trickery. I feared some omen lurked in the flames. The ink remained in its pot, untouched by my power.

Where I wanted to go wasn't on the map, so I lowered my gaze to the asphalt. Pink, sparkling light illuminated the ground where the chalk had fallen and surrounded my hands in a pale nimbus. Great. I was glowing again. At least the ambrosia's influence had worn off.

The chalk writhed on the ground in sparkling tendrils, waiting for my command.

"Go," I ordered.

One day, I would learn how to better control my powers—or at least understand what happened and why. If my magic worked, the chalk would guide me. It slithered along the road, stretched out twenty feet, and halted. Snatching the burning map, I gave it a good shake to extinguish it and folded it up. "If you're going, get in the truck."

Fortunately for everyone involved, Kevin's truck had an extended cab. I took the man's keys, loaded the box with the phoenix feathers into the back, and got behind the wheel.

Only an idiot would join me, but I had somehow found five of them. Kevin and the three cops opted for the backseats while Quinn's grandfather took shotgun. I cracked up laughing at the loud but brief argument over how four men would fit on a bench made for three. The two losers were Chief Hollands and his youngest cop.

"Perhaps one of you would like to stay here," I suggested.

"No," they snapped.

Chief Hollands ended up sitting on his cop's lap, and I considered it a miracle I didn't laugh in their faces. I turned around first. "Buckle up, boys."

A chorus of curses in the back made me smile, but they obeyed.

Kevin's truck rumbled to life, and I followed the pink, glittery glow. Since I was using a map as a focal point, my magic would hopefully acknowledge the existence of roads. Maybe one day I'd figure out why it worked.

Then again, maybe I wouldn't. It was magic, after all.

THE TRAIL OF PINK, glowing chalk led me far from civilization, up a mountain, through a river, and into the woods. The 'river' was only a few inches deep, but that didn't stop me from singing annoying Christmas songs to irk my passengers.

Grandma apparently lived in a stone fortress. I whistled. "Who the hell builds a three-story gothic mausoleum out in the middle of nowhere? Are those gargoyles on the roof?"

"Those are called crenelations, darling girl. And no, those would be petrified incubi and succubi." Quinn's grandfather sighed. "How is it *my* grandson discovered a wayfinder and married her without realizing what she is? How is this even possible?"

Kevin snickered. "Probably the way the CDC had no idea what she was for a decade. You're no vanilla human, Mrs. Quinn. How naughty of you. Don't do it again—and come in for a proper evaluation of your talents."

I had a feeling Kevin would be added to

the short list of people I actually liked. "Non-invasive evaluation?"

"We save the invasive evaluations for those with immunities."

I narrowed my eyes and turned in my seat to glare at the man. "Remember, Kevin. I turn into a unicorn and can breathe fire."

"I don't believe in unicorns."

Annoyance and amusement waged a cruel war, and I ended up cracking a grin. "When you have the seat of your pants lit on fire by an angry unicorn, remember it's your fault for your lack of belief."

"You're going to be so entertaining to evaluate."

"Any evaluations will have to wait until after she gets her extravagant honeymoon with her groom."

"What honeymoon?" After killing the engine and pocketing the keys, I shot a glare at my grandfather-in-law. "I was unaware there was going to be a honeymoon."

"I may have suggested little Samuel plan something nice to distract him. It kept him from attempting to kill people for not finding you faster."

Kevin chuckled. "Still, I'm pretty impressed, Bailey. That's the nicest piece of wayfinding magic I've seen in my entire life. Direct, best route, no detours, and you even used the roads efficiently. That's something special."

I blushed. "Really? It's not magic. It's a curse. We're going to walk inside and bad things will happen. Actually, only the gorgon is coming inside with me. He's expendable."

In reality, he was immune to gorgon dust, but I didn't want to risk anyone else being exposed.

"I regret my inability to petrify your tongue."

"My life is complete. I have annoyed a gorgon king. Come on, Your Most Royal Majesty, Archambault Quinn. If you end up petrified, I won't laugh too hard while I'm dumping neutralizer on your statue. Then again, you would make a pretty decoration. Curse you and your family's good looks. I'm a crow stuck among peacocks. This is not fair." I threw open the truck door, jumped out, and retrieved the phoenix feathers from the back. Tucking them under my arm, I marched towards the doors.

Quinn's grandfather was nice enough to close the driver's side door for me before following me. "Have you had a psychiatric evaluation yet? If you haven't, you should have one."

Nice. I'd been deemed insane by a member of the crazy Quinn menagerie. "Says the gorgon following me into a building contaminated with gorgon dust. I'll laugh so hard if you end up a statue. I'll never let you forget it. I will call you in the middle of the night, and when you answer, all you'll hear is my laughter."

"You left the meter in the car."

"Don't need one. There's only one way to deal with this sort of problem."

"Oh?"

"Fire. Lots and lots of fire. Phoenix fire, to be specific. You may want to stand back. Thirty feet's a single phoenix's blast radius. I don't think anyone has ever tried to activate two feathers at the same time."

I loved when people listened to me, but I wasn't a fan of Quinn's grandfather reaching his hand into my pocket to take the truck's keys. "Hey!"

"I'll move the vehicle to a safer place while you work. I'd rather not have to explain how we killed a CDC representative and three cops."

With a light, fast stride, the gorgon returned to the truck, hopped in, and fishtailed the vehicle in his haste to get away. After a few hundred feet, the vehicle disappeared into the trees.

"Cowards," I muttered.

As long as I held the two baby blankets, I

would be protected. Part of my certification with the CDC involved handling phoenix feathers, although the feathers had been used with the living bird's permission, on loan to the CDC for training purposes.

Most students had gotten singed. I'd been one of the few to dodge any burns. Now I could better appreciate the phoenix's amused 'don't die' since I faced the possibility of resurrecting two of its kind in one fell swoop. Since I had used my magic to locate the gorgon hive, I expected to have my hands full of squirming baby birds soon.

I also expected Quinn would show up—or was already in the gorgon hive somewhere. What else could go wrong? I grimaced at the numerous possibilities. An angel could show up, or an incubus, or a succubus—or all of them.

Ah, I knew: the entirety of Quinn's family could arrive. I sighed, shoved my shoulder into the front door, and slipped inside. An empty stone entry disappeared into darkness, and the place reeked of gorgons. Surprise, surprise. My footsteps echoed. Relying on the light from the open door behind me, I headed deeper inside.

Why hadn't I gone to a more traditional school, earned a proper degree, and taken a job as a secretary or something else sane and safe? A few math courses would have helped; I could have determined the potential blast radius of resurrecting two phoenixes.

I should have made a pitstop for coffee on the way. Sighing, I crossed the entry to where it opened into a grand chamber, so large I couldn't spot the far wall through the gloom. At least the fire would have plenty of places to go.

As long as I held onto the baby blankets, I wouldn't have to worry about the flames, the heat, *or* asphyxiating. Setting the glass box down, I regarded the feathers inside. "Please don't kill me, baby birds. I have a yummy treat of ambrosia in my pocket for you. Please don't kill me, baby birds."

All I had to do was hold onto both baby blankets, grip the feathers by their shafts, uncover the vanes, and wait. The knitted yarn would protect me as the temperature went from safe to *holy shit on a stick, everything's on fire*. If I ended up with baby birds, I'd have to hold onto them for at least ten seconds until they cooled.

No problem.

I shivered, removed the bundles from their storage container, and slid the box away. When the explosion happened, the last thing I needed was molten glass shards tearing through my skin. "Please don't kill me, baby birds. Please don't collapse the mausoleum around my ears, either."

What sort of idiot brought a pair of phoenixes to a gorgon fight, anyway? Oh, right. The kind who could transform into a fire-breathing unicorn and was banned from having access to napalm. I sighed at my own lunacy, prayed I wasn't about to die, and began the nerve-wracking process of handling the blankets in the dark so I could locate the shaft and vanes of each feather without uncovering them.

Each feather was a little over two feet long. A full-grown phoenix had primary feathers up to six and a half feet in length, which made the ones I held likely secondary feathers from the wing. Body feathers often burned out fast, surviving a single use before crumbling into a pile of soot.

I wished I hadn't looked at the tags on the blankets at the police station. Knowing the names of the babies didn't make things easier on me. Someone had decided to give the blankets to me, respecting the wishes of two fathers bereft of their wives and children. When the phoenixes rose and took the blankets with them, the two men would have, in a sad way, the miracle denied to them years ago.

No one could bring back the dead, not really. When a vampire rose, it never returned to its old life. Everything that made them human died with their mortal body, leaving precious few memories behind. With a phoenix, the lost unborn lived on as a cherished memory rather than in body and soul.

Why had I looked in the first place? It made the blankets hard to hold and harder still to use as a tool so I wouldn't be incinerated.

Damn it, I was so stupid sometimes. Later, I'd blame Quinn—and stress—for making me cry. I wasn't supposed to be the sentimental type. It hurt too much.

Yet there I was, crying my eyes out like I'd lost my puppy, not that I'd ever had a pet in the first place, but I imagined the chest-tightening pain had to be similar. If there was ever a next time, I wouldn't read the tags. That way, I wouldn't have to acknowledge why the blankets could suppress the magic of a phoenix.

I gripped the feathers below the vanes and took several long breaths to steady my nerves.

Blinding light and warmth erupted beneath my hands, and darkness smothered me. Pain stabbed through my eyes, deep into my head.

Fuck. I had forgotten to close my eyes *before* handling the blankets. Next time, I'd remember phoenix feathers, much like the birds, had minds of their own. I spat curses at my idiocy. The unlucky became permanently blind without someone with strong magic around to restore their vision. The majority recovered after a few hours to a few days.

Wiggling bodies beneath my hands confirmed my suspicions; I'd gotten two birds with one stone all right. The pain receded, but thunder rolled in my ears. I bet the little bastards squawked, not that I could hear them.

Idiot me had forgotten to request earplugs. Yippee.

"Please don't eat me, pretty birds. Pretty please?" Oh. I wasn't totally deaf. "Uh, good morning. I hope you slept well?"

Great. Not only was I an idiot, I sounded like one, too. I shook my head, and through the ringing, I heard disgruntled avian squawks. Yippee, the baby fire birds were unhappy.

"If you don't kill me, peck me to death, or light me on fire, I have ambrosia. You can have some. You like ambrosia, right?"

The squawks softened to inquisitive chirps. Had ten seconds gone by? I sure hoped so, because if it hadn't—or my information was wrong—I'd soon become a crispy critter. Bracing for the worst, I released the newborn phoenixes.

I waited.

Huh. I lived. Fancy that.

"Nice baby birdies," I murmured, fumbling for my pocket so I could pull out the bottle of ambrosia pills. At least I'd been smart enough to put the sedatives in my *other* pocket, else I'd be playing Russian roulette with a pair of flaming baby birds preparing to molt and evolve into flying cataclysms. "I made these treats just for you, but if you want them all, I need a little bit of help."

The birds kept chirping, and I felt two small, warm bodies press against my legs.

They didn't feel very big to me, much smaller than the feathers that had birthed them.

I fumbled with the bottle, muttering curses at my shaking hands and blindness. "Just give me a minute. Turns out if you keep your eyes open doing this, the lights go out."

The chirps rose in pitch to the peeps of baby chickens.

One of the little bastards pecked me in the shin, and the stone castle blinked back into existence around me as though someone had flipped a light switch. The stone around me had melted, stained black from soot. Pressed against my legs, tangled in the baby blankets, were two birds. One was white with red flames marking her feathers, so realistic I expected it—she—would burst into fire while I watched. The other was red, and its—his—

feathers were tipped with the blue-white of the hottest, purest flames.

In their previous life, they had been a mated pair, and in their rebirth, they would remain a family. When they took flight, they would take with them the hopes and dreams of two fathers left with nothing else.

Both looked like they'd been dunked in water and wrung out before sticking their beaks in electric outlets.

Too cute.

Part of me really wanted to grab them both and snuggle with them like I did with Quinn's blanket and take them home with me. How could anyone get upset with me for wanting to keep them? I bit my lip, fumbled with the bottle's cap, and eventually managed to pop it off so I could dig out a pair of the ambrosia capsules. Once I secured the lid and returned the bottle to my pocket, I offered one capsule to each bird. "One each for not killing me. I have more for you if you don't fry me or my friends when you molt."

My negotiation skills were top notch. I barely resisted the urge to snort.

The little bastards pecked the shit out of my hand in their hurry to gobble down the ambrosia. The female broke her capsule, spilling the golden fluid on my skin, and then went to work licking it up with her surprisingly soft and pliable tongue.

Some of the ambrosia mixed with my blood. I froze, staring while holding my breath. The phoenixes drank up their ambrosia, and they licked at where they'd punctured my skin. A shiver ran through me, and the wounds itched.

Then they closed.

I regretted not bringing a meter. Had I gotten ambrosia in my bloodstream, or had the phoenixes licked it all up first? I wasn't dead—yet. Would I fall over and die in a few minutes? Would I have a spectacular death, a slow one, or a fast one?

Quinn was going to kill me when he found out, assuming the ambrosia didn't do the job first.

What *did* ambrosia poisoning feel like? No one really knew, since victims tended to kick the bucket before they could tell anyone they'd been contaminated. Great. Just what I needed on top of everything else.

The phoenixes stared up at me with black, beady eyes, chirping before opening their beaks in a demand for food. Their infancy wouldn't last long, but until their first molt, the baby birds were my problem.

Yippee.

"Is it safe to come in yet?" Quinn's grandfather asked from the doorway.

"One pill each not to kill Quinn's grandfather."

Greedy chirps answered me, and I pulled out the bottle and dropped a capsule into the gullet of each of the scrawny demon chickens. "Sure, old man. I think I'm going to name the girl Annie and the boy Peter."

"The names on the tags."

I bristled. "Got a problem with it?"

"Not at all. It's a very sweet gesture. They probably have their own names already, considering they're immortal phoenixes. They've probably been alive longer than most of our family combined. Looks like Kevin guessed correctly. You even survived. Well done. I wouldn't have liked having to explain to my little grandson I let his wife get herself killed trying to be heroic."

The phoenixes gave a final chirp before cooing and burrowing into their blankets.

Demon chickens weren't supposed to be so damned adorable. "I want to keep them," I whispered.

"Pick up the baby nuclear bombs so we can find the dust and get rid of it. Little Samuel would not be pleased if I allowed you to bring the baby nuclear bombs home with you. There are limits, and I'm pretty sure this goes beyond the permissible."

I gathered the birds and their blankets, tucking them into the crook of my arm. They weren't much bigger than baseballs, and they radiated a soothing warmth. "Won't the dust petrify them?"

"Bailey, they're immortal. You gave them enough ambrosia in one of those little capsules for them to take on a god and possibly win. They'll be fine. That said, no, you may not take them home with you.

The black of the phoenixes' eyes paled to a vibrant sky blue. They chirped, and wiggling in my hold, they rubbed their beaks against my arm, scratching hard enough to break the skin.

I bled, and my blood gave off a faint golden luminescence.

"But they're so cute."

"Are we looking at—" Quinn's grandfather blinked. "Oh. Little Samuel must be nearby."

"What? Really? He is? How do you know?" I could worry about the glowing blood problem later. I needed Quinn. Surely I could talk Quinn into taking the phoenixes home. Someone had to feed them and care for them.

"Bailey, those two birds are uglier than sin. They'll be gorgeous when they molt, but right now? They're pretty hideous, and that says a lot coming from a gorgon."

I cuddled the birds closer. "They are not!"

"Bailey, you have approximately six minutes before they grow up, torch the hive, and probably eat us before flying off to nest somewhere."

"They—" The little bastards pecked my arm. "Hey!"

My grandfather-in-law chuckled. "Six minutes, Bailey."

They pecked me again, and then they licked my blood. "You're probably right."

"Good girl. Take a deep breath. We need to find the dust, then you need to nicely ask those two phoenixes if they'll take care of it for us. Then you can take your husband to the nearest hotel and get some rest."

Why did I need to take a deep breath? I frowned.

"The dust, Bailey."

Dust? Oh, the gorgon dust. Where was it? I chewed on my lip, staring around the entry. "It's too dark."

The phoenixes chirped, and golden light and warmth radiated from them.

Four walls, four corners, four doors, but no dust. "Where's the dust?"

"Find it."

"Find it? But how?"

"Oh boy. Earth to Bailey."

I shook my head. I hated gorgon dust. Why did I have to go find it again? A flash of pink drew my eye, and a streamer of sparkling light slipped through an open doorway. "I hate gorgon dust."

"I know. Show us the way, then we can make it disappear."

"Burn," a little girl's voice whispered in my ear, accompanied by the crackle of flame. *"We burn it. We play with fire. Yes! We like playing with fire."*

Yes, I liked playing with fire, too. I remembered the rush, the feel of it washing over me, and its roar as it consumed everything around me.

"Burn," a little boy's voice agreed.

The birds chirped, and I cradled them closer to me.

That was right. I needed to reward the birds. I needed to convince them to help without burning my Quinn's grandfather—without burning my Quinn. "Ambrosia, if you burn the dust." Thinking hurt, as though I had run a marathon, sat down after the race, and waited for a few hours before trying to get up and run again.

I didn't want to think about anything, but I did it anyway. "Burn only the dust."

"No fun," the children wailed. *"Burn, burn, burn!"*

"Only the dust. Twenty pills of ambrosia each, if you burn only the dust."

The birds quieted, their chirps softening to pleased coos.

I followed the light.

"Twenty-five," they demanded.

"Twenty-five," I agreed.

"Playing with fire fun! Burn, burn, burn."

I remembered playing with fire and dancing within the flames, and I envied them for what I could no longer have.

THE LIGHT LED ME UNDERGROUND. The phoenixes I cradled squawked and shrieked their complaints. The shimmering pink ribbon weaved through twisting corridors of rough-carved stone. Every step I took, the temperature dropped until my breath emerged in white clouds and I shivered.

Not even the phoenixes' glow warmed me.

"A minute and a half, Bailey." Quinn's grandfather sounded worried.

A minute and a half until what? I frowned and decided to ignore the interloping gorgon. Had I paid ambrosia to keep him alive? Whatever for? He wasn't fire.

"*Not fire,*" the children agreed. "*Burn?*"

"No. Only the dust. For twenty-five pills of ambrosia each." I remembered. Yes, that was important. My baby phoenixes needed their ambrosia. I also needed Quinn.

I couldn't let my babies burn Quinn.

They snuggled against me, their beaks scraping my arm again so they could dip their soft little tongues into my blood.

The tunnel opened to a cavern with a steep staircase carved into the wall which descended to the ground far below. At its center, a vat filled with dark brown fluid bubbled.

"Look there." The gorgon touched my arm and pointed at something beside the vat. "He is Ozmose, a middling prince of the Rockwell family. A strong enough line."

What did I care for gorgon princes? I couldn't burn them. The vat could burn, however. "If you burn the vat but nothing living here, thirty pills each. The rest of the bottle, all yours, if you purge this whole place of dust," I murmured to the precious birds I cradled in my arms.

Yes, that was what I needed to do. Everything needed to burn so the dust would never bother me again.

"*Yes,*" they whispered, and the air shimmered with heat. "*You live. He live. You all live. The rest burns!*"

Flame burst to life around me, blinding me with its intensity. Heat enveloped me, but it didn't sear my skin. Sharp beaks and talons pierced me, and my arm dropped limp to my side. The blankets fell, and the phoenixes went with them.

Sharp claws I couldn't see tore at my hip, and as I blinked away the bright spots in my vision, living fire shaped like birds winged down into the cavern below, blankets clutched in their claws. One held the bottle of ambrosia in its beak.

A pillar of flame spiraled from them and engulfed the cavern. The phoenixes cried, their song shrill and piercing. Then, in a flare of blue-white light, they disappeared.

TWENTY-FOUR

Why was everyone so happy?

THE PHOENIXES LURKED in the flames, beyond the limitations of my human eyes, but they must have stolen their light from the heavens along with the voices of angels. When they weren't crooning the notes of some melody only they knew, they shrieked, and their cries tore at my soul. I flinched at the sound, covered my ears, and squeezed my eyes shut.

I didn't want to see heaven, and I didn't want to hear it, either.

The very air caught on fire and flooded my lungs, but its heat didn't burn me when I breathed.

What had I done? I hadn't resurrected mere *birds*. I had summoned living gods, and they cawed their laughter. In it, I heard their amusement and mockery. In it, I heard an echo of their promise, the bargain we had made, which they would keep—for now.

"Well, that's one way to do it. That batch of gorgon dust isn't going to last long." Quinn's grandfather also sounded amused.

Why was everyone so happy? My babies were gone, and they had become gods. There was nothing okay about the situation.

The phoenixes screeched, and red, yellow, and white light pierced through my closed eyelids. I sucked in a breath, turning my head. Underneath the roaring of the flames, someone—no, a chorus—sang.

I remembered the notes and the angels who had sang them, and the melody tugged at my soul. I swayed to its rhythm, holding my breath so I wouldn't miss anything.

Angels greeted the phoenixes with a triumphant song, one filled with welcome, love, and jubilation. When the final distant notes faded, the light dimmed and left me in darkness. A choked sound emerged from my throat.

"It would help if you opened your eyes, little one."

Oh, right. I did.

What had once been stone gleamed in the light of a pair of burning feathers, which drifted over the floor where the vat had once been. Of Prince Ozmose, I saw no sign. "Oh no."

Quinn's grandfather touched my shoulder. "It's all right. He was long dead. He sacrificed himself to make that dust, by his choice, the fool. Everything makes sense to me now. There are two ways dust can be—"

"No," Quinn growled behind me. "I'm pretty sure nothing about you two being here makes any sense at all."

Uh oh. While I loved the way my husband growled, he sounded pissed. I considered my options. Pixie dust? Sedative? Both? If I ignored him, would he go away? I ran fast, but I doubted I could outrun Quinn for long.

Warm arms slid around me and my back pressed against Quinn's chest. Running lost its appeal, and with a pleased murmur, I leaned against him. Soft, hot lips brushed the side of my throat. "Where did you get two phoenixes from, Bailey Quinn?"

I closed my eyes, tilted my head back, and made myself comfortable against my husband.

"She's probably a little tired," Quinn's grandfather murmured. "She requested them from the CDC because they wouldn't give her napalm. She was very concerned about the dust."

Quinn nibbled on my neck, and his teeth scraped against my skin, sharper than I expected. Sucking in a breath, I tilted my head to the side to give him easier access. "Quinn, they made the dust go away."

"I see. Well, I'm not finished here. You,

however, are." Quinn shoved me forward, grabbed my wrist, and spun me around. The instant I caught my balance, he pushed me back against the tunnel's stone wall, melted smooth by the phoenixes' flame. Capturing my other wrist in his hand, he forced my arms over my head.

Twelve crimson-hooded cobras swayed from Quinn's dark hair. They stared at me, their forked tongues flicking and tasting the air. While incubi had black wings, instead of the leathery black ones I expected, his were feathered and banded with sky blue. His tail, unlike his incubus brethren's, was covered with down. With startling strength, it constricted around my knees and forced my legs together.

"Quinn!" I squealed.

Kissing was his favorite way to shut me up, and the desperate heat of incubus-inspired desire flooded through me. I needed him, and I whimpered, struggling to pull free of his hold on me so I could reach for him, pull him closer, and make him mine all over again.

Breaking our kiss, he brushed his lips against mine, released my wrists, and unwound his tail from my legs. I strained to reach for him, but something cold and hard held me in place. I twisted to see what was stopping me from getting closer to Quinn and ripping off the rest of his shirt so I could touch his bare skin.

Stone encased my arms from wrist to elbow and trapped my ankles and feet.

"Quinn, you fr—"

He covered my mouth with his and swallowed my words, smothering my protests. Another surge of heat washed through me, and as always, he left me breathless. When he pulled away, I panted, and a soft, desperate moan slipped out of me.

"How did you get here, you sneaky woman?"

I wanted to kick him for being so far away. I wanted to run my hands over his chest, stroke his wings, and explore every inch of him. A sane woman would've been at least a little concerned about being close to twelve cobras. I had no idea if their crimson hoods signified anything, but unlike his gorgon grandfather, Quinn's skin remained a rich golden tan.

When I broke free, I'd give him a piece of my mind about tying me up and leaving me hanging. "If you hadn't left, I—"

Damn him and his kisses. I closed my eyes, and without the stone holding me up, I would've melted into his arms.

Quinn's grandfather cleared his throat. "Little Samuel, perhaps now is not the best time to be doing such a thorough examination of your wife's mouth with your tongue."

No, it was the perfect time for Quinn to do a very thorough examination of me with his tongue, and I groaned when Quinn pulled away. He cupped my face with his hands. "They hurt you. They took you from me."

"You have a one-track mind, little Samuel. Bailey, it might be easier if you let him have his way, especially since he went through all the effort to tie you to the wall. While it's a good idea on how to keep her out of trouble, you may want to move her upstairs where the air is fresher, little Samuel. You might want to know she has sedatives in her pocket along with a vial of pixie dust. The sedatives in particular might help keep her from doing something we regret."

"Traitor!"

"I view it as pursuing my grandson's interests."

Quinn smirked, gave a playful lick of his lips that made my toes curl in my shoes, and peeked down my shirt. "I see you haven't used your beautiful breasts as a most royal treasury this time."

"*Quinn*!"

A single touch of his lips to the side of my throat left me whimpering and needing more. "You're so beautiful," he murmured.

His hands skimmed down my sides and

dipped into my pocket. He retrieved the vial and bottle of sedatives. "This could work nicely. Sedatives for here." He paused, leaned towards me, and whispered in my ear, "How does a little bit of dust and a whole lot of lust later sound to you?"

Yes, please.

Quinn's grandfather chuckled. "Save your loving reunion for later, little ones. Have you learned how many of them are here?"

"Audrey has five sisters. They're all in torpor. Audrey's awake, and she's caring for the hive's sole young, a female, maybe two or three years old." Something about Quinn's tone changed, and the growl I so loved took on a frightening edge. "There are at least ten petrified surrogates who may be with whelp or child. The phoenixes avoided them. I can't say the same for the incubi and succubi on the roof. I suspect they were infected with dust."

Quinn's grandfather sighed. "Our family will take care of the whelp and the unborn. The sins of the parents are not the sins of the child. What else do you know?"

For a long moment, Quinn's dark eyes stared into mine, and he lifted his hands to run his fingers through my hair. "They tried to take her from me. They meant to try again, and again, and again, until they succeeded. They won't."

"You have her safely trapped now. Separate her from the wall so we can take her to a better—safer—place. Where are the females nesting?"

"Upstairs, top floor. Their nest is there. They might have eggs." Quinn's snakes hissed and flared their hoods. "New eggs. It looked like Audrey was settling in to guard the nest."

"The eggs will be safe. If you ask your bride to hold them and keep them warm, I'm sure she won't mind. After all, she mothered a pair of phoenixes. You chose well."

"The little bastards pecked me," I mumbled.

Quinn's gaze snapped to my arm, which was still stained with my blood. The orange tint to my blood hadn't faded. "The phoenixes did that to you?"

"They're phoenixes, little Samuel, and she has a hint of ambrosia in her blood."

"Ambrosia?" Quinn pulled away, turned to his grandfather, and tensed, his feathered wings rustling and his tail lashing from side to side. "She's been poisoned with ambrosia?"

"She seemed rather distant for a while but hasn't suffered any harm as far as I can tell. Either her immunities are far stronger than I ever imagined, or someone in her ancestry had a romp with a god. All things considered, I suspect one of her relatives wasn't truthful on the identity of a father. Perhaps a grandfather or a great-grandfather? It would explain where her immunities came from." With a chuckle, Quinn's grandfather stepped on my husband's tail. "Do settle, little Samuel. We have work to do. If there are live eggs, we need to get them into a proper nest and soon. This place is far too cold for healthy eggs."

Quinn growled. "I don't know if there are any eggs, only that the five females are in torpor on the nest."

"Remove your bride from the wall so we can take her somewhere safer and warmer. It's chilly and damp here. It wouldn't do to let her get cold."

The stone released me, and with a startled cry, I fell against Quinn. My wrists remained bound together with bands of glossy stone. Wrapping his arms around me, my husband pulled me close, pressed his nose to my shoulder, and breathed in deep.

His cobras vied for the right to nuzzle me, snapping at each other and hissing until they all had a turn rubbing their scaled heads against my cheek.

"Quinn?"

"All you have to do is hold the eggs in your hands for a while and keep them warm. Would that bother you?" he murmured.

"What? No, of course not." I had held two phoenixes. "That's it? I just need to hold them?"

"That's all."

Quinn's grandfather released my husband's tail, and it coiled around my legs. "Bailey, what little Samuel isn't telling you is that gorgons are like birds in some ways. Our young require warmth while they are still in the egg. When they're young, they're very small. Their eggs grow as they do. I suspect he didn't kill the hive because he refused to risk hurting any live eggs. We're like that. We'll do almost anything to prevent the death of the unborn."

"Yes," Quinn hissed, as did his cobras.

"Be calm, little Samuel. There are four male humans in the truck outside. We'll have no problems keeping even a full clutch of eggs warm." My grandfather-in-law pulled out a bottle from his pocket. "Should heat become a concern, we can have a unicorn in short order."

"No." Pulling me closer, Quinn dug his fingers into my back hard enough I held my breath. "Mine."

The possessiveness in his tone and hands startled me almost as much as my reaction to him. The grandfather-in-law needed to go away, and the fool gorgon kept distracting Quinn.

My mouth on my husband's throat recaptured his attention, and I mimicked one of his growls. His, far more sensual than mine, spread intoxicating heat through me. "We need to get rid of those gorgons so I can take you." I gave him a light lick to give him an idea of what I had in mind. "Home," I added as an afterthought.

"You'll have plenty of time to stretch your wings after the hive's been dealt with. We must rescue the living eggs and the little whelp."

Quinn chuckled, a low, breathy sound, and nipped my ear. "Soon," he promised in a whisper. "Soon, I'll take you." I felt him smile. "Home, of course."

Of course. If we could ditch the grandfather-in-law, the tunnel would do, too. So would the cavern, and the entry, and the woods, and…

QUINN CHEATED.

How had I not noticed him pop a sedative until after he kissed me? The gel capsule hit my tongue, and with a throaty chuckle, my husband stroked his hand down my side to my hip and dug his fingers in hard enough I gasped and swallowed.

I wouldn't blame myself. Any sane, hot-blooded American woman with functioning ovaries would have fallen prey to him. It hurt to pull away from him. "You bastard."

A smile curved his lips. "You should have been paying more attention to me then, my beautiful."

Why had I asked the CDC for sedatives? At least I'd been careful in the dosing; according to Kevin, within a minute, the pill would numb me and leave me pliable but conscious—perfect for what Quinn wanted. A tingle spread from my stomach, and as it reached my extremities, the slow burn of my desire winked out, and my breath left me in a sigh. I slumped against him, surrendering to the inevitable. "Cheater," I mumbled.

Quinn worked his arms beneath my back and knees and lifted me up. The stone bands circling my wrists parted. The clever man used his downy-soft tail to arrange me to his liking—and my comfort—in his hold. Useful thing, his tail.

I'd have to remember that later—and find out if he could take on his wings and beautiful crimson cobras without the help of gorgon dust. As though aware I admired them, the serpents cooed at me.

If real snakes didn't coo, I'd be greatly disappointed. I loved their sounds, from the rasp of their scales to their soft hisses.

"I will keep you safe," he promised.

I didn't want to be safe. I wanted to help him. "Not fair. I want to help."

He ducked his head and kissed my brow.

"You'll be able to help soon. You'll have the most important job of all. You'll protect the eggs. You'll keep them warm. You'll help the petrified surrogates, and should any of them have eggs, you'll save them. I can't do that."

Unable to understand why he couldn't hold them, I asked, "Just hold them?"

"That's all you have to do."

Quinn's grandfather cleared his throat. "Are there any bedrooms upstairs? If so, that may be the best place for your bride until we're finished."

"No. She should watch. She should be nearby in case any of the eggs live. The little whelp may be afraid of us males, too."

"It won't be safe with her drugged like this, little Samuel."

With his cobra's hissing and spitting venom, Quinn shot a glare at his grandfather. "I'll keep her safe."

Score. Who knew I'd enjoy the idea of someone wanting to protect me? When I could get my body to do what I wanted, I'd have to remind him I was perfectly capable of taking care of myself. For the moment, however, I'd enjoy every minute of his possessive protectiveness. "Your snakes can't do that," I informed my grandfather-in-law.

"I'm aware. Believe me, little one, there are few things little Samuel does better than me. He has good reason to be proud of his snakes.

Even his father is jealous. While asps are plenty lethal, crimson hooded cobras are fit for a future king."

"Ha, you won a round against your crazy family, Quinn."

He rewarded me with another kiss. "And to think I was worried about how you would react."

"Are you serious? My husband can become an incubus. I have no problem with this."

"Most girls don't like snakes—or gorgons."

"Are you going to make me clean up after you?"

Quinn bristled. "Of course not!"

"I don't see what the problem is. Okay, I see one problem. You sedated me, you bastard!"

"You weren't paying enough attention to me. If you had been paying enough attention to me, I wouldn't have gotten away with it." With a smug smile, he shifted me in his arms. "You're so pretty when you're angry."

"You're crazy."

"For you."

I blushed.

Quinn's grandfather sighed and cleared his throat again. "Instead of standing here flirting, we really should deal with the nest. You'll have plenty of time to seduce your bride later, little Samuel. First, you must take her somewhere safe, then you can deal with the females."

"No one will hurt her."

"And should they try?"

"I'll rip their heads off."

Sexy or creepy, sexy or creepy—I went with very sexy with a side dish of creepy. "That sounds messy."

Quinn's chuckle had a rather villainous quality to it. "I'll petrify them first, if that'll make you feel better."

While breaking a statue would be a lot less bloody, I wasn't sure the thought of Quinn being able to tear stone apart with his bare hands helped any. The tension in his body and the way he tightened his grip warned me he meant every word.

A flash of resentment partnered with the rekindling of my desire to strip him of the shredded ruins of his shirt and make certain he understood he belonged to me and only me. A frustrated sigh burst out of me.

"Shh, my beautiful. Soon."

Quinn carried me upstairs to the main entry hall, across the room to the opposite door, and hesitated at the hallway lined with archways. Judging from the flame-scorched walls, the phoenixes had blasted the doors into ash. "Their 'guest' suites. Most were occupied by statues, but I suspect they were infected."

I heard the warning in his voice, but I looked anyway.

If there had been statues in the chambers, very little remained of them, and guilt clawed away at my chest. I had been the one to bargain with the phoenixes. They had agreed to abide by my wishes.

I had asked them to destroy the dust and spare the living, but the statues, technically, hadn't been alive when the birds had destroyed them. How many could have been saved? How many would have become carriers?

If I had thought things through a little better, things would be different. Now, no one would ever know.

"Did you get a count?"

"Yes." Quinn didn't elaborate, for which I was grateful. He shifted me in his arms and carried me down the hall to a spiral staircase, which opened to a massive room littered with the naked statues of women, a few incubi, and a single succubus. At the center of the room, six gray-green figures curled together in a nest of torn mattresses, shredded sheets and blankets, and clothing.

Snakes hissed while scales scraped on stone, but only one of the figures moved.

Audrey. I curled my lip in a silent snarl. Quinn eased me out of his hold and leaned me against the cold stone wall. It shifted behind me. I struggled to escape so I could beat the hell out of my husband's ex-wife for everything she had done.

Without any sign of noticing my efforts, Quinn forced my arms to my sides and brushed his lips to mine. A blend of fury and desire swept through me and stole my breath.

Stone crackled and covered my wrists before banding across my chest and spreading, imprisoning me from hips to knees. "You wretch. Let me go!"

Quinn kissed me again. If misbehaving got me more of him and his touch, I'd have to be a very bad girl, often. With a low chuckle, he trailed kisses along my cheek and down my throat. "She's watching, and she's jealous. She wants you, but she doesn't dare leave the nest while there are males here. Of course, she may also see a use for us males. You know what they say about blind squirrels and nuts."

Yeah, I knew all about blind squirrels finding a nut every now and then. I'd managed to con Quinn into marrying me, after all, with a little help from his insane family. After I figured out how to get free of the stone pinning me to the wall, I'd teach Audrey a lesson or two, then I'd deal with my husband for pinning me to the wall in the first place.

I clacked my teeth and swallowed a frustrated scream. "Let me go so I can kick her ass, Quinn."

"No. It's my turn. You already had your chance. Don't worry. She's not going to touch me—or you."

I wasn't worried about Audrey stealing my man. She'd already messed up her chance with him, and he seemed perfectly content toying with me, making me hot and achy with desire, and leaving me tied to a wall.

He'd regret that, later—and I'd enjoy every moment I spent punishing him.

Quinn gave me a final kiss before turning to face his ex-wife. He brushed the tip of his downy tail beneath my chin, and I shivered at the sinfully soft touch. Maybe I'd amend my initial plans and schedule a great deal of time cuddling with his tail and wings. Soft things were meant to be enjoyed, and I could see myself spending hours stroking my hands over him just for the pleasure of the plush texture on my skin.

Unable to do anything to free myself, I voiced my frustration as a hiss through clenched teeth.

Quinn's grandfather stayed with me and watched his grandson, his arms crossed over his chest. "I understand why you're angry, but he needs to do this, and you need to watch. He needs to prove himself to you. You can blame my side of the family for this. Gorgons are well-known for posturing, and while us males may have many females, we only have one bride."

I hadn't known, but that was what I got for sleeping through my gorgon biology and sociology classes. "He doesn't need to prove anything. He needs to untie me from this wall so I can kick that bitch in the face."

"What can I say? He's a man, and as my queen and bride says, men are stupid. Especially me, for having taught our son to be a man, too, who in turn taught his son. We're a plague, us men. At least we're handsome enough to keep around despite being stupid enough to tempt our women to murder us."

The whole Quinn family needed to see a psychologist. "There are doctors for that, you know. I can recommend a few through the CDC."

I bet Professor Yale would love a chance to psychoanalyze my husband, his father, and his grandfather.

"Audrey, you fool." Quinn halted on the edge of the nest, sighed, and shook his head. I grimaced at the disappointment in his tone; he sounded as if he had truly expected better of the woman—gorgon—who had murdered her own brother and left his body to be found in a horrific and humiliating fashion.

"My dust did turn you." Audrey sat up, her black snakes framed her face and draped over her shoulders. "My dust gave you cobras. Maybe you won't turn to stone when you make my children."

Silence.

Quinn's grandfather slapped his forehead and sighed. "You have got to be kidding me."

"I'd do the same, but my hands are tied. Do it for me," I ordered.

He did. Ouch.

"Audrey, you bombed Bailey's apartment with gorgon dust. Did… did you really do that to infect me with the dust?"

Either Quinn was a really good actor, or he really couldn't believe his ex-wife could be that reckless.

"Yes," she hissed. "I had to know if she was the one. She is. Isn't she beautiful? Our children will rule this world—and all the others, too—even the heavens."

Quinn's body quivered with tension, and his cobras swayed overhead, their hoods flared while they stayed eerily silent. "She is beautiful, but she's mine. You hurt her. You scared her." The tip of his tail twitched. "You frightened her. You destroyed her home. You threatened her neighbors. You threatened her friends."

With a snort and wave of her hand, Audrey dismissed his words. "Those worthy will become like us. The rest will die. They are of no concern to me. You've become beautiful, you know. Those black wings. Those glorious snakes. So lovely. Had I known you would turn into such a prize, I would have come for you sooner."

I wondered if Audrey realized she was signing her own death warrant, and the grim reaper stood in front of her. Probably not.

"You killed your brother because he wanted to remain a human."

And she had left him the way I had found her in Central Park with her college stud.

The pleasant tone of Quinn's voice set me on edge. I clenched my teeth. He sounded like he spoke to an old friend—or worse, someone he loved but was disappointed in.

"He mocked me. He insulted me." Audrey's voice rose in pitch, and her snakes hissed. "He told me I wanted a good-for-nothing washout. I considered petrifying him, but that would have been too easy. No, I made him regret his choice. He'd already outlived his usefulness, anyway. Yes, I killed him. Did you like how I left his body for you to find?"

"He had better technique."

My eyes widened. Wow. And Quinn called *me* mouthy. "That was so catty," I whispered to his grandfather.

"And rather below the belt," he agreed.

"You'll regret that, Samuel."

"No, I won't." Quinn nodded towards a corner of the room, and I realized there was a young child hiding in the corner, as far away from the statues and the nest as she could get. She wore rags, dirty, torn rags that barely covered her.

I balled my hands into fists, clacked my teeth together, and waited, my fury burning through me until nothing else remained.

"Is the whelp yours?"

Audrey snorted. "Of course not. I wouldn't produce such—"

Quinn darted forward, and my grandfather-in-law covered my eyes with a hand. "I don't think you need to see this part."

Audrey screamed, the shrill cry of a dying animal, and the crack of bone cut the sound off. Okay. I could deal with broken statues and piles of ashes that'd once been people. Wet crunches, however, went right over the line into the realm of the stomach churning. "That sounds gross."

With a sigh, Quinn's grandfather adjusted his hand over my eyes, and a moment later, he stroked his hand over my hair, the gesture oddly comforting. "It is. Killing a gorgon can be done in many ways. He's making sure Audrey and her sisters don't return—and that their bodies can't be used to create more dust."

Something tore, and I shuddered. "That's good."

"It is. Bear with it a little longer. It'll be

over soon. Ah, that's promising. The little whelp is crying, but she's clapping her hands. Good."

"I fail to see how that's a good thing."

"She celebrates. Perhaps she is the prince's whelp? Or stolen. She's not of their blood or hive; had she been, she would only cry. She's happy, as are her snakes."

Crunch.

"Do I want to know what he's doing?"

"No."

Oh boy. I gulped. "What about the other gorgons in the nest?"

"They're in torpor. They won't feel a thing."

"What *is* torpor?" Maybe if I talked about something—anything—else, I could ignore the sounds.

"Are you sure you're certified to handle gorgon affairs?"

I wrinkled my nose. "I may have slept during the biology and sociology courses. It was a guaranteed pass. I sometimes did homework for other classes during it. Sorry. I wasn't expecting to actually *need* it."

Quinn's grandfather chuckled. "I suppose I can't blame you for that. Newly mated females will often hibernate while nesting. They curl around their eggs and sleep while the eggs grow, preparing for when they need to care for the young after they hatch. It is the responsibility of the male or hive sisters to care for the females in torpor. Torpor helps elevate a female's body to a suitable temperature for incubating the eggs. Outside of torpor, gorgon females have a body temperature about twenty degrees below humans. During torpor, their temperature is closer to a human's."

That explained why Quinn worried about having someone hold the eggs. I didn't need a biology degree to understand how eggs required a certain temperature to remain viable.

"Are there eggs?"

"Certainly. Living ones, however, is a different matter. Audrey isn't the nurturing kind, and I expect her hive sisters starved while nesting. After two weeks without feeding, a female in torpor will cool too much for the eggs to remain viable."

I clenched my teeth so tightly my jaw ached. "You think if there are eggs, they're dead, don't you?"

"Very likely. Quinn understands it's unlikely there are surviving eggs. He's quite displeased. We'll find out soon enough. He's almost finished. Ah, no, little Samuel. Take their bodies away from the nest before you petrify the remains. Don't get too excited." My grandfather-in-law chuckled. "Now that's adorable. The little whelp's helping, and she's almost as enthusiastic as little Samuel. Do be careful of the eggs, children."

I decided I really didn't want to know.

It felt like an eternity had passed before my grandfather-in-law uncovered my eyes. Of the female gorgons, I saw no sign. "What happened to them?"

The former gorgon king pointed at a far corner of the room. "He buried their petrified remains within the walls so they can't be used by someone else to create dust. He's a very thorough child."

The young whelp hopped along at Quinn's heels, flailing her too thin arms. The pair halted at the nest.

"Any viable eggs, little Samuel?"

"I don't know."

"Come release your bride. She can help us look for any survivors, then she can help reverse the surrogates' petrification."

Quinn scowled and lashed his tail from side to side.

"She's hardly going to get into any trouble here."

"Someone's going to be in a lot of trouble if you don't let me loose!"

His cobras hissed at me and flared their hoods. I hissed back.

"Samuel Leviticus Quinn, unseal your bride this instant."

Leviticus? And I had thought Ember was a

terrible middle name. A giggle tickled my throat. Screw it. I laughed until I cried. If he had a problem with my mirth, I'd blame it on the sedative.

TO RESCUE THE PETRIFIED SURROGATES, the incubi, and the succubus, I had to call the CDC on Quinn's phone and request backup. I explained the incident with both phoenixes, endured the twenty-minute long scolding in silence, and sighed while listening to the supervisor tear into me for failing to secure the immortal birds following their first molting.

What were they expecting from me, a miracle?

While I dealt with the CDC, Quinn and his grandfather went through the nest, conferring over each and every egg. I stopped counting at thirty, and my chest tightened each time they set one aside, knowing it hadn't survived Audrey's neglect and scheming.

Quinn's grandfather found the only viable egg about ten minutes after I hung up with the CDC, and he rose to his feet, showing it to his grandson. "This one lives. See the mottling on the stone? The green and gray hasn't dulled or paled."

I held my breath and stared with wide

eyes as my husband took the egg from his grandfather, lifting it to his lips and breathing on it. "It can't be more than a week old at this size."

"Bailey must not have been the only one kidnapped from New York. We might be able to learn who the surrogate is, if she survived. Go on. Take the little one to your bride."

Quinn stepped around the dull pale eggs and approached me, holding out his hands.

How could something so tiny become a gorgon? Most marbles were larger. Swallowing, I cupped my hands together and held them out so I could take the egg. "Is there anything wrong with it? It's so small."

"It's quite normal. She'll probably be a girl; the eggs of males tend to have splashes of other colors, often correlating with their snakes' patterning. She's maybe a week old. Is that right, Grandfather? A week old at this size? How long does Grandmother normally hold your whelps?"

Quinn's grandfather chuckled. "She prefers a month. By then, the eggs are a little smaller than a golf ball. She says the whelps have an easier hatch the longer they stay in the womb. The eggs can be nested right after fertilization, but she believes the little ones are weaker at hatching. I've learned not to argue with your grandmother on such things"

I closed my fingers over the egg, worried

it felt so cool against my skin. "What's going to happen to her?"

Quinn kissed my cheek. "Don't worry. We'll find her a home, probably with a couple lacking a surrogate. A newly hatched whelp draws new females to the male, which in turn encourages the male to locate a permanent surrogate. She'll find a good home quickly."

While I had my doubts, especially after the lengths my parents had gone to in their efforts to get rid of me, I kept my mouth shut.

"He's telling the truth. We're not human, little one. We don't treat our young the same way humans treat theirs. I'll handle finding petitioners. Since I'm a former king, more new couples will be willing to approach me for a chance to claim the egg. If it makes you feel better, you and little Samuel can help consider the petitioners and oversee the meet and greets."

"Meet and greets?"

Quinn's grandfather chuckled, a low, wicked sound. "You'll appreciate this. Prospective parents will come and battle for the right to be named parent of the unborn hatchling. When it's your turn, you and little Samuel will decide if they're worthy."

With a huge grin, Quinn flicked my nose. "You'll like this. We get to beat the living snot out of the prospective parents. The most determined pair wins the egg. That's how gorgons handle adoption. Nothing tells a young whelp they're treasured more than their new parents withstanding the most vicious beating of their lives for the right to claim a child."

Oh. My eyes widened, and I held the egg close to my chest so it wouldn't get cold. "We get to beat up a bunch of gorgons?"

"There are only two rules: we don't kill, nor do we maim. The pair to withstand the worst beating goes home with the egg, once they've recovered. We'll contact the CDC and hire someone talented with healing magics to speed their recovery."

"And they want us to do this to them?"

Quinn's grandfather laughed. "It's considered a grave insult if they aren't beaten sufficiently so they can prove they deserve to win the egg. An orphan in gorgon society is rare. While we can be vile in many ways, we get this right. Nothing is more sacred than a whelp."

I glanced in the direction of the young whelp. She curled on the stone floor, sleeping with her snakes coiled on her shoulder. "And what about her?"

"It's the same, with a small caveat. *She* will witness every interview, and she will decide who fought the hardest for the right to call her their child. She picks her own fate."

Huh. I wondered how much human society would change if parents had to fight for the right to bring a new child into their home. "How long will it take?"

"I'd give it a few weeks. I'll ask your grandmother if she'll serve as a surrogate for the little one. That should give us time to make arrangements and find out if there are any health issues we'll need to be aware of. It'll also help the little one recover if the nest was too cold. I expect your grandmother will insist on three to four weeks to give the little one the best chance at a healthy hatching."

Quinn seemed pleased.

I stifled a yawn. "Can any human keep a gorgon egg warm?"

"Yes. Gender isn't important when humans hold gorgon eggs. Why?"

I nodded my head towards the statues. "There are four men in the truck who can take turns holding this egg for a while. Unlike you two, I still have work to do. No rest for the wicked."

At Quinn's low, seductive chuckle, which was partnered by the tell-tale heat of his incubus nature washing over me, I glared at him. "You'll just have to wait, sir."

"It'd also help if you reversed back to human first, little Samuel, unless you want everyone to know your deep, dark, dirty secret."

I didn't think his crimson cobras, beautiful, glossy black wings, or soft tail were anything to be ashamed of, but I kept quiet.

"Damn it," my husband muttered.

Unable to help myself, I laughed at the displeasure in Quinn's voice.

QUINN'S GRANDFATHER raided the truck for supplies and took the egg to Chief Hollands for safe keeping, bringing back a meter and a spray bottle of concentrated neutralizer. Squirting Quinn with it did nothing, and I frowned at the bottle while he laughed.

"That's not going to work."

"Dust and other gorgon materials can trigger his transformation, little one, but he controls when he returns to his human form."

Narrowing my eyes, I prodded his chest with the bottle. "Change back."

"No. I don't want to." The gleam in his eye informed me he had something in mind, something I probably wanted as much as he did.

"He can also transform from human whenever he wants," his grandfather added. "You have your very own on-demand incubus."

"Traitor," Quinn hissed, and his cobras joined in.

"This time, I'm working in my lovely

granddaughter's favor. Of course she should enjoy you at your prime at her leisure."

Sometimes, I really liked the old man.

It took a bit of bullying and a lot of bribing to convince Quinn to transform before the CDC arrived. I'd have to pretend I didn't actually have the vial of A grade pixie dust anymore, but I figured it was for a good cause.

Dealing with the surrogates turned sour fast, as Quinn's grandfather discovered four more viable eggs. With a little help from a CDC representative and the privacy of one of the downstairs rooms, the eggs were retrieved and left in my custody.

I worried for the pea-sized eggs, one of which I believed was a male, its stone shell a vibrant green and gold. The surrogate identified Prince Ozmose as the father, but she didn't remember who had mothered the eggs.

I was pretty certain she was lying about not knowing who had mothered the eggs, but I said nothing, and no one else did, either.

Before Audrey had ruined everything, the woman had been Ozmose's bride. When she had been turned to stone and left with the eggs entombed within her, she had been held hostage so the hive could sacrifice Prince Ozmose and have their source of potent gorgon dust.

Her four eggs would be given up for adoption, as a human surrogate couldn't care for the needs of gorgon whelps. Pain haunted her eyes. Once she left with the CDC reps to go to the nearest hospital, Quinn and his grandfather sighed.

"She didn't want them." My throat tightened, and I swallowed.

Quinn's grandfather rubbed my shoulder. "Don't judge her too harshly, little one. To you, they're unborn children. To her, they're bad memories and represent the loss of her husband—and the loss of her hive, her friends, and the rest of her family. Ozmose would not have left his other females while they still lived, and they would not have left him. I have no doubt they were killed. That's a lot of grief for one woman to bear. She knows the eggs will find homes with those who truly want them, something she can't give them right now."

"What will happen to the eggs?"

"The Rockwell family will be offered a chance to fight first for the eggs. While you will help beat them as is proper, it will be understood if their determination is strong enough, the eggs will remain with their clan. I know Ozmose's father well, and he will fight hard to protect the whelps of his whelp."

We left the incubi and the succubus for last after clearing everyone out of the area. Since I had the most luck with escaping their influence, I got the job of hosing them down with neutralizer and hightailing it out of the area.

Leaving them a note, a charged cell phone, and instructions to call for a pickup once they were in full control of themselves seemed a little rude in my opinion. However, even with all the precautions I took, they managed to influence me before I made it back to the truck.

The way Quinn smirked at me warned me he knew it, too, and would enjoy himself a great deal later. I feigned anger, but he saw right through me.

At least holding the five gorgon eggs kept me distracted and busy while Quinn kept the young whelp entertained in the backseat. She wore the shreds of Quinn's shirt as a blindfold and scarf to keep from petrifying anyone.

All in all, she handled it a lot better than I expected, spending most of the ride back to civilization giggling and laughing at Quinn's antics.

Quinn's grandmother met us at the police station. She claimed the eggs from me, cradled them in one hand near her chest, and snagged his grandfather by a handful of his snakes and dragged him off.

I really didn't want to know why my

grandfather-in-law grinned like a maniac on a sugar high.

The next couple of hours tested my patience, and I cursed the CDC and the police in equal measure. I snarled at every single delay, gnashing my teeth together so I wouldn't say something I'd regret later.

When we finally escaped the break room, which had been functioning as an interrogation room, I grabbed Quinn's hand and dragged him to the nearest bathroom. "You, me, and a bed. Now. I'll accept a hallway, or the wall, or I'm sure we could make use of a bathroom stall if necessary…"

With a gleam in his eye, Quinn pulled out his phone and dialed a number. "Hey, old man. I'm taking my wife to a hotel now. She's tired, she's cranky, and we've both had a long day. Can you get those pesky CDC agents and the Vermont State Police off our backs for a while? Just tell them I kidnapped her and we're going on our honeymoon. If they really need to know how many feathers each phoenix had, they can ask us when we return to New York."

I had forgotten Quinn had been planning something for a honeymoon. Would he accept a delay for the nearest hotel room?

Stupid incubi. Stupid incubi realizing they were in the same room with a succubus.

Quinn hung up. "Can you survive thirty minutes?"

"If I have to."

"Got everything you need?"

I nodded.

With a grin, he pulled me in the direction of the staircase. "Let's bail before the cops catch us."

I laughed. "You're such a bad cop."

VERMONT SUCKED.

While there were hotels near the police station, none of them met Quinn's standards, and we had to drive thirty minutes to find one he could live with. He wanted a room with a jacuzzi, which was unavailable. I swore if he delayed my shower any longer, he'd die a slow and painful death.

I won.

While I meant to do a lot of things to and with Quinn, hot water, relaxing in the tub plenty big for two, and sedative equalled an instant nap. I didn't mind, especially when Quinn woke me with gentle kisses, which led to far better things.

Later, after I made myself comfortable using his shoulder for a pillow, I murmured, "I'm still mad you ran off without me."

"Yet you still managed to show up and

scare a few years off my life. Really, Bailey? Phoenixes? Since one wasn't bad enough, you had to go and wake two of them. Next time, I hope the CDC rethinks their tactics and just gives you the napalm. It'd be safer."

I giggled. "If you think that's bad, wait until you find out my vanilla human ranking is being revoked. If surviving ambrosia contamination wasn't sufficient, my new magic rating will bump me off the list."

"So what is your trick?"

"Wayfinder, apparently."

Quinn didn't seem impressed. "So?"

"When I use my magic, bad things happen, like resurrecting two phoenixes at the same time."

"And?"

"How do you think I found Audrey?"

"A lot of good things happened because of that." Quinn held me closer and kissed the top of my head. "It just took a while is all."

"My apartment was bombed when I tried to find out what McGee was up to."

"You got to move in with me."

"120 Wall Street."

"I seem to recall you earned a spanking because of that, which led to one of the best days of my life. In case you've forgotten, I spent it worshipping your body."

He sure had. "Incubus in a bar."

"We got married. I think I like this. Every

time you try to convince me your magic causes some sort of catastrophe, you mention things that directly benefit me. I think that means the best is yet to come. Of course, now that you've had your well-earned nap, I think you need to feed me a little powdered joy, then we're going to be very, very busy for the rest of the day. Tomorrow morning, I'm stealing you away for a while, and we'll enjoy even more time alone together with no one around to bother us. Then, next month, we'll get to beat up a bunch of gorgons trying to prove they're worthy of parenting whelps. It'll be therapeutic. Best of all, we'll be at my grandfather's house. I know firsthand his guest suite is soundproofed and well away from any watchful eyes, so I won't have to transform before we go to bed. We'll have a great time. What do you say to that?"

Was he really expecting me to refuse? I wiggled out of his hold and reached for the tiny vial of pixie dust waiting on the night-stand. "Convince me."

He did.

Want more? Hoofin' It is the next book in the series. But if you're looking for some more fire-breathing unicorns, Bailey and Quinn are back in Burn, Baby, Burn: A Magical

Romantic Comedy (with a body count.) Their final novel, The Flame Game, releases in October 2020.

If you're looking for a more sinful reading experience, the Devil meets his match in A Chip on Her Shoulder, releasing September 1, 2020.

Like mystery, magic, and books? Keep reading to sample Booked for Murder: Vigilante Magical Librarians Book One.

About R.J. Blain

Want to hear from the author when a new book releases? Sign up here! Please note this newsletter is operated by the Furred & Frond Management. Expect to be sassed by a cat. (With guest features of other animals, including dogs.)

For a complete list of books written by RJ and her various pen names, please click here.

RJ Blain suffers from a Moleskine journal obsession, a pen fixation, and a terrible tendency to pun without warning.

When she isn't playing pretend, she likes to think she's a cartographer and a sumi-e painter.

In her spare time, she daydreams about being a spy. Should that fail, her contingency plan involves tying her best of enemies to spinning wheels and quoting James Bond villains until she is satisfied.

RJ also writes as Susan Copperfield and Bernadette Franklin. Visit RJ and her pets (the Management) at thesneakykittycritic.com.

Follow RJ & her alter egos on Bookbub:

RJ Blain

Susan Copperfield

Bernadette Franklin

CPSIA information can be obtained
at www.ICGtesting.com
Printed in the USA
LVHW091631180122
708386LV00033B/602